W9-BZL-103

DATE DUE

Jane and the Stillroom Maid

Jane and the Stillroom Maid

~*Being the Fifth Jane Austen Mystery*~

by Stephanie Barron

BANTAM BOOKS

NEW YORK · TORONTO · LONDON · SYDNEY · AUCKLAND

JANE AND THE STILLROOM MAID
A Bantam Book / August 2000

Library of Congress Cataloging-in-Publication Data
Barron, Stephanie.
Jane and the stillroom maid / by Stephanie Barron.
p.   cm. — (Jane Austen mystery ; 5th)
ISBN 0-553-10734-8
1. Austen, Jane, 1775–1817—Fiction.   2. Women novelists, English—Fiction.
3. Women detectives—England—Bakewell—Fiction.   4. Women domestics—
Fiction.   5. Bakewell (England)—Fiction.   I. Title.
PS3563.A8357 J35 2000
813'.54—dc21
00-037837

Published simultaneously in the United States and Canada

Bantam Books are published by Bantam Books, a division of Random
House, Inc. Its trademark, consisting of the words "Bantam Books" and
the portrayal of a rooster, is Registered in U.S. Patent and Trademark
Office and in other countries. Marca Registrada. Bantam Books,
1540 Broadway, New York, New York 10036.

*Dedicated to Carol Bauer Bowron, friend and writer,
who carries a certain Pemberley in her heart*

Editor's Foreword

THIS IS THE FIFTH OF THE AUSTEN MANUSCRIPTS I HAVE BEEN PRIVI-leged to edit for publication since their discovery, in 1992, in the cellar of a Georgian manor house outside of Baltimore. I may say that I find it by far the most exciting, for it sheds light on Jane Austen's life and travels in 1806 that helps to confirm events only suspected before.

One of the most vividly described and memorable locations in all of Austen's novels must be the county of Derbyshire, where Fitz-william Darcy, the reticent hero of *Pride and Prejudice,* makes his home. Here Elizabeth Bennet is privileged to travel in the company of her relations, the Gardiners. The party tours Matlock and Dove-dale before visiting Darcy's estate of Pemberley, where they unac-countably stumble across the owner. Elizabeth, in conversation with Darcy, refers to the inn at Bakewell, where she has been staying with the Gardiners—and to this day there is a tradition in Bakewell that Jane Austen was once a guest at the town's principal Georgian inn, The Rutland Arms. She must have been to Bakewell, the local inhabi-tants reason; her description of the landscape surrounding Pember-ley accords so closely to the town's physical reality. Furthermore, she imputes to Elizabeth Bennet an enthusiasm for the beauties of the Peaks that sounds entirely genuine.

Austen scholars, however, have contested for years The Rutland Arms' claim that Jane was a guest during the summer of 1811; for in

1811, as all good Austen scholars know, she was far from the Midlands and the Peaks.

A few voices, however, have lately suggested that Jane might have visited Derbyshire during the summer of 1806, while staying with her cousin Edward Cooper in neighboring Staffordshire. During the seven weeks she spent in a rectory in Hamstall Ridware. Staffordshire, Austen would have been but forty miles from the sites she later describes in *Pride and Prejudice*. George Holbert Tucker, author of *Jane Austen the Woman,* is inclined to support fellow academic Donald Greene, who argues that Darcy's fictitious home corresponds in its broad outlines to Chatsworth, the great estate of the dukes of Devonshire. Certainly it is true that the entire Cooper family succumbed to whooping cough during the Austens' visit—and for this reason, as well as from a possible desire to tour the Peak District, Edward Cooper may have carried the Austen ladies into Derbyshire. No letter has survived in Jane's hand, dated late August 1806 from the town of Bakewell, but that should hardly be surprising. She was, after all, traveling with her chief correspondent, her sister Cassandra—and any number of Austen's letters have been destroyed over the years.

Jane and the Stillroom Maid thus comes as a revelation. Here is the complete story of that singular week in 1806, when Austen saw the original of the great house she would use as one of her models for Pemberley. She was writing sporadically, if at all, during this period, having abandoned *The Watsons*—a decision most Austen scholars ascribe to persistent grief for her late father and the unsettled nature of the Austen ladies' domestic arrangements. Some part of Jane's Derbyshire experiences must have lingered powerfully in memory, however. When she once more took up her pen, the outlines of Bakewell and Derbyshire would be traced in the landscape of Pemberley House, and a bit of Charles Danforth in the character of Fitzwilliam Darcy. Is it too great a leap of the imagination to claim, indeed, that but for this 1806 trip to Derbyshire we might never have seen a revision of *First Impressions*—the novel we now know as *Pride and Prejudice?*

STEPHANIE BARRON
GOLDEN, COLORADO
SEPTEMBER 1999

Jane and the Stillroom Maid

Chapter 1

The Butterfly
on the Stone

MR. EDWARD COOPER—RECTOR OF HAMSTALL RIDWARE, STAFFORD-shire, Fellow of All Souls, devoted supplicant before his noble patron, Sir George Mumps, and my first cousin—is possessed of a taste for hymns. He sings without the slightest encouragement or provocation, in a key entirely of his own choosing. Were he content to sing alone, in a subdued undertone befitting one of his dignity and station, all might be well. But Mr. Cooper has achieved a modest sort of fame as the composer of sacred music; and like the ardent shepherd of many a flock, must needs have company in his rejoicing. There are those who profess to admire my cousin's wistful baritone and remarkable lyrics—Sir George Mumps himself is said to have presented the Staffordshire living on the strength of his esteem—but Jane Austen is not among them. Were Mr. Cooper to sing airs in the Italian, before an audience of five hundred, I should still blush for his execution and taste. My cousin is a very good sort of man, his compassion and understanding quite equal to the duties of his parish; but his strains are not for the enduring, of an early hour of the morning.

I was blushing now, as I rolled towards Miller's Dale in the heart of

Derbyshire behind the horse of Mr. Cooper's excellent friend, Mr. George Hemming; and I foresaw a morning's-worth of mortification in store, did my cousin continue to sing as he had begun. I had borne with Mr. Cooper's hymns through his dawn ablutions; I had borne with a determined humming over our morning coffee. And as the pony trap rolled west through a remarkable spread of country, I now reflected that I had borne with a stream of liturgical ditty for nearly a fortnight. To say that I possessed an entire hymnal of Mr. Cooper's work writ large upon my brain was the merest understatement. I heard his powerful strains in my sleep.

"Is it not a beautiful morning, Jane? Does not the heart leap in the human breast for the greater glorification of God?" Mr. Cooper cried. "Pray sing with me, Cousin, that the Lord might hear us and be glad!"

Poor Mr. Hemming cast a troubled glance my way. He was but an instant from a similar application, and I read his distress in his looks. My cousin's talent, we may suspect, had progressed unnoticed by his friend during the long years that interceded between their first acquaintance, and this latest renewal; had Mr. Hemming known of the recital we were to receive during our journey to Miller's Dale, he might well have retracted his invitation. I had long ago learned the surest remedy for Mr. Cooper, however, and I now hastened to employ it. Even the least worldly of men may be prey to vanity.

"Do not destroy all my pleasure in hearing you, Cousin, by requiring me to sing myself!" I cried. "My voice should never be joined with yours; it is not equal to the demands of the performance. Nor, I am certain, is Mr. Hemming's. Pray let us rest a little in your art, and be satisfied."

Mr. Cooper beamed, and commenced a tedious five verses of "The Breath That Breathed O'er Eden."

I endured it in silence; for I owed Mr. Cooper every measure of gratitude and respect. But for my cousin, I should never have set foot in Derbyshire at all. And Derbyshire—with all its wild beauty and untamed peaks—had long been the dearest object of my travels. What was a little singing, however off-key, to the grandeur of lakes and mountains?

Mr. Cooper had long despaired of my mother's ever paying a visit to Staffordshire and her dearest nephew's rectory. It was many years, now, since he had first urged the scheme; his family had annually increased, his honours as a vicar and homilist multiplied; Mr. Cooper himself was approaching a complaisant middle-age—and still the Austen ladies remained insensibly at home.

But so lately as June my mother determined to quit the environs of Bath—the town in which we have lived more than three years—it being entirely unsuitable now that my beloved father is laid to rest. Being three women of modest means, and having endeavoured to live respectably on a pittance in the midst of a most expensive town, we at last declared defeat and determined to exchange *Bath* for anywhere else in England. An interval of rest and refreshment, in the form of an extended tour among our relations, was deemed suitable for the summer months; October should find us in Southampton, where we were to set up housekeeping with my dearest brother, Captain Francis Austen. We should serve as company for his new bride, Mary, when duty called Frank to sea.

And so it was decided—we shook off the dust of Bath on the second of July, with what happy feelings of Escape!—and bent all our energies to a summer of idleness.

We travelled first to Clifton, and from thence to Adlestrop and my mother's cousin, the clergyman Mr. Thomas Leigh. We had not been settled in that gentleman's home five days, when the sudden death of a distant relation sent Mr. Leigh flying to Stoneleigh Abbey in Warwickshire, with the intent of laying claim to a disputed inheritance. After a highly diverting week in the company of Mr. Leigh's solicitor, Mr. Hill, and the absurd Lady Saye and Sele, we parted from the intimates of Stoneleigh and turned our carriage north, towards Staffordshire.[1]

Hamstall Ridware is a prosperous little village lost in a depth of hedgerows, with a very fine Rectory and a finer church spire. Our cousin Mr. Cooper and his dutiful wife, Caroline, possess no less than

[1] Jane's adventures while with the Reverend Thomas Leigh in Warwickshire may be found in "Jane and the Spoils of Stoneleigh," in *Malice Domestic 7,* Avon Books, 1998. *—Editor's note.*

eight children, the eldest of whom is but twelve and the youngest barely a year. Some little difficulty in the matter of bedchambers was apparent from the moment of our arrival. Cassandra and I were forced to shift together; my mother claimed a bed in the next room. The little boys were grouped in pallets on the nursery floor, and it was likewise with the little girls, while the baby was taken up in its parents' chamber. And so we contrived to be comfortable; and so we should have been, despite the heat of August and the closeness of such a populous house, had not the whooping cough presently put in an appearance. After three days of Christian endurance, of instruction from the apothecary and draughts that did little good, Mr. Cooper proposed a journey into Derbyshire, with the intent of touring Chatsworth and the principal beauties of the region.

My mother acceded thankfully to the scheme. The harassed Caroline Cooper, beset with ailing children on every side, was relieved of the burden of guests, and the Austens of the fear of contagion. Having set out from the Rectory steps on the Saturday previous, we achieved Bakewell yesterday in the forenoon, very well satisfied with our progress north. But for one aspect of the journey—my cousin's unsuspected ardour for the sport of angling, which has entirely determined our course through Derbyshire—we should have found nothing in our prospects but delight.

Bakewell is a bustling, if modest, collection of stone buildings and paved streets, of ancient bridges spanning the Wye and sheep-pens ranged along the banks of the river. The town is remarkable for enjoying the patronage of no less than two ducal houses—that of the Duke of Rutland, who is a great landowner hereabouts, and of the Duke of Devonshire, whose principal seat of Chatsworth is but three miles to the east. A brush with nobility and Fashion has lent the town an air of importance unusual in this wild, high country. A few hours sufficed to reveal its charms, however; by dinner I was surfeited with commerce and linen-draping; I yearned for a landscape of disorder, for a riot of water and stone. Too little activity, and too great a period in the confines of a carriage, had conspired to render me peevish and melancholy. When Mr. George Hemming proffered his invitation to Miller's Dale over our evening tea, I accepted with alacrity. My mother could not be persuaded; and upon ascertaining that the intended equipage was a pony trap, Cassandra, too, declined. I should be left to all the luxury of solitude, once my cousin and his friend were established over their rods.

Mr. Hemming is a solicitor in Bakewell: a prosperous and congenial gentleman, whose quiet manners must always make him amiable, though he should never be called handsome. He is confirmed in middle-age, being nearly twenty years my cousin's senior. He possesses no family, his wife having died in childbed a decade ago. Having found occasion to perform some little service for the Duke of Devonshire, he may claim an intimacy with so august an institution as Chatsworth; and this alone would ensure that he is regarded in Bakewell as a person of some respectability. To my cousin, he is chiefly valuable in being addicted to the sport of angling; to myself, he appears more in the guise of social saviour. Possessed of conversation, and not entirely ignorant of the world, Mr. Hemming must be regarded as a decided advantage—particularly after too many days in the confines of a closed carriage, with a vigorous soloist for company.

This morning Mr. Hemming came, at the reins of his admirable trap; he displayed no irritation at the company of a female; and his comments during the course of the hour's journey from Bakewell to Miller's Dale were always sensible, and sometimes droll. I quite liked him, for the amiability of spirit that urged the revival of a friendship of such ancient formation, as much as for the evenness of temper that marked all his conduct. The conversation of well-informed men falls but too rarely in my way, and I intended to profit from Mr. Hemming's company.

"Are you Derbyshire born and bred, sir?" I enquired, when my cousin's five verses were done.

"I am," he replied, "and have never found a cause to repine. Other than a brief period in the South, when I was so fortunate as to make Mr. Cooper's acquaintance, I have been happy to call Bakewell my home these thirty years and more. I should never exchange it for another."

My cousin closed his eyes, as though lost in contemplation or prayer; I knew he should soon be asleep. The gig had not progressed another mile before the gentle sound of snoring fell upon my ear.

"I think I should be content to live my whole life in Derbyshire, Mr. Hemming," I said. "Never have I seen a country so blest in the marriage of the tame and the wild, so replete at once with romance and comfort."

"You do not share the opinion of so many fine ladies, then, that these hills and rocks lack refinement?"

"What is refinement," I cried, "when one has glimpsed the whole force of Nature? Who, having witnessed the Dove toiling amidst her course, could wish for the quieter banks of the Stour? If by refinement you would offer me the dull, Mr. Hemming—if you presume that having spent my life in Hampshire, I know nothing of Beauty—then I must assure you to the contrary."

"What is it Cowper writes?" he mused. "That 'Nature is but a name for an effect,/Whose cause is God'?"

Admirable fellow, to have looked into Cowper! "I have always supposed him to mean that true Beauty, true *perfection*—which is the essence of God, is it not?—may only be found in what is *simple*. A life of artifice and affectation *must* prove hollow, and incapable of granting happiness."

"You shall not win an argument from me, Miss Austen," replied Hemming. "I have seen your life of artifice in my younger days; and I assure you it will break its victim as a butterfly on a stone."

His words were heavy; they belied the sunshine of the morning. Abruptly Mr. Hemming fell silent. Some memory he had stirred, of bitterness or regret; it was not for me to probe the wound. I turned my energy to an enjoyment of the landscape beyond the gig, and found everything to delight.

We travelled west for a time through a lovely passage of country, along the banks of the River Wye. The water gurgled in its bed, the horse's hooves clopped comfortably along the dusty August road, and the green Derbyshire hills rose up around us. It is a northern custom to divide the fields with stone walls, rather than the hedgerows so suitable to the flat meadows of the South. I found the practise charming, and longed for a hut among the rocks, where I might survey the entire country of a morning, and breathe the clear sweet air. We rolled on, through Ashford-in-the-Water, while my cousin Mr. Cooper was yet lost in slumber, and the sun climbed higher in the cup of sky.

Near Blackwell, the road turns north and plunges into the Dale it-self, a precipitous and winding drop among the crags towards the tor-rent of water below. I had grown accustomed to such a pitch in the course of our Derbyshire travels; and I prided myself upon a measure of complaisance. It should not be said that Jane Austen was so little fa-miliar with the world, that a smart stretch of road might reduce her to hysterics. Upon reflection, however, it was greatly to be thanked that *Cassandra* had remained in Bakewell.

I gripped the leather seat of Mr. Hemming's equipage more firmly, and trained my eyes upon his hands as they managed the reins. He spoke in a low voice to his horse, holding the animal in, and we descended by degrees to the Wye, and Miller's Dale itself. I had a moment for the drawing of breath, and a swift prayer of thanks, when Mr. Hemming brought the gig to rest under the shade of a venerable oak.

He roused my cousin with a few jocular remarks, and the threat of a dose of river water to clear Mr. Cooper's head; then led our party to a secluded spot some distance downstream, where the lime-stone crags rose in harsh and fantastic shapes. An ancient mill stood beside a weir; and the picturesque was so delightful that I gasped with pleasure.

"You must not neglect to form an acquaintance with the miller," Mr. Hemming informed me with a smile, "for he is the purveyor of an excellent cordial. We shall all be desirous of a glass before the day is out."

The gentlemen disposed themselves with their rods and tackle, their figures quite charming amidst the willows and reeds. It was a bu-colic scene that had grown quite familiar. Fishing, I will own, is one of the more healthful and least vicious of gentlemen's pursuits; but it is unfortunate that it should produce such a number of fish, that must be consumed or otherwise disposed of, before they rot. The rivers that spring from the High Peaks are justly celebrated for their quanti-ties of trout; they have provided generations of gentlemen with sport, well before Mr. Izaak Walton wrote of their charms in *The Compleat Angler* over a century ago. Our progress through Derby had been marked by an assay of waters: the Trent, the Derwent, the Dove, and at last the Wye. It was through a tangle of line and tackle that I first espied Dove Dale; it was in the odour of fish that I descended upon Burghley House, and was granted permission to tour the estate. By the time we achieved Matlock, I was heartily sick of trout, and utterly refused it for dinner in Buxton.

I set about the business of unpacking Mr. Hemming's commodious hamper, which contained a generous store of bread and cheese, a packet of sliced ham, and some peaches—all of it warm and fragrant with the heat of the day. He had considered of cutlery and napkins, and a cloth to lay upon the ground; an admirable host in every respect. It was as I laid out the fruit knives that my cousin Mr. Cooper commenced to sing.

> *"Hear us, oh hear us Lord; to thee*
> *A sinner is more music, when he prays*
> *Than spheres, or angels' praises be*
> *In panegyric alleluiaaaas."*

Mr. Hemming was at a little remove, between my cousin and the bend in the river, where the mill was situated; he glanced over his shoulder as my cousin achieved a fulsome baritone, looked a trifle uneasy, and then glanced at me. I waggled a gloved hand in salutation.

Mr. Hemming returned his gaze to his rod; but I observed that the set of his back was rather more rigid than before. "Do you always sing, Edward, when angling?" he enquired.

"There are few pursuits, I suppose, that are not improved by a hymn," replied my cousin gaily. "I may assure you, George, that a burst of song is highly beneficial to the lungs. My esteemed patron, Sir George Mumps, has condescended to follow my example— and Sir George survived the whole of last winter without so much as a cold. You must attempt it."

"I am unfamiliar with your tune," Mr. Hemming managed.

My cousin's countenance was suffused with delight. "But the words themselves you certainly recognise. They are Donne's, from the *Divine Poems*. My ambition is to set all of his work to music, in the course of time."

Mr. Hemming did not vouchsafe a reply. His brow was furrowed and his attention claimed by the tying of a fly.

"As no doubt you comprehend," Mr. Cooper continued, in happy oblivion of his effect, "Donne is sometimes problematical. What is one to do with 'And through that bitter agony/Which is still the agony of pious wits/Disputing what distorted thee/And interrupted evenness, with fits'?"

Mr. Hemming's rod twitched; so, too, did his jaw; and then the line broke free of the river and was swiftly reeled in. He was keeping a check on his temper, I perceived; but the excess of his feeling was visible in his handling of the rod. There would be few fish to catch, at this present rate.

"Not to mention 'as wise as serpents, diversely/Most slipperiness, yet most entanglings hath,' " I murmured.

"Exactly." My cousin wheeled about, jerking his line from the river with a spattering of drops. "I have been forced to abandon those for a time, Jane, until the Lord provides for their arrangement. But I have infinite faith in His devising."

Mr. Hemming raised his rod in preparation for a cast, his gaze trained upon the coursing river. "If I might make a suggestion, Edward—the counsel of an old friend—"

"But I should be delighted, George!"

"I believe your singing—excellent though it may be in its way—is driving off the trout."

A look of the most extreme mortification clouded Mr. Cooper's countenance. "I had not the slightest notion the creatures possessed ears."

"I am not convinced that ears are entirely necessary. The . . . vigour of your performance—"

"Perhaps the fish do not approve of Donne," I suggested.

Mr. Hemming threw a glance my way. "It must be said that there are many who do not," he observed.

My cousin looked from my serene countenance to the blacker one of his friend. "If I have offended you in any way, George, I humbly beg leave to apologise—."

"Pray do not mention it," Mr. Hemming retorted abruptly. He cast, and the line tangled upon a tree branch. Mr. Hemming stifled an oath.

The waters of the Wye lapped at our feet; a curlew called in the crags somewhere above; and off in the distance I caught the clatter of crows. It was a distinctly mournful sound, rife with dispute and acrimony; and for an instant, a shade was thrown over the brightness of the summer day. I lifted my head, and studied the heights. Nothing but a soaring of rock and green things among them, a footpath winding above. I was not yet seized with hunger, and now that my cousin was cowed to silence, the gentlemen were absorbed in their sport. It was time to attempt the heights of Miller's Dale.

THE WAY WAS GENTLE ENOUGH IN ITS EARLY STAGES, BUT STEEPened inexorably even as it narrowed, until with the passage of three-quarters of an hour, I felt myself to be a sort of sheep or mountain goat, clinging with my half-boots to the edge of the earth. All about me swung the green hills and stone walls of Derbyshire, with the river a bright ribbon below. I looked my fill upon this corner of the sceptre'd isle; saw, as with the eye of Heaven, the flocks of sheep like clouds against the pasturage, the rapid gallop of a distant horse, the tumbled stones of ancient habitation. Smoke curled from the miller's chimney. I felt as Henry, my brother, must once have done, marshalling toy soldiers. I commanded all that was at my feet.

And then the crows rose up in a great black cloud and tore the peace of morning into fragments. I focused my gaze upon a massive crag of rock, some distance further up the path. The birds were gathered there, a darkling company.

Small heaps of cloth—the remnants of a pleasure party, perhaps—were tossed about the crag's base. There would be crusts of bread amidst the refuse, enough sustenance for a crow to squabble over. I schooled my gaze to pierce the shadows thrown by the great rock, but the glitter of sunlight on limestone pained my eyes. The crows were settled on the limbs of a tree at the crag's foot. But surely a tree branch would have no use for a gentleman's shoe? And yet it *was* a gentleman's shoe I espied—

Without hesitation I hurried forward, the beauties of the day forgotten in a sudden access of anxiety. My breath came in tearing gasps, as though born of great exertion, and yet here the pitch of the slope was in my favour, and I might have flown the distance on winged feet. To reach him required but a few moments.

He lay in the shelter of the great rock as though seeking relief from the sun, one hand serving as pillow under his head—a young man, with a delicate countenance and golden curls, dressed entirely in black. He might almost have been asleep. But to my sorrow, I knew better. The stench of blood was heavy in my nostrils, and the raven tearing at the man's entrails did not suffer itself to move, even when I screamed.

For the Staunching of a Wound, Where There Be Great Blood

If the wound be deep or a great vein cut, take a piece of lean salt beef and lay it in hot ashes until heated through. Then press the hot stuff entirely into the wound and bind with clean linen. A good piece of roasted beef, heated on the coals, will serve as well.

—From the Stillroom Book of Tess Arnold,
Penfolds Hall, Derbyshire, 1802–1806

Chapter 2

The Devil
of Water Street

THE STENCH OF BLOOD AT THE FOOT OF THE CRAG WAS NEARLY overwhelming—a hot, sweet, animal smell that engulfed the senses and obliterated thought. I pressed one gloved hand to my nostrils and closed my eyes. A feeling of faintness was inevitable, but I *would* not give way. It was imperative that help should be sought from my cousin and Mr. Hemming—but they were fixed at the riverbank, perhaps a half-hour back along the path already traversed. My scream of terror had not alerted them. I opened my eyes and allowed my gaze to travel over the form sprawled in the dust. A round hole in the center of the forehead, black with crusted blood, suggested first how the man had died; there would be a lead ball lodged in the skull. But other wounds he had sustained, more grotesque and inexplicable: blood seeped from his parted lips, spilling gore over the folds of his cravat and his white shirt-front. The shirt itself was rucked-up over the fastening of his black pantaloons, and his bowels spilled out upon the rock—a sight that must urge a desperate retching. I turned away, and caused myself to bend nearly double in an effort to contain the wave of sickness. At length the black haze subsided; the blood pounding in my temples returned to its wonted course. I stood up, my back to the savaged corpse, and stared dully at a raven triumphant on a rock. The bird had alighted perhaps five feet from my position, sunlight glinting blue on its sooty feathers; one cruel yellow eye surveyed me with indifference. In the raven's beak was an oblong of flesh—sandy pink, amorphous, and yet not dissimilar from the breakfast fare on every farmyard table. It was *tongue.* A human tongue. From the cleanness of the wound at the severed end, I should judge that a knife had cut it out.

I began to move down the path away from the body, unable to look at it again. I stumbled once, saved myself from a bruising fall, and then broke into a run.

"MISS AUSTEN! ARE YOU ILL?"

George Hemming cast aside his rod and hastened towards my breathless figure. Mr. Cooper, it appeared, was in the midst of landing a determined trout; his countenance was o'erspread with a fierce scowl, and he did not spare me so much as a glance.

"I am perfectly well," I assured Mr. Hemming in a feverish accent, "but there is a man lying among the rocks above who is not. I have found a corpse, Mr. Hemming—so viciously worked upon, I dare not trust myself to relate the particulars. We must fetch a surgeon at once! And the Law, if such exists in these wretched hills—"

Mr. Hemming could not be insensible to my wild appearance; in an instant, he was all solicitude, and led me to a broad, flat rock some yards from the river. There I sat down in gratitude and relief. Mr. Hemming pressed a handkerchief into my hands. I found that I was trembling uncontrollably, and that a feeling of nausea would not be denied. "Do not regard my indisposition," I cried, "but send at once for aid."

"Pray calm yourself, Miss Austen," Mr. Hemming urged. "I will go myself in a moment—or seek help from the miller's hut—but first, I must insist that you partake of my French brandy. It cannot but prove restorative to one in your condition."

At this, the admirable Mr. Hemming produced a silver flask from among his fishing tackle and administered a modest draught. I spluttered, choked, and raised a hand to my mouth.

"That's better," he said approvingly. "The colour has returned to your cheeks."

I very much doubted that it had ever been absent—a complexion such as mine does not show to advantage under the twin forces of exertion and summer weather—but I forbore to dispute his gallantry.

"The corpse of a man, you say." His eyes were fixed upon my countenance with an expression of trouble and anxiety. "A shepherd, perhaps? Or a jagger who lost his way?"

"Jagger?" I was momentarily diverted by the strangeness of the word.

"The packhorse pedlars who roam the Peaks," Hemming replied. "They bring all manner of goods to more remote villages of Derbyshire, and a fair measure of gossip as well. The jaggers are to be found everywhere among these hills in the summer months."

"This man was not a pedlar," I told him, "but a gentleman by his appearance. I should judge his clothes and shoes to be of the first quality, and fairly new."

Mr. Hemming's expression changed. From one of interest in myself, it turned to disquiet for another. I saw that he should have preferred to dismiss this death as a misadventure among the lower orders—and with it, all burden to himself. But such was not to be. The claims of a gentleman *must* be felt.

"How old a gentleman should you judge him to be, Miss Austen?"

The face had been clean-shaven, the skin delicate. "He cannot be much above twenty."

A whoop from the riverbank then attracted our notice. Mr. Cooper raised high his severed line, an enormous trout depending from its length.

"Edward! We have need of you!" Mr. Hemming cried.

My cousin frowned, then set his fish carefully upon the grass at his feet and ambled towards us.

"Was there any sign of a horse?" Mr. Hemming returned to me with urgency. "Hoofprints, perhaps? —Could he have found his death from a fall?"

I shook my head. "He has been brutally and most savagely murdered, sir. There is nothing else to be said."

"My dear Jane," my cousin observed as he achieved our position, "you look remarkably unwell."

"Miss Austen has sustained a shock," Mr. Hemming informed him. "She has discovered a gentleman in the rocks above, quite dead."

"A corpse?" Mr. Cooper exclaimed, with a look of consternation. "Not *again*, Jane! However shall we explain this to my aunt?"

BUT I WAS SAVED THE NECESSITY OF UNPLEASANT EXPLANATION SOME hours more. Mr. Hemming conveyed me to the relative comfort of the miller's cottage, where I was seated in a hard wooden chair by an ancient woman of obscure dialect. There I sipped some water from a chipped earthenware mug, and gazed out of the unglazed window, and felt my terror ease with the water slipping noisily over the mill-wheel's vanes. It should have been the perfect pastoral scene, of a kind beloved of my favored poets, but for the preparations under-gone a few moments before: the miller's waggon readied, and his sole draught horse lured from the fields; a pallet laid out between two poles, and secured with a length of rope; the miller's wife dispensing a spare sheet, worn quite through in places by time and the marriage bed. A few moments only saw the work completed, and then my cousin, the miller, and Mr. Hemming toiled up the craggy path in search of the ravaged body. They should not miss it for the crows.

Perhaps an hour passed before they reappeared, bearing a draped mass on the pallet between them. The countenances of all three, labourer and gentlemen alike, were stamped with grave disquiet. They set the pallet in the bed of the miller's waggon with grunts of exertion and relief. The miller's wife stood in her doorway, twisting her hands in her apron and considering, no doubt, of her sheet.

Mr. Cooper drew a tremulous breath. "May God have mercy on his soul," he murmured, and wiped his streaming brow with a handkerchief.

"Did you recognise the face?" I enquired of Mr. Hemming.

"I did not," he brusquely replied. "The poor wretch might hail from anywhere—he need not be a gentleman of this county. There are many who pass through Derbyshire in the summer months."

He failed to meet my gaze with steadiness, and seemed most anxious to encourage the thought of the murdered man's alienation from his final resting place. A dim note of warning sounded in the recesses of my brain—but suspicion of such a man as George Hemming must be absurd. His desire to regard the murdered fellow as foreign to Derbyshire should not be extraordinary. It is one thing to witness the mutilation of a stranger—death might have occurred as the result of a thousand grievances and enmities unknown. But the brutal end of an acquaintance is quite another matter. Such an end cannot be readily forgot.

"Are you well enough to attempt a journey, Jane?" Mr. Cooper enquired.

"I am. What is to be done with the corpse?"

Mr. Hemming stared at me in surprise; not one in an hundred ladies, perhaps, should have considered it her place to pursue such a matter. But then he recollected that I had discovered the poor soul myself, and must naturally feel an interest.

"I think it best to convey the body into Buxton," he said. "It is no greater distance than Bakewell, although in the opposite direction; and chances are good that Deceased will be known there. Many strangers to the district put up in Buxton, intending to take the waters."

"And does the Coroner for this district also reside in that town?"

"He does not," Mr. Hemming replied, "but that is no very great matter. Tivey may ride over from Bakewell if he chuses; he does so often enough."

"The choice appears to have been made already for him, sir," I returned with some surprise. "He cannot help but ride over; he cannot neglect of so painful a duty! Is the local Justice, perhaps, a resident of Buxton rather than Bakewell?"

"Sir James may be said to reside in neither," Mr. Hemming replied shortly, "his estate being at Monyash."

"Monyash! But that is a good deal south of here, and only a few miles from Bakewell, is it not?"

Mr. Hemming turned towards the waggon with a suggestion of angry impatience in his countenance, and retorted that he preferred to carry the body into Buxton, and there was an *end* to the matter. He hoped to divert some greater misfortune, I guessed, in directing the

corpse into a neighbourhood not his own. But why? Gone were the
happy manners of the morning; he had become taciturn, preoccupied, closed in his confidence. I read some great trouble in Mr. Hemming's looks—a greater unease than even the ravaged corpse had
produced. Was it possible that the solicitor detected something in the
gentleman's aspect—or in the gruesome manner of his death—that
gave rise to the gravest anxiety?

Did he suspect, perhaps, the hand that had done these acts?

Or was Mr. Hemming merely desirous of being rid of interfer-
ing females?

"Would you wish us to accompany you, Hemming?" enquired my
cousin Mr. Cooper. He made the offer most unwillingly; we should
lose the better part of the morning in traversing the hills, first west to
Buxton, and then east again to Bakewell.

"Pray escort Miss Austen back to your inn, Edward, and leave this
unhappy affair to me." Mr. Hemming did not deign to look at my
cousin as he said this, but kept his eyes resolutely turned towards the
harness of his pony. "You shall take my trap, and leave it in The Rutland Arms' stableyard. I shall send for it later."

"But how shall you return to Bakewell from Buxton, Mr. Hemming?" I said in exasperation, "if we have commanded your horse?
Why should we not all proceed companionably together towards
Bakewell, and allow the Coroner and the Justice to exert their authority within their own district? Is not this diversion to Buxton a
great deal of trouble, for no very good reason?"

"My reasons are my own, Miss Austen—" Mr. Hemming began
abruptly, when he was interrupted by my cousin.

"I confess I must agree with Jane," Mr. Cooper admitted doubtfully. "I cannot see the purpose of such needless activity, when so
many of the principals reside in Bakewell. And we cannot know for
certain, after all, that this poor unfortunate was staying in Buxton; he
might as readily have taken a room at The Rutland Arms, like ourselves! I am sure that the Justice shall wonder at your decision,
George. He will like to know—as we do—why you are so desirous of
sending him over hill and dale in pursuit of his duty!"

The solicitor opened his mouth as though to speak, looked from
the miller to ourselves without uttering a word, and then shrugged in

resignation. "Very well," he muttered, "let it be Bakewell, then, and the Devil take the consequences!"

With which impenetrable remark, he pulled himself up into the seat of his trap, and reached for the reins.

We made our progress towards Bakewell in the heat of the day, the miller's waggon following slowly behind. The air was oppressive with the promise of thunder, and a mass of cloud hovered over Dark Peak. Our passage was utterly silent but for the sound of the horses' hooves; even my cousin was unmoved to send Heavenward a sacred song. Heavy as our spirits were, I was mistress enough of my faculties by the time we reached Bakewell to urge Mr. Hemming onward in search of the surgeon, when he would first have set me down at The Rutland Arms. And so it was that we came into Water Street.

Hemming pulled up in the midst of a dozen equipages; the miller's waggon ground to a halt behind. Tuesday is market day in Bakewell, and Water Street was at a standstill. The solicitor craned his head over the sheep farmers and lead miners, the quarry workers and tradesmen lounging in the doorways, and cried out, "Mr. Tivey! I want the surgeon, Mr. Tivey!"

All conversation ceased. The tradesmen straightened; the farmers stared. I felt suddenly as though I were condemned to death by exposure. My cousin gave a little sigh of exasperation. And then, with a clang of iron and sparks from the blacksmith's forge opposite, a broad-shouldered devil of a man set down his hammer.

He was not much above thirty, with powerful forearms and heavy dark brows, a living embodiment of the fabled Vulcan. He wiped blackened palms on his leather apron and studied our faces. "What's so great a matter, George Hemming, that it warrants a summons on market day? Tha' knows I'm not my own man of a Tuesday."

Mr. Hemming jumped down from his gig, and the crowd parted to permit his passage. He spoke in a lowered tone to Michael Tivey, while the men standing nearest did not attempt to conceal their interest. However bent upon discretion Mr. Hemming might be, however, it appeared that Mr. Tivey did not share his inclination. He turned away from the solicitor's urgent intelligence, and whistled appreciatively, his eyes on the shrouded burden in the miller's wag-gon. "If no one claims 'im, ah'll be wanting the body for study, mind."

"He will certainly be claimed," Mr. Hemming said sternly. "This is no itinerant labourer you might anatomise, Tivey. You have a gentle-man in your hands."

"That's as may be. Tha'd best take him along to the Snake and Hind. Jacob Patter will give me the use of his scullery."

A murmur of debate and excitement swelled around us. No one present could be in doubt as to the nature of the blacksmith's direc-tion; the Snake and Hind was a coaching inn at the head of Water Street, and Jacob Patter its proprietor. Mr. Tivey intended the use of the scullery as a resting place for the dead. It was there he would ex-amine the corpse, with the curious of Bakewell struggling for a view through the chinks in the publican's shutters. We were, I thought drily, rather remote from civilisation in the depths of Derbyshire.

"Damn Tivey and his love of sensation," Mr. Hemming muttered. He had returned to the gig and now offered his hand. "I might have passed the matter off with credit, but for his indiscretion. Pray forgive me, Miss Austen, for deserting you at such a time. Have you courage enough to attempt the town on foot, or shall I send Mr. Cooper as escort?"

"Mr. Cooper had far better attend you to the Snake and Hind," I replied. "The offices of a clergyman must be in greater demand *there* than at The Rutland Arms. I shall be quite all right, I assure you."

My cousin did not look as though he appreciated my sacrifice.

Dr. Bascomb's Water to
Strengthen a Woman after Travel

Steep equal parts pomegranate buds, oak bark, and rose leaves in boiling spring water until very strong. Then add to each pint of the tea a quarter-pint of red wine. Dip clean cotton in the posset and apply hot to the Sufferer's forehead, or anywhere on the body that is pained. Applications in evening are most beneficial.

—From the Stillroom Book of Tess Arnold,
Penfolds Hall, Derbyshire, 1802–1806

Chapter 3

A Turn at Fancy Dress

26 August 1806, cont.

~

A CRUSH OF THE POPULACE MILLED ABOUT THE STREETS OF BAKEWELL in happy confusion: farm women and domestic servants bustling with purpose and large twig baskets; young boys singing the praises of tin and soap and bristle brushes made of boar. There were cheese sellers and egg sellers and a man who held a pair of squealing piglets high for inspection; and I should have enjoyed the hurly-burly of market day, were it not for the picture of horror that still lingered in my mind. A profusion of odours mingled in the August heat— the sweat of men and of horses, the deep mustiness of sheep's wool. Roasting sausage and spoiling hay. Bruised peaches. And the smell of butcher's blood.

It was everywhere in the folds of my light muslin gown and the damp curls of my hair, that warm, sweet, engulfing odour from the heights of Miller's Dale. I felt a wretched desire to be sick, and steadied myself against a hitching post.

There is a madman loose in the hills. Only this could explain the savagery visited upon the poor fellow lying among the rocks. The attack seemed very nearly inhuman, as though a wild beast had come upon the gentleman unawares, and torn him asunder.

That he *was* a gentleman, I had no doubt. His clothing was well-made, and near enough in style to my fashionable brothers' to suggest that he was a person of some means. A traveller such as ourselves, perhaps. An admirer of the beauties of the Peaks. Certainly not an angler, for there had been no sign of abandoned tackle. But what traveller wandered alone through hill and dale, so far from Bakewell, and without an equipage or a mount? And where were his party—the friends who might have put a name to his broken form?

Not a traveller, then. A person long familiar with the Peaks. An excellent walker, who had come from a farm or a nearby estate in the first light of morning and mounted the path above the Wye by slow degrees, lost in heavy thought, until he achieved the heights—and a meeting that had brought his death.

"Jane!"

It was my sister Cassandra's voice. I turned and espied her in the doorway of the confectioner's opposite, waving a gloved hand. Her chestnut curls peeked demurely from a lace cap, and the cut of her gown was sober; for the briefest instant I might have been gazing upon the image of my mother, drawn from life a score of years ago. *How old we are become,* I thought, and waited for the passage of a waggon before traversing the paving stones.

"You must sample one of Mrs. Carver's puddings," my sister urged. "Only think—they are called Bakewell puddings, and are peculiar to the region. I have been enjoying mine this quarter-hour, but I am certain Mrs. Carver would not hesitate to bring another for yourself."

I sank onto a stool in a corner of the close room and placed my head in my hands. "I could not bear the sight of food at present."

"What has happened?" Cassandra enquired. "I did not look for you in Bakewell until the dinner hour, at least. Are you unwell, Jane?"

Her gentle hand was upon my shoulder. A great weariness had me in its grip, and it was enough to rest there amidst the warm smells of pastry and jam and say nothing. But Cassandra would have an answer.

"Where is my cousin?"

"With the blacksmith."

"Has Mr. Hemming's pony thrown a shoe?"

"The blacksmith, Cassandra, is also the surgeon. There has been . . . an accident." I raised my head and looked at her; she was all anxiety.

"Mr. Cooper," she breathed in horror.

"No." I gripped her wrist in reassurance. "A person quite unknown to us all. A gentleman, rather young, with blond curls and the face of an angel. He had the look of a poet about him—rather as Cowper ought to look, and never could. He was murdered, Cassandra."

"Murdered! Oh, surely not—"

"It was horrible." I shuddered with all the force of memory. "A great wound to the temple from a lead ball, and his bowels entirely cut out. His tongue had been severed, and there was a welter of blood about the rocks. I shall never forget the cawing of those crows—"

A stifled scream alerted me to the presence of Mrs. Carver behind her counter, and to the rising tendency of my own conversation. It would not do to cause a fit of public hysterics.

Cassandra's right eyebrow rose in reproof. "It sounds to be a scene drawn straight from a horrid novel," she observed. "One of Mrs. Radcliffe's. Only it should have been in Italy, several centuries ago, and the victim a wandering prince. Take some tea, Jane. I find that it is delightfully restoring, despite the heat of the day. Or perhaps Mrs. Carver might compound a cordial."

"When she is done imparting the news of murder to her neighbours," I replied.

THE RUTLAND ARMS IS A FINE, MODERN BUILDING OF STONE COMmanding the top of Matlock Street, with all of Bakewell falling away before it. A posting-house named The White Horse was formerly upon the site, but some two years since the Duke of Rutland, who owns the land upon which the old inn sat, pulled down the building and threw up this new one, to our infinite satisfaction. I find myself in possession of an airy bedchamber overlooking Matlock Street, where every carriage of consequence is subject to my view; and as the principal London stages must change horses here before proceeding on to Manchester, the parade of the fashionable, the frivolous, the indigent, and the wary must be a source of constant amusement. Add to this the luxury of a snug upstairs parlour set aside for our party's use, and the wild beauty of the surrounding country—and we are considerably more comfortable than we should have been among the victims of whooping cough.

My cousin Mr. Cooper did not return until our dinner was very nearly laid—which at The Rutland Arms occurs at the grand, unfashionable hour of four o'clock. I was sufficiently recovered to quit my bedchamber and join Cassandra and my mother in the parlour a few moments before Mr. Cooper alighted wearily from George Hemming's trap. Heavy dark clouds had rolled in from the hills, ominous with the threat of rain; thunder bruited in the distance. The air was oppressive and increasingly close—hardly uncommon of an August afternoon. Today, however, I read portents in the storm. The natural order had been violated—a man despatched as one might butcher a calf—and all of Heaven knew it.

My mother was attempting to mend the lace on one of her caps; she had drawn her chair quite close to the window in a vain search for available light. At the sound of carriage wheels in the cobbled street below, she set down her muslin and peered through the storm-darkened panes.

"Well. There he is at last, Jane," she said, "and not a hint of a corpse about him. I do hope the inn boasts a laundress. The smell of blood can be most persistent."

"Yes, ma'am," I replied. I had ordered a bath myself upon returning to The Rutland Arms, and scrubbed my skin raw.

"He does not bring his friend with him," she observed. "Pity. I had marked out Mr. Hemming for one of you."

"Thank you for my part of the favour, Mamma, but I do not wish to spend the rest of my days in Derbyshire," Cassandra said plaintively. "Although a trifle advanced in years, and undoubtedly given to the wearing of flannel during the winter months, Mr. Hemming will do very well for Jane. She may learn to prepare any manner of fish in five different ways, and exclaim continually over the glories of the Peaks."

"I think I might be equal to the latter," I mused, "did the gentleman consume his fish himself."

The door to the hall was flung open, and Mr. Cooper appeared. My cousin's hair was disarranged and his countenance drawn and pale. His good worsted suiting was smeared with dark stains that could only be blood.

"Dear ladies," he said faintly, and bowed.

"My poor Edward." My mother's accent was more brisk than fond.

"Pray take a chair. The roast shall be sent up presently. Unless you should prefer a cold dinner today on account of the juices," she added obscurely.

"It makes no odds," Mr. Cooper replied absently, "my appetite is fled. I commend your Christian charity, however, for considering of it, Aunt. My cousin has informed you of the sad events of this morning?"

"You must know that Jane loves nothing so well as a tale of murder," my mother replied comfortably. "I blame her father, Mr. Cooper. George Austen was an excellent man and an accomplished sermonist—quite lauded in his day, and besieged with offers of publication, which he would not hear of, except insomuch as his fame contributed to his supply of students, for he was always disposed to the tempering of young minds—particularly when their patrons were generous with board, and paid on time. But where was I?"

"You were about to say, ma'am, that my father disposed me to relish a tale of murder," I supplied.

"And so he did. All that novel-reading of a winter's eve! The more horrid the better. And she has gone from bad to worse, Mr. Cooper— she practically chooses her friends from among the intimates of the dock. First it was the Countess of Scargrave, who must place herself in Newgate for poisoning of her first husband; and then it was Lord Harold's nephew, the one who shall inherit the Dukedom. Not to mention French spies. I should not be surprised to learn that Jane has taken up with Whigs," she added darkly, as though this was tantamount to running naked through the streets, "and no respectable man will have her *then*."

"Lord Harold?" my cousin enquired, with a faint line between his brows. The allusion to the fifth Duke of Wilborough's second son was lost upon him.

"Well you may look shocked," my mother retorted, with a triumphant air. "You see, Jane, how that man's reputation has preceded him? Even in the rectories of Staffordshire, his name is uttered with dread!"

At this juncture the serving girl put in her appearance, bearing high a covered tureen. All discourse was naturally suspended some moments. Sally laid the cloth, set out the various dishes, and waited until we should be seated. When she had served us all, I gave her leave to quit the parlour. Left to himself, I believe my cousin should never have considered of it. He appeared insensible to everything but a brown stain upon the tablecloth, which he studied earnestly. His plate he left untouched.

Cassandra sent me a look of mute enquiry. I lifted my shoulders a fraction in dismay. My mother continued to talk of her late husband— of students long absent from our lives, and the disproportionate fortunes of their patrons—of her youth in Oxford, and her uncle Theophilus Leigh, the Master of Balliol College, who was renowned for his wit. When at length she had drawn breath to repeat one of the Master's most cherished aphorisms, I hastily intervened.

"Was the Coroner able to put a name to that unfortunate young man, Cousin?"

"Eh?" Mr. Cooper came to his senses with a start. "What young man?"

"The one I discovered murdered this morning," I reminded him gently.

Cassandra's expression of concern had deepened; her gaze was fixed anxiously on Mr. Cooper. She appeared ready to leap to his aid in the instant, should he fall into a swoon.

"I suppose there is no harm in relating the intelligence," Mr. Cooper conceded heavily, "and, indeed, it will be on every tradesman's lips by morning. I shudder to think what my esteemed and noble patron, Sir George Mumps, will say when he learns of the affair."

We waited in some suspense.

His eyes came up to meet my own, with a look of profound confusion. "The corpse of Miller's Dale was not that of a gentleman, Jane, but one who had borrowed a gentleman's clothes."

"An imposter?" I enquired. "The matter gains in interest."

"And delicacy," Mr. Cooper added. "For no one can say what the poor girl was about, or who might have used her so foully."

I stood up abruptly and thrust back my chair. "Would you tell me that the young man so savagely murdered this morning—"

"Was, in fact, a woman," my cousin said.

Against Disorders of the Head

Chop two ounces of wild Valerian Root, and add to it an ounce of freshly-gathered Sage. Pour over two quarts of boiling water, and let stand till it be cold. Strain off the water, and give the Sufferer a quarter of a pint, twice each day.

This is most useful against Giddiness and Pains, and all disorders of the Head, especially Nervous Cases.

—From the Stillroom Book of Tess Arnold,
Penfolds Hall, Derbyshire, 1802–1806

Chapter 4

The Witch of
Penfolds Hall

26 August 1806, cont.

~

"BUT HOW EXTRAORDINARY!" I CRIED. "CAN SUCH A THING BE possible?"

"It can, Cousin, and it is," Mr. Cooper replied gloomily. "Mr. Tivey discovered the truth directly he examined the corpse. There is no denying that a woman's body is very unlike to a man's, you know, and furthermore, he recognised the girl at once. She is Bakewell born and bred."

"Indeed?" There had been elegance in her looks—that delicacy of feature, the cropped golden curls. She might well have been a gentleman's daughter, abroad on some lark in the dead of night. That would explain the fancy-dress. "And did she belong to one of the estates in the neighbourhood?"

"To a place called Penfolds," my cousin said, "some five miles distant. She was a stillroom maid."

"A servant!"

"By the name of Tess Arnold."

I glanced over my shoulder at the parlour door, concerned lest word of the girl's unhappy end should travel unbeknownst into the hallway; Sally might be hovering there, her ears grown large with the intelligence. I shut the door firmly and placed my back against it.

"Was Mr. Tivey able to determine when she was killed?"

My cousin's eyes moved blankly to meet my own. "He thinks it possible that life was extinguished some hours before the body was discovered, but cannot tell exactly when. The maid probably met her end in the middle of the night."

"Quite alone and far from home"—Cassandra shuddered—"where her cries for assistance must certainly go unheeded. How dreadful, to be sure!"

"You say that Penfolds is five miles from Bakewell, Cousin," I said. "But how great a distance separates it from Miller's Dale, and the place of the maid's gruesome end?"

"Less than a mile, Sir James Villiers tells me. Sir James is in commission of the peace for Bakewell, and a very fine gentleman; he has known Charles Danforth from birth."

"Mr. Danforth, I conclude, is the owner of Penfolds?"

"And a man of very easy circumstances—a clear ten thousand a year. The Danforth family is an ancient one in Derbyshire, and boasts a considerable reputation and influence; Sir James assures me that they are everywhere esteemed and valued." The respectability of the Penfolds family appeared of some importance to my cousin, as though it might blot out the savagery of their dependant's murder.

"I knew a Danforth once," my mother offered, "but he was killed at sea in the year 'sixty-nine. They carried his body in the hold of his ship for six weeks together, pickled in a hogshead of rum, so that his wife might have the burying of him. Unsavoury business. I cannot think that any wife should wish to see her husband so thoroughly disguised in drink."

"But how came this young woman to be from home so late at night?" Cassandra enquired. "And attired as a man?"

"And whose," I added, "were the clothes? It must be tolerably difficult for a serving girl to obtain the articles of a gentleman."

"Unless she were intimate with the Penfolds laundress," my mother observed—a point not without its merits.

"One does not wish to speak ill of the dead—particularly when death was achieved in so hideous a manner," Cassandra began hesitantly. "One does not like to place an unpleasant construction on events—"

"But clearly duplicity was the maid's object. You may speak freely, Cassandra; your words cannot harm Tess Arnold now."

"I fear I cannot agree, Jane," objected Mr. Cooper. "It is not for us to canvass the matter of the girl's death. It is an affair for the Justice."

Impossible for my cousin to comprehend the restless agitation that had held me in its grip throughout the morning; or the feverish activity of my intellect, in its effort to make sense of so much brutality. He could not be expected to apprehend that having seen the blood on the rock, I must be *doing* something to rid myself of nightmare. Such behaviour in a lady was beyond Mr. Cooper's experience, and, indeed, beyond what he might consider the bounds of decorum. But I would not submit willingly to nightmare for anyone.

I took a turn before the unlit grate and came to a halt at my cousin's chair. "Did Mr. Tivey offer his opinion of the girl? Or any views that might throw some light on this dreadful business?"

Mr. Cooper drew a laboured breath, and failed to meet my eyes. "Tivey is the sort who would consign his own mother to the Devil, Jane," he said with surprising vehemence, "and I would not give a farthing for his opinion of anybody."

SIR JAMES VILLIERS, HOWEVER, WAS ANOTHER KETTLE OF FISH—AS MY mother, in an angling spirit, might have been disposed to say. Sir James appeared in The Rutland Arms at so advanced an hour of the evening, however, that my mother was long since gone to bed, and Cassandra hard on her heels; only my cousin and I kept vigil with the lamps. Though the subject went unbroached between us, I rather fancy that neither of us was in haste to shut his eyes that evening, being uncertain what visions of horror might descend.

Mr. Cooper was bent over his travelling desk, composing a letter to his wife or perhaps a sermon on the day's events—a natural expression of relief after so trying a period. I was engrossed in a slim volume of George Crabbe's, discovered on a shelf in a corner of our parlour—a book of verse, unknown to me before, entitled *The Village*. Its tone was so like to a bitter wind that blights the first faint flowers of spring, that I quite admired the poet. He might have captured my very spirit of trouble and melancholy. I had just concluded the passage that begins "amid such pleasing scenes I trace/the poor laborious natives of the place," when Sally announced Sir James.

He was not a tall man; but his figure was so elegantly spare, and so swooningly attired, that he might have been the lengthiest reed, a veritable whip of a fellow. He slid lithely into the room and bowed low over my hand before I had even thought to make my curtsey—before, indeed, my cousin Mr. Cooper had gained his feet. In another instant, Sir James had sent the serving girl for a bottle of Madeira—had made himself comfortable in our parlour—and was conversing so cordially with Mr. Cooper and myself that we might all have been acquainted this last age.

Sir James's fair hair was artfully curled over his forehead *à la Titus* and the leathers of his Hussar boots gleamed. I observed the cut of his dark blue pantaloons, the narrow shoulders of his olive coat, and the remarkable extravagance of his necktie—and knew myself in the presence of a Pink of the *ton,* a Sprig of Fashion, a True Corinthian. My brother Henry had long ago taught me the mark of such a man.

"Have you lived long in Derbyshire, Sir James?" I enquired as Sally reappeared with his wine.

"All my life," he replied. "I was born and raised at Villiers Hall, and absent a few years of schooling and a Season or two in London, have been happy to call it home. I am the fourth Villiers to bear the title of baronet, and the second to serve as Justice for Bakewell."

"And does your commission generally give you so much trouble?"

He grinned—an easy, languorous expression not unlike a hound's. "There has not been a serious offence in the vicinity for years, Miss Austen. The duties of Justice are more honoured in the breach than the observance. We may account Tess Arnold's murder the result of an extraordinary run of bad luck."

"Have there been other incidents, then, predating this murder?"

"Not in Bakewell itself," Sir James replied. "But the owner of Penfolds Hall—Mr. Charles Danforth—has suffered grievous misfortune in recent months. He has lost no less than four children, the last a stillborn son. His wife passed away a fortnight after her lying-in."

"It is a wonder the people of Bakewell do not believe him cursed," I murmured.

"Ah—but they do! And the maid's murder will be taken as further proof of it." Sir James looked to my cousin. "It is a most distressing business, whatever the cause. It seems your passion for angling, Mr. Cooper, has placed us all at the center of a maelstrom. What have you to say for yourself?"

Mr. Cooper opened and shut his mouth without a word escaping him. It was fortunate, I thought, that no hymn sprang forth.

"A maelstrom," I repeated. "Has news of the girl's murder spread so quickly?"

"Recollect that it was market day, and all the countryside gathered in town," Sir James replied. "If there is a resident within twenty miles of Bakewell yet in ignorance of the events, I should be greatly surprised."

"Is Mr. Tivey so little to be trusted?"

Sir James hesitated. "Michael Tivey is well enough in his way—a good surgeon, and a better blacksmith—but he is also a native of this country, reared in all the superstition and ignorance for which these hills are known."

"And what does superstition argue, Sir James?" I enquired.

"Tivey would have it the girl was killed in sacrifice—that she was butchered like a spring lamb to appease a vengeful god. He is crying out in every publican's house against the heretics who walk among us—against infidels, and idolators, and destroyers of respectable faith. In short, Tivey would have it that Tess Arnold was murdered by Freemasons."

"Freemasons!" I cried. And was bereft of further speech.

A Freemasons' lodge is so much a part of life in a country village—a gathering place for local gentlemen, and a focus for their benevolent works—that it might rival the Church in sanctity. Indeed, not a few of the most distinguished clerics in the Church of England espouse the Brotherhood's Christian principles; to be a politician is almost synonymous with membership; the Prince of Wales has lent the order an air of Fashion; and advancement in the world of the professions, whether in London or the counties, might well turn upon the influence of one's fellow Masons. In short, the lodge is the most powerful of gentlemen's clubs—than which, in England, little else is *more* powerful. The idea of a surgeon-blacksmith inciting public opinion against such a creditable institution strained the bounds of belief.

"Freemasons," Sir James repeated with a hint of irony in his voice. "I suspect the local lodge has rejected Tivey as a member. However excellent his hands with horses and broken sinews, he is not what our Derbyshire gentry would like to call *one of ourselves;* and so he seizes this opportunity to paint us all with a grisly brush. He shall certainly do some damage, to be sure—there are many enough among the Bakewell rabble who are willing to believe the rankest sort of nonsense."

"But Masons have long been regarded as pillars of respectability," objected my cousin Mr. Cooper. "I do not mean to say that this was always the case; there was a time, indeed, when God-fearing folk understood the Brethren to have formed a dark cabal, a sort of heretical sect, and the Masonic affection for obscure symbols did not recommend their cause. But such ignorance must be a thing of the past. To be a Freemason is to be recognised as a decent and benevolent fellow— and one who moves in the first circles. Even so exalted a gentleman as my esteemed patron, Sir George Mumps, is not above joining a lodge. He pressed me most flatteringly only last winter to become a member; but, however, I could not spare the time from my parish duties. It is impossible that a Mason should be connected with so disgraceful an affair as the maid's murder—and if such accusations were to reach Sir George's ears, I am sure he would refute them most indignantly!"

"But as Tivey has seen fit to point out, there is a ritual execution prescribed for traitors to the lodge," Sir James replied, "and the maidservant's case is very like in nearly every particular. Tivey has published the nature of the girl's wounds in Bakewell's streets, and many are now crying revenge against the Secret Brotherhood."

"In what way does the maid's case appear similar, Sir James?" I enquired.

"When a man betrays his brother Masons, he is to be executed in a rather grim and unhappy manner. His throat is slit, his bowels cut out, and his tongue torn from his mouth. You see the resemblance to Tess Arnold's case."

"But for the throat-cutting," I murmured, "and the addition of a lead ball to the forehead. And do you credit Mr. Tivey's accusation?"

Sir James shrugged expressively. "I am a member of the Duke's lodge myself, Miss Austen. I cannot be considered impartial. But I may attest that the maidservant's name was never broached in our proceedings, and that no formal decision was taken to murder her in this way. What a rogue Mason may have done, however . . ."

The Justice allowed his thought to trail away; the conclusion was evident enough. Sir James Villiers was placed in a most awkward position. As a Mason in commission of the peace, he must judge the very institution of which he was himself a member—a fact that should not be lost upon the common folk of Bakewell. The matter of the maid's brutal end should become a cause for politics.

"The Duke's lodge, you say?" Mr. Cooper's interest had been swiftly regained. Here was influence to rival Sir George Mumps's.

"His Grace the Duke of Devonshire has long been a member of two lodges—the Prince of Wales's, which he attends while resident in London; and the Bakewell Brotherhood founded by his father, the fourth Duke."

"But a woman should never be admitted to either," I observed, "unless she went disguised as a man."

Sir James surveyed my countenance narrowly. "You have hit upon the very point, Miss Austen, that most supports Tivey's wildest suppositions. Tess Arnold was arrayed as a gentleman on the night of her death; and I will not disguise that her master, Charles Danforth, is a Mason like his neighbours. It is our custom to go masked into certain of our ceremonies; and with her face concealed, the girl might credibly have passed for an absent Brother."

"And did the local lodge convene that night?"

"It did," Sir James replied. "But certainly not among the rocks above Miller's Dale."

"Was Charles Danforth present?"

"I believe that he was. His brother, Andrew, however, did not appear, having an engagement to dine at Chatsworth that evening."

"—Though the Duke is a fellow Mason?"

Sir James smiled. "Indolence marks nearly every endeavour in which His Grace is engaged, Miss Austen. It should not be extraordinary for the Brotherhood to meet, and Devonshire to remain comfortably at home."

I rose restlessly and took a turn about the room. What possible interest could a mere maid have felt in the proceedings of gentlemen?

As Sir James acknowledged, Freemasons cloaked their meetings in an air of mystery. They trafficked in rituals and signs. Had Tess Arnold attempted to pierce the veil as a sort of joke? But I could not believe she had stumbled upon the idea herself. Someone—some man, who might possibly have supplied her extraordinary clothes—had suggested the plan; and it was probably *he* who killed her.

"What use does Mr. Tivey intend to make of the sensation he has caused?" my cousin enquired.

Sir James pursed his lips. "He may simply enjoy the discomfiture of his betters. Or hope to see an institution destroyed, that determined to reject him."

"So you regard his malice as having a general, rather than a particular, target in view?" I observed.

The Justice lifted a satiric brow. "Miss Austen, where Michael Tivey is concerned, I cannot profess to apprehend anything. If you believe he hopes to discredit one person—I will not say you nay."

"Mr. George Hemming was very loath to carry the body into Bakewell," I said slowly. "I rather wonder if he expected Mr. Tivey's accusation."

"Mr. Hemming is a Freemason as well as a solicitor; and highly regarded in both realms."

"But he was not in attendance at the lodge Monday evening—for he took tea with us in this very room that night! Something of ritual murder he must suspect, however. I can think of no other objection, no other explanation for his anxiety towards a stranger."

"He did not recognise the maid?" Sir James enquired searchingly.

"Emphatically not. He was at great pains to underline that the young man—as we then believed Deceased to be—was foreign to him."

"I confess I am surprised to hear it. George Hemming has served as Charles Danforth's solicitor for many years, and old Mr. Danforth before him; he must be familiar with every person attached to Penfolds Hall."

Sir James's intelligence must be such as to astonish. If Michael Tivey had known the girl at a glance, then George Hemming could not be excused by the fact of men's clothes and a fearful mutilation. His every action must now be weighed in light of this deceit. I glanced at my cousin, but Mr. Cooper's countenance revealed nothing of anxiety.

"Has the wretched girl any family?" he asked the Justice.

"Yes, indeed. Once Tivey had put a name to the corpse, Tess Arnold's mother besieged the Snake and Hind with a demand for the girl's body, and no amount of explanation on Tivey's part—no mention of inquests or the mysteries of the Law—would satisfy her. She was required to be physically restrained, and uttered all manner of abuse."

"How dreadful!" I replied. "But it is to be expected, perhaps, that a mother should wish to see her child in such a circumstance. Her distress does not bear thinking of."

"Mrs. Arnold is blind," Sir James returned succinctly, "and has seen nothing for a score of years. I rather think her object in display was to make as much trouble as possible for all concerned. You may imagine how the townsfolk relished the scene. I was very nearly struck down this evening in my passage through the streets, with cries of 'Murderer!' and 'Vengeance against the Dark Brotherhood!' "

My cousin looked all his indignation. "We shall believe ourselves in France by and by, if order is not established. When I consider what Sir George Mumps, my noble patron, would say—"

"Could Mrs. Arnold offer an account of the girl's movements, Sir James?" I broke in hastily. "Could she explain her daughter's extraordinary mode of dress?"

Sir James replied in the negative. "Betty Arnold knew little of Tess's life at the Great House. The woman lives with her younger daughter in a tenant cottage, while Tess shared a bed with two other maids in the servants' wing of Penfolds Hall."

"Did the other maids observe the girl's direction Monday night? Could they name, perhaps, the owner of her borrowed feathers?"

Sir James paused in the act of replying, and eyed me dubiously; and only then did I recollect that a Justice should never share his knowledge before an Inquest, particularly with a person so wholly unconnected to the neighbourhood as myself.

"Pray forgive me," I managed. "My interest borders on the unseemly. It is only that having discovered the poor girl, I am naturally anxious—"

"I do understand. But I must beg you to await the Coroner's panel."

"When is it to meet?" Mr. Cooper enquired.

"Thursday morning—and it cannot be too soon for my liking," Sir James said frankly. "Tivey made no effort to conceal the extent of the girl's wounds; and the mood of the townspeople is grown quite ugly. The savagery of her end has given rise to fear and speculation; both will work a hideous change in the quietest folk. All manner of accusation and rumour fly about."

"A good deal of it must concern ourselves," I observed. "Though I assure you we know little of Freemasonry, we are nonetheless strangers in the neighbourhood, and must consequently draw every eye."

"Nonsense!" my cousin cried; but his colour had heightened unhealthily.

"I fear you view the matter only too clearly, Miss Austen," the Justice replied. "It is to your benefit that Mr. George Hemming—a local man of some consequence—was of your party, but suspicions will remain. The corpse was found at such a remove from the gentlemen's position on the riverbank, and a good deal of time elapsed from its initial discovery to its eventual appearance in Water Street—"

"But this is absurd!" Mr. Cooper protested. "Would you have it that Miss Austen despatched the abominable maid? *Miss Austen*, who never laid eyes on the girl in her life, and should have no cause to murder, if she had?"

"Pray contain yourself, sir," I begged him. "You would not wish to awaken my mother."

"I rather think," Sir James assured my cousin, "that not the slightest suspicion has been visited upon Miss Austen's head. Recollect that her gloves and gown were entirely free of blood."

Unlike Mr. Cooper's own, which were splashed with the maid's gore by the time he achieved Water Street. My cousin considered of this; took the point that the respectable George Hemming should not be the object of local calumny—and his countenance drained of colour.

"But I am a man of God!"

"And may undoubtedly prove that you were in your hired bedchamber at the exact hour of the maidservant's end," Sir James concluded briskly. "You will, however, be required to speak to the disposition of the body. Whatever misunderstandings are presently in circulation, must be silenced by the Inquest. Have you sufficient courage, Miss Austen, to face the Bakewell worthies? You shall not be charged with Freemasonry, at least."

"I think I may say that I am equal to Bakewell's worst, Sir James," I replied.

"I fear you have not yet seen it; but, however, a few days of patience, Mr. Cooper"—this, to my apoplectic cousin—"and the matter should be resolved."

"Miss Austen certainly shall *not* appear before a Coroner's panel," Mr. Cooper protested. "To stand in front of Mr. Tivey and the very lowest sort of folk, in a public inn, and answer all manner of impertinent questions! It does not bear thinking of."

"I have done so before," I observed.

"Have you, indeed?" Sir James bestowed upon me a penetrating look.

"You were not then under my protection," my cousin replied. "I cannot allow it. What condemnation should I justly merit, from Sir George Mumps, for so exposing a young lady to the public eye!"

"But the matter, Cousin, is hardly in Sir George's keeping," I reminded him. "And if you will insist upon using such words as *protection,* in the absence of your excellent wife, I do not know what Sir James will think of us!"

This final declaration—carrying with it all manner of scandalous implication, as though the discomfitted clergyman had offered me *carte blanche* in return for my favours—so shocked Mr. Cooper, that he was speechless for several minutes.

"It is unfortunate that Miss Austen should have found the body, Cooper," Sir James went on, "but there is nothing for it. Her testimony must be invaluable. I could wish Miss Austen greater felicity in the nature of her victim, but there again, we are but sport for circumstance."

"You know something of the girl's history?" I asked him curiously. "Pray divulge it, if you will."

"There are few in Bakewell who can be ignorant of her character. Tess Arnold was the subject of considerable gossip, you understand. She was not entirely a respectable creature. And there are some who would have it she was a witch."

"A witch?" I was startled. "Surely not!"

"Mr. Cooper might be the soundest judge of such matters," returned Sir James with a pleasing deference for my cousin. "I cannot pretend to a spiritual court; my powers are purely temporal."

"But whence arises such a charge?" I enquired. "Surely the people of Bakewell are not so simple as to believe a serving girl possessed of the Devil."

"She was, after all, a stillroom maid."

"Which tells me nothing more than that she was an adept at the preservation of peaches," I retorted peevishly. "There is nothing very wonderful in this."

"An adept, too, at the compounding of simple medicines," Sir James supplied. "Tess Arnold was reputed to know everything about healing the sick. There are some who claim that she had mastered still greater arts—that she sold charms for lovers, and curses for enemies; that she could blight crops and cause sheep to drop their lambs stillborn. The power of her look would sap the strength from a man, so the women of Bakewell say."

"And now they would have it that she died at the Devil's hand," I concluded. "Is that the sum of the tale? That an incubus destroyed Tess Arnold on the rock?"

In the flickering light of the lamps, I saw my cousin's eyes, wide and grave; and then he crossed himself once against the Evil Eye.

"Incubus or Freemason—such things have been rumoured in country towns before this," Sir James observed. "It is far more comfortable to throw the guilt upon mysteries one cannot understand, than upon a human being disturbingly like oneself."

I threw up my hands in exasperation. "There is another force at work in country towns, Sir James—a force of greater power than witchcraft, and certainly as deadly: jealousy, and the malice that it will breed. You said, I think, that Tess Arnold was not considered respectable. Is that because the people of Bakewell believed her a witch? Or because she was a woman of easy virtue?"

My cousin Mr. Cooper uttered a scandalised snort. "Remember where you are, Jane, and do not run on in the wild way you are suffered to do at home!" he cried.

Sir James appeared not to have heard his injunction. "You are anxious to defend her, though totally unknown to you before," he observed.

"Recollect that I saw her face," I told him. "When I believed it to be a man's, I was struck by the delicacy of feature; now that I know it to have belonged to a woman, I can comprehend the envy it might arouse."

"She was reported to be liberal in the granting of her favours," Sir James conceded, "although in that instance, too, a jealous tongue may do much with little matter."

"She was foully and cruelly murdered, and she cannot have been more than five-and-twenty! How is such a creature to possess the depth of art you would describe?"

He said nothing for a moment; and then, setting down his glass, he shook his head. "I should be the last to deny the evil weight of a jealous tongue, Miss Austen. But it is my experience that few women of any age or social station end as Tess Arnold did. And that must give one pause. Her death was achieved in a kind of fury, as though the gods themselves had spread her bowels upon the rock."

To Find if a Body be Dead or Not

Stick a needle an inch or so into the corpus. If it is alive, the needle will become tarnished whilst in the truly dead the needle will retain its polish.

—From the Stillroom Book of Tess Arnold,
Penfolds Hall, Derbyshire, 1802–1806

Chapter 5

A Consultation
with the Solicitor

Wednesday
27 August 1806
~

"I THINK, MR. COOPER," I SAID WHEN WE HAD ALL ASSEMBLED IN THE parlour for breakfast this morning, "that our first object should be to pay a call upon your friend Mr. Hemming."

My cousin looked up from his buttered toast in astonishment. "Upon George? I am sure that he is hard at work, Cousin, in his solicitor's offices. However much Mr. Hemming may look the gentleman, he is not entirely at leisure. His time is not his own to command, but must await the pleasure of his clients, upon whom his sustenance depends. We shall certainly not find him at home."

"Very well," I replied, "then let us seek him at his place of business if we must. It is imperative, I think, that we discover what Mr. Hemming truly knows of the maid Tess Arnold. The Inquest cannot hope to be a pleasant affair in any case—"

"I am sure you love nothing better than a Coroner's panel, Jane," my mother objected.

"—but if we appear in ignorance of your friend's purpose, in concealing from us the truth of the maid's identity when he must surely have known it, we shall feel ourselves the objects of a very poor joke, indeed."

Mr. Cooper set down his teacup with a clatter of crockery. "You cannot really intend to make such a display of yourself, Cousin, as to appear before Mr. Tivey at the Snake and Hind tomorrow morning!"

"My dear Mr. Cooper," I replied, "can *you* really know so little of the English system of justice, as to believe I am offered any choice?"

George Hemming keeps his offices in Carding Street, less than half a mile from The Rutland Arms; and it was thither we repaired after breakfast. My mother declined the errand, but Cassandra consented to make a third of the party, the day being very fine, and our time in Bakewell all too short.

"Do you really intend to quit this place on Friday?" she enquired of our cousin. "I suppose you must believe your admirable wife sorely in want of you. I must own that were I to consult only myself, I should prolong the visit—I have not seen a tenth of the region's beauties! Not a standing stone nor a cavern have we explored, Jane! And how I long to open my sketchbook before a chasm or a torrent, and attempt to seize them in crayons!"

"My dear cousin—we cannot throw off the dust of Derbyshire too soon," Mr. Cooper replied indignantly. "I shudder to think what Sir George Mumps should say, did he know of our entanglement in this dreadful affair; and he shall know of it very soon, for I related the whole to my dearest Caroline, and she will feel herself obliged to publish the intelligence throughout Hamstall Ridware. It must make a very great piece of news, indeed. I daresay she will be asked to dine on the strength of it."

Being momentarily torn between the most sublime gratification, at the thought of himself as the object of general admiration and pity within his parish—and the gravest anxiety for his noble patron's good opinion—my cousin very nearly lost his way. I steered him gently back from the turning into Water Street, and said, "Just here, Mr. Cooper, I believe we shall find Mr. Hemming."

A painted sign in a prosperous shade of bottle green announced the premises to all of Derbyshire: *George Hemming Esquire, Solicitor at the Bar.* Mr. Cooper begged us to precede him onto the doorstep, then did the honour of the brass doorknocker; it made a hollow, echoing sound, as though the offices burrowed deep.

"There is your cavern, Cassandra," I murmured, "and mind you make the most of it."

The door swung open to reveal a tall, thin heron of a fellow arrayed in rusty suiting and a well-worn collar. He clutched a quill in one hand; the fingertips of the other were stained dark blue. His head was bare and balding; his eyes were of a watery brown; what hair he possessed was already grey. Mr. Hemming's clerk. He had spent all his life apprenticed to the Law, and should carry ink-stained fingers to his coffin because of it.

"No appointments today," he said firmly, and made as though to shut the door.

I put out my hand and grasped the handle. "But we are not here on business, Mr. . . ."

"Bartles," he replied. "Joseph Bartles, Mr. Hemming's chief clerk. Mr. Hemming is not at leisure at present."

"George has spoken so very highly of you," my sister Cassandra put in warmly, to Mr. Cooper's astonishment. " 'I should be nowhere at all without Mr. Bartles' he said, only Monday evening. 'Mr. Bartles is the man I depend upon'—isn't that right, Jane?"

"Oh—yes, yes, indeed," I replied, with an eye for the clerk. His ancient chest had visibly swelled with pride. "I do not know where our excellent friend George would be without you. How *well* I recall Mr. Hemming's words, as we all drove towards the Dale only yesterday: 'So dependable in every respect! So entirely worthy of trust! If I have earned some small measure of success, it must all be laid to Bartles's account!' "

"I do not recall—" my cousin began, in tones of the greatest disapprobation.

"—You were asleep, Edward, you always are. We shan't be a moment, Mr. Bartles. Is Mr. Hemming within?"

"Certainly, miss," Bartles replied, and drew wide the door.

We were ushered to a bare little anteroom, where the scriveners' desks stood bleakly in a wash of sunlight; a young man was arranged behind one, his face pale and his brow furrowed as he shifted from foot to foot. Unlike Mr. Bartles, this fellow's collar points were enormous and his neckcloth elaborately tied; they quite prohibited him from lowering his chin over his work, so that he was forced to peer down his nose at the foolscap before him, in a manner that I wondered did not drive him mad.

"If you will please to wait," Mr. Bartles said formally, and bowed to my cousin. "The name again, sir?"

"Edward Cooper."

"And the Miss Austens," Cassandra added with a brilliant smile.

"Good God, Edward, whatever are you doing here?" exclaimed George Hemming from the doorway of an inner chamber. "I'm most deucedly pressed this morning. I cannot possibly spare a moment—"

"I think perhaps you must, sir." I moved towards him swiftly, and Cassandra followed. "Sir James Villiers paid us a most delightful call last evening, and your company was sorely missed. You should have added so much to the general tone of conversation—to the brilliance of the party! Do you not wish to hear what the Justice had to say, on the subject of angling?"

Mr. Hemming hesitated; he glanced from ourselves to his two clerks, who were attempting to overlisten the conversation without appearing to do so; and then the cast of his countenance changed.

"How delightful to see you again, Miss Jane Austen," he said. "I can certainly spare a quarter-hour for any news you might bring."

We filed through the doorway and found ourselves in a comfortable room, with a broad mahogany desk and a quantity of volumes bound in leather, a decanter of spirits, and a painting in oils of a gentleman from the last century. Two chairs were pushed back against the wall; but Mr. Hemming made no gesture towards them, and I preferred to stand in any case.

The solicitor surveyed us with a tight and uneasy smile. "I had not looked for such a visit," he observed, "but I must assume that circumstances urge it. You are come, Edward, about this business of the maid?"

"Indeed, I hardly know why we are come, George—unless it be that my cousin Jane insisted upon it," Mr. Cooper replied. "I am sure that the demands of your work are many, and if the ladies disturbed you in this extraordinary application, I must beg leave to apologise."

Mr. Hemming leaned against the edge of his desk, his fingers gripping the wood painfully. But his countenance and his voice were all that was easy. "Miss Jane Austen would interrogate Mr. Hemming. From what I know of Miss Jane Austen, I should have looked for the honour. Very well, my dear lady—how would you be satisfied?"

"We are to appear before the Coroner's Inquest tomorrow, Mr. Hemming, as no doubt you must yourself. My past experience of similar authority has taught me that honesty before a panel invariably saves a good deal of trouble."

He crossed his arms over his chest and peered at me with amusement. "And have you a *good deal* of such experience, Miss Jane Austen?"

"Enough," I replied succinctly, "to apprehend that you lied, Mr. Hemming, when you failed to identify the corpse above Miller's Dale as being that of Tess Arnold—a young woman with whom, I understand, you have been acquainted for most of her life."

He went pale, and clutched convulsively at the desk; then thrust himself to his feet. "I could not know what I saw in Miller's Dale. In such a scene of horror, who should not be confused? The girl's clothes—the savage wounds to her body—I barely spared a moment to study the face. I was as astonished as yourselves to learn last evening that she was not the gentleman she appeared, and a complete stranger."

"Then why did you behave so oddly at the time? I distinctly recall every word and action. You appeared distracted and oppressed in your manner; you insisted that Deceased must be a traveller like ourselves, and undoubtedly from Buxton. And when we prevailed upon you to return with us to Bakewell, you washed your hands of the affair—'Devil take the consequences,' I believe you said. There was nothing of confusion in all this, Mr. Hemming, but rather a measure of conscious deceit."

"That is absurd!" he burst out.

"Sir James Villiers does not appear to think so," I replied. "And we may presume that he has no reason to prevaricate, when he suggests you were acquainted with the maid for years."

"I have never denied that. I merely failed to recognise the girl in death."

"But I would put it to you, sir, that you *did*—and that the fear her murder occasioned arose from some other cause, than merely horror at her wounds."

"Jane!" my cousin cried, aghast. "How *can* you be so shameless! Mr. Hemming has given us his word as a gentleman!"

George Hemming stared at me, his features working; then he turned away, and put his face in his hands.

"Would you care to offer an explanation for your extraordinary behaviour, sir, before Mr. Tivey requires it of you?" I pressed.

"I cannot see that I owe any young lady so wholly unconnected with me as yourself, the slightest word in regard to the matter," the solicitor said bleakly. "Whatever I may *then* have felt and done, stands between me and my God."

"Very well, George," said Mr. Cooper hurriedly. He turned towards the door. "We shall not disturb you further."

"I can think of only two explanations," I persisted, my eyes on Mr. Hemming's face. "That in recognising the maid, you guessed at the hand of the murderer, and were so wretchedly anxious on *his* account, that you sought to throw the entire affair into Buxton, a district far from the maid's home."

"Not at all!"

"Or, that you played a role *yourself* in Tess Arnold's death, and carried us into Miller's Dale yesterday with the design of establishing yourself creditably in the minds of the chief witnesses to her discovery!"

"Jane!" my cousin cried again. "You have said quite enough!"

"In either eventuality, you cannot have thought very clearly, Mr. Hemming. We were bound to remark your singular conduct, and to discover that you knew quite well who the young 'gentleman' was. We *must* find your appearance of guilt and dismay peculiar in the extreme. If Mr. Tivey enquires as to your reaction, Mr. Hemming—what exactly are we to say?"

The solicitor did not reply. His pallor was dreadful, and sweat had broken out upon his forehead. Cassandra stared from Mr. Hemming to myself with an expression of the most intense anxiety; even my cousin looked all his consternation.

"If you know anything at all, Mr. Hemming, regarding the maid's death, you would do well to disclose it," I advised. "There can be no loyalty so deep as to permit of such a crime. If you will not speak to us, in the privacy of your chambers—then pray determine to speak on the morrow, before the eyes of God and the Law! I beg of you, sir, do not perjure yourself *then*."

"Forgive me, Madam—but I believe that *I* am the solicitor in this company," Mr. Hemming managed with a ghastly smile. "And now if you will excuse me—I have an appointment that cannot wait. I must ride to Penfolds Hall today, and offer my client Mr. Danforth what counsel I may."

"Charles Danforth?" my cousin enquired. "I suppose he is greatly disturbed by this dreadful affair."

"As you would be, too, my good Cooper," the solicitor replied grimly, "if all your neighbours were calling you murderer and fiend. Miss Jane Austen had better counsel what she may of Truth in Danforth's ear."

"DO YOU BELIEVE THAT MR. HEMMING FEARS FOR HIS CLIENT, JANE?" Cassandra mused as we made our way back towards The Rutland Arms, "and that an immediate suspicion of Charles Danforth's guilt urged him to profess ignorance of the maid's identity?"

"It is possible, I suppose—"

"It is utterly *im*possible," my cousin broke in, with remarkable heat. "George Hemming is a highly respectable man! He holds the trust of a considerable number of the Great! He is a gentleman of reputation and no little decency—"

"And his behaviour is in every way calculated to ruin him," I replied. "Do you believe it likely, Cassandra, that the loyalty of a solicitor to a client should extend so far as perjury?"

"As to that—he has not exactly perjured himself as yet," she replied. "He has only offered falsehoods to his friends. We must await the outcome of the Inquest, and then observe how far Mr. Hemming's allegiance—or his guilt—shall drive him."

"Guilt! Perjury!" cried Mr. Cooper in consternation. "When I consider the abominable fashion in which you have served my esteemed friend, Jane, I cannot find it in me to regret that we shall leave this place as soon as may be!"

"There must be something greater at issue," I told my sister;

"something more personal than allegiance to a client, or even a valued friend. A man should not compromise his honour so lightly."

"You have disgraced me before one of my oldest fellows," Mr. Cooper continued hotly, "and you have conducted yourself in a manner that must lay you open to accusations of vulgarity and impertinence."

"I cannot think that Mr. Tivey is the sort to treat a gentleman's honour with respect," observed Cassandra thoughtfully. Her gaze was arrested by a scene played out at the foot of Matlock Street, some hundred feet distant: a crowd of common folk, both men and women, were gathered before the town's well. A single figure was mounted on the well-head; even at this distance I could discern the massive forearms, the darkly-knit brows. Michael Tivey would harangue his fellows about the vicious propensities of the Masonic lodge. To what purpose? Had he named Charles Danforth the maid's murderer? What cause had Tivey to so hound a gentleman, when nothing could yet be known of Tess Arnold's enemies, or the reasons for her death? And with so strong a conviction towards the guilt of another—how could Tivey remain, in conscience, Coroner for the Inquest?

"But why I should find your behaviour astonishing *now*," my cousin cried, "is worthy of question. You have never comported yourself with the modest humility becoming to one of your sex and station, Jane. I may only count myself fortunate that I did not chuse to throw you in the way of Sir George Mumps, my esteemed patron, who must find you unlike his idea of a gently-bred female in every particular."

"My dear Cousin!" Cassandra cried, in a shocked accent. "Consider the violence of your expressions, before it is too late! Our dear Jane has operated from the best intentions in the world."

"She is an insufferable busybody," my cousin retorted, "and will never get a husband if she does not mend her ways. George Hemming seemed so disposed to admire her, too—I thought it very promising that he carried her with us for the angling party. And now it will all come to naught. When I consider of the chances you have thrown away, Jane, I despair of the future of matrimony!"

For a Sour Humour
on the Stomach

Take an ounce of fine white chalk and three-quarters of an ounce of finest white sugar, and rub them to a powder. Add to these two drams of powder of gum Arabick; when all these are well rubbed together, add to a quart of water in a large bottle and shake it up. The dose is a large spoonful at a time.

—From the Stillroom Book of Tess Arnold,
Penfolds Hall, Derbyshire, 1802–1806

Chapter 6

The Curse
of the Damned

Thursday
28 August 1806
~

"AND THA' DETERMINED TO WALK UP INTO THE HILLS ABOVE MILLER'S Dale, Miss Austen, quite alone and with no other object than healthful exercise? Was that entirely wise?"

Mr. Tivey, the blacksmith-cum-surgeon-cum-coroner of Bakewell, threw me a stern look as he posed this question before his empanelled jury of twelve men; but I was not the sort of lady to suffer a diminution of composure on *his* account.

"As to the wisdom of my course, Mr. Tivey, I cannot say—but it is customary to walk through the dales of Derbyshire while embarked on a pleasure tour of the county. Thousands of ladies, I am sure, have done so before this."

"Tha' did not expect, then, to encounter Deceased in the course of thy rambles?"

"If you would enquire whether I mounted the path with Deceased as my object—then no, sir, I did not. The discovery of the maid's body came as quite a shock."

"Could tha' describe for the jury thy actions upon first perceiving Deceased?"

I looked at the Coroner's panel assembled on their benches. A stalwart lot—small farmers and landowners by the looks of them, and careful to preserve their countenances free of expression.

"A murder of crows first attracted my interest," I replied, "and upon attaining the place where the corpse was laid, I perceived that the person was quite dead."

"How did Deceased lie?"

"At the foot of a crag, some distance upwards along the path."

"And how did the body appear?"

He offered the question easily enough; but I could not avoid a hesitation—an indrawn breath—a desire to drop my eyes. Thoughts of the most distressing nature *would* obtrude.

"Miss Austen?"

I lifted my gaze to meet Mr. Tivey's. "It appeared to be the corpse of a young gentleman, savagely murdered. A lead ball had lodged in the center of the forehead; and the bowels had been quite cut out, as had the person's tongue. A great welter of blood had stained the corpse's clothes and the surrounding rocks."

"Would tha' judge the blood to have been freshly-spilt?"

"I cannot say. It appeared quite congealed and dried."

"Did tha' touch the body in any way?"

"I did not, sir."

"Did tha' observe the marks of a horse, or perhaps of another person, anywhere on the path?"

"I did not, sir."

"Pray describe for us the condition of the ground."

"It was quite dry and dusty, as should not be unusual in August; the path was hard-packed, and the grasses withered."

"So tha' should have been unlikely to discern either the marks of Deceased's passage, or those of any other person in the vicinity?"

"I cannot say. Certainly I did not discern such marks."

"Did Deceased appear to have discarded any belongings? A trunk or a bundle of some sort?"

"Not that I could discover."

Mr. Tivey peered at me from under his brows. "Very well. Miss Austen, what did tha' next do?"

"I ran back along the path in search of aid. I summoned the gentlemen of my party—Mr. George Hemming of Bakewell, and my cousin Mr. Edward Cooper, who were fishing along the Wye—and urged them to make all possible haste towards the crag, and the unfortunate person lying there."

"Very well, Miss Austen. Tha' may retire."

I rose from the witness chair and made my way back through the assembled throng in the Snake and Hind's main room. The eyes of the curious roamed over my person; but I was accustomed to impertinence—it could not be avoided in the course of an Inquest. I was no longer an anonymous pleasure-seeker bent upon a summer of idleness; I was a local Sensation. I found a seat at the rear of the room, and prepared to observe all that ensued.

"Mr. George Hemming!"

Mr. Tivey's voice rang through the chamber, but no answering shuffle of feet prepared to meet it. I craned my head in search of the solicitor's form. Mr. Hemming, I felt certain, was not in the Snake and Hind; but was such a lapse of duty possible? Had he unaccountably avoided the Inquest?

A stab of doubt, akin to the warning note that had sounded in my brain at Miller's Dale, coursed through my blood. Mr. Hemming was *not* to be suspected of murder. He was too much the gentleman, and too much my cousin's old friend. Besides, there had been a gentleness in all his ways—an ease of manner—that was utterly at variance with violence. That ease had fled instantly once the maid's body was discovered. Why was the solicitor determined to act as one burdened by guilt?

"Mr. Hemming! I call Mr. George Hemming!"

The stir of speculation throughout the room was considerable. Lacking a gavel, Mr. Tivey hammered upon the table with the flat of his broad palm. "Very well—then I call Mr. Edward Cooper, clergyman of Hamstall Ridware!"

My cousin opened his mouth and began to sing.

He made his way in stately procession to the head of the airless room, his eyes uplifted to the rafters, and his face beatified. The lowness of the public room's ceiling rather spoiled the effect; but his strains carried into every available corner in a most gratifying way. I thought I should sink under the misery of Mr. Cooper's example, but that I was a stranger to most of the observers present. He took his place in the witness's chair, and gazed solemnly at the assembly as he concluded his first verse. I felt sure that he intended to go on with a second—he filled his lungs with air—but Mr. Tivey swooped down to administer the oath, and forestalled another chorus of "Jesu, Joy of Man's Desiring."

In answer to the Coroner's questions, Mr. Cooper related how he had retrieved the body in the company of the miller and his friend Mr. Hemming, and how our party had conveyed its sad burden into Bakewell. He made no mention of Mr. Hemming's extreme reluctance to do so, and from this, I determined that my cousin was anxious on his friend's behalf as well. Mr. Tivey addressed some further questions, regarding time elapsed between my discovery of the body, and its conveyance into Water Street; and then dismissed Mr. Cooper, who retreated to his seat in fulsome song.

Mr. Tivey pounded upon his table.

My cousin bowed his head in supplication, but happily ceased his caroling.

Black brows drawn down over his harshly-graven features, Mr. Tivey paused to compose his thoughts.

"As the surgeon called in attendance upon Deceased," he informed the jury, "I proceeded to examine the corpse. It is well known by now that my first discovery was an interesting one—namely, that Deceased was not a young gentleman of unknown origin, but a maidservant by the name of Tess Arnold—" At this, a murmur arose from the assembled townsfolk, more of satisfaction at having previously possessed the remarkable intelligence than any surprise at its publication. Mr. Tivey stared balefully at the crowd. He refused to speak further until the comment had subsided.

"The maid Arnold belonged to Penfolds Hall, the estate of Mr. Charles Danforth, near Tideswell. It will be observed that Tideswell is little over a mile north of Miller's Dale, an easy enough distance for an accomplished walker.

"Deceased had suffered grievous harm. As the previous witnesses have described, her tongue was cut out and her entrails torn from her body. It is my opinion, however, that these dreadful wounds were inflicted *after* death."

This had the power to surprise me; and it spurred a further wave of murmuring in Jacob Patter's inn. Few in Bakewell had known the Coroner's judgement, it would seem. Mr. Tivey's dark eyes glittered with satisfaction.

"The blood observed to be congealed in such amounts did not flow directly from the mouth or abdomen—although the marks of blood were on them—but from the wound to the head created by the lead ball. The shot, I believe, was fired from a fowling piece at some remove from Deceased. From the condition of the body when I viewed it at one o'clock Tuesday, I should judge the girl was killed the previous night—but when exactly she was killed, who can say? Certainly not Michael Tivey."

That Tess Arnold should have died from the firing of a gun some distance from herself, while climbing about the rocks above Miller's Dale in the utter dark, defied belief. I had comforted myself with the notion that only a madman could have destroyed the maid—but no madman had aimed the piece that killed her. Only a most accomplished marksman could effect such a shot; the calculation and coolness necessary for the deed's success, argued premeditation. And once the girl was dead—why cut out her tongue and bowels? Here was a tangle, indeed.

The Coroner sat back with a grin, very well pleased by his own performance. The recital was calculated to excite the townspeople in Jacob Patter's public house; it was for this that they had come. They were mostly common folk, of the sort that might have claimed Tess Arnold's station; and they were mostly men. Their faces were burnt brown by the sun, and their nankeen breeches, though generally clean, were worn and mended in places. They had greeted the witnesses' accounts with a stolid gravity—but Mr. Tivey's gruesome testimony must be apprehended and exclaimed over.

The few women in the room *must* draw my interest, from the singularity of their presence. They were four in number: the first, a respectable-looking individual with a tight mouth, shrewd eyes, and a gown of dark grey, worn less in respect of Deceased, I surmised, than as a matter of custom. She sat apart from the other three, with her gloved hands laced tightly through the strings of her reticule; her posture was exceedingly upright. She looked neither to right nor left, but kept her eyes fixed upon Mr. Tivey at his table.

The remaining women formed a loose knot at the head of the room, barely a yard removed from the coroner's panel. The eldest—a crone whose crazed, unfocused stare betrayed her blindness—was undoubtedly Betty Arnold, the maid's mother. The girl to her right was disposed to maintain a determined weeping, and I utterly failed to glimpse her face, it being smothered by a large checked handkerchief throughout the proceeding. The young woman to the left kept her hand firmly on the old woman's elbow and stared malevolently at Mr. Tivey, her face like stone and her cold eyes unblinking. What was she, then? Friend of the bosom or sister to Tess Arnold? Her profile was fine, and I thought I traced a semblance of the dead girl's features—until she turned, and I saw that her face was utterly disfigured by a wine-coloured stain that mottled one cheek.

"Pray allow Mr. Charles Danforth to approach the panel," Mr. Tivey intoned.

I turned my head, in company with every other person in the chamber—and watched as Tess Arnold's employer made his slow progress towards the coroner. He was perhaps five- or six-and-thirty, a man not above medium height, with powerful shoulders encased in a well-cut green coat of superfine; his hair was chestnut, and his features regular. An expression of pain was writ upon his brow, however; and he walked with the aid of a stout length of oak. The widower Charles Danforth—handsome, rich, and the object of either a curse or a singular run of bad luck in his personal affairs—was also lame.

"Tha'rt Mr. Charles Danforth of Penfolds Hall?" Mr. Tivey enquired.

"I am." The voice was surprising in its depth—a rich voice of decided timbre, the voice of politics or of God; but there was a languor about the man that suggested illness or deep sorrow. Little of a worldly nature was capable of stirring Charles Danforth's passion.

"And tha' held the maid Tess Arnold in thy employ?"

"I did. She was raised on the estate during my father's time, and entered into service at the age of twelve."

"That would be ten years ago, Mr. Danforth?"

"Closer to twelve or thirteen, I imagine."

"And did she give satisfaction?"

"So far as I could tell," he replied indifferently. "Mrs. Danforth—my late wife—and the housekeeper were responsible for the management of servants' affairs, as I was often absent on business a good part of the year."

"Very well. Would tha' describe for the panel what tha' did on Monday evening?"

"I dined early, and at home," he said slowly, "and retired around ten o'clock."

"What does tha' regard as early, Mr. Danforth?"

The gentleman gave the barest suggestion of a shrug. "Five o'clock."

"And between the hours of five o'clock and ten o'clock tha' stopped at home, alone?"

"Certainly not. Monday is the night upon which it is customary for the Masonic lodge to meet"—a low rumble, as of great guns fired upon a distant front, moved through the room—"and it was for this reason I dined early."

"Tha' went to the Freemasons' meeting?" If words may be said to pounce, then Michael Tivey's all but seized hold of Mr. Danforth's neck. The gentleman appeared impervious to the sensation his words must cause.

"Of course. I should judge that I left the Hall on horseback at six o'clock, and reached the Lodge—it is on the Buxton road, perhaps three miles out of Buxton itself—around half-past the hour."

"Very well," Mr. Tivey said expansively. "Mr. Danforth admits to forming one of that insidious cabal; he admits to entering the Lodge. I will not ask him what he did there—I know he is sworn never to divulge the workings of his brother Masons. But perhaps he will tell the panel when he quitted that fearsome place."

"Fearsome?" Mr. Danforth repeated. "Whatever are you saying, man? That stretch of road into Buxton is in better repair than most. I should judge that I turned towards home no later than nine o'clock, because I wound my watch before retiring; and saw then that it was nigh on ten."

"Ten o'clock," Mr. Tivey repeated. "And was tha' quite alone for the rest of the evening, Mr. Danforth?"

"I was," he replied, "my brother—Mr. Andrew Danforth—having dined that evening at Chatsworth House, in the company of a large party. I could not say when he returned to Penfolds—well after midnight, I should think. Mrs. Haskell will know the hour."

"Mrs. Haskell is housekeeper up t'a Hall?"

"She is."

"Very well. Tha' has stated for the panel that tha' retired at ten o'clock, or near enough. When did tha' rise?"

"Rise?" said Mr. Danforth hesitantly. "At what hour of the morning, would you mean—or . . . or that night?"

Michael Tivey's small eyes narrowed. "Tha' wert abroad during the night?"

Mr. Danforth shifted in the hard wooden chair. "I often have difficulty sleeping."

"And on Monday night, Mr. Danforth?"

"I attempted to find repose for several hours. At length I abandoned the effort, got up and dressed, and took a turn out-of-doors. I find that a walk will often relieve an unquiet mind."

"And does tha' possess an unquiet mind, Mr. Danforth?"

"I am in mourning, Tivey," the gentleman retorted. "For no less than my whole family. If a man is at peace in such dreadful circumstances, then he can possess no heart!"

I felt a surge of pain and sympathy for Charles Danforth at this burst of feeling; but from the aspect of my neighbours in the Snake and Hind, few others were animated by a like sensation.

"Tha' admits to having walked out of thy house," Mr. Tivey said insidiously. "Where did thy ramble take tha'?"

For the first time, Charles Danforth seemed to apprehend his danger. He hesitated. "I cannot say. When wandering in that fashion, all sense of time and place may be lost."

"Did tha' bide within the bounds o' Penfolds?"

"Possibly. Possibly not."

"I see." Mr. Tivey stared balefully at his witness, and then gazed out at the assembled folk of Bakewell with an air of significance. "Mr. Danforth says as he were abroad in the middle of the night, but cannot state where he may have been." He reached for a canvas-wrapped bundle. "Is the gentleman able to identify these?"

Charles Danforth stared at the black coat and pantaloons the coroner held forth. He half rose from his chair, reached for his stick, and bent to the inspection with an air of disbelief.

"Those are mine," he said. "I should recognise the tailor's mark anywhere. How did they fall into your hands, Tivey?"

Every man and woman in the room could have answered that question. Was it possible Mr. Danforth was so ignorant of events?

"They were found on the body of Tess Arnold Tuesday morning," the Coroner replied. "Let the panel observe that Deceased was attired in Mr. Charles Danforth's clothing at the time of her death."

"But that is impossible!" Mr. Danforth cried. He fell heavily back into the witness chair. "What would Tess want with my things?"

"Tha' did not make a . . . *gift* . . . to the young woman?"

"Of my clothes? Certainly not!" The scorn in Charles Danforth's voice was scalding, and his features were distorted, of a sudden, with a spasm of fury. My first estimation of the gentleman had been in error. This gross invasion of his privacy, it seemed, had brought the dragon to life.

"And tha' canst think of no reason why the maid should have taken them?"

"None whatsoever."

"Did any sort of relations—for good or ill—subsist between thyself and the stillroom maid?"

A mottled band of colour swept over Charles Danforth's handsome countenance. "What in God's name would you suggest, Tivey? I should call you out for that!"

"Pray answer the question, Mr. Danforth," the coroner replied coolly.

"I never looked at the girl, nor considered of her existence," the gentleman replied angrily.

"Very well." The Coroner spoke easily—as though Charles Danforth had supplied all the reply that was necessary. "Thank'ee, Mr. Danforth. Tha' may step down."

Charles Danforth thrust himself to his feet with the aid of his stick, and made a stately passage through the assembled townsfolk. He did not look to the right or the left, and the expression of dignity on his countenance should have wrung the heart of the coldest person; but the people of Bakewell showed him no pity. Not a few of them crossed themselves hurriedly as he passed, or made the sign against the evil eye. The gentleman chose not to observe this; and I wondered if it was a practise long familiar of old.

He did not wait for the conclusion of the panel, but left the inn immediately, the broad oak door slamming harshly in his wake. This little display of petulance, I fear, did not recommend him to the assembled crowd; and his conduct on the night of Tess Arnold's death—blameless though it may in fact have been—laid him open to the worst sort of public conjecture. It was a great pity that Charles Danforth could summon not a single witness to his cause; and I wondered, as I considered of the evidence Mr. Tivey would build against him, what George Hemming had urged his client to say. What words had passed between the two men during their consultation yesterday, that Charles Danforth should seem so ill-prepared for the Coroner's questions?

I followed the man in thought as he made his way from Bakewell—in a closed carriage, perhaps, to defy the gaze of the curious. What emotions roiled in that melancholy breast? And whither was he bound, while his neighbours canvassed his troubled mind, his midnight rambles, his well-tailored clothes and their curious theft?

"Coroner calls Mrs. Augusta Haskell!"

The matron in grey rose with dignity and proceeded towards the panel. The girl with the disfigured face—Tess Arnold's sister?—followed Mrs. Haskell's progress with an expression of purest hatred on her stony countenance.

"Tha'rt Mrs. Augusta Haskell?"

"I am, Michael Tivey, as tha've known since tha' wert in leading strings."

Mr. Tivey made no gesture of acknowledgement to this sally.

"And tha' keeps house up t'a Hall?"

"These three-and-twenty year."

"Deceased was employed by tha'?"

"She were."

"In what position?"

"Stillroom maid." Mrs. Haskell shifted in her seat and allowed her eyes to drift over the three women grouped at the front of the room; a curious lapse, I thought, in her iron self-command. She looked almost uneasy.

"And could'ee relate for the panel what tha' told Sir James Villiers on Tuesday, ma'am?"

"I said as how I'd dismissed Tess Arnold without a character," she declared, "and good riddance to a bad seed."

A slight murmur, as the wind sighing through the trees, made its way through the inquest chamber. Of indignation or surprise, I could not tell.

"Though Tess Arnold had been in thy employ some years?" Mr. Tivey persisted.

"Twelve year or more. Ever since she were twelve year old."

"And though she had been raised as a child on the Penfolds estate?"

"I did what I had to do," Mrs. Haskell returned defiantly, "and I'll not be beggin' pardon of anybody."

"And because of it, our Tess were murdered," came another voice—chill, bereft, and filled with suppressed violence. The stony-eyed girl rose to her feet and pointed a trembling hand directly at the Penfolds housekeeper. "Because of thy unfeeling heart and malicious soul, Augusta Haskell, my sister were cast out of her home and sent abroad in the dead of night, without even the clothes she earned upon her back. She were cast out, and died a brutal death alone and far from aid. Because of tha'! May her unquiet ghost haunt thy sleep, Augusta Haskell, and cry vengeance for what tha' did! May tha' never find another night's peace, until the end of thy days!"

The girl's cry fell in the midst of total silence, and the manner in which she uttered it gave her imprecation all the weight of a curse. I felt a cold finger trail along my spine, and sensed a greater power than Sir James Villiers's take command of the chamber.

Augusta Haskell's countenance turned ghastly and her lips went blue. She pressed a gloved hand to her bosom. "My heart—oh, Lord, my heart—"

And then her eyes rolled Heavenward, and she slumped insensible to the floor.

The furor that then ensued was indescribable. Mr. Tivey might pound with his hand in vain, for the hubbub went on unceasing; sev-

eral of the empanelled jury rushed to Mrs. Haskell's aid; and still others moved to adjure the Arnold girl. But I judged that they were a little afraid of her—and when she stared defiantly at one man, and
moved to guide her mother towards the door, the wall of townsfolk
fell back. A parting was made, and a fearful silence fell, broken only
by the sound of the third woman's weeping. The three passed like a
cabal of Furies from the room. An air of menace—or was it grief?—
moved with them, and stirred the dust long after they were gone.

The Coroner's Inquest was adjourned, for pursuit of further information, and the crowd of the curious gladly filed outside into fresh
air and sunlight.

I was perhaps one of the few who noticed that Mrs. Haskell had
been prevented, by the depth of her fear and a strategic swoon, from
publicly disclosing the cause of the stillroom maid's dismissal.

For Swooning Fits

Rub to powder three grains of Cochineal, and mix thoroughly with a little sugar. Add a spoonful of burnt wine, and take the dose immediately. Follow with a glass of the same burnt wine afterwards.

—From the Stillroom Book of Tess Arnold,
Penfolds Hall, Derbyshire, 1802–1806

Chapter 7

Old Friends Well Met

"You acquitted yourself well, Miss Austen." Sir James Villiers appeared before me in all the splendour of yellow pantaloons and a striped waistcoat, his fair hair carefully disarranged. "And without the display of nerves or sensibility so many young ladies should have thought necessary! I feel myself moved to offer you refreshment. Shall we adjourn to Mr. Patter's front parlour, and send the maid-servant in search of victuals? I should like to discuss the particulars of this extraordinary case."

"Though I am as much a friend to an innkeeper's larder as any man," interposed my cousin Mr. Cooper, "I confess, Sir James, that we cannot quit these premises too soon for my taste." Mr. Cooper's first experience of a Coroner's Inquest had been an unhappy one; his brown eyes were deeply shadowed, and an unaccustomed frowziness distinguished his sparse hair. "I cannot feel easy in Miss Austen's association with this unfortunate affair. I must beg to remove myself and my party from Derbyshire at the nearest opportunity, Sir James, and cannot apprehend why you believe it in your power to thwart my wishes—"

"My dear Mr. Cooper," exclaimed Sir James, "pray do not let us quarrel! Circumstances at present are disagreeable enough. I suggest you find comfort in a spot of angling, and throw off the cares of this sordid world in fresh air and exercise. Your friend Mr. Hemming will undoubtedly oblige you—if he can be found."

"Fishing!" Mr. Cooper cried indignantly. "You would have me to fish, when the whole world is run mad? I should rather spend an interval on my knees in the parish church. I am sure that *someone* should consider of his God."

"Very well," returned Sir James briskly, "then I may recommend most highly the offices of Mr. Dean, the rector of All Saints, should you desire a companion in your spiritual ablutions. But I am most anxious for Miss Austen—she appears in danger of swooning"—this was purest fabrication on the Justice's part, although the closeness of the crowded room at such a season was considerable—"and I cannot think it wise for her to forgo a nuncheon. You will find Mr. Dean at The Elms, Mr. Cooper—a lovely little stone cottage directly across from the churchyard. He is sure to be at home, and happy to welcome a fellow man of the cloth. Do not neglect the Vernon Chapel in the South Transept. The tombs are quite fine. Come along, Miss Austen!"

And so I was led, without chance of argument, towards the neat front parlour of Jacob Patter, publican, while my cousin stared after, open-mouthed.

THE TABLE HAD BEEN LAID WITH A CLEAN WHITE CLOTH AND A TRAY of victuals—cold roasted capon, fresh Derbyshire cheese of the blue-veined variety, and the cherished Bakewell puddings of my sister's preference. Next to these stood a pitcher of ale and one that proved to be filled with ginger beer. Sir James drew forth my chair and I settled myself with a sigh.

"You are very good to think of my comfort, Sir James," I told him. "I am afraid my cousin is not at present equal to consideration of anything but his own misery. He must be overwhelmed by present events, and cannot offer an accurate picture of his true character."

"We are not all the masters of every circumstance that life presents," Sir James replied equably. "I am sure that Mr. Cooper is a very good sort of man, in his own neighbourhood and his own church particularly."

"Among the people of Hamstall Ridware I believe my cousin is esteemed and valued," I replied. "His character is unblemished and his conduct entirely respectable. If he is unequal to the present horror, so much the better. I should not like to meet a man who could view Tess Arnold's corpse with equanimity."

"Could I despatch him to his rectory without comment tomorrow, I should do so," the Justice declared, "and all his party with him. But I fear the kindness would not be worth the talk it should occasion in the town. I must beg you to remain a little in Derbyshire, Miss Austen, until the present affair is concluded."

"Would this necessity have arisen, Sir James, if Mr. George Hemming had not disappeared? You spoke just now as though you had sought the gentleman, and found him from home."

"He was certainly not in evidence at the Inquest," Sir James replied, "and having sent a messenger to his establishment in Carding Street, and having found Mr. Hemming away—I am not entirely certain what to think. He might have chosen a more suitable hour for his absence."

"You do not know any real ill of him, however?"

"As to that—I do not think I should open my mind even to you, Miss Austen. I have a dangerous tendency to disclose far more than is safe, under the influence of so subtle a lady."

"Flattery, Sir James, must satisfy me for the present," I told him archly. "Mr. Hemming's nature—his power for good or ill—shall remain a mystery, and my cousin shall bear all the weight of his disgrace, by standing firm in Mr. Hemming's stead. Mr. Cooper must endure his purgatory, whatever the just horror his noble patron may feel; and offer up his suffering to God." As my cousin had yet to cast his suffering in lyrics, I saw no reason to dread the event. "I am sure that upon reflection, Mr. Cooper will comprehend the necessity of your prohibition."

"I fear that he has arrived at a very unnatural conclusion—that he is himself under present suspicion of effecting Tess Arnold's death."

"And so should he be." I accepted a serving of capon from the Justice and met his gaze unflinchingly. "So must we all. From your particular acquaintance with events, Sir James, you may determine only this: that the maidservant, Tess Arnold, met her death at midnight in a place peculiarly remote from her home, and in clothes that

are determined to have belonged to her employer. She died as the result of a prodigious shot, fired at some remove from her corpse's resting place. You never met my cousin before Tuesday; and as he and
some part of his party were the first to discover the dreadful scene, we
might reasonably have done so to appear in innocence before your
eyes. You know nothing whatsoever of Mr. Cooper—or if it comes
to that, myself. He might be a desperate cutthroat in the guise of a
clergyman, and I his paramour. We might have quitted The Rutland
Arms in stealth at ten o'clock of a Monday evening, with the intention of seeing murder done. I leave it to your considerable understanding to devise a motive for our doing so."

"And as a sporting fellow, I should accept the challenge," Sir James
cried, "but for the excellent report of both your characters I received
from George Hemming, whom I have known these three decades
and more."

"Mr. Hemming I never met before Monday evening," I declared,
"and my cousin has not seen him this age. Besides, Mr. Hemming
may stand in testament to nobody; his own actions at present will not
bear scrutiny. No, no, Sir James—you must preserve the cold judicial
eye of the Law. We are none of us above suspicion, and I for one am
glad of it. Only the most discerning and impartial mind shall discover
the truth in this sad tangle."

"Well said." He poured out a tankard of ale for himself and
quaffed it deeply before replying. In the silence I could hear a slight
noise in the passage beyond the parlour's closed door, and wondered
if Jacob Patter or his serving girl was lingering there, in respect of Sir
James's conversation.

"Have you an idea where Mr. Hemming could have got to?"
I enquired.

The Justice shook his head. "I may say that I am most uneasy in
my mind, that he should have neglected of his duty. Indeed, his conduct throughout this affair must lay him open to the most uncom-
fortable scrutiny; it is unlike anything I have witnessed in George
Hemming before. He certainly does not serve Charles Danforth as I
should like."

"Not at all! The gentleman seemed astonished at the tenor of
the Coroner's questioning, and that anyone in Bakewell should re-

main so in ignorance of the facts, or of his own peril, is in every way remarkable."

"Except, perhaps, when his solicitor conspires to keep him so," Sir James observed. "Though Danforth summoned Mr. Hemming to Penfolds yesterday, to my knowledge the solicitor did not appear; and so poor Charles went forward to the Inquest without the slightest sensation of danger."

"Mr. Hemming did not appear? But surely—" I stopped short, uncertain of what should be said. Might Mr. Hemming's sudden disappearance creditably be laid to my own account? I had bullied the man unmercifully, and it seemed that he had fled.

Sir James smiled grimly. "I could wish Mr. Danforth greater fortune in his movements that night; he possesses not a single person who may testify to his presence at the house, or about the fields. But still he may claim *some* friends. His housekeeper is surely one of these. Had Augusta Haskell not fainted dead away, we must have seen her master charged with murder."

"Given the direction of Mr. Tivey's questions, the panel may be excused for believing no other course left open to them," I agreed. "But what do you know of Mr. Danforth's brother, Sir James? For he was also abroad that night. Is he a man to be trusted?"

"As to that, I cannot presume to say whether any man is entirely to be trusted, Miss Austen. Andrew Danforth was certainly present at Chatsworth on Monday evening, however. He appeared at the house at six o'clock, and sat down to dinner at seven; the last course was cleared at half-past ten, and the ladies quitted the dining-room. The gentlemen rejoined them at a quarter to twelve, when the card tables were set out—"

"What late hours these Whigs do keep, to be sure!" I murmured. It was the Austen habit to retire early; I was generally abed by ten o'clock.

"—and the entire party broke up after supper, at approximately half-past one o'clock in the morning. Andrew Danforth cannot have reached his bed before half-past two, I should judge, in travelling at that hour; and by that time, it seems safe to say, the maid was already dead."

"You were prevented from saying it, however, by the sudden end of

the Inquest," I mused. "But perhaps it is just as well. I have long determined that an Inquest is no place for justice—it serves no greater
purpose than to satisfy the local worthies that they may manage the
affair themselves. Impartial judgement may only be won from impartial judges; and for them, we must look to the Assizes."

Sir James drew his chair somewhat closer to mine. "You referred
Tuesday evening, Miss Austen, to a former intimacy with the investi-
gation of murder. I must confess that I have not been so unfortunate.
My experience of such tangles is . . . limited. I should dearly love to
learn your opinion of this dreadful affair."

"My opinion, sir?" I returned with some surprise. "But I know
nothing of the country or its inhabitants. I am acquainted neither
with the victim, nor with the family that employed her. I cannot be allowed to have formed an opinion."

"From what little I know of your character and understanding,
Miss Austen, I doubt very much that this is the case." Sir James was
studying my countenance over the rim of his tankard; the directness
of his gaze brought the colour to my cheeks.

"What can you mean, sir?"

"Your understanding and good sense were recommended to me
in the most fulsome terms last evening—and from a source that I
should consider unimpeachable."

"Were they, indeed!" I could not suppress a stirring of curiosity.
"You have been speaking again with my cousin, I perceive."

"Such events in your life as were then unfolded," he continued
without a yea or nay, "confirmed my good opinion of your penetra-
tion and firmness of mind—and determined me in my course of so-
liciting your aid in the present affair."

"Good God!" I cried. "What *can* my cousin have told you, Sir
James? I fear that he has grossly exaggerated my talents, for some mis-
chievous purpose of his own."

"Mr. Cooper would never presume to impart particulars so injuri-
ous to the reputation of a lady, and a lady so closely connected to
himself," Sir James said quietly. "In the present instance, indeed, he
would not wish it known that you have been associated with past cases
of murder. It might enflame the gossip already circulating about
the town."

I coloured, doubted, and was silent.

"The intelligence I received, Miss Austen, was from a very old acquaintance we hold in common. He is presently residing at Chatsworth, being an intimate of the Duke."

"Chatsworth!" I cried. "I must believe you to have been imposed upon, Sir James! For I know no one in Derbyshire."

At that moment, the rustling in the passage increased and the parlour door was thrust open. I turned, gazed, and rose immediately from my chair. A spare, tall figure, exquisitely dressed in the garb of a gentleman, was caught in a shaft of sunlight. He lifted his hat from his silver hair and bowed low over my hand.

"It is a pleasure to see you again, Miss Austen. We have not met this age."

Nor had we. But I must confess that the gentleman had lately been much in my thoughts.

"Lord Harold," I replied a trifle unsteadily. "The honour is entirely mine."

A Way of Getting Sons

*A*ll babes are male in the womb, and turn weak and female only through the humours of the Mother. Therefore, if a girl child be desired, the Lady must spend her time of increase in lying upon the Sopha, and drink only warmed milk with little egg in it. If a boy child be the object, then the Lady is advised to eat heartily of chopped beef and mutton boiled in Claret nearly every day. She must rise early, and spend her Mornings in healthful exercise, such as walking about the country or riding to hounds; her evenings should be principally spent among friends, with the diversion of dancing and conversation. At no time should she waste more than seven hours in sleep, for a male child will not require it.

—From the Stillroom Book of Tess Arnold,
Penfolds Hall, Derbyshire, 1802–1806

Chapter 8

A Period of Mourning

THE APPEARANCE OF LORD HAROLD TROWBRIDGE HAS EVER BEEN A source of astonishment in my life, the sudden intercession of a breathless world, imperfectly understood. His taste for fashionable intrigue and clandestine statecraft, when allied with a character already prone to discretion, make him an elusive figure. Although an intimacy of sorts subsists between us—as much as any such condition may, when the lady is single and impoverished and the gentleman one of the most pursued *partis* on the marriage circuit—I never know when he is on the Continent or in Town; in danger of his life on behalf of the Crown, or dying of boredom at a country retreat. Ours is not the sort of footing that might encourage a voluminous correspondence. The exchange of letters between a lady of my station, and a gentleman of his, might suggest an improper liaison or a secret understanding. I have never enjoyed either in my association with Lord Harold.

On the present occasion we met after a silence of above eight months, and the absence, on his part, of nearly a year. I had seen vague reports in the public journals of diplomatic sallies in the Baltic, and visits to the Prussian Court; I had snatched at rumours of romantic alliance with a certain Russian Princess, and the whiff of scandal in the Montalban chit's elopement. I knew not what to credit, what to deny, what to approve, or what should give me pain.

I cannot presume upon Lord Harold's notice, or even look for the continuance of his friendship. But he is, without exception, the most intriguing member of my acquaintance; to move in his circle is to drink a kind of elixir, not necessary to the maintenance of life, but sparkling in its effect and invariably invigorating.

Though my mother and sister disapprove Lord Harold's influence, I consider my intimacy with the Gentleman Rogue to be a considerable honour, and one not lightly bestowed. On certain occasions, and in certain circumstances, I have known some part of Lord Harold's confidence and his counsel—and in this, I understand myself to have been the keeper of his trust. Should he disappear from the face of the earth and persist in silence the better part of a decade, I should still meet his renewed attentions with cordiality.

"I understand your mother and sister are also in Bakewell," he said to me now, and I replied in the affirmative. "They are well?"

"Perfectly well, I thank you."

"Despite the intrusion of a murderer in their midst?"

"I do not think my mother has afforded the Arnold girl more than a quarter-hour of consideration," I said drily, "and my sister, though greatly distressed by the reports she has heard, was spared all sight of the corpse. We must remember, Lord Harold, that it is August. The world's concerns cannot be too deeply felt when the weather is fine."

This sally won the barest ghost of a smile. "What brings you into Derbyshire? I should have thought to find you in Kent, at Mr. Edward Austen's estate, in such a season."

"My brother is from home at present," I told him, "having taken a house at Ramsgate; but I may find it in my power to visit Godmersham again in the autumn. We intend a removal in October to Southampton, my lord."

"Southampton?" he repeated, with a slight frown; "I should not have thought your character any more suited to a watering place, Jane, than it has been to the dissipations of Bath. Of what is your mother thinking?"

"Of economy," I returned, "and of my brother, Captain Francis Austen, who makes his home our own. Southampton is but seventeen miles from Portsmouth, and the naval stores; wherever Frank's duties may take him in the world, he shall always return to the Hampshire coast."

"I see." Lord Harold declined Sir James's offer of refreshment and drew forward a chair. "It was very wrong of me to speak as I did—the effect of surprise alone must explain it. But what brings you then to Bakewell? It is rather more northwards than Southampton, surely?"

The Gentleman Rogue had never been given to idle chatter, and if I wondered at his distracted air, and his random pursuit of subject, I forbore from comment. I found his appearance to be remarkably ill. I had never seen him so obviously prey to an inner torment as he now appeared, and I experienced the most lively anxiety on his behalf. His beak of a nose looked sharper than ever, the skin being stretched tightly across the bone; his eyes were hollow, and I should judge that his rest had been disturbed for some nights past. Perhaps the affair of the Russian Countess—so vaguely alluded to, in the slyest of morning papers—had exacted a greater toll than I realised. Had there been a duel? A suicide? An illicit birth in a small town on the Continent? It seemed as though a great sickness or a desperate sorrow must gnaw at the man. Lord Harold looked all his eight-and-forty years at least.

"We have been embarked on a journey of pleasure this summer," I told him gently, "and being so near to the Peaks as my cousin's home in Staffordshire, could not defer a glimpse of Derbyshire's beauties."

"I rather imagine it is a chance you will forego next time it offers," observed Sir James. "If Mr. Cooper is to be consulted, you should better have stayed at home."

"Tess Arnold would still be as dead," I replied.

Lord Harold said nothing. His grey eyes were fixed upon my face. In the usual way I would never have presumed to enquire as to his movements, but he was so little master of himself that the question sprang thoughtlessly to my lips. "And you, my lord? What brings *you* to Derbyshire?"

His eyelids flickered. "A visit of condolence," he said. "The heaviest I have ever been called upon to pay. You will have heard, naturally, of the Duchess's death."

"The Duchess of Devonshire?"

Lord Harold dropped his gaze to the pair of gloves he clutched tightly in his hands; and it was then that I troubled myself to notice that he was arrayed entirely in black. It had often been a habit of his—a kind of elegance of attire—but on the present occasion was accompanied by a total lack of adornment. He was plunged into the deepest mourning. Was this, then, the source of his trouble?

The passing of Georgiana, Duchess of Devonshire, so recently as March, had been the sensation of the Season. Not only was she the most powerful hostess of the great Whig families, a lady who had presided over a veritable court to rival King George's, but she had been the most fashionable figure of the past age, almost a queen in her own right. It was Georgiana and her circle at Devonshire House that Richard Brinsley Sheridan burlesqued in *A School for Scandal,* and it was Georgiana, not Queen Charlotte, whom the public followed in blind adoration. Her blond curls, her sweetness of temper, and her youth—she was a Duchess at seventeen—had recommended her to the multitude; and no gown was adopted, no style or habit worn, that Georgiana did not set. More than this, however, had been her ambition. Her intellect ranged beyond the frivolities of Fashion. Some two decades ago, in the Westminster election of 1784, she had discarded the reserve so usually associated with great ladies of her station and fortune, and had condescended to campaign on behalf of the Whigs' political light, the Genius of the Rabble, the Monster of Richmond, Charles James Fox. It had been rumoured in broadsheets that the two were lovers; Her Grace had been everywhere reviled, for buying votes on the hustings in return for kisses; but Fox prevailed in his parliamentary contest, and went on to sustain a brilliant career. With the death of the Tory leader, William Pitt, this past January, Fox at last bid fair to win the post of Prime Minister for which he had apprenticed all his life—and he owed his ascendancy in no small part to the Duchess of Devonshire.

When a liver ailment at last would claim her, huge crowds stood vigil with flaming torches before the gates of Devonshire House in London. The Prince of Wales paid a death-bed call. And the newspapers squandered oceans of ink for ensuing weeks, in eulogizing her fame.

I had known, of course, of Georgiana's death—much as I had known of Marie Antoinette's, and with as little personal sensibility.

Although my brother Henry and his little wife, Eliza, the Comtesse de Feuillide, may have attended her routs at Devonshire House, the Austens were not in general a Whiggish family. My mother regarded the great ducal families, and their determination to control their King, as a select form of heathenry—one that possessed more wealth and influence than any heathen ought. Georgiana was as remote from my world as might be the moon.

But she had not been remote from Lord Harold's. He was, after all, the son of a duke.

"You were intimately acquainted, sir?"

"From our infancy," he replied. "I am Devonshire's junior, of course—he is eight years older than his late wife—but with Georgiana I was always of an age."

"My deepest sympathy, my lord."

He shrugged slightly, as though from embarrassment at his own emotion. "The best-natured and best-bred woman in England is gone, Jane. There is nothing more to be said."

"Hear, hear," murmured Sir James. I glanced at him, and found an unwonted gravity in his looks. It was to be expected, I suppose, that a baronet and a native of the country would be acquainted with the Cavendish family—he must often have been invited to dine at Chatsworth when the Duke was in residence.

"Do you make a long stay in the neighbourhood?" I enquired.

Lord Harold seemed to rouse himself from a brown study. "Unhappily, not so long as I could wish. Parliament is at present recessed, but when it sits again we shall have much to do, if Fox is to prevail. Napoleon's victories in Austria have satisfied the Emperor's appetite, for a time; but more of Europe, and its armies, and its resources, are in thrall to the Monster, and he has never been a man to let fall a weapon when he might rather use it. Worse is yet to come, and we must be prepared to meet the Empire with force on both land and sea. I am come to Chatsworth, Miss Austen, to consult with His Grace the Duke—for no one may move the Whigs as Devonshire, if only he will give himself the trouble."

I smiled faintly at Lord Harold. "You would do well to guard your tongue, my lord. You speak to a respectable Tory, who must declare with Pitt that the map of Europe had better be rolled up again, for we shall not be wanting it this decade or more. I will not listen to the schemes and stratagems of a Whig! And I rather wonder whether His Grace is in any condition to hear you? Is not the Duke at present prostrate with grief?"

Lord Harold exchanged a look with Sir James, and both men were silent a moment. "His Grace must feel his wife's passing, to be sure. But his consolation in life has always been the friendship of Lady Elizabeth Foster; and she is presently his guest at Chatsworth."

"I see," I said, although I saw nothing but that Lord Harold would dissemble, and that he moved in deeper waters than I had previously understood. A change of conversation appeared advisable. "Pray tell me, my lord, how does your family?"

"Very well, thank you. My nephew Lord Kinsfell is very lately married."

"I wish him joy! And your delightful niece? Is the Countess of Swithin in health and beauty?"

"Desdemona is blooming," he replied, with more of lightness than I had yet seen; "indeed, she is increasing. We expect the child to put in its appearance at Christmas."

"How delightful!" I cried, and marvelled inwardly at the effect of time. I had first made the acquaintance of Lady Desdemona Trow-bridge some two years before, in Bath, when she was a girl of eighteen and all unmarried. Now she was a lady of fashion—a formidable host-ess in Town—a Countess in her own right, and soon to be a mother. Life for Lady Swithin had only grown more dazzling, while life for Jane Austen had contracted yet further. I had survived the passage of my thirtieth birthday, the loss of my father and a very dear friend; I was soon to give up my abode of three years, and venture forth into the unknown. I possessed even less inclination for marriage, and fewer prospects of achieving that state; I must live upon the princely sum of fifty pounds per annum—the probable cost of one of Lady Desdemona's gowns—and did I dwell too long upon the impoverish-ment of my circumstances, I should grow unutterably depressed.

"It was precisely this that drew me to your side today, Miss Austen," Lord Harold was saying. "My niece is come with me to Chatsworth, to condole with Lady Harriot Cavendish, who is of an age with Mona and a friend from her earliest years. The Countess learned of your presence in Derbyshire only last evening, from Sir James"—this, with a glance for the Justice—"and could not know of it, without desiring to renew the acquaintance. My niece would have waited upon you this morning, indeed, but that Sir James assured us you were to appear as witness at the Inquest; and so it was settled that I should seek you out and bring you back to Chatsworth when all was concluded. Lady Swithin is wild to meet with you again—I say no more than she would herself," he added with a smile, "for those were her very words."

Chatsworth! Second only to Blenheim as the most venerable and exalted estate in the land! That I should be invited, the acquaintance of one of its intimates—that I should walk into its grand foyer, not as a member of the touring public, but as a guest desired and welcomed! I might stroll through its extensive grounds, arm-in-arm with a Countess, and admire the fabled fountains and the Spanish oaks scattered about the lawns—I might take tea at a table set out on the grass, or sample fruit from a hothouse tree. I might fancy myself an equal with such a man as Lord Harold, and turn to find his gaze upon me. I, Jane Austen, an intimate of Chatsworth—and of the heathen Whigs it harboured!

Whatever would Cassandra say?

But then, with an inward sinking, I considered my state of dress. I had donned a respectable muslin gown of pale blue that morning, and had gone so far as to submit to a navy-blue spencer, despite the heat, in deference to the austerity of the occasion. I was very nearly suffocating. My gown, moreover, was not in the first stare of fashion, and grossly unequal to the grandeur of the Cavendishes.

And I was emphatically *not* in mourning.

"The Countess is very good," I told Lord Harold haltingly, "but it is beyond my power to accept her invitation. Perhaps, if she intends to prolong her stay in the neighbourhood, we might walk together in Bakewell—"

"Courage, Jane," said Lord Harold quietly. "You always possessed it of old. Do not fail me now."

His grey eyes met my own, and held—and for the barest instant, I saw deep into his soul. Lord Harold was oppressed with worry, an anxiety so fearful he could not share it before Sir James; and I knew

To Make a Tart that is Courage to a Man or Woman

*B*oil two peeled quinces, three peeled burdock roots, and a pared potato in a quart of wine until tender. Put in an ounce of dates, and when these are tender, force the whole through a strainer. Add the yolks of eight eggs, and the brains of four cock sparrows, or mourning doves if sparrows be not handy, and add a little rose or orange water.

Next stir in some sugar, cinnamon, and ginger. Add cloves and mace if they be close at hand. Put in some sweet butter, and place the whole in a copper pudding mold. Tie the mold with cloth and string, and boil until done.

If courage be not found in the eating, then a dose of strong spirits be advised.

—From the Stillroom Book of Tess Arnold,
Penfolds Hall, Derbyshire, 1802–1806

Chapter 9

A Fine House
Richly Furnished

28 August 1806, cont.
~

THE CAVENDISH FAMILY ARE WITHOUT QUESTION AMONG THE GREAT in Derbyshire—indeed, throughout all of England. It may fairly be said that the Whig party was born among these peaks in 1688; for it was the Cavendishes who conspired with their near neighbours, the Manners family—later the Dukes of Rutland—to call William of Orange and his consort, Mary, from Holland in a Glorious Revolution. Having seized the throne of England from James II, William III rewarded his king-makers with dukedoms; and they served him in turn, by reminding him that though the throne might be his, the kingdom was now *theirs*. It is a Whig tenet that the monarch serves at the pleasure of the people—if one considers the people to be solely those who own a vast deal of property. The Whigs will court the common rabble in order to preserve their own heads secure upon their shoulders, without ever intending to do very much to ameliorate the rabble's condition—other than to set them against their kings.

I write all this in the pages of my journal despite my deep regard for Lord Harold Trowbridge, a Whig if ever there were one. The Dukes of Wilborough, having always possessed a keen sense of interest, were no more slow to champion William than their Cavendish brothers; and thus fortunes were made, influence won, and Lord Harold preserved from want from the moment of his birth. It should not be remarkable that such a man is an adept at the manipulation of faction, and at the preservation of his own life, regardless of the tempests of warfare and politics; he was formed in intrigue, schooled in calculation, and took the cynic's breath with his mother's milk.

And now he was to carry a respectable Tory Austen into the very heart of Cavendish territory. If I must storm the gates of Chatsworth, then no one but Lord Harold would do for my lieutenant.

At our first entering the country, my mother determined that we should view Chatsworth's grounds and some part of the house, which by custom are made open to the public. But upon learning that the family were down for the summer, and thrown into the deepest of mourning, we gave up the scheme in excessive disappointment. A sense of delicacy would not allow even Mrs. George Austen to invade the Cavendishes' privacy at such a time.

Her surprise would be great indeed upon learning that I had now secured an invitation to the house. In anticipation of the fevered exclamations such intelligence would excite—the inordinate concern for my state of dress, my speech, my manners, and my looks—and fearful that my mother would end by determining that she must accompany her younger daughter on so august an occasion—I undertook to leave my dearest relation in ignorance of events until they should be entirely past repair. I settled it with Sir James Villiers that he should call upon my cousin Mr. Cooper at The Rutland Arms, and convey to my mother a note I swiftly penned, explaining the nature of my absence.

I might trust Sir James to make all my party easy as to the propriety of my visit, and the considerable honour of the Countess of Swithin's notice—for he is possessed of exactly that buoyant self-assurance, that familiarity with the Great World, calculated to impress my mother and comfort my sister. When Sir James is done, I might well be the object of envy for having glimpsed Chatsworth on so intimate a scale—despite having entangled myself once more with Lord Harold.

His lordship had come to Bakewell in an elegant landau, drawn by four matched bays, the panels and doors emblazoned with the

Devonshire serpent and stag. A liveried coachman handed me into the carriage, and I settled myself opposite Lord Harold with all the sensations of delight attendant upon an airing in such an equipage, behind such a team, and through such splendid country. It was useless to attempt much conversation amidst all the bustle of the village; and until we had descended the length of the town, and crossed the ancient stone bridge that led towards Chatsworth, Lord Harold said nothing. But a journey of three miles cannot be passed entirely in silence; and presently, in a lowered tone, he enquired how I did.

"Perfectly well, my lord, I thank you."

"The breeze is not too distressing?"

"Not at all. I find it most refreshing. You will recollect that I have my spencer."

He then enquired whether I had yet ventured the Baslow road, and upon my answering in the negative, observed, "Then you may expect nothing but delight. This part of the country is known as Manners Wood, after the Rutland family. Do not neglect the view, Jane, as we achieve the top of the hill."

"I am sure I shall find it charming, Lord Harold."

He studied my countenance an instant, and then ventured, "You look very well, Jane. I rejoice to find you so obviously in health. It has been too long since we last met; and yet you appear not a day older."

"You flatter me, sir," I chided him.

"Not at all. I merely detect in you a resilience I am far from feeling myself."

"You *do* appear to have sustained a trying period."

"Most trying. From a variety of causes, this past twelvemonth has proved the most difficult of my life." His gaze wandered over the woody hills to left and right, the gentle slopes of pasturage fading now in late summer, without appearing to register their beauty. "And now this brutal death in Miller's Dale. It is by far too much."

I frowned. "I had not expected you to feel the maid's murder with any personal sensibility, my lord."

"I confess I do not," he returned, with a brusque laugh. "Indeed, I have entirely failed to consider of the wretched girl. She is nothing to me. It is for those who might be encompassed in the affair, that my anxiety is all alive. If I but knew what Georgiana would do—how she would wish me to act—" He broke off, and raised his hand to his lips in mute frustration.

The late Duchess. Comprehension and astonishment broke upon my head at once. I leaned forward and spoke in no more than a whisper, conscious of the footman behind and the coachman before.

"Would you suggest, my lord, that an intimate of Chatsworth is somehow entangled in the murder of Tess Arnold? But her death was an act of savagery—an act of madness! Surely no one from that exalted family—"

He looked at me with pain. "I am not master enough of the circumstances, Jane—I am too much in the dark on several fronts—to know what can or ought to be disclosed. Would that I might share the worst torments, the most despicable of my fears! But such are not for your hearing."

I sat back against the squabs and studied him narrowly. "Why was it so necessary for me to call at Chatsworth, my lord?"

"Because Mr. Andrew Danforth, the younger son of Penfolds Hall, rode out with His Grace the Duke this morning; and shall certainly be attendant upon the ladies at this hour."

"I have not seen the younger brother," I mused, "though I was so fortunate as to observe Charles Danforth only a few hours since. He is a . . . singular gentleman. I have rarely remarked so much grief and suffering upon so contained a brow."

"Charles Danforth is an exceptional fellow. You know that he is descended on his mother's side from the d'Arcy family, and in Charles one might almost discern the d'Arcy powers reborn."

"I confess I am unacquainted with the name. Are they well known in Derbyshire?"

"It was the d'Arcys who conspired with the Cavendishes and the Rutlands to bring about the Glorious Revolution," Lord Harold informed me, "in an alehouse in Whittington named the Cock and Pynot. It was there the Whig party was born, Jane."[1]

"And has not escaped the air of the alehouse from that time to

---

[1] The Cock and Pynot of Old Whittington is now the Revolution House, a museum dedicated to the conspirators of 1688, where Mr. John d'Arcy's contribution is duly noted. —*Editor's note.*

this," I murmured. "But you were speaking of Mr. Andrew Danforth, I believe."

"Unlike his brother, Andrew was raised on the Penfolds estate. He is said to have been Tess Arnold's playfellow when they were both in their infancy."

"Was he, indeed? Then is Andrew a good deal younger than his brother?"

"By some eight years, I believe. He is but a *half*-brother, being the son of old Danforth's second wife. I would dearly love your opinion of both gentlemen, Jane." He hesitated, then plunged on. "I suspect them of being rivals for the hand of the Duke's younger daughter— Lady Harriot Cavendish. Which of the brothers she prefers is yet in doubt—Charles Danforth, though far superior to Andrew in almost every respect, has age and unhappiness and a widowhood against him—but I shall leave you to judge. Charles being detained at the maidservant's Inquest, and Andrew being claimed by His Grace, they shall both be served up *now* on the back lawn, over ratafia and rout cakes."

My lord's countenance was inscrutable as always. The grey eyes were fixed upon the road falling away behind us; he had placed himself at the coachman's back, in deference to a lady's sensibility and abhorrence at being driven by another.

"Do you suspect one of the Danforths," I enquired in very nearly a whisper, "of having done away with his maid? And is your concern, then, all alive for the feelings and prospects of Lady Harriot Cavendish? But surely the fact of Tess Arnold's having stolen Mr. Danforth's clothing would preclude *that* gentleman's involvement. A more careful assassin, in severing her tongue, would have severed all connexion with himself."

Lord Harold's gaze dropped to his hands. As always, they were spare and elegant; not for him the marks of distress, in torn and bitten fingernails. "I scarcely know what I suspect, Jane. You have heard the rumours of Freemasonry, no doubt?"

"Who in Derbyshire has not? The Coroner is most anxious to discredit his neighbours; but his reasons for doing so remain obscure."

"Why should any man throw mud upon his superiors in birth and fortune? From hatred—resentment—a conviction of inferiority.

Tivey cannot possibly credit the accusations he has formed. They are in every way absurd. But that will not prevent them from working a hideous change in the peace of this village. And for that I cannot forgive him."

I cast Lord Harold a sidelong glance. "You speak with real feeling, my lord. I might almost imagine you injured yourself."

"If you would enquire whether I am a Freemason, Jane, then I shall not hesitate to answer in the affirmative. I have no compunction in proclaiming my pride in an institution that may trace its origins to the Knights Templar themselves; had I lived in the world in the twelfth century, I should have been a Templar in any case."

"But for the vow of celibacy," I murmured.

"When the Templars were cast out and denied their worldly powers, their tradition of service to God and country was forced into secrecy, Jane," Lord Harold continued, "and took upon itself another name. That is why it is death to betray the Masonic Brotherhood; lives once depended upon such protection. The obligations of Brotherhood transcend the ties of nations and their allegiance. If the Monster Napoleon is ever thwarted, my dear girl, it will be due in large part to the work of enlightened men of every country in Europe— and no few of them Masons."

It was the longest outburst he had yet managed; in his voice I detected something of the Gentleman Rogue, that from his looks, might have been banished forever. I was quietly gratified at having excited so energetic a defence of the gentleman's realm.

"I understand His Grace the Duke is a member of the local lodge."

"It was founded in his father's time. You perceive, now, the cause of my anxiety. The murder of the stillroom maid bids fair to involve the Great very far above her station."

And it was Lord Harold's practise to defend the Great from harm. "You are afraid, perhaps, that the men of Chatsworth and those of Penfolds Hall are somehow united—not only in being members of a lodge, but in Tess Arnold's murder?"

"I do not know, Jane. I cannot possibly say. What I may fear, however—"

"Lord Harold," I attempted, "surely you take too much upon yourself. If the girl were murdered as a traitor to Freemasonry—then what did she hope to betray? The gentry are all members in good standing; and the common folk of the town should never credit Tess Arnold's story!"

Lord Harold inclined his head; but he remained unconvinced.

"His Grace has been described as far too indolent to stir himself in any cause," I persisted, "and he was dining at home in company with Andrew Danforth on the night of the murder. Besides—the wounds to the girl's body did not entirely correspond to those prescribed for ritual execution."

My companion stared at me in surprise. "Have you been overlistening the ritual yourself, Jane, in a suit of your brother's clothes?"

"Sir James Villiers supplied the intelligence. Had she been killed by a true Mason, Tess Arnold should have died of a cut throat, and not a lead ball. Very well—a true Mason did not kill her; or not for the reasons described. The Masonic mutilation is by way of subterfuge, visited upon her body after death."

"By her murderer—or another person altogether?" Lord Harold enquired, with a narrowing of his eyes.

"I cannot say. I believe, however, that it is a diversion—intended to direct our gaze from the true nature of the crime."

"And what would you have that to be, Jane?"

I lifted my shoulders impatiently. "The Inquest was scuttled by the performance of the Penfolds housekeeper and the maid's family between them. But we learned this much: Tess Arnold's situation was compromised, and her subsequent flight may be imputed to her dismissal from the household. It should be Sir James's first object to learn the cause of the maid's disgrace."

"He has done so," Lord Harold told me.

I looked all my chagrin. "Then he was very remiss in not informing me at once! I have come to depend upon Sir James's indiscretions. They form the principal matter I possess for consideration. But *you* will not torture me, my lord. *You* will not consign me to suspense."

"Tess Arnold was dismissed because she found her way into Andrew Danforth's bed. Mrs. Haskell discovered it, and turned the girl away without a character."

Trust the Gentleman Rogue not to mince words, even with a lady. I was too old an acquaintance to merit the usual deference; we had long adopted the habit of plain-speaking. I revolved the intelligence in my mind. It was, after all, one of the oldest stories in the world, and murder had been done on so slim an account before.

"Tell me a little of Penfolds Hall," I commanded Lord Harold, "and of the Danforth family history."

"Charles Danforth is the son of a very respectable man who passed from this life nearly fifteen years ago, leaving a considerable estate in Mr. Danforth's care. The family is ancient, though untitled, in Derby-shire; and Penfolds itself is a venerable place, dating from the time of Elizabeth. Charles Danforth's mother was, as I have said, a d'Arcy—the Honourable Anne, a very elegant but fragile woman. She died when the boy was still quite young. Charles was her only child.

"Old Danforth married again not long after his first wife's death. The second Mrs. Danforth was reckoned a beauty; she was certainly over twenty years his junior; and though perhaps amiable, had not a wit in her head. Andrew was the child of that union, and so delighted his fond parents, that Charles fell into disfavour. Andrew was dandled, spoilt, indulged beyond what was good for him—and raised to believe himself the rightful heir to Penfolds. Charles was sent away to school, and later, to Cambridge. At his parents' death, he had not seen Penfolds for over a decade."

"What a dreadful story!" I cried. "That the father should prove so unfeeling to his own child! It is in every way unpardonable!"

Lord Harold shrugged. "Charles Danforth was always of a taciturn disposition, as might repulse the affections of a parent. He was born with a clubbed foot, Jane; and the infirmity, and its singularity, worked early upon his sensibility. It is said that the second Mrs. Danforth—Andrew's mother—was afraid of the boy, believing his deformity to be the mark of the Devil."

"Then she was a much stupider person than reputation allows," I returned crisply. "And Andrew himself? How does he conduct himself towards the usurper of his fortune?"

"With becoming affection," said Lord Harold. "Without Charles, you understand, Andrew should possess not a farthing. I feel his situation keenly; it is rather like to my own."

A sidelong glance, to judge how I should take this. I rejoiced in the return of Lord Harold's wit, and forbore to comment on the sad case of younger sons.

"Do not pretend to being in charity with the fellow," I cried. "You dislike Andrew Danforth excessively, I feel it in your words. You have said nothing to encourage prejudice; and yet prejudice runs rank throughout your narrative. Because he chuses to dally with his own maids?"

"Young Mr. Danforth's manners are very pleasing, Jane—I am certain you will find them so. Certainly Lady Harriot enjoys his attentions; and she is nothing if not a discerning character."

"You believe that he aspires to her ladyship's hand," I mused. "If word were put abroad of his liaison with the maid—"

"Who knows what the result might be?"

"It admits enough of doubt, perhaps, to warrant murder—if the gentleman's case is desperate."

"He aspires to a career in Parliament," Lord Harold observed, "and possesses neither fortune nor influence. Lady Harriot, however, might be the saving of him in both respects."

"I wonder if Tess Arnold's witchcraft ran to blackmail?"

"A girl who has been dismissed from service must make her way in the world," Lord Harold replied drily.

"Were I Andrew Danforth, ambitious as to love and fortune, I believe I should murder the maid myself. I should arrange to meet her in the wildest country, upon my return from a respectable engagement; and I should make it appear that her death was the work of a madman."

"But if Tess Arnold walked out into Miller's Dale at Andrew Danforth's urging—why borrow Charles Danforth's clothes?"

My gaze held Lord Harold's impenetrable one. "Because Andrew wished her to do so, of course."

"To throw suspicion for her death upon his brother?"

"If Charles Danforth were to hang," I suggested, "surely Andrew would inherit the Hall."

"He has no other heir." Lord Harold revolved the idea in his mind; then slowly shook his head. "It cannot explain the attempt at Masonic mutilation, Jane. You may answer the clothes, or answer the wounds, with a number of attractive theories—but you cannot answer them *both*, in the person of Andrew Danforth. It will not do."

"Sir James would have it that she was the victim of vengeance," I said slowly.

"Then why deprive oneself of the pleasure of witnessing her pain, by despatching her with a lead ball prior to inflicting it?" Lord Harold persisted.

"Have you considered, my lord, that the girl's death might be nothing more than a hideous mistake?"

His glance travelled over my countenance. "You would suggest that she was killed in Charles Danforth's stead?"

"Why not? The moon that evening was only at the half; in variable darkness, wearing the clothes of mourning, Tess Arnold might well be taken for a man. I credited the ruse myself, in the full light of day."

"Someone might well fire upon the figure of a man in the belief that it was Charles Danforth," Lord Harold conceded, "but to then mutilate the body in ignorance? Impossible!"

"Unless, being horrified at his discovery of his mistake, the murderer then proceeded to create a diversion," I offered equably.

"Freemasonry." Lord Harold sighed.

"What else? We might justly charge Michael Tivey with the maid's death, on the strength of his diversions alone!"

I had intended the jibe to be taken in jest; but Lord Harold considered it thoughtfully. "We should enquire whether Tivey has reason to wish Charles Danforth dead."

"A question the Justice might better pursue. If Charles Danforth is the surgeon's enemy, then all the world shall know of it. Anyone might employ a man such as Tivey."

"Andrew?" Lord Harold enquired.

"He *does* stand to inherit," I concluded pensively. "What better method of ridding himself of a double vice, than to set Tivey on to his brother, and so quit himself of the maid? I begin to admire the cast of young Mr. Danforth's mind. It is subtle and calculating. Has Sir James considered of the gun-room at Penfolds Hall? Are all the fowling pieces in order?"

"Even if the Justice had secured it with stout men from the first whisper of the maid's passing, Jane, the fowling piece would not be found," Lord Harold replied. "It is probably at the bottom of one of Derbyshire's deepest caverns, and no one shall bring it up again."

BY THE TIME WE TURNED IN AT THE LODGE, MY SPIRITS WERE IN A high flutter. The park was very large, and contained great variety of ground. We entered it in one of its lowest points, from the west, and drove for some time through a beautiful wood stretching over a wide extent.[2]

"Have I stumbled upon Paradise?" I murmured.

"It was not always thus," Lord Harold replied. "The approach was formerly from the east, in Elizabeth's time. The present Duke's father determined that it had better be changed to the west, and so pulled down some old stables and offices on this side that interfered with the view. He razed the cottages of Edensor Village as well, which used to sit near the river."

This, I supposed, was the privilege of a Duke—to destroy the homes of his dependants in order to enclose his park. How admirably the Whigs did manage the people! "How large is the estate, my lord?"

"Some thirty-five thousand acres. But I presume you would mean the park itself. Dawson?" Lord Harold threw the word over his shoulder. "How many miles round is the park?"

"Near ten mile, sir," the coachman replied.

We gradually ascended for half-a-mile, and then found ourselves at the top of a considerable eminence, where the wood ceased, and the eye was instantly caught by Chatsworth House, situated on the opposite side of a valley, into which the road with some abruptness wound. It was a large, handsome stone building, standing well on rising ground, and backed by a ridge of high woody hills.

"Observe the river," Lord Harold commanded. "The course of it has been altered, and swelled into greater, but without any artificial appearance. This stone bridge"—as the horses' hooves clattered across it—"was also built in the last Duke's time."

[2] Much of Jane Austen's description of her first view of Chatsworth echoes wording she would later employ to describe Elizabeth Bennet's first glimpse of Pemberley, the Derbyshire estate of Fitzwilliam Darcy, in *Pride and Prejudice*. —*Editor's note*.

"I have never seen a place for which nature has done more, or where natural beauty has been so little counteracted by an awkward taste." In this, I might hope to judge Chatsworth entirely without prejudice, as Lord Harold had preferred; my whole heart was filled with delight at its beauty, and at everything that proclaimed the elegance of its owner.

"You detect the hand of Capability Brown," Lord Harold replied. "There was no man for designing a park quite like him."

Sheep scattered at the curricle's approach; the splendid façade of the house drew near, with its masses of windows, its central pediment blazing with the Devonshire arms, its ornate pilasters and casement stonework—and above all, surmounting the broad, flat roof, a parade of urns and statues from antique climes. It was a picture of elegance and taste that rivalled everything I had ever seen; and to think that I should enter through the great portals of Chatsworth, and attempt to pass myself off with credit, must strike terror to the very bone.

The curricle pulled up—a waiting footman stepped forward—and I was handed down to the sweep before the massive divided stair that led to the very door.

"Thank you, Dawson," Lord Harold said absently to the coachman; and offered me his arm.

To Beautify the Hands

Take two ounces of Venice soap and dissolve it in two ounces of lemon juice. Add one ounce of the oil of bitter almonds, and a like quantity of oil of tartar. Mix the whole, and stir it well, until it is like to cream; then use it as such for the hands.

—From the Stillroom Book of Tess Arnold,
Penfolds Hall, Derbyshire, 1802–1806

Chapter 10

Among the Serpents, and the Stag

28 August 1806, cont.

~

A FOOTMAN IN SKY BLUE AND BUFF LIVERY LED US FROM THE WEST ENtrance through an open colonnade, to a great hall with a painted ceiling and branching twin staircases.[1] I should have liked, at that moment, to be a stranger even to Lord Harold—a mere pleasure-seeker escorted by the Chatsworth housekeeper, who might be expected to stare boldly upwards at the vivid frescoes. A multitude of classical figures—in the usual state of undress—reclined on a swirling bed of painted clouds, without taking the slightest notice of my existence far below: a metaphor, one might say, for the entire Whig view of Society.

"You shall gaze upon Caesar until you are sick of him, my dear Jane," murmured Lord Harold at my ear, "once you have been properly introduced. The State Apartments, too, are not to be missed; but they are well above, on the second floor. Pray attend to the footman!"

---

[1] Present-day visitors to Chatsworth will detect a discrepancy here between Jane's description of its interior and grounds and the manner in which both now appear. The sixth Duke of Devonshire made extensive renovations and additions to the estate after his accession in 1811. The colonnade through which Jane passed was then enclosed, and the twin staircases replaced with a single flight and matching galleries along the east and west walls. —*Editor's note.*

I tore my eyes from the Painted Hall and hurried resolutely after the servant. He led us through a passage to the rear of the great house and from thence to a stone terrace. Beyond it lay a sweep of lawn, more verdant and inviting even than the formal parterres that lay to the east of the building; and there, like the Muses themselves, were arranged the figures of three ladies.

"Uncle! And my dear Miss Austen! It has been an *age*!"

It was the Countess of Swithin who first distinguished me, as should be only natural—rising from her chair beneath a spreading oak, where she had been disposed with an easel and crayons, intent upon capturing the scene. Lord Harold drew me forward across the flags, up a short flight of steps to the lawn, past several flower beds, where some late blooms were charmingly grouped among the lavender—and bowed low upon achieving the ladies.

"I dared not dream that Uncle would prevail upon you to pay a call today," said Lady Swithin. "It is very good of you, and far more than we deserve, after all that you have been through. You must be utterly fagged!"

Lord Harold's niece was considerably altered since I had last seen her—for two years, in the life of such a young lady, must make a distinct change. Her countenance was less open, less touched by innocence, but still as glowing; her figure, though full with the burden of her approaching child, yet managed a youthful grace. Her hair was as golden, and her gown as before the fashion, as ever they had been; but where once her attire had possessed the simplicity of youth, there was now an elegance and refinement due entirely to her familiarity with the Great. I was pleased to detect no sign of weariness or sorrow about the eyes, no suggestion of a private pain. The Earl of Swithin was always a difficult companion, and the love that united him to Desdemona of a jealous and fitful kind; but it appeared that the two had learned to suit, and that no spectre of unhappiness could dog their union.

Two other ladies were seated near the Countess, on chairs set out upon the lawn. One was fast approaching middle age, and wore the decent but unadorned dark grey cambric of a lesser relation or superior domestic; the other was a strong-boned, fresh-faced, alert young woman of middle height, with a figure fully-formed, and a wild cascade of gingery curls about her nape.

How shall I relate my first impression of Lady Harriot Cavendish, second child of the Duke of Devonshire? She is not a beauty by any means, but her face has a certain intelligent distinction; it shall be called "handsome" with time, and her character will stamp it. The nose is a defiant blade, the chin square and stubborn; her round eyes and full lips, I later learned, she received from the Cavendish side of the family, but her temperament is entirely Spencer.[2] I should judge her to be of an age with the Countess of Swithin, but being yet a dependant in her father's home, she wants Lady Desdemona's easy assurance. Her countenance, too, is bereft of Mona's happy glow; she is altogether a more subdued and reflective companion than I should look to find at the Countess's side.

Lady Harriot's gown was of sheer grey Alençon lace, over a dark grey underskirt; it was trimmed in white soutache, which offered some relief from the austerity of mourning. But the languor of grief clung about her still—she moved with the weariness of a spent child.

Lord Harold drew me forward. "Lady Harriot, may I have the honour of introducing Miss Jane Austen to your acquaintance? Lady Harriot Cavendish."

The Duke's daughter closed the volume she had been reading and nodded austerely. Those round eyes, deeply shadowed, swept the length of my person. "Welcome to Chatsworth, Miss Austen. You find us in a melancholy state, I own, but we are glad you are come to lighten it."

"You have my deepest sympathy, Lady Harriot, and my gratitude for allowing this trespass upon your kindness at such a time." I curtseyed deeply.

Lady Harriot made an impatient little movement—a plucking with one hand at the lace of her gown—and then recovered her countenance. If she had heard my words, she had already dismissed them as a commonplace—the muttered decencies of the Polite World—and accorded them no other significance beyond an irritant. I had not known her mother; I could not possibly comprehend what Georgiana Duchess, nor her passing, had meant in this household, and

[2] Spencer was the maiden name of Georgiana Cavendish, Duchess of Devonshire. —Editor's note.

every attempt at condolence must be regarded as the grossest impertinence. I wondered if Harriot Cavendish was often prone to dismiss the goodwill of others. Her life must be full of sycophants and toad-eaters.

"May I introduce Miss Trimmer to your acquaintance?" Lord Harold directed my steps towards the creature in grey cambric and inclined his head with a certain fond deference. "Miss Jane Austen—Miss Selina Trimmer. Miss Trimmer has been Lady Harriot's governess from her earliest years, and now serves by way of companion."

"It is a pleasure," Miss Trimmer said, with a nod of her head. "Any friend of our excellent Lord Harold must always find a welcome at Chatsworth."

"Do you make a long visit in the neighbourhood, Miss Austen?" enquired the Countess of Swithin. "Do say that you intend a few weeks, at the very least!"

"I fear it is beyond my power to name the length of my stay, Lady Swithin," I replied with a smile, "since I remain at the pleasure of my cousin Mr. Cooper, who was so good as to bring me into Derbyshire."

"I do not know that name," Lady Harriot observed with a frown. "Is he a gentleman of Bakewell? I do not believe that we have ever met."

"Mr. Cooper is a clergyman, Lady Harriot, with a living in Staffordshire, and I fear his interest in this county does not extend beyond its trout streams! I have seen very little else, I assure you, during the three days I have spent at Bakewell."

"Then you must remain another week complete," Desdemona said warmly, "and allow us to show you the wonders of Derbyshire. There are said to be at least seven, are there not, Uncle?"

"Only by the county's detractors, Mona. I could name an hundred, and never tire of discovering more."

"There is Cresswell Crag, and the Heights of Abraham," she began, numbering them upon her fingers, "and the Nine Ladies—they are monstrous great stones, Jane, rather like to the Henge—and the Blue John Cavern! Have you ever descended into the depths of the earth, and seen stone carved by nature into the semblance of a cathedral?"

"I confess that I have not."

Lady Swithin clapped her hands. "Then we shall make up a party and spend the day. You must and shall see the Blue John!"[3]

"If your cousin is an angler, Miss Austen," Lady Harriot interposed, "then you may assure him that the very best streams are on the Chatsworth estate. Mr. Cooper must come one day and fish with the other gentlemen, before he quits the neighbourhood."

"You are very good, my lady," I replied, "but I fear Mr. Cooper is lately surfeited with trout streams. I do not think he will be fishing very much in future. Miller's Dale has put paid to his passion."

She gazed at me in some little puzzlement, then said, "Why, of course! You are the lady who stumbled over the dead maidservant!"

"If Miss Austen *was* so unfortunate, Hary-O," said Miss Trimmer briskly, "I cannot think she would wish to be reminded of it."

The governess's words barely checked her former charge. "Mona informed us of it only yesterday! An extraordinary business, was it not?"

"Extraordinary," I murmured in assent, though there were many other words I might have chosen to describe Tess Arnold's end.

"I cannot remember the like in all my days in Derbyshire! And the Inquest was held this morning, I believe. Did the panel put a name to the murderer?"

"Unhappily, they could not. The Inquest was adjourned."

"I cannot recall that I ever encountered that maid," Lady Harriot mused, "though I have often been at Penfolds Hall."

"Have you, indeed?" I enquired, with a quickening of interest.

"Of course. A tie of the deepest respect subsists between Chatsworth and the Danforth family. Its basis is nearly two hundred years old. I feel this . . . misfortune of theirs . . . quite deeply."

"I understand that they have suffered much in recent months."

Her head came swiftly round, and she studied me acutely. "Have you been listening, then, to gossip in the streets of Bakewell, Miss Austen? I would not credit everything you hear. More superstition is

---

[3] Blue John is a blue-colored fluorspar peculiar to Derbyshire. During the eighteenth and nineteenth centuries, it was often carved into vases and ornamental figures, examples of which may be seen at Chatsworth today. —*Editor's note.*

bred in those stone cottages than miners' whelps, and ignorance is the commonest form of barter. We trade in everything but charity, in these wretched hills."

Startled, I glanced at Lord Harold. For a lady nearly ten years my junior, the Duke's daughter had a tongue swift as a viper's. I must be on my guard in future, did I hope to pry any secrets from Chatsworth's walls.

"It was Sir James Villiers who first repeated something of the Danforths' history," I replied.

"Mr. Charles Danforth but lately lost his wife—having lost, in turn, the four children she had borne," Lady Harriot informed me. "First little Emma was taken, in the midst of a virulent fever, when she was but five years old. That would be last November. She was a beautiful child—very pretty in her ways."

Lady Harriot rose restlessly from her chair and began to pace about the lawn, her eyes fixed upon the grass and her tone growing ever more strident. "Then Julia died suddenly in February, of acute gastric attacks. Mr. Danforth was from home at the time—and the illness came on suddenly. My father called a physician from London, and sent the man express at his own expense. Everything was done for her—purges, draughts, bloodletting." Lady Harriot shook her head. "Nothing could save the child.

"John d'Arcy Danforth died in March. He was no more than two, the darling of his father. And in the midst of her grief and despair, Lydia Danforth was brought to bed of a stillborn son in April, several weeks before she expected."

A gasp from Lady Swithin; I looked, and saw that she was unwontedly pale. Lady Harriot was too engrossed in her tale to notice its effect on her friend. She stared at me hotly.

"Do you know what the townspeople said of Lydia Danforth, with all her children dead about her? They declared that she was cursed. That she had mated with the Devil, and must reap her reward. And when she followed her babe to the grave a few days after, they mouthed pious comforts, assuring all and sundry that her death was the will of God!"

Unable to contain her rage, Lady Harriot took refuge in mimicry. " 'The pore missus is at peace, now, wit' 'er little 'uns,' " she spat out in a broad Derby accent; and turned her furious gaze upon Lord Harold. "We may give thanks at least that she is beyond the spite of her neighbours!"

"So many children. It does not bear thinking of," whispered Lady Swithin. Her right hand was pressed against her stomach, as though she might protect the babe within, and her grey eyes—so like Lord Harold's—were wide with fear. It would be as well, I thought, did Lady Harriot consider of those who were present, as well as those who were gone.

Something in Mona's voice must have alerted her; Lady Harriot summoned a smile, and reached for the Countess's hand. "If you do not sleep a wink this night, Mona, you may lay the account at my door. Swithin will pillory me for putting such dreadful notions in your head. Forgive your Hary-O, my darling—if I am a wild beast sometimes, I cannot help it."

Lady Swithin pressed her friend's hand and attempted something of her usual manner. "No beast ever had such a heart, my dear. Yours is the largest in the world, as I have cause to know."

Lady Harriot glanced diffidently away, as though to disguise her emotion, and said in a lowered tone, "One always feels the sufferings of the bereaved, when one has lost the dearest creature in the world! It pains me to see this fresh cloud hanging over the Penfolds family. I could shake that stillroom maid until her teeth fell out, for having brought this misfortune upon Charles!" Her jaw was set so fiercely I felt I glimpsed for an instant the spirit in Lady Harriot's blood that had moved her forebears to Whiggish revolt.

"I believe your warm heart urges a greater anxiety for the Danforths than is necessary, Hary-O." Lord Harold's tone was unaccustomedly gentle. "The girl was probably despatched by a spurned lover. Sir James will have the villain out in a fortnight, and all will be forgot."

It was something to catch Lord Harold in a barefaced lie.

"Yes," she replied with effort. "I am sure that you are right, Lord Harold—you always are, it is your special talent."

Lady Harriot turned to me with the ghost of a smile. "I do not need to tell you, Miss Austen, that Sir James Villiers is an excellent man—far less frivolous than his appearance would suggest, and shrewder than his friends will allow. He holds his commission at my father's request. But I cannot help thinking that the Justice moves rather *slowly*. What is your opinion, Lord Harold?"

"I believe Sir James moves no faster or slower than the pace of a one-horse dray, Lady Harriot; and as that is the accustomed pace of a country town, he is exactly suited to his company. His mind, however, is formed of swifter stuff; and I should be very much surprised to learn that Sir James was not before events."

Miss Trimmer set aside her needlework and, with a severe look for Lady Harriot, said, "Remember your duties as a hostess, Hary-O. I am gone in search of Lady Elizabeth."

"Go, then," her charge muttered at Miss Trimmer's departing figure, "and if such is your errand, my dear Trimmy, I cannot wish you back again. Are you perishing for a glass of iced lemon-water, Miss Austen? For if you are, pray advise me at once and have done. I cannot abide the sort of people who stand upon ceremony, as though I were a bit of porcelain, and might break when handled."

"Who can possibly have mistaken your character so completely, Hary-O, as to think you fragile?" enquired Lord Harold.

She flashed him a look of scorn meant entirely for another. "Forget my duties as a hostess, indeed! As though I *could* forget them now, when they have been utterly usurped—"

He shook his head once; she bit her lip, and struggled for self-control.

"I should very much enjoy a glass of iced lemon-water," I said, in an effort to turn the conversation, "for Lord Harold loves nothing better than an open carriage, and you must know the dust on the roads at such a season is dreadful. I shudder to think how I must appear to you all."

"Heaven-sent, I assure you"—Lady Swithin laughed, her colour recovered—"for the gentlemen have been riding all the morning, and two women cannot endure an entire day's *tête-à-tête* together without coming to blows. You must sit between us, Miss Austen, and tell me all your news since last we met. Do you still find Bath as disagreeable as ever? I have not set foot inside the town, you know, since my marriage!"

And thus in sparkling reminiscence, with many introductions of her own adventures and good jokes, did Desdemona contrive to amuse us all for a half-hour together, while the shadows lengthened on the verdant lawn. A chair was brought for my comfort, and the promised lemon-water; Lord Harold tossed his hat aside and threw his length along the grass, resting carelessly at Hary-O's feet, and adding a word or two when the conversation required it. He bent his efforts to peeling a series of peaches, the long, curling, golden skin lengthening under the ministrations of his pocketknife; and I watched the subtle movements of his hands, the delicate fingers roaming over the surface of the fruit, while attending to Desdemona's chatter with half my mind. There was trouble here in Paradise, something greater even than the grief of mourning; the anxiety behind all their looks revealed it.

I was the first to perceive Charles Danforth as he made his way across the lawn; and Lord Harold, in following my gaze, rose abruptly to his feet.

"It would appear that Trimmy has found someone besides Lady E.," he observed to Hary-O. "I thought Charles Danforth should have arrived well before myself and Miss Austen; but perhaps he had an errand along the way."

"Charles!" Lady Harriot cried, an unsuspected warmth in her voice; and she ran forward to seize his hand, as unaffected as a girl. "I am so glad you are come! I cannot bear to think of you, alone in that house on such a fine summer's day! You *will* stay to dinner? I do not think you have been at our table three times this summer—and yet Andrew is never absent!"

"And thus we manage to achieve a balance," Mr. Danforth replied, "Andrew, by his excess, and I in my restraint. In this you may read the nature of our characters, Lady Harriot." The judgement was offered coolly, but there was a smile about the gentleman's lips; whatever his inward trouble, he could not regard Lady Harriot's eager countenance and remain unaffected.

"And were you always so measured, Mr. Danforth?" enquired Lady Swithin with a teasing glance, "or was your youth as ardent, and as misspent, as your brother's? Come and meet my very great friend, Miss Jane Austen. She is travelling through Derbyshire, to our good fortune."

"Miss Austen," Charles Danforth said correctly—and was then arrested when he would have bowed, and studied my countenance keenly. "But surely—I cannot be so mistaken—surely we have already met?"

"We have had a glimpse of each other," I replied. "In Bakewell this morning, at the Snake and Hind."

"Good Lord! You are the lady who discovered poor Tess."

I inclined my head. That he could speak of the maid with such charity—after the imputations the Coroner had laid at his door, and all the malice of the townsfolk—spoke to his amiable temperament.

"Was the Inquest horrid, Charles?" Lady Harriot enquired. "Miss Austen is too well-bred—or too in awe of Trimmy's disapproval—to speak of it."

"Then I am for Miss Austen," he quietly replied. "Such unpleasant scenes cannot be too quickly forgotten."

"And have they no notion of who may have injured the poor maid?"

"None whatsoever, Lady Swithin. It is in every way inexplicable. I had not so much as known that she was dismissed from my service, before I learned of her death."

"Dismissed?" Lady Harriot cried.

"Indeed! Mrs. Haskell turned Tess Arnold away, on the grounds of some grievous infraction, on the very night she was killed—although she made no such confession to *me*. The servants all conspire to respect my privacy, you know." He offered this last for my benefit, who could not be presumed to know anything of Penfolds Hall.

So Charles Danforth would have us believe he knew nothing of his brother's affairs; and perhaps, indeed, he did not. My gaze drifted towards Lord Harold; but his eyes were fixed on the gentleman's face. His own disclosed nothing of his inward thought.

"Poor Haskell seems to feel herself in some wise responsible for the maid's death," Danforth continued. "It is only natural, I suppose, that she should take so much upon herself; but I cannot believe it reasonable. The girl was murdered by a wandering lunatic. That is the only explanation possible—and Haskell must learn to forgive herself."

"It is a difficult lesson for any of us to learn," I observed.

"Yes." He gazed at my countenance, and his own altered slightly.

From a studied air of ease that had been meant to reassure the ladies—to suggest that he was in no way affected by the Inquest—it saddened perceptibly, and his thoughts fled far afield. Had Charles Danforth forgiven himself, I wondered, for the deaths of his little children? For the despair and agony of his late wife? A man might take every grief in the world upon his shoulders—might stand as God within the bounds of his own kingdom—and feel how futile his power to alter the balance of life and death. Charles Danforth could do nothing to prevent his daughters failing before him; he could not keep back his son from the brink. Such a man might well believe the whispered mutterings he heard on every side—and cry out that he was cursed. What had kept Charles Danforth from falling headlong into the grave?

"And how have you been amusing yourself, Charles?" Lady Harriot demanded. "Playing the gentleman farmer, I suppose? Or reading great tomes of philosophy in your dusty old library?"

The look of nagging melancholy softened, and was gone; he smiled at Lady Harriot. "I have been planning a great journey, you know. You will have heard, I think, that I intend to sail for the West Indies in the spring."

"Not really!" The sudden access of delight—of wistful longing—was startling in Lady Harriot's face. "How I should *love* to throw off the wet and cold of England, and sail towards the sun! What freedom you men possess—and how I detest you all!"

He held her gaze, and measured his words with care. "I am sure that if Lady Harriot Cavendish wished to go anywhere in the world, she might command the will of any man."

Lady Harriot drew a sharp breath, and glanced away. Colour flooded into her cheeks; she affected indifference. "It has been ages and ages since I've been anywhere but London. And the Continent is entirely closed to us now, unless one considers Oporto, which I cannot regard. But the Indies—! Oh, Charles, how *fortunate* you are!"

"Or would be, were my estates in better order. But that is to talk of business, and I shall not try your patience with sugar and accounts. My lord," he observed with a nod to Lord Harold, "what have you attempted, for the amusement of these ladies? I had heard from Andrew that archery had been taken up, and targets secured on the lawn; but I can observe nothing so novel in the landscape. Chatsworth rolls on, as it has ever done, serene in its breadth of green."

"The only novel you shall find, my dear Charles, is presently in Lady Elizabeth's work basket," Hary-O retorted before Lord Harold could speak. "The bows and arrows were dismissed from her sight so lately as yesterday; we may presume that she feared they offered too much temptation. With one murder in the air, you know, the effect may be catching; and dear Bess will not play the bull's-eye for anyone."

"You are very *bad*, Lady Harriot," Danforth assured her with a half-choked laugh; and as he bent over her chair to admire her work, I had the strongest impression of collusion among Hary-O and Danforth and Lady Swithin. They were all of them shaking with guilty amusement; and I wondered that I had ever found Charles Danforth a figure of melancholy. The effects of sadness—of profound loss—were etched upon his countenance, to be sure; but in this place, and among these young women, he was able to set aside his care. Like Lady Harriot, I was suddenly glad that he had come; and I disliked to think of him alone amidst the many ghosts of Penfolds Hall.

The sound of a barking dog drew Lady Harriot sharply around, to gaze towards a gravelled avenue; three horsemen and several great hounds—bull mastiffs, by their appearance—approached at a walk. The eldest of the three, whose venerable head and resemblance to Lady Harriot proclaimed him her near relation, I judged to be His Grace the Duke of Devonshire. The second was a boyish figure of perhaps fifteen, with auburn hair, a bearing quite stiff and correct, and an unsmiling countenance; he was arrayed entirely in the profoundest black. William, Marquess of Hartington, it must be presumed—the sole Cavendish son and heir to a king's ransom. He did not look to me to be very promising; but allowances must be made for youth, and for the effects of grief. Lord Hartington was said by all the world to have been devoted to his mother.

The last was a gentleman of sober dress and easy appearance, a decade older than the boy at his side. This must be Andrew Danforth, though I could trace not the slightest resemblance to his brother. Where Charles Danforth was dark and sombre, this man was fair-haired and easy; where the weight of suffering lent nobility to Charles's brow, his brother could offer only good-humoured charm. Whatever of tragedy had been visited upon Penfolds Hall, it had not laid low this elegant figure.

He swung himself carelessly from the saddle, nodded at his brother by way of greeting, and strode towards our party before his companions had even dismounted.

"You have been eating peaches, Lady Harriot!" he cried, "and were so cruel as to leave us nothing but stones! You see us returned as from a desert. We are utterly parched. Has there ever been an August so hot and brown?"

"There were peaches a-plenty, had you returned in good time." Lady Harriot proffered a glass of iced lemon-water. "We expected you this last hour, Mr. Danforth, and had no recourse but to devour all the fruit when you failed us."

"Were I a scrub," he confided, "I should lay all the blame upon His Grace. There was the matter of a dog to be visited—a bitch with a new litter—and you know what Canis is when he is among his fellows."

"Not really, Father!" she cried, with a look for the Duke. "Visiting the stables, when you meant to persuade Mr. Danforth to stand for Parliament! It is too bad!"

"Possible to persuade and visit all at once, m'dear," observed His Grace the Duke. "He's agreed to stand."

Lady Harriot threw up her arms in delight and pirouetted on the lawn. "Glorious!" she cried. "The very thing for you, Andrew, had you but eyes to see it!"

"Apparently he does," observed Lord Harold drily, and drew me forward. "May I present Miss Austen, Your Grace? An old family friend from Bath."

The Duke inclined his head with a faint air of boredom and proceeded to fondle his dog. The Marquess of Hartington entered more fully into the *forms* of polite address, without greatly embracing their spirit; he bowed low, but failed to utter a word.

Mr. Andrew Danforth, however, was another matter entirely.

He bent over my hand with an expression of pleasure, smiled warmly into my eyes, and said, "Your servant, Miss Austen. I am *delighted* to make your acquaintance. Lady Swithin cannot stop praising your merits—and as you know, Lady Swithin is never wrong."

"Although perhaps she is sometimes a little kinder than I deserve," I replied with a laugh. "I should not wish my worth to stand a closer scrutiny!"

"Are you the one who found the body?"

The voice was curious—muffled, heavy and halting, as though the speaker must measure every word. I turned, and saw that it was Lord Hartington who addressed me; his expression was quite intent, his eyes fixed upon my face.

"I am, my lord," I replied.

He stared at me uncomprehendingly, the eyes acute and agonized.

"Lord Hartington is a trifle hard of hearing," Desdemona breathed in my ear. "Pray repeat your words a bit louder, Jane."

"Yes, my lord, I found the body of Tess Arnold," I said distinctly, and saw from the change in the boy's expression that he had understood.

"Do you think she suffered?"

They were all listening to us now, silent and watchful—Lady Harriot and the Danforths, Lord Harold and the Duke. I felt that they waited with breath suspended, as though something extraordinary were about to happen.

"The shot that despatched her was deadly and true," I replied. "She can have suffered no more than a dog that is put down."

Lord Hartington approached until he was barely a foot from my form. His youthful visage twisted suddenly with bitterness.

"Bloody hell," he burst out. The words were like a gun report in that bated stillness. "I'd hoped the witch had died in agony!"

A Remedy for Deafness

*R*oast a fine fresh oyster and when it is moder-ately done, open it and preserve the Liquor. Warm a spoon and put a little of the warm Liquor in it. When it is blood-warm, let the Sufferer lie on one side, turning the deaf ear uppermost, and let four drops of Liquor be dropped in from the spoon. Let him lie thus upon the same side half an hour, leaving the Liquor to operate on the Obstruction.

If both ears be deaf, the same must be repeated half an hour afterwards on the other Ear.

—From the Stillroom Book of Tess Arnold
Penfolds Hall, Derbyshire, 1802–1806

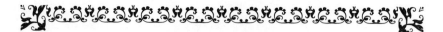

Chapter 11

Enter the Usurper

"GOOD GOD, HART, WHAT IS IT YOU HAVE SAID? WHAT CAN YOU HAVE been thinking?"

Lord Hartington wheeled around and stared at the woman standing just beyond our circle, her figure indistinct in the heavy shade thrown by the Spanish chestnuts. The Marquess's pallor was suddenly dreadful and his features worked furiously; then, with a strangled word that might have been an oath—or a cry of despair—he ran to his horse and sprang into the saddle.

"Hart!" cried Lady Harriot.

He hauled savagely on the reins, pulled the animal's head around, and, with a kick to the horse's flanks, cantered off in the direction he had come.

"I shall follow him." Andrew Danforth pressed Hary-O's hand and made for his horse.

"You shall do nothing of the kind, Mr. Danforth," ordered the lady who had caused the Marquess's flight. "Hart is master enough of himself and his mount; he cannot possibly come to harm at Chatsworth. He *will* enjoy his fit of the sullens, you know, though it be at the expense of those dearest to him in the world! Never have I seen the boy so blue-deviled as this summer! Canis and I agree that nothing he says should be taken in the least account. I do not regard his ill-behaviour towards myself, I assure you."

"You were always the best-tempered creature in the world, Bess," said the Duke with fondness. "And what have you found to occupy yourself this morning?"

"I have been perusing dear Georgiana's letters." Her voice faltered, and she stepped forward into the last rays of sunlight.

She was a frail, fine-boned creature with a heart-shaped face, a cascade of pale curls, and large eyes deeply set. The inky black of her clothing threw the translucent skin of her face into ghastly relief; but one might almost declare that mourning became her. Lady Elizabeth Foster, I should judge, would never allow herself to appear to disadvantage, no matter how real her grief, or how deeply felt her loss.

"How pretty you all look!" she cried, as she surveyed our party. "Such colour! Such gaiety!" One speaking, long-fingered hand carried a piece of silk to her eyes. "Had I known you were all to be so happy, I should have forced myself to leave my little room, and sought some comfort here. But alas . . ."

"Dear old Racky." The Duke rose and went to the lady. "Have you been moping yourself again?"

"Do not regard it," Lady Elizabeth returned with apparent effort. She fluttered her delicate hand and again pressed the handkerchief to her eyes. "When I gaze upon Hary-O, the merest girl, flush with all the dreams and hopes of a girl's heart—I might almost think myself transported, to those happy days of old! But they are gone—gone, Canis, with our dear one, into the grave!"

Lady Harriot rolled her eyes towards Heaven with an expression of intense irritation. A faint smile played about Andrew Danforth's lips; but I noticed that he had not returned to his horse. Lady Elizabeth's injunction, it appeared, would be obeyed.

"Lady Elizabeth," said Lord Harold, "may I intrude upon your cares long enough to present a very great acquaintance—Miss Jane Austen—to your notice?"

Lady Elizabeth's gaze strayed over me, and she attempted the faintest curtsey; but fell almost into a swoon, so that the Duke was forced to support her rather heavily. With an exclamation of concern, Charles Danforth seized a chair, and set it close to the swaying pair.

His Grace disposed of his fair burden, and Miss Trimmer—sensible, forthright Miss Trimmer, who had followed in Lady Elizabeth's train bearing a remarkable encumbrance of fringe-work, sketching book, and circulating library novels—produced a bottle of hartshorn, and waved it under the lady's nostrils. A start—a failing cry—a dramatic lifting of hands to eyes—and Lady Elizabeth was once more among the living.

"And so, while I had descended into the tenderest reflections in the world, you have all been enjoying a *social* call," she murmured, as one amazed. "No, no—do not think to offer an explanation, Hary-O. It is exactly as your mother should have wished. I, who knew the smallest concerns of her excellent heart—who cared for her as a sister even unto death—I must comprehend better than anyone that Georgiana would not wish you to repine."

"Indeed," I said hastily, "I have no wish to intrude upon your privacy, Lady Elizabeth, and duties of my own call me immediately back to Bakewell. I shall take my leave, and offer deepest thanks for the hospitality of all at Chatsworth."

"Well . . ." Lady Elizabeth inclined her head and summoned a smile. "Now that you have paid this first call, pray do not hesitate to come often. I am sure the Duke will join me in assuring you, Miss Austen, that we do not begrudge our Hary-O her little pleasures. She is very young, after all, and cannot always be expected to conduct herself with the propriety of her elders."

"No," Lady Harriot murmured ironically, "*that* would be unthinkable." Her countenance had acquired a markedly set expression; and I observed that both the Countess of Swithin and Lord Harold had moved closer to the Duke's daughter, so that they were arrayed as one against the lady enthroned near His Grace.

"Good Lord!" exclaimed the Duke. "Should be passing strange, Bess, if the chit didn't enjoy her pleasures! Not an old shade like ourselves! Girl wants dissipation—life—a home and family of her own! Only natural. Not getting any younger, what?"

"I ask for nothing more than the home I have known all my life, Father," retorted Lady Harriot. Her lips were compressed into a thin line; she was checking her temper with difficulty.

"And how fortunate you are that such a home is open to you!"

observed Lady Elizabeth faintly. "I was not so happy in my own situation in life, dear Hary-O. I rejoice to see the case is different for you. Could I prevent you feeling one-tenth of the suffering I had endured by the time I was your age—"

"You shall achieve that prevention, madam, by ceasing to speak of it. And now, pray forgive me, but I should be remiss in my duties did I not conduct Miss Austen to her carriage."

Lady Harriot moved to my side as though we were already the greatest of friends and slipped her hand through my arm. Lord Harold followed a few paces behind; his niece impulsively kissed my cheek in farewell.

"I rejoice to see you in such health, Jane, and shall call upon you in Bakewell at the first opportunity," she whispered.

Charles Danforth bowed low, his expression correct; his brother's was more satiric; but both remained, like Mona, with the Duke and his lady. I curtseyed to the entire party, and allowed myself to be drawn across the verdant lawn towards the flag terrace.

"Insufferable presumption!" Lady Harriot burst out when we had achieved the Painted Hall. "To condescend, *in my presence*, to offer me a place in my own household! When it is *I* who should be suffering *her* to remain! I, who should assume the role of hostess now in my father's home! Good God, could my mother only see it! Can His Grace be so miserably blind to the insults that are daily offered me?"

Lord Harold placed his hands on Lady Harriot's shoulders and looked directly into her eyes.

"She is no longer young, Hary-O, and she is very much afraid of losing all that she possesses. Consider how precarious is her position! While your mother lived, she might remain here as the bosom friend of a Duchess. But now? She has no position, no protection, no tacit veil between Society and herself; all the world must know what Lady Elizabeth is, and comment upon her indelicacy. Do not allow such a woman to drive you to the gravest error—an error you might regret all your life! You cannot flee one misery by choosing another. Do you understand me?"

Lady Harriot glared into his face rebelliously; she started to speak, and Lord Harold laid his finger against her lips.

"Quell your delicious temper, my sweet, and play the pretty to your father's guests. The duties of a hostess fall to those who seize them. Every notice you desire, Hary-O, is within your reach. It is Lady Elizabeth who exceeds her grasp."

Lady Harriot took Lord Harold's hand, planted a kiss in the palm, and then turned hurriedly to me. "We are to have a trifling dinner on Saturday, Miss Austen, in respect of my twenty-first birthday. Do I presume too much—or may I beg you to make another of the party?"

"With the greatest pleasure," I replied. I was sensible of the signal honour Lady Harriot thus did me, in extending the invitation to a relative stranger; her warmth must be all on Lord Harold's behalf.

"Until Saturday, then."

She moved swiftly back towards the terrace and the waiting Danforth brothers without another glance at Lord Harold; and so I was free to witness the expression that swept across his countenance. It was hollow, and yearning—the palm she had kissed still cupped at air—and I recognised the look for what it was: the pain of a man denied his very breath of life.

A Charm for the
Preservation of Love

T ake one ounce of dried foxglove, one ounce of comfrey, and one of the shredded bark of wild cherry; pound all together in a mortar, and secure in a small pouch of blue silk. Let the pouch rest close to the heart for seven days together, and then infuse the whole in a cup of strong tea. Give the tea to your Beloved on a night of full moon.

—From the Stillroom Book of Tess Arnold,
Penfolds Hall, Derbyshire, 1802–1806

Chapter 12

A Rough Justice

~

LADY ELIZABETH FOSTER WAS BORN A HERVEY; AND AS LADY MARY Wortley Montagu once famously observed, the world is divided into three sorts of people: men, women, and Herveys. They are a family marked by considerable beauty, by varied talents, and by eccentric behaviour; by a whining nasal tone to the voice, and a bird-like frame; by a thread of insanity and a singularity of character that inevitably embroil them in scandal. Divorces, bigamy, and the murder of duelling opponents have dogged the Hervey clan; there have been Herveys estranged from their wives, Herveys who die without recognising their children, Herveys who clutch at greatness and fall rather short. Lady Elizabeth Foster may be deemed one of these.

As the Cavendish carriage conveyed me steadily towards Bakewell, I reflected upon the nature of The Adventuress's career. Its broad outlines were known to me, as they must be to anyone who has lived in the world.

Lady Elizabeth Foster is approaching the age of fifty. She was married when still quite young to an Irishman whose violent temper and habit of seducing his wife's maids had early estranged her affections. Divorced by Mr. Foster after only a few years of marriage, she was deprived of her two sons, then in their infancy, and forced to live on a pittance. Her father, Lord Bristol—one of the more bizarre of the Hervey clan—then threw off Lady Elizabeth and her sister, whose marriage had also failed; and the two ladies moved forlornly about the watering-places of Europe, presuming upon the privileges of birth, and clinging to a threadbare decency. It was then that Lady Elizabeth fell in with the Duke and Duchess of Devonshire—childless, not long married, and not entirely able to suit one another.

She lived with the pair for over twenty years, acknowledged as the Duchess's dearest friend and the Duke's principal mistress. The perfect delight of the three in each other was not unmarred by comment; in the salons of the Great, eyebrows and questions were raised regarding the Duke's behaviour, and rather more gossip concerning the Devonshire progeny. Georgiana's daughters were deemed above suspicion; but Georgiana had also condescended to rescue several "orphans" from war-torn Europe, and had raised them as her own in the Devonshire nurseries. The Duchess, moreover, had gone so far as the Continent to produce *her* son and heir, Lord Hartington—accompanied by none other than Lady Elizabeth. The Vicious in Society wondered aloud whether Lord Hartington was Georgiana's son—or a Hervey bastard, exchanged for an unwelcome daughter at birth.[1]

Lady Elizabeth's continuance in the Chatsworth household after Georgiana's death must be perceived as awkward, both by intimates of the Cavendish family and by those more hostile to their circumstances. Convention held that Lady Harriot should assume the duties of her father's household, her elder sister being already several years married; and yet there was Lady Elizabeth—senior to Lady Harriot, clearly held in preference by the Duke, and determined to wrest at last some acknowledgement of her claims and position from the Great World.

She would continue to make life painful for Lady Harriot until the

---

[1] Although the Duke of Devonshire had not yet acknowledged his paternity of Lady Elizabeth Foster's children by 1806, he was to do so several years later. Lady Elizabeth bore the duke a daughter, named Caroline St. Jules, in 1785, and a son, named Augustus William Clifford, in 1788. The Cavendish family has always maintained, however, that William Cavendish, born 1790 and here referred to as the Marquess of Hartington, was indeed Georgiana's son.—*Editor's note.*

girl fled the Devonshire *ménage* for a suitable household of her own. Was it this that Lord Harold had meant, when he advised Hary-O not to exchange one misery for another? Could any young woman, raised in so divided a household, regard *marriage* as a form of salvation?

Lord Harold would not allow Georgiana's daughter to fall prey to a man who had brutally despatched his own maid. But which did he fear most: the easy charm of Andrew Danforth, or the subtle warmth of his brother, Charles?

As we descended the Baslow road towards Bakewell, my thoughts turned from Lady Elizabeth to the scene that had preceded her entrance. Whatever had been her principal object in engrossing all our attention, Lady Elizabeth had certainly succeeded in diverting us from the Marquess. Young Lord Hartington had behaved in a most extraordinary manner; but I suspected that such was often the case. He had the look of a boy tormented: by grief, by the deafness his family seemed determined to ignore, by the rumours that had dogged his birth. He must often be flying alone on horseback through the fields of his father's estate.

I'd hoped the witch had died in agony!

Disturbing sentiments to voice aloud, even in the company of one's friends. It must be impossible that Lord Hartington would expose himself in such a way, were Tess Arnold a complete stranger to him. The bitterness of the pronouncement—his rejoicing at the maid's death—suggested rather that the boy harboured some deep grievance towards the woman that found satisfaction in her gruesome murder. What could possibly inspire so profound a hate?

Madness. Madness born of grief and despair, madness born of unrequited love. Which had stirred in the Marquess's breast with those final, fatal words?

A madman is loose in the hills. And Lord Harold, it seemed, was afraid that the madman was the Duke of Devonshire's heir. It was for this he had begged me to observe the household; not for Lord Harold the unhappy duty of naming Georgiana's son a murderer. He would leave that to strangers.

I sighed in exasperation. Impossible, to consider any part of the whole with clarity. I was too much unsettled in my mind—too little familiar with the habits of Whigs—too greatly troubled by the secret

Lord Harold's countenance had lately betrayed. *The Gentleman Rogue was in love with his oldest friend's daughter.* Did he find Georgiana's bewitching charms revived once more in Lady Harriot?

And what did *she* think of *him?*

Or say rather—what did Lady Harriot think of any man?

Charles Danforth was marked in his reserve; yet there had been meaning in all his words to Hary-O. He had told her, in effect, that his will was hers to command. But so much dignity and suffering—such a weight of years and loves already outworn—might well terrify a girl of one-and-twenty. Andrew Danforth—the maid's seducer—had no such reserve; his back was unbowed by sorrow, he had charm and looks enough. He was ambitious in the field of politics, which Hary-O's entire world had taught her to admire. Andrew sought the Duke's patronage, and he desired the Duke's daughter. It would be a brilliant match for the younger son of an untitled family, however respectable. *He* would gain everything—a formidable Whig hostess, practised in Parliament and Society; a considerable fortune; and the sponsorship of one of the greatest Powers in the land. *She* would escape from the misery of living under Lady Elizabeth's reign, and acquire a gentleman with pleasing manners, an air of affection, and the best humour in the world.

But Tess Arnold had stood, quite possibly, in the way of it all—

By the time the carriage achieved The Rutland Arms, I was in the grip of a severe head-ache.

"And so you have renewed your acquaintance with the Countess of Swithin, Jane," my mother observed as I entered the parlour. "And how did you find her? Wasting away from a life of dissipation and vice?"

"Indeed not, ma'am. Lady Swithin is presently increasing," I remarked, as I removed my hat and spencer. "She was in excellent looks, I assure you, and begged to be remembered most fondly to yourself and my sister."

"Increasing! And so she gets on, does she, with her scoundrel of a husband?"

"As to that, I cannot say. The Earl did not put in his appearance."

"He leads her a merry dance, I've no doubt," observed my mother in satisfaction. "It is some comfort to reflect, Jane, that however sad your situation in being as yet unmarried, you have not chosen a man solely to disoblige your family. It is a great thing, now I am in my failing years, to find you are not the mother of ten children, and all ill-provided for."

"And Lord Harold?" enquired Cassandra, as though the word *scoundrel* had given rise to an idea of that gentleman. "He is well, I trust?"

"Not so well as I could wish." I settled myself in a chair and observed the linen Cassandra was embroidering. "He is presently in mourning for the Duchess of Devonshire. She was a great friend of his youth, it seems."

"*Great* is but the first of the superlatives to describe her," intoned my cousin Mr. Cooper from his chair in the corner. "One cannot escape hearing her spoken of in this town. Her death has been most deeply felt; and yet, I rather wonder at such a figure being held in high esteem by the common folk! My noble patron, Sir George Mumps, was a little acquainted with Her Grace—such people of Fashion are always aware of one another, you know—and Sir George assures me that the Duchess owed no less than an hundred thousand pounds at her death—and all, debts accrued at the gaming tables!"

"A gamester!" cried Cassandra, horrified. "How is half such a sum to be repaid?"

"Very readily," I murmured, "if the riches of Chatsworth are a token of the Duke's wealth. I suspect he should no more regard the debt than you should moan over your laundry bill, Cassandra."

"I am sure that the Duchess was everything that is pleasing," my mother observed, "but she was a Whig, my dear, and you know they cannot be respectable."

"It is dreadful, indeed," my cousin reflected, "to consider the course of her life. Such great gifts, and so little principle; such riches, and yet such a squander of what might have gone to the greater Glory of God! I hope you were sensible, Cousin, that in entering that house you visited a place of lamentation—a place where Death has taught the most awful lesson it may bestow: that of waste, and misery, and a life struck down in its very prime!"

"I am afraid, sir, that I observed only the natural grief for a beloved parent gone too early to the grave," I rejoined. "And as I have endured a similar loss myself in recent months, it could not seem extraordinary."

"Was the estate very grand, Jane?" enquired Cassandra eagerly.

"What little I saw of the house was almost oppressive in its grandeur," I said thoughtfully, "and not what I should consider a home. But for a family of Whigs I am sure it would do very well. And the grounds are magnificent. I could wish for a week together to ramble over the estate; a phaeton and a pair of ponies would be the very thing."

"And may you hope for a second invitation?"

"I have already received one. Lady Harriot Cavendish has asked me to dine at Chatsworth on Saturday, in respect of her twenty-first birthday; and I have agreed to go."

"Saturday!" Mr. Cooper cried in horror. "But I had intended to quit this dreadful place as early as tomorrow, or Saturday morning at the very latest!" He waved an unsealed letter in the air. "My dear Caroline writes that the whooping cough has taken hold of the entire family; several of the little ones are in a most parlous state. Her mother urges draughts of black cherry water, but the apothecary, Mr. Greene, will have none of it, and abuses the good woman for her interference. It is imperative that I return to Staffordshire immediately. I am certain that Sir George Mumps would wish it."

"But has Sir James given us leave to go?" I enquired, surprised.

My cousin flushed. "I have not the least intention of conducting my affairs at that gentleman's behest," he retorted. "It lends a most unseemly air to my conduct, to kick my heels in Bakewell like a guilty party when I might better be in attendance upon my family."

"If you *do* mean to throw yourself in Lord Harold's way again, Jane, you had better have the wearing of Cassandra's grey silk," my mother observed in a resigned accent. "Its tone should soften the ill effect of your blushes, and pay some deference to mourning. Unhappily, it can do nothing further for your complexion; you are most disgracefully tanned!"

"Such contrivings shall hardly be necessary," Mr. Cooper broke in. "You must refuse the invitation, Cousin. Express all that is proper to

Lady Harriot—show yourself sensible of the very great honour you have been done—but refuse it in any case."

"I could not deprive Cassandra of her silk—"

"Fiddle!" my mother cried. "You will never get Lord Harold, Jane, in a washed-out muslin! With Mr. Hemming fled in fear of his life, it cannot matter what Cassandra wears!"

"Fled?" I repeated. "Not truly?"

Mr. Cooper was approaching apoplexy in his looks. "If Jane were to dine at Chatsworth on Saturday, we should be incapable of quitting this miserable place until Monday at the earliest—for I *trust* you are not intending to subject me to Sunday travel."

Sunday travel, the horror of every person who professed to keep the Sabbath—and an opportunity, did we force my cousin to it, for an unremitting martyrdom of hymn singing. "Certainly not," I replied. "We might perfectly quit this place on Monday. Have you communicated your intentions, Cousin, to Sir James?"

Mr. Cooper slapped his wife's missive down upon the table. "I have no opinion of Sir James Villiers. He does not deserve such attention. I am certain that he has led the people of this despicable hamlet to believe the very worst sort of nonsense. In moving through the streets today, Cousin, I felt as though an hundred eyes were upon me, and the most malicious falsehoods whispered in my train."

"Indeed, Mr. Cooper, I am sure you take too much upon yourself. The unsettled nature of events has given rise to unnatural fears. You must endeavour to calm yourself, and consider where your duty lies."

"My duty! *My* duty!" Mr. Cooper's countenance was purple with rage. "Let us better consider of Sir James's duty, Jane! Any person of sound understanding would counsel the Justice to lay that villain Charles Danforth directly by the heels! If Sir James does not effect it soon, the local folk will achieve justice in his stead!"

"Of what are you speaking, Mr. Cooper?" My entire body felt suddenly cold, although the heat had not yet faded from the day.

"Of that cursed and misbegotten soul," my cousin retorted, "the maid's employer! It was Danforth's clothes she wore at the moment of her death; and he is everywhere acknowledged as a Freemason, and an excellent shot. Clearly he was sent to destroy the girl when she would have published the dark secrets of the Masons' lodge!"

"Good Heaven, Edward, do you truly believe such rank nonsense? What would your noble patron, Sir George Mumps, say if he did hear you? He should reconsider his pressing invitation to join the Staffordshire lodge!"

My cousin faltered an instant, then summoned energy for a final retort. "Charles Danforth has the mark of the Devil upon him, Jane, and he shall be strung up on a tree before the night is out. There are the torches in evidence!"

I looked through the windowpane at Mr. Cooper's direction. A grim band of local men was assembled at the head of Matlock Street. There were thirty of them at least, some mounted and some on foot, with burning staffs raised high. At their head was Michael Tivey, the coroner and surgeon; and it was clear from all aspects they meant nothing but mischief.

"Are they bound for Penfolds Hall?" I enquired in a breathless accent.

"As soon as darkness will descend." Even my cousin had left off his bluster, at the sight of the milling men.

"Then someone," I said with decision, "had better send word to Chatsworth. The Danforths are from home tonight, and would not wish their house burnt down in their absence."

"But it is none of our affair!" my cousin cried. "We are strangers to Bakewell and everyone in it. If these vicious fellows would string one of their company from the nearest tree, then I for one shall not risk my neck to stop them."

"And is this the issue of a day spent humbly on your knees, Cousin?" I enquired with scorn. "You had better have devoted the hours to your fishing rod. If you do not chuse to sound the alarm, when all of Bakewell must know what these ruffians are about, then I shall do so."

"I beg you will not," snapped Mr. Cooper, now white-faced. "You will bring the whole town in arms to the inn, and then who shall save us all? Charles Danforth is entirely unknown to us, and very likely a murderer. He can be nothing to *you*."

"Nothing, sir, but a fellow creature and a gentleman," I cried. "If Mr. Danforth *is* a murderer, let an English court pronounce him so! Come, come, Mr. Cooper! Do you think that rabble below has any notion of justice? They are moved solely by superstition and the most appalling ignorance. I despise that sort of public tyranny!"

My cousin had the grace to look somewhat ashamed. My sister Cassandra, who had overheard the whole, turned her gaze intently from one to the other of us, her troubled countenance betraying her dismay at family discord. I am always firm, however, when I know myself to be in the right. I reached for the inn's supply of paper and searched among my things for a well-trimmed pen.

"Rough justice made a mockery of peace in France," I told Mr. Cooper. "I shall not stand idly by while it has its way with England, sir!"

Remedies for Whooping Cough

$\mathcal{S}$tew one gill sliced onion and one gill sliced garlic in one gill sweet oil, until the juices are rendered. Strain, and add one gill honey, a half-ounce paregoric*, and a half-ounce spirits of camphor. Bottle and cork tightly. For a child of two to three years, the dose is one teaspoon three or four times daily, increasing with the severity of the attack or the age of the child.

—From the Stillroom Book of Tess Arnold,
Penfolds Hall, Derbyshire, 1802–1806

*By *paregoric,* the stillroom maid probably meant paregoric elixir—an apothecary's compound of camphorated tincture of opium flavored with aniseed and benzoic acid.—*Editor's note.*

Chapter 13

A Sinner
in the Night

SALLY, OUR PARLOUR-MAID, WAS DEEMED WORTHY OF BEARING SE-
crets; and so she was summoned, and requested to despatch two mis-
sives, hastily penned and sealed up with wax. The first bore the name
of Lord Harold Trowbridge; he should know better than anyone how
to convey the news of a hanging party to the Danforth brothers, without alarming the Duke's entire household. I did not feel secure in
communicating directly with Charles Danforth—did the bearer read
his name upon the letter, even one despatched to Chatsworth, Mr.
Danforth might never receive it.

The second letter was directed to Sir James Villiers, at his ancestral
home near Monyash. If violent men were abroad in Derbyshire at
night, the local Justice was the most proper person to rout them; but
I chafed at the delay necessitated by so indirect an approach. Could I
have sent immediately to Penfolds Hall, and warned the steward, I
should have done so; but the likelihood of a messenger's being prevented from travelling the same road as the men he hoped to fore-
stall, argued against that course of action.

Sally solemnly assured us that she would see the letters into the
hands of her male relations, who might be trusted to carry them
safely through the dusk. I pressed three coins into her palm, and of-

fered fervent thanks; and so, with a wide-eyed impression of her own importance, Sally ventured forth on an errand whose nature remained obscure to her. Those of us privileged to know the evil that men may do, were forced to wait in painful suspense, while the darkness gathered and the company of ruffians increased in the streets below.

"I fear there is a poisonous quantity of gin in circulation," observed my mother resignedly. "They will all be wanting coddled eggs in the morning."

THE TORCHES MADE THEIR WAY OUT OF BAKEWELL ALONG THE ROAD I had last travelled in Mr. George Hemming's pony trap, towards Ashford-in-the-Water and Miller's Dale and the small town of Tideswell just beyond, where Penfolds Hall was said to be situated. It was a considerable distance for such a party, a fact that Mr. Tivey the surgeon must have anticipated—for several drays and waggons were pressed into service, and those without mounts of their own obliged to crouch in the springless bottoms of their fellows' equipages. I watched them quit Matlock Street in silence, for Mr. Cooper had abandoned his post by the window and was now established over his writing desk. My mother and Cassandra had gone to bed. I was considering of a sleepless night myself, when a small tap came at the parlour door, and Sally peered into the room.

"Please, miss, and I thought I did ought to tell tha' as me broother Jack is come home."

"And what has he to say?"

Sally grinned. "He's been nearly run off his legs, the past three hour. First he took the road to Chatsworth, while Nate undertook the road to Monyash—Nate's me cousin, and fair put out about his dinner he were, but I don't pay no mind to that, he were happy enough to have the coin, and Sir James paying him handsome to boot—"

"Sir James was at home?"

"He were," Sally said carefully, "and at his dinner, too, but Nate says as how he seemed fair flummoxed and called for his horse direckly. The whole country is wanting their nags tonight—it's like an army moving, miss."

"And your brother Jack?"

"He never laid eyes on the gentleman as tha' were wanting," Sally said doubtfully, "but gave the note to the housekeeper and was asked to wait for a reply. He sat in the servants' hall at Chatsworth, miss, and his eyes were fair round as cups when he did describe it, so grand as it were! Like a fairy castle, Jack says, and they'm gave him bread and cold chicken—"

"Did he carry a reply?"

"Tha'll never guess!" Sally grinned, triumphant. "Sent out in a great carriage, he were, to the constables in Buxton, with a letter penned by the Duke himself! Jack's not likely to get over it! He's strutting like a gamecock, he is, down in me moother's kitchen, and telling anyone who'll listen about the Duke's horses."

"Thank you, Sally. You have prevented a very grievous harm, you and your family, and I am sure that the Duke himself would thank you. But I would urge young Jack not to crow too loudly. There are violent men abroad tonight, and some of them may resent your part in thwarting their plans. Tell your brother he has done a noble thing, and that it is a very great secret. *Important gentlemen rely upon his silence.* That should guard his safety."

"Aye, miss," said the girl, bobbing a curtsey. She pulled the door closed behind her.

I was relieved enough in my mind to seek my own bed, and lay there in fitful slumber nearly three hours. If Sir James Villiers and the Duke's men could not deter the rabble of Bakewell from firing Penfolds Hall, then Jane Austen's attempts should be hopeless. Yet sleep remained elusive, a haze of impressions half-dreamt and half-understood, in which the figures of Chatsworth moved with the grace of knights and queens, across a chessboard of mown lawn and gravel.

THE TOWN CLOCK HAD JUST TOLLED THE HOUR OF TWO, WHEN A CLATter in the hallway and a stifled oath brought me bolt upright in the darkness. Someone was attempting to lift the latch on my bedroom door.

Heart pounding wildly, I reached for a taper, and then recollected that I had no embers in the summer grate by which to light it. Thoughts of the masked men in the square—of the quantity of gin they had consumed—of Sally's brother Jack boasting of his errand behind the Duke's horses—flitted rapidly through my brain. I weighed the merits of screaming for aid, or retreating into the clothes cupboard, where my four muslin gowns now hung limply; neither course, upon reflection, should do me credit. The person seeking entry might be none other than my sister, Cassandra. But she should have knocked first, and called out my name; and in over thirty years of living, I could not recall a time when she had emitted a drunken oath.

I threw back the bedclothes and stepped lightly on the floor. The boards, though fairly new in their construction, creaked beneath my feet. The man—for I had concluded the intruder *was* a man—did not falter, however, in his fumbling at my latch. To his misfortune, I had thrown a bolt before retiring for the evening, and the latch itself availed him nothing; my door remained obdurately closed. The intruder's invective flowed swift and furious, though it remained unintelligible; the speech was slurred and the sense fragmented. He must be completely disguised in drink.

When barely a yard from the doorway I called out in a harsh voice, "Who is it? What do you want at this hour of the night?"

All movement beyond the oak planks immediately ceased.

And then, to my horror, I heard a shrill scream and the crash of a heavy china object upon the floor. I pulled back the bolt, threw open the door—and found my sister, Cassandra, standing in the hall, well wrapped up in a dressing gown. Mr. George Hemming lay inert at her feet.

She had broken her chamber pot upon his head.

WE SUMMONED MY COUSIN MR. COOPER, AND BADE HIM CARRY HIS friend into the comparative privacy of our communal parlour, where Mr. Hemming was laid across two armchairs. The tumult in our passage had disturbed the innkeeper's rest; he shuffled up the narrow back stairs from his quarters with a lighted lamp, and begged to know why decent people could not keep to their beds of an evening. At the sight of Mr. Hemming lying still insensible across his comfortable armchairs, Mr. Davies's mouth dropped open, and the hand holding his lamp began to shake.

"It's nivver anoother murther?"

"No, sir, it is not," retorted my cousin. "Mr. Hemming has merely indulged too much in drink, and suffered an unfortunate blow to the head in navigating his way through your narrow corridors! He requires a vial of hartshorn, a damp cloth, and a quantity of hot coffee, which I trust an inn as reputable as The Rutland Arms should be capable of supplying."

"And a fresh chamber pot, I think, Mr. Davies." Cassandra cast the innkeeper a winning smile as he turned to go. "Mine has unaccountably shattered. Pray leave your lamp, as well—"

"How does Mr. Hemming appear, Edward?" I asked my cousin. "Are the bones of the skull at all injured?"

"I think not, Jane. But his brain must be sorely addled by the quantity of Blue Lightning he has consumed. His very clothes reek of gin!"

"I am quite well, damn it—or would be, if you'd leave off hovering!" muttered the solicitor, his eyes opening. "What in God's name connected with my head, Cooper? It felt as though the house itself fell upon me!"

"I fear you struck your skull against the lintel of my door, sir, in attempting to open it," I told him primly. The blow had succeeded in sobering the gentleman more swiftly than any coffee could do. "Perhaps you would explain what you meant by such a visit, and at such an hour? We are all agog at the honour of it."

"*Your* door?" He had the indelicacy to look horrified. "I was assured it was Cooper's."

"Unhappily, he is presently occupying the next room down. But you have secured his attention, Mr. Hemming, as well as my own, by the manner of your approach. Pray tell us in what way we may serve you."

George Hemming gazed around the circle of faces staring down at him, and the belligerence died out of his countenance. "I came to confess," he told us. "I thought it best to seek out Cooper, and make a clean breast of it. Clergyman, you know—adept at this sort of thing. Shriving."

"Confess?" I repeated, puzzled. "To playing truant? Avoiding the

Inquest? Or to indulging in spirits beyond what any sound person should tolerate?"

Mr. Hemming began to shake his head, then stopped short as the pain in his skull seized hold of his senses.

"To the murder of the stillroom maid," he said.

Remedies for Drunkenness

Take ½ oz gentian root, 1 drachm valerian root, 2 drachms best rhubarb root, 3 drachms bitter orange peel, ½ oz cardamom seeds, and 1 drachm cinnamon bark. Bruise all together in a mortar, then steep in 1½ pints boiling water, and cover tightly. Let stand until cold. Then strain, bottle, and cork securely. Keep in a dark place. Two tablespoonfuls may be taken every hour before meals.

Another cure is to compel the patient to drink nothing but strong spirits for a week. He is sure to be thoroughly disgusted.

—From the Stillroom Book of Tess Arnold,
Penfolds Hall, Derbyshire, 1802–1806

Chapter 14

An Unlikely Story

"IMPOSSIBLE!" I CRIED.

Mr. Hemming scowled up at me, then struggled to a sitting position. "It is all too possible, I assure you, Miss Austen—though I admit myself quite gratified to discover you believe me incapable of violence."

His speech was still somewhat slurred with drink, and he pressed a palm to one eye. As he did so, a small gold trinket slipped from his hand and fell with a clatter to the floor. I bent swiftly to retrieve it: the miniature portrait of a golden-haired lady, arrayed in the style of perhaps thirty years before. Even shown thus, in the poorest likeness of watercolour on ivory, she was a beautiful creature, her glance imperious, her cheekbones high under slanting green eyes. The late Mrs. Hemming, I must suppose.

"Lord, how my head aches!" Hemming muttered. "Where the Devil is that coffee?"

My cousin Mr. Cooper dropped to his knees beside his friend's chair and grasped his free hand firmly. It was not an attitude of dignity in the best of circumstances, but when adopted in nightshirt and cap, must verge on the ridiculous. "The Lord is rejoicing, George, though your misery be great; for He loveth nothing so well as repentance. Sing with me, brother! For the time of your sinning is at an end."

"Bosh," said Mr. Hemming succinctly. He kicked out at the chair directly opposite and struggled to his feet. "Be so good as to inform me where I might find Sir James and have done."

"I believe he was called away on urgent business this evening," I replied with circumspection, and held out the miniature.

Hemming stared as though he had seen a ghost, and accepted it with trembling fingers. His eyes, replete with shame and misery, slid away from mine. Aware, of a sudden, of my immodesty in standing before such a figure in my chemise, I sashed my dressing gown.

"I sought Sir James at Monyash before returning to Bakewell," he said. "Having screwed up my courage before the prospect of the gallows, I was afforded no opportunity to throw myself upon the Law; and thus took solace in bottled spirits. I drank the health of the Snake and Hind's last patron, and should be there still if Jacob Patter had not shown me the door. Do you know Sir James's direction?"

"Even if I did, I should not offer it to you now. You *cannot* intend to inform him of your absurd claim, Mr. Hemming! He will have no choice but to send you to Derby, to await the sitting of the Assizes."[1]

"Having done my duty, I cannot fault him for performing his," the solicitor retorted carelessly.

Mr. Davies, our long-suffering landlord, materialised in the doorway with a steaming pot of coffee. All conversation was necessarily suspended some moments; but having seen Mr. Hemming furnished with a cup, and having supplied Cassandra with a fresh chamber pot, Mr. Davies soon bowed his way back to bed.

"Pray sit down, Mr. Hemming, and explain yourself," I urged the

---

[1] The Assizes, in the British legal system of Austen's time, was a court convened by a superior judge for each county; it was this judge's duty to hear civil and criminal cases remanded by local magistrates, including capital crimes. The Assizes were held aperiodically, and the accused could wait months for a trial. Austen's aunt, Mrs. Leigh-Perrot, spent more than seven months in the Somerset County jail awaiting trial on a charge of shoplifting, which at the time was considered grand larceny, and carried a sentence of death or transportation. She was acquitted in March 1800.—*Editor's note.*

solicitor, when the door had shut soundly behind the innkeeper; "for nothing will satisfy me that you are guilty of this horror."

"What is there to explain?" he airily returned. "I waited in the rocks above Miller's Dale on the Monday night, and shot the maid as she walked up the path."

"Merciful Heaven!" whispered Mr. Cooper. "Knowing that she was Tess Arnold, arrayed as a man?"

"Naturally," he replied defiantly. "She had come out from Penfolds Hall at my urging; and the decision to adopt her master's clothes was taken by way of security. A maid abroad at such an hour, and in such a place, might well give rise to comment, were she seen; but a gentleman, never."

"That is very true," Cassandra murmured.

"Did you then proceed to mutilate her person?" I enquired.

Mr. Hemming hesitated, and his gaze fell.

Of firing a shot, I could believe him guilty; but of cutting out Tess Arnold's tongue or her bowels—this, George Hemming should never do. I sat down on the chair he had quitted. "And why should Tess Arnold come at your urging, Mr. Hemming?"

"Because I paid her a great deal of money, Miss Austen." He passed a hand wearily over his eyes. "Tess had been sure of me for many years, you understand; our relations were so predictable and easy, she never thought to preserve a necessary caution. That is the one mistake I have known Tess Arnold to commit—she failed to regard me with fear—and it cost her life."

"George!" my cousin cried in horror, "would you add to the list of your sins the debauchery of this woman—a woman in every way your inferior, and thus dependent upon your honour as a gentleman?"

"It was not her favours Mr. Hemming would purchase," I told my cousin, "but her silence. Am I correct, Mr. Hemming, in believing that Tess Arnold held your very honour over your head?"

"She did," he replied, "and to preserve it—and the delicate reputation of another creature, far too vulnerable in spirit for such as Tess Arnold—I have paid dearly, and in more than coin. How many years of sorrow and denial have I suffered! But I will not attempt to compel your pity—such tender feelings are not mine to claim. When the maid's demands for money became importunate, I determined to put an end to the business. I considered carefully of the sin; I weighed the gravity of murder against the evil her blackmail ensured; and set myself upon the course of violence."

Cassandra shuddered, and turned her face away.

"And so you arranged to meet her at Miller's Dale on Monday last," I persisted. "Why that night, above all others? Why not the one evening each month when the maid had secured her leave?"

The solicitor hesitated. "I wished the affair to be quickly achieved. Having taken my decision, I could not bear to linger in suspense. I sent the girl a note at Penfolds, and received her reply within hours."

It would be well, I thought, to determine whether the maid had ever received such a note. Tess must have been summoned from home by someone. "But having killed her with a single shot," I persisted, "—a remarkable shot, indeed—why did you feel compelled to visit such savagery upon her person?"

The solicitor looked at me directly. "I hoped her death would be imputed to a madman."

Cassandra placed her hand upon her throat. "I cannot think it Christian, Jane, to recall these hideous memories of the maid, and particularly in the middle of the night, when such ravaged souls may walk the earth in torment. I beg of you, leave Mr. Hemming's explanations for the Justice! The guilty are properly Sir James's province."

"But Mr. Hemming is *not* guilty, Cassandra. He merely hopes to shield another from discovery—and if I am not mistaken, it is his client, Mr. Charles Danforth. What cause have you, sir, to suspect that gentleman of guilt? Do you know aught of the man's movements on Monday night, that will not bear an honest scrutiny? Pray speak, before your own case is desperate! The loyalty of a solicitor should not extend so far as the gallows!"

My sister's face was yet averted from Hemming's; he observed it, and his countenance paled. Cassandra's distress should be nothing, however, to the public aversion in which he would be held, did he persist in proclaiming his guilt. That such a man, of reputation and standing in Bakewell, should risk everything on a whim—!

"If I *did* visit the hideous wounds upon the maid's body," he said, in a voice less steady than it had been, "I may only claim a profound disturbance of spirit."

"You will not disclose the nature of Tess Arnold's hold upon you?"

"I cannot."

"Nor why you effected the mutilation in such a manner, as to throw suspicion upon your brother Masons?"

To this he made no reply whatsoever.

"Will you produce the note you received from the maid, or the fowling piece that killed her?"

George Hemming raised his head, and in his looks I read a seizure of doubt. Whether fuddled by drink or the torments of his own mind, he had not considered of this point when he constructed his confession.

"In the darkness above Miller's Dale," he said, "a man may lose his reason. When I stood over Tess Arnold's body, I was not then myself. I cannot frankly say what I may have done, or why."

"To use your own term, sir," I cried, "*bosh!* You cannot expect me to believe, that having undertaken to kill Tess Arnold—having drawn her out in the dead of night by subterfuge—you then left her body in plain view of the walker's path above the Dale, and returned to the river so soon as the following morning! Recollect that you were seen to have taken tea here at the inn with us on the night of the maid's death; and it was then you extended the invitation to all our party for a drive to Miller's Dale! Are we to believe you so cold-blooded a killer, that you may drink tea and propose the angling scheme, mere hours before despatching your blackmailer? Never, sir! I refuse to credit it!"

"Perhaps I hoped that you would discover her body," he attempted. "Is it not the way of the sinner to wish his disgrace to be known?"

"Had you felt so deep a remorse, you might have led Sir James to the body yourself on that dreadful morning. It will not do, sir. If discovery was your object, you should have killed Tess Arnold in the middle of the Bakewell green, and have done!"

Mr. Hemming stared at me; and then he summoned the faintest of smiles. "It is a pity you were not born a man, Jane Austen," he observed, "for I certainly know whom I should hire for my defence."

"IT IS UNACCOUNTABLE," I TOLD LORD HAROLD THIS MORNING, AS he sat in the inn's parlour, one elegantly-clad leg caught in a stream of late-summer sunlight; "in every way, it is unaccountable! What can he mean by confessing to a murder it is impossible he should have committed?"

"Surely you have already found the answer, Jane," the gentleman replied. "He intends to shield another by taking the burden of guilt upon himself."

"But whom? Charles Danforth? No one else has been so openly the object of suspicion. Why should George Hemming sacrifice his life for Danforth's?"

Lord Harold shrugged indolently. His face this morning was less ravaged than it had been; the activity of the past few hours agreed with him. He was not the sort of man to spend many days together in attendance upon a group of females, arranged about a well-clipped lawn. Dissipation was to Lord Harold a kind of disease.

He had ridden early into town to inform me of the outcome of last night's events. The constabulary from Buxton had arrived post-haste at Penfolds Hall, due to Devonshire's urgent instruction; and they had been in time to mount guard over the household, and prevent the more egregious damage intended by the hanging party. Charles Danforth had been most eager to ride upon the scoundrels himself, and had been required to be restrained by his brother, when he would have gone in pursuit; but eventually the pleading of Lady Harriot, and the calmer counsel of Lord Harold, had urged caution. Both the Danforths had gratefully accepted the Duke's offer of aid, and of bedchambers for the duration of the siege.

At about midnight, Michael Tivey had led his men up to the door of the Danforth estate, and demanded to parley with its owner; Charles Danforth must show his face, as a Mason and a murderer, or be burnt in his bed. It was left to the Penfolds steward—a respectable man by the name of Wickham—to admit that the master was from home; and the rage of the assembled drunkards was then unimaginable. Bricks were hurled, and windows smashed; a very valuable vase of Blue John was dashed upon the front steps, and several of the raiding party gained entrance to the house itself, where they commenced to tear at draperies and harry the terrified servants, most of whom had been torn from their beds. The introduction of flaming torches to the interiors might have caused considerable destruction, had Sir James Villiers not arrived.

The Justice came upon the scene, admirably mounted and entirely cool of temper, just as the assembly were in the act of thrusting a rope over the unfortunate Wickham's head. The rabble intended, Lord Harold told me, to hang the steward from a venerable oak that stood on the verge of the sweep. The Justice fired his gun in the air, however, summoning the constabulary at his rear, and the hanging party were swiftly routed. Several were even now sleeping off the effects of gin and blows in the Bakewell gaol; while others—including the disreputable Tivey—had fled through the darkness to the obscurity of their homes, and were unlikely to show their faces in town for some days to come. But it had been a very near thing: had the Danforths been sitting quietly at Penfolds last evening—had I failed to mount the alarm—had Sir James or the Duke been called away—who knew the event of such rough justice?

And the intervention of the Law had done nothing to allay suspicion against Charles Danforth: it still ran at full tide through the streets of Bakewell. The gentleman was protected, so the townsfolk said, by Influence. A murdered maid, without connexion or consequence, could not hope to find justice in an English court of law; Danforth's fellow Freemasons would ensure that the crime remained obscure. The common folk of Bakewell should never sleep safe in their beds until the pernicious Brotherhood was banished from the Peaks.

They had not considered, perhaps, that they should be forced to rout the Prince of Wales as well, and most of the kingdom's Great, if an end to Masonic influence was their object.

"Your friend George Hemming having barely diverted the public eye from his client," Lord Harold observed, "we may assume there are not many in Derbyshire who credit the truth of his confession. But in asking whom he would shield, my dear Jane, you would beg the question of the entire affair. Who was burdened enough by Tess Arnold's existence, that he should take up a knife and a gun to cut off her young life?"

"Whoever that person may be," I observed, "he has gone free, while Mr. Hemming is presently in gaol." The solicitor, I learned upon

Lord Harold's entrance just after breakfast, had pounded upon Sir James's door at five o'clock this morning, and had begged to be put in irons. So much for the sobering effects of coffee and common sense.

"Then if you would have their cases reversed," Lord Harold returned, "you must find the guilty party. Sir James is under no obligation to do so, I assure you. A confessed killer has walked up to his door. All that he must now do is declare the matter of Tess Arnold's death resolved, and await the Assizes."

"It will not do," I replied. "You know that no sane man would pursue revenge in so haphazard a manner."

"Many a hot-blooded gentleman has killed before this, Jane, without due consideration of the consequences," said his lordship gently.

"I am sure that is what the jury will find in the present case," I retorted, "but we will both know it to be absurd! Mr. Hemming's professed method does not fit the circumstances; and his character, moreover, is quite unsuited to the manner of the maid's death."

"Do you know so much about him, Jane, on the basis of a few hours' conversation? There was a time when you considered his behaviour decidedly odd."

"And so do I still—though perhaps for different reasons." Hard scrutiny must find that I knew little of George Hemming beyond his friendship with my cousin, and a taste for angling and Cowper. My heart declared that he was a man of merit, and my reason rebelled at the poverty of his explanation for the murder of the stillroom maid. Where reason and heart are aligned, conviction will follow.

"Do you know very much, Lord Harold, about your friends at Chatsworth—though you have been acquainted with them this age?"

I had been fixed by the window as we conversed, my gaze moving restlessly over the herd of townspeople below—the good folk of Bakewell, all agog with the news of a respectable man's misery. Lord Harold arose, and joined me at the view.

"I know enough to be deeply troubled, Jane," he replied. "What exactly did you observe during your interval under the Spanish oaks?"

"A household in some upheaval," I replied, "spurred by the twin influences of jealousy and competition. Lady Elizabeth has much to answer for."

"Say, rather, the *Duke*, since it is the result of his perennial weaknesses that disorder is allowed to flourish. Could you apprehend, Jane, the qualities for good in that man—the immense talents, so indolently employed—your heart would surge with indignation at all he has squandered. The late Duchess's gaming debts are nothing to it. *There*, we speak merely of money."

"That such a character as Lady Harriot's could be formed in so pernicious an atmosphere, is a testament to her breeding," I observed.

"In her we see again the strength of her noble family, rather than its decline." Lord Harold fidgeted restlessly with a signet ring on his left hand, his countenance for once unguarded. "Harriot is very much like her aunt, Lady Bessborough—keen of wit, sharp of tongue, utterly discerning, and blessed with a singular understanding. Had she been born a man—" He broke off, and allowed his hands to fall to his sides.

"And in the Marquess, Lord Harold? What do we observe in Devonshire's heir?"

"The callowness of youth, and a depth of misery unimaginable to ourselves." He looked at me keenly. "Georgiana's death is a blow from which her youngest child has not recovered. I may say so much; the rest you will discern for yourself. The very circumstance to which you refer—my long acquaintance and friendship with the Devonshire household—must prohibit me from speaking rashly now. But I will admit, Jane, that I am most distressed in my soul about Lord Hartington."

"His words to me were indisputably singular," I persisted. " *'I'd hoped the witch had died in agony.'* What can his lordship have meant by so frank and brutal a sentiment?"

"You are not alone in posing such a question," Lord Harold replied. "Lady Harriot is most uneasy for her brother. He has been too much alone this summer at Chatsworth; he barely speaks a word to anyone. You saw how all his family regarded you with amazement, when he deigned to question you concerning the maid's death; only the most ardent interest could have moved Lord Hartington to address a stranger."

"And I thought them merely appalled at his conversation." I studied Lord Harold's countenance; but as ever, it revealed only what he would have me to know. "Would you make me your proxy, sir, in this dreadful business? Am I to be forced to the unhappy duty of examining that privileged household—one of the most exalted in England—because your honour forbids you do it?"

"Remember that you possess a motive I lack," he replied. "If you would save George Hemming's neck, my dear Jane, you must place another in the noose."

"The discovery of guilt and innocence is more properly Sir James's province." And yet, as Lord Harold observed, Sir James was compelled to do nothing further. An honest man had come forth to claim his share of blame; the Law was satisfied, and Sir James might take up his old schoolfellow's invitation, to shoot grouse in Scotland.

"I do not mean to suggest that George Hemming is entirely blameless," I attempted. "He is certainly most determined upon shielding another, and may even possess a dangerous knowledge—knowledge that torments him. But I do not believe that he killed Tess Arnold. Though he was anxious and preoccupied at the moment of the corpse's discovery, it was not the anxiety of guilt. He was startled, he was amazed, he was determined to conceal the whole—but he was not fearful for the salvation of his soul."

"Prove it, Jane," Lord Harold retorted with a smile.

"How, my lord?"

"You must first comprehend the nature of the woman Hemming claims to have killed. You know already that she was hated by some, and feared by others. But you know nothing of what *Tess Arnold* regarded with ambition and dread. When we comprehend so much, we may claim to understand why she died."

"You urge me to this, though you know full well that whatever I learn may harm the people you love best in all the world?"

His eyes did not waver. "I cannot sit by and watch a good man go to his death without cause. Neither will I countenance evil with equanimity. I cannot undertake to betray my friends, Jane. But if you choose to probe the nature of Tess Arnold, I shall support your endeavour. You must attempt the matter soon, however: I understand that your cousin, Mr. Cooper, hopes to quit Bakewell as soon as may be."

"He has forbidden me to dine at Chatsworth tomorrow," I told his lordship with a smile. "My mother, however, has secured me borrowed feathers; and from this we may assume that my attendance is certain. The next day being Sunday, we are entirely fixed—Mr. Cooper would never profane the Sabbath with travel. I shall remain in Bakewell until Monday at the very least."

"Excellent," Lord Harold cried. "That wins us nearly three days. How shall you use them?"

"First, by returning to Miller's Dale. I wish to review the ground where the maidservant died, and consider where her murderer might have hid. And if energy enough remains, I intend to walk the path she might have taken from Penfolds Hall. Much may be learned from the country itself, if one has but the courage to ask."

"You will require a carriage," he added thoughtfully, "and a broad-brimmed sunbonnet, if you hope to do so much of an August morning. Pray leave the business to me."

To Avoid Apoplexy

This illness occurs most frequently in the corpulent or obese. To treat, raise the head to a nearly upright position. Unloose all the clothes. Apply cold water to the head and warm cloths to the feet. Give nothing by mouth until the breathing is relieved, and then only draughts of cold water.

—From the Stillroom Book of Tess Arnold,
Penfolds Hall, Derbyshire, 1802–1806

Chapter 15

In the Footsteps of the Dead

29 August 1806, cont.

~

THERE ARE MOMENTS IN LIFE THAT SHOULD JUSTIFIABLY LIVE LONG IN memory—moments of experience so deeply felt, whether of pain or pleasure, that they mark the human soul even unto the grave. I am long familiar with such intimate scars. I may recall with the vividness of yesterday, the happy agitation of being first asked to dance—though by entirely the wrong gentleman; the pain of Tom Lefroy's defection for Ireland, and a lady of greater fortune; the oppression of spirits at the death of Cassandra's betrothed. My father's laugh, ringing out again in memory, will bring both tears and joy; so, too, will the idea of reading aloud in Madam Lefroy's front parlour of a winter afternoon, long ago. What is life, but an accumulation of such memories, a gathering of sensibility?

And yet, not *all* that is precious must be alloyed with pain. I have also these moments in Lord Harold's company, on a golden day in the High Peaks, with the swift shadows of clouds chasing the sheep on the hillsides and the babble of torrents curling whitely over stone. The soul may be as indelibly marked by such impressions of peace—by a conversable man of elegant appearance and the clop of a well-shod hoof—as by an experience of the most shattering emotion.

146 ~ STEPHANIE BARRON

When the rains of January have overtaken Southampton, the Gentle-man Rogue will rise in memory as one of the better gifts of the past year.

"You are lost in reverie, Jane," Lord Harold remarked as we descended the final curve of road towards Miller's Dale. "You are hardly attending to what I have said."

"I freely confess that I have heard not a word," I admitted, "though you speak so well and so knowledgeably, my lord, on every subject. It is one of your talents, is it not? The judicious employment of silence and volubility. It is an aspect of your character that must make you a friend to every *salon*. I have an idea of the scene: Lord Harold enters upon a fashionable rout; he takes the measure of his company, and determines in an instant whether the taciturn or the feckless is most suited to the occasion."

Lord Harold drew up his horses not far from the miller's cottage. "I appear to have misjudged the present instance lamentably."

"Not at all," I protested. "Your voice gave the perfect foil to thought—so insinuating, so low, so charming in every respect. I have been gazing upon the beauties of the Peaks, and considering of Andrew Danforth's bed."

"Jane!"

"Do not *Jane* me! Everyone is always doing it—particularly my cousin Mr. Cooper, who seems to feel himself my moral arbiter now my father is gone to rest. The presumption is most trying, I do assure you."

"You have the advantage of me, dear lady," Lord Harold replied, as he swung himself down from our hired curricle; "for I have never considered of Andrew Danforth's bed in the whole course of our acquaintance."

"A palpable falsehood. It was first brought to my notice by your own communications."

He looked up, and offered his hand. "You would mean the fact of Tess Arnold's having been discovered in it?"

"Exactly." I stepped lightly from the curricle and smoothed the creases from my rose-coloured gown. "The housekeeper claims the maid was dismissed for an indiscretion. Sir James would have it that the indiscretion was Andrew Danforth's. The gentleman, I may add, does not seem unduly grieved by Tess Arnold's death, so there cannot have been much affection in the case—at least on Andrew Danforth's side."

"But we know nothing of the maidservant's heart. She may have allowed herself to regard anything as possible. She may have aspired even to becoming *Mrs.* Andrew Danforth. He is, after all, only a *younger* son."

"And must therefore make his fortune through marriage! It has been my experience, my lord, that the habits of younger sons run to considerable expense. Andrew Danforth intends to have a Duke's daughter, and all of Parliament at his feet; and with such ambitions, Tess Arnold *must* prove a shameful impediment."

"Lady Harriot and her role in Danforth's brilliant career may have been utterly unknown to the stillroom maid," Lord Harold objected.

"I very much doubt that there was anything toward in the Peaks that Tess Arnold did not know. From what I hear of her character, she was a woman to regard intelligence as gold."

"Very well. Proceed with the fruits of reverie, Jane. I expect to be amply repaid for my wasted chatter along the road."

"George Hemming confessed to having called Tess Arnold out on Monday night, with the intention of murdering her," I declared, "and yet, she is *known to have been dismissed.* Did she quit Penfolds Hall that evening at the housekeeper's injunction? Or George Hemming's?"

"That is the first of many flaws in the solicitor's story."

"And one reason I do not believe it—entirely."

Lord Harold looked at me swiftly. "Then you credit some part of the tale?"

"I have observed, Lord Harold, that when a man would plausibly lie—as George Hemming has done—he is inclined to present a patchwork, not a tale made of whole cloth. I believe him when he says that the girl would blackmail him—that she *had* blackmailed him, for years together. So much of his confession bears the ring of truth."

"Then we must consider what the maidservant might be in a position to learn," Lord Harold mused, "and turn to profitable account."

"She was a stillroom maid. She was everywhere regarded as a sort of country apothecary—the compounder of draughts, of ointments, of remedies for common ills. Therein lay her knowledge and her power. We must find the cause of Hemming's grievance among the herbs and simples of Tess Arnold's storeroom. I know, for example, that he lost his wife in childbed nearly a decade ago."

Lord Harold surveyed my countenance. "If the lady's death was due to any error of the maid's, it should rather be Hemming's case to blackmail *her*."

"True. I doubt, however, that Tess Arnold was in attendance upon Mrs. Hemming. She would have been only fifteen or so at the time. But perhaps Betty Arnold may recall the circumstances."

"How may the revival of such a grievance further our purpose, Jane? For you would have it that Hemming is innocent of the maid's death. You have declared him incapable of the act."

"And so I believe him to be. But in the patches of truth Mr. Hemming has tossed us, we may learn much of Tess Arnold's life and purpose."

"For example—why she left Penfolds Hall Monday in the dead of night."

"We cannot be certain that she did," I objected. "We know only that she was dismissed from service sometime during the course of Monday, and met her death a mile from Penfolds Hall late that night. I do not imagine Mr. Tivey's estimation of the hour of the murder to be exact; and Mrs. Haskell was prevented, by her timely swoon, from outlining the facts of the maid's disgrace."

"But if Tess was dismissed for a dalliance with her employer's brother," Lord Harold observed, "then we may certainly set the earliest limit of her departure. Andrew Danforth is known to have quitted Penfolds for Chatsworth at roughly five o'clock. If the maid was turned away, her infraction must have been discovered before that hour."

"Did Danforth come on horseback?" I enquired curiously.

"He did," Lord Harold replied, "and an impressive animal it was. However varied his taste in young women, Andrew Danforth has a superior eye for horseflesh. The gelding could not have done less than twelve, and not more than sixteen miles an hour over the fields between Penfolds Hall and Chatsworth; and the distance to be traversed is no more than six or eight miles. I should judge that Danforth was perhaps half an hour upon his road—three-quarters, if he took the horse at a trot."

"And when did he appear?"

"I cannot swear to the hour. I was dressing at the time."

The admission shocked me. Lord Harold was always so perfectly turned-out, I had grown to believe he was somehow beyond the common human endeavour of dressing. The idea of the Gentleman Rogue in small-clothes, before his valet and his mirror, brought a bubble of laughter to my lips. I averted my gaze, lest he espy it. "I believe Sir James was told that Danforth arrived at six o'clock. There might be time enough, I suppose, to beat a hasty course into the hills, slay the maid, and turn the horse towards Chatsworth before dinner."

"So early as half-past five? In August, when the light does not fade until after nine o'clock? Why run the risk of such exposure?"

"Very well. Then let us consider his opportunity along the road home. At what time did the Chatsworth party break up?"

"Dinner was served at seven o'clock—the Duke keeps the hours of Town, even in Derbyshire—and between the demands of cards, conversation, and Lady Harriot's instrument, Danforth cannot have called for his mount until after one o'clock."

"What dreadful habits of dissipation! But he may have made his way, under a fitful moon, to the hills above Miller's Dale no later than two o'clock."

"I understood that was the hour he is said to have arrived at home." Lord Harold studied my countenance with interest. "You believe the maid to have been waiting at the place of her death, at Danforth's instruction? It seems a tedious business, and little to the point. If he wished to be considered as beyond suspicion, due to his engagement at Chatsworth, then he should take care to fix the hour of Tess's death during the period he was known to be safely away."

"—Provided he were as cunning as yourself, my lord," I observed, "but I should never assume so much. Does Miller's Dale lie in the way from Chatsworth?"

"Not directly. He should lose valuable moments in crossing a tortuous bit of country. I do not think he could possibly have done it, along the road home, and yet appeared at the stated hour."

"Let us leave, then, the whole tangle of the maid's flight," I suggested, "and take up instead the question of her clothes. Why choose

Charles Danforth's attire? For choice it must have been. I do not be-lieve, as Arnold's sister declared at the Inquest, that Tess was sent naked into the world."

"Perhaps she did not wish to give rise to comment if she were seen—as Mr. Hemming avows."

"Then why not wear *Andrew* Danforth's clothing? It would be more the style of a besotted female, to sport the attire of her beloved."

"He is somewhat taller than his brother, and undoubtedly taller than the maid."

"I cannot recall her relative height," I admitted, "but surely, if dis-guise alone was the maid's object, she might have found ample re-sources enough within the servants' wing. Danforth must possess at least one manservant." I shook my head obstinately. "No, Lord Harold, there is a purpose to her masquerade that worries me greatly. I cannot help believing that she was intended to be mistaken for Charles Danforth. And that George Hemming perceives it."

Lord Harold studied me gravely. "You think that Hemming is Charles Danforth's enemy?—That Hemming was here, in the rocks above our path, with the view to killing Charles Danforth? And that he shot the stillroom maid in error?"

"Not at all," I returned, "though such an admirable theory would explain his extreme disquiet upon viewing the body, his avoidance of the Inquest, and his recent confession. I admire your thinking greatly, my lord, but I cannot agree with it. George Hemming is too prosper-ous a man of affairs, to commence killing off his oldest clients."

"Then let us have your own view of the case."

"George Hemming is well-acquainted with Charles Danforth's enemy—and fears that it was this person's hand that despatched the maid in error."

"Jane—Jane! Must you complicate the business so dreadfully?"

I sighed. "It *is* a woman's duty in life."

Lord Harold did not reply. We were just then breasting one of the heights of Miller's Dale—the very spot where I had paused to draw breath on Tuesday morning, and had considered of the crows.

"But why should anyone expect Mr. Danforth to appear at such an hour, in such a place? He mentioned no summons in the course of the Inquest."

"He *does* admit to having dined alone, and to being a restless sleeper. He visited the Masonic Lodge, and thus is known to have been abroad on the Buxton road on Monday night. He admits to having retired, and then to rising once more with the intention of walking through his estate sometime near midnight. —What if that pattern is not unusual? What if it is known to all his domestics, and a good part of his acquaintance? Perhaps the man who killed Tess Arnold *expected* to find Charles Danforth—and in the variable light of a half-moon, fired upon a single figure toiling up the path from Penfolds in a gentleman's pantaloons."

"You said, I think, that Tess Arnold was *intended* to be mistaken." Lord Harold had come to a full stop at the brow of the hill, and stood there, breathing lightly, his eyes upon the tips of his Hessians. The gleaming dark leathers were clouded with dust. "If you would mean what I suspect—then *someone* must have directed the murderer to lie in wait."

"Of course. The person who wished Tess Arnold dead—as she so decidedly is."

Lord Harold's grey eyes flicked over to my own. "The same person who took her into his bed?"

"Why not? Who else could know of both the maid's circumstances, and Charles Danforth's habits? Who else should be so admirably suited to setting a snare—but Andrew Danforth?"

"Why not shoot the maid himself? Surely such a course would require less subterfuge than this proxy killer, and a victim in disguise."

"Remember that Mr. Andrew aspires to politics. Such characters will be marked by their subtlety; outright murder is not in their style. It should be far too dangerous for an impecunious younger son, and might place him, rather than his brother, on the gallows. Better to dine at Chatsworth on the night in question and have one's movements vouchsafed by a Duke. I'll wager that Andrew would not go so near a fowling piece as the gun room at Penfolds, before the first of next month."[1]

---

[1] The partridge season opened September 1, and pheasant season October 1. —*Editor's note.*

"You think it was *he* who urged the maid to wear Charles Danforth's clothes," Lord Harold remarked.

"Provided it was he who procured the gunman. Only in Charles Danforth's pantaloons could Tess Arnold be killed by Charles Danforth's enemy. Moreover, local suspicion has turned swiftly on Danforth himself, in no small part because of the maid's clothes."

"You believe that Andrew intended his brother, Charles, to wear a noose, so that Andrew might come into his inheritance with the same stroke that rid him of the maid."

"Charles Danforth has been a most inconvenient figure for the better part of Andrew's life. But for Charles, he might have inherited all his fond parents intended for him."

"And but for Tess—he might have had Lady Harriot."

"—Or so he may be suspected of fearing."

Lord Harold considered all this in silence, his gaze fixed upon the limestone crag a hundred yards distant.

"And that," I told him quietly, "is where the poor wretch died."

THE SCATTERED STONES WERE STILL SPLASHED WITH DRIED BLOOD, but the birds had departed, and the stench was nearly gone. Lord Harold doubled his elegant frame, his hands upon his knees, and narrowly surveyed the earth about the maidservant's place of sacrifice.

"Your theory, Jane—excellent though it is—does not explain the mutilation," he observed.

"No more it does," I replied serenely. "I was so kind as to leave you matter for thought, my lord. You must have something to engage your restless understanding."

He smiled crookedly and stood up. "Let us throw blame upon the long-suffering Freemasons," he suggested, "and be satisfied. I can observe nothing on the ground, Jane—the earth hereabouts is too trampled."

"But surely you are sportsman enough to study the surrounding landscape, and determine where her killer was fixed?"

"The lead ball found its mark in the center of her forehead, I think you said."

Unbidden, the memory of that visage—so untroubled in the sleep of Death, the ragged hole of the wound so incongruous above the fair curls—rose like a spectre in my mind. I said with difficulty, "A remarkable shot."

"Too remarkable by half. Were there scorings in the dust, suggestive of the body's having been dragged?"

"—As though she were struck by the ball elsewhere, and brought here to the base of the rock for . . . anatomisation?"

"If that is the case"—he scrabbled swiftly back along the path we had already traversed, then forward again some distance, along the way Tess Arnold might have come—"there would be blood spilled where she first fell."

We cast about, eyes narrowed, for the space of several moments. The sun beat down fiercely, and not a breath of air stirred; the sound of a bird's strident call brought a prickling of gooseflesh along my arm.

"Ah ha!"

Lord Harold was crouching in a patch of crushed bracken perhaps fifteen yards from where I stood. I hastened to join him.

"The ball hit her here, Jane, and she fell heavily across that rock." He pointed to a crimson smear on a broad, dimpled boulder. "She must have lain dead some time—observe how much blood has soaked into the earth. It would naturally be disguised by the grasses"—he poked at them with his ebony walking stick, and revealed a broad brown stain—"and Sir James would hardly think to look for it; it cannot really concern him where the maid fell."

"I doubt he has even visited this place."

"But who moved her—and why did he carve up her corpse so brutally?"

I'd hoped the witch had died in agony.

The Marquess of Hartington—the Duke's unhappy young heir— had nothing to do with Andrew Danforth's ambitions. How, then, was he concerned with Tess Arnold?

"For the ball to find her so precisely," Lord Harold observed, "she cannot have been moving along the path, as we had surmised. She must have been standing still, just here—"

"Waiting for someone. By previous arrangement."

He looked up at me from his position on the ground, the grey eyes intent. "Yes. We must assume that she was summoned here, Jane. So much for the theory of the maid's dismissal."

"Do you believe it a fabrication? Put forth by Mrs. Haskell to protect her employer?"

Lord Harold shook his head. "No. I credit the notion of the maid's disgrace. Certainly her sister knew of it, and resented the result. We may adjudge Mrs. Haskell's heartlessness a mere coincidence with whatever drew Tess here."

"A coincidence Andrew Danforth may have seized. With Tess Arnold in disgrace—impecunious, thrown off by her employer—he may have thought her too dangerous for keeping."

"Blackmail, again."

"She would know the way to Lady Harriot's door as readily as anyone in Bakewell."

Frowning, Lord Harold gazed over my head. "We must assume that the maid's murderer was in position anywhere within a radius of perhaps twenty-five feet, Jane. No shot in the dark could be so accurate at a greater remove. Let us pace off the distance, and cover the ground within that circle, in the hope of discovering some token of the killer."

I had grown quite hot despite the broad brim of my leghorn straw, and the delicate protection of a sunshade; and toiling through the parched grasses, which stood so high as my knees, was not the easiest of tasks; but it was for this I had brought Lord Harold out into the hills, and I was not about to deny the consequences of my own ardour. Sunshade raised firmly above my head, I measured the distance of twenty-five feet, and proceeded in the direction opposite to his lordship's.

I had not gone more than seven paces towards Penfolds Hall, when I came upon a tumble of gritstone boulders—the sort of a perfection for fashioning the stone walls so prevalent in the district—and bent down to study the surrounding ground. To the rear of the pile—which, I may add, was admirably suited to the steadying of a gun—the grasses were heavily matted, as though someone of considerable weight had settled there for a time. I condescended so far as to sit myself down in a similar position, and called to Lord Harold.

He could not at first discern me for the rocks. And in his confusion as he looked for my form, I learned all I needed to know. Under the shifting light of a half-moon, Tess Arnold might have stood securely before her killer, while the sights of his gun were levelled upon her head.

For the Preservation
of Shoe-Soles

*M*elt together two parts tallow and one part common resin, and apply hot to the soles of boots or shoes, as much of it as the leather will absorb. The shoes will last for miles of walking over any sort of ground.

—*From the Stillroom Book of Tess Arnold*
Penfolds Hall, Derbyshire, 1802–1806

Chapter 16

What the Sister Knew

29 August 1806, cont.

~

WE THOROUGHLY SEARCHED THE GROUND SURROUNDING THE PILE OF rock, but discovered nothing more than a considerable amount of matted grass, a few broken stems of late daisies, and the evidence of a large stone's having been dislodged. This last article Lord Harold examined on every side, even withdrawing a quizzing glass from his waistcoat pocket to scrutinise the surface more intently. At length he was satisfied.

"Observe, Jane," he said, with a gesture towards a dark speckling on the rock indistinguishable to my eye from the usual grey mottling of gritstone. "Grains of black powder from the firing of a fowling piece. We must look for the wad to have been expelled somewhere between this spot and the place where the maid fell."

I had often watched the gentlemen shoot at Godmersham, my brother Edward's principal estate in Kent. A party of servants was required for the endeavour—first and foremost the gamekeeper and his beaters, who flushed the birds from the fields; and then the men consigned to loading the guns, with their horns of powder, their pouches of shot, their squares of clean rag cotton. It was an elaborate business, the bagging of a dozen brace; and the gentlemen achieved a sort of poetic power, lifting their barrels to follow the flight of the bird, while the gamekeeper's fellows stumbled with bent backs through the chill air and bracken. I saw in memory my brother James— puffed-up, important, somewhat silly James—raffishly elegant in his long hunting coat of drab; and admirable in his silence. A report, the jerk of his shoulder, the puff of smoke at the gun's mouth—

"And here it is, Jane," Lord Harold said softly. "The usual bit of cotton, soiled with powder and oil. It tells us nothing of our sportsman, unfortunately, but that he was *here*."

He drew a handkerchief from his coat and wrapped the spent wad carefully in its depths. Then he gazed swiftly around, eyes creased against the sun. "There. That oak. Come, Jane."

I followed him through the dried grass and tumbled stones until we had reached the shade of the tree; but relief from sunstroke should never be Lord Harold's object. He crouched down and studied the ground at the trunk's foot, much as he had done near the cairn of stones.

"Hoofprints," he muttered. "I expected as much. Fairly-worn shoes, and slightly sunk into the earth, despite the dryness all around—the rider was no stripling. The horse stands fourteen hands and is slightly lame in the off hind. That tells us something, at least. The murderer did not come by foot."

He threw me an appraising look. "Are you the sort of lady who carries a sketchbook about you, Jane, and hastens to cry admiration at every picturesque?"

"You mistake me for my sister, sir."

"A great pity. Had you adhered to the usual female type, we might usefully have recorded the disposition of the body as it fell, the place where the powder marked the stone, and the trajectory of the spent wad."

"To what purpose, my lord?"

"The catching of Mr. Hemming in a lie. For if your theory is correct, my dear Jane, he will describe an entirely different location for each of these events. And I imagine he neglected to mention a horse."

"So he did, indeed! And thus we may prove him never to have approached the scene at all!" I cried. "Admirable."

"I see you reserve your enthusiasm for matters of duplicity,"

Lord Harold said briskly. "Very well. What subterfuge remains for our undertaking?"

"A social call, I believe. To Penfolds Hall."

"But the Danforths are as yet at Chatsworth—and shall be fixed there, so long as the mood of the countryside remains uncertain."

"Exactly. And being unaware of that circumstance, we shall be thrown upon the offices of Mrs. Haskell and Mr. Wickham. You appear admirably suited to the management of the former, while I shall attempt to disarm the latter. Everything on your side, of the power of command; and on mine, the blush of a single young woman uncertain of her reception. We cannot admit of failure."

Lord Harold readily agreed, but would have it that we should return along the path already traversed, in order to retrieve the hired curricle and horses turned out to grass behind the miller's cottage. I demurred, with a view to walking the path Tess Arnold had taken from Penfolds Hall on the night of her death. His lordship comprehended the utility of such an attempt, but could not abandon the hired equipage; neither did he wish to abandon *me*. I assured him I should do perfectly well in solitude, as I was often given to rambling alone about the countryside; he protested that in the present air of violence, solitude was most unsafe, and offered to traverse the ground in my stead. I observed that it was foolhardy in the extreme for us to exchange places; being a far better walker than a driver of a team, I should more readily come to grief in handling the equipage than in enduring another mile through the fields. I had no intention, moreover, of passing a tedious hour in the company of the miller's wife, while Lord Harold covered the distance and returned to the Dale. And so we ended as we often did: with a mutual respect for our several abilities, and the determination to leave one another in peace. Not for Lord Harold the expansion of his own self-importance, by a commensurate diminution of *mine.*

He set off for the Wye, and our patient equipage; I held my sunshade at a jaunty angle, and turned my steps northwards along the footpath towards Tideswell. It ran desultorily through the high grasses and waving flowers, plunged into a little wood, and presumably emerged on the nether side, in full view of Tideswell Dale and Penfolds Hall.

From the position of the sun in the sky, the abating of the breeze, and the sultry oppression of the day even so high in the hills, I should judge that it was very near noon, or somewhat thereafter. If I were to present a decent appearance at dinner, I must be returned to Bakewell no later than half-past three, my mother persisting in dining at the unfashionable hour of four o'clock. I hastened my steps, and hoped that Lord Harold might do the same. He must travel a greater distance along the Tideswell road than I should face across the fields; but he possessed all the advantage of speed.

Perhaps a quarter of an hour was suffered to wear away, and my arms in the service of my sunshade began to tire. As I was even now approaching the little wood, I allowed the sunshade to falter, and employed it instead as a sort of walking stick, for the swatting of undergrowth to either side of the path. A light film of sweat had dampened my curls under the close brim of my sunbonnet; my hands were sticky in their cotton-net gloves, and the muslin of my gown clung to my warm back. I was already rather tanned—hardly extraordinary when one travels in summer; but I should never emerge from this morning's adventure without a sun-burn. Such an appearance as I should make in the elegant dining parlour at Chatsworth tomorrow evening, with a scattering of freckles across my nose! Lady Elizabeth should condescend to pity me; Lady Swithin, to forgive me; while the correct Miss Trimmer should regard the whole with contempt, and confide to Lady Harriot that, however intimate a friend of Lord Harold Trowbridge's, she could not find me nice in my taste or habits.

It was cooler here beneath the trees; curlews called from the green shadows, and a cloud of midges danced before my eyes. I observed an arc of sunlight just ahead—an opening out of the forest—and there, in the lee of a large shrub, crouched a young woman.

She wore a mulberry-coloured gown of India cotton, and her hair was loose about her shoulders. She had set a large willow basket on a convenient stump, and was busily gathering berries from the shrub. I stopped short some thirty paces from her position and studied her. Something in her aspect was familiar, even at this distance; and then she turned her head, and I saw the wine-dark stain upon her cheek.

Tess Arnold's sister.

"Hello, there!" I called out, and stepped forward with my sun-shade raised.

She stood up, and bobbed a curtsey, waiting in silence until I should have passed. If my decision to greet her—she, whose dress and entire figure proclaimed her my social inferior—caused her any astonishment, she did not betray as much in her countenance.

"Pray tell me," I attempted, with a little gasp of exertion, "whether this is the way to Penfolds Hall?"

"So it be," she returned, in a voice entirely without affect.

"And is it very far? I fear the heat is most cruel today."

She stared at me, taking in my close bonnet, the gloves, the folds of my muslin gown, and my stout boots. She was thinking, no doubt, that her own simple attire should be much cooler.

"Jus' a ways on, miss."

"Thank you. I am most obliged."

She bent towards the tangle of branches once more, and I knew myself dismissed.

"That is an elder," I observed of the shrub she was busily harvesting, "and not good for eating. What use do you find for the berries?"

Her hands arrested, she stared at me. "Doesn't tha' know? Poultice for burns."

"Indeed? That is a remedy that has not made its way to the south. We use an infusion of elder flowers for feverishness and a sore throat; or the bark, when mixed with a little butter, is useful for healing sores. The berries we leave to the birds."

"Tha's the lady from th' Inquest." She straightened, and rubbed her hands carefully on her skirt.

"And you are Tess Arnold's sister."

We studied one another an instant. Her countenance was less stony; her curiosity, I should judge, was piqued.

"What is your name?"

"Jennet."

"Very well. I am Miss Austen. Are you also a stillroom maid?"

"I know the ways of simples." She searched my face, clearly troubled in her mind. "Tha's been lookin' o'er the ground. Where she was killed. Wha' fer?"

"A gentleman of my acquaintance has confessed to murder. I do not believe he killed your sister. Do you ever recall her mentioning a Mr. Hemming?"

"George Hemming? 'A course. We've known 'im twenty year or more."

"And known him rather well, I should judge."

Jennet shrugged, her expression inscrutable. "Did for old Master— and his last Missus, until they died. Almost one of the family, Hemming were. It's never 'im as says he shot our Tess?"

She read the answer in my eyes. Her own closed abruptly. "I'd made sure t'were Danforth."

"Why?"

The eyes flashed open. They were dark blue, I noticed, the colour of flags by the riverbank. "He's a Mason, in't 'e? An' Tess were carved up like a new lamb. They Masons be done fer all sorts of evil. Murdering babies. Burnin' 'em on an altar at midnight. But never none of their own. It's the common folk as suffer, when evil walks the land."

"Wherever did you hear such a story?" I exclaimed. "Mr. Danforth burning babies, indeed! A man who has lost his own children!"

"It's a judgement," she declared, "them little'uns. They went to they graves in torment, on account o' 'is sins! Tess said so. She knowed it. That's why she were killed. She'd been watchin' they Masons right here, above the Dale."

"Here," I repeated, much struck. Was it possible that Tess Arnold had made a habit of creeping out to spy on her betters, wearing gentlemen's clothes?

"The altar be somewhere in the rocks above the Dale," Jennet said darkly, "and Tess told me of the babe she saw them take, and how it were crying as if its heart would break. Two weeks before she died, t'were, and when I heard her blood were spread upon the crag, a traitor's death, I knowed the reason why."

"You said nothing of this at the Inquest," I observed.

"I want nothing wit' thy justice." Jennet spat upon the ground. "Tha' thinks yon Michael Tivey cares fer Law? Him what was always sniffin' like a dog at our Tess's heels? Bringin' her medicines, givin' her books, simperin' and smilin' and saying, 'Eh, Mistress Tess, tha's lookin' mighty fine the mornin'!' And her laughin' up her sleeve all the while, and never givin' him as much as he wanted. The Snake and Hind's no court o' law. Michael Tivey called our Tess a slut and a wanton when he wasn't hangin' by her bodice-lace."

"And what did Andrew Danforth call her?"

Jennet drew breath sharply and bit her lip. "Don't you go speakin' against Mr. Andrew. He's more a friend to us than anyone up t'a Big House, and always were."

"And yet your sister lost her place because of him."

"Tess? Dismissed on Mr. Andrew's account? Go on!"

So she had not known the particulars of her sister's disgrace.

"It's just like Haskell to think the worst of our Tess," Jennet muttered. "Her what's known Mr. Andrew from a child. Who else should play with the boy, I ask you, in such a great lonely place? And the old Master dying like he did, and his second Missus, too! Our moother thought that Master Andrew would fair run mad with grief. We all done what we could, to make him happy again. Our grandfer, him what's been gardener up t'Hall these fifty year and more, right took'm under his wing. And then Andrew's broother come home, and sent him off to school—"

Tess Arnold, the playfellow of Andrew Danforth. Naturally it should be so. I had forgotten that they had been children together. But a vast deal of ground must separate the maid and her master, once the child was grown to a man.

"He's a very charming gentleman," I observed.

"Aye—and so good-humoured! Full o' jokes and teazing, Mr. Andrew is."

"Jokes and teazing. And—playacting, perhaps?"

"Aye."

"Is it possible, Jennet, that Mr. Andrew persuaded your sister to wear Charles Danforth's clothes?"

The girl took a step backwards. "Why should he?"

"I don't know. Can you think of a reason why she was dressed as a man? Another joke, perhaps? An attempt at playacting?"

Jennet turned her head away and reached for her basket.

"Mr. Andrew is also a Freemason, Jennet. Like his brother."

She did not answer; but her limbs were rigid with fear. She had re-volved the idea already in her mind. For no one should wonder as Jennet why her sister had worn a man's clothes.

"Would Andrew think it a joke to bring Tess to the Lodge, arrayed as a gentleman, under cover of darkness? Could your sister have died, Jennet, by way of a mistake? A bit of teazing gone wrong?"

Her eyes, when she turned back to me, were ablaze with pain and anger. Not only Tess Arnold had been fond of her playfellow; this girl with the ugly stain across her cheek had yearned for years in silence, and watched as Master Andrew escaped the Penfolds estate, and grew into a man, and considered of her no more than he should an old piece of drugget beneath his feet.

"Did Tess tell you where this meeting place was—the place in the rocks where the Masons gather?"

She shook her head.

"Might she have told anyone—a friend perhaps, another girl in service at the house?"

"She'd have told me if she told anybody," Jennet said defiantly; then some of the anger drained from her frame. "Our Tess were close-mouthed. But happen it'll be in her book."

"Her book?—Tess could read and write?"

Jennet's head came up with a dangerous pride. "Tha' thinks we're all simple as the remedies we make? Tess knew her letters. She kept a book, she did, all filled wit' writin'. Receipts for ills, and the days she gave 'em out. The names of the ones as paid her."

A stillroom book. One received, perhaps, from her mother before her, a veritable history of life and death at Penfolds Hall. "And have you looked into it, Jennet?"

The young woman averted her gaze. "I don't have Tess's learning."

And her mother was blind.

"But you possess the book."

All that was visible of her face was the wine-dark map.

"If you showed me it, Jennet—we might read it together."

The young woman did not reply. Silent tears were rolling down her cheeks; and with a sensation of pity, I saw that at least one person in the world had truly loved Tess Arnold, and deeply mourned her loss.

I reached out a hand, but stopped short of touching Jennet. Such containment—such inward suffering—commanded respect.

"I am no Michael Tivey," I told her, "and all I seek is justice for your sister."

"And a noose for Mr. Andrew," she whispered miserably.

For the Carrying-Off of Freckles

*T*ake an ounce of lemon-juice and a quarter of a dram of distilled elder-flower water. Bathe the skin with it five or ten minutes, and wash afterwards with clear water, night and morning.

—From the Stillroom Book of Tess Arnold,
Penfolds Hall, Derbyshire, 1802–1806

Chapter 17

The Stillroom Book
of Penfolds Hall

29 August 1806, cont.
~

JENNET ARNOLD LED ME SWIFTLY DOWN THE NORTHERN SLOPE OF Miller's Dale, speaking not a word, while I struggled to keep her in view and abandoned all attempts to shelter my complexion with the tedious sunshade. Where the line of distant fields met the sapphire arc of sky, I could just make out a cluster of buildings and a church spire—Tideswell, I presumed. Well before it, rising from the fields like a fortress, were the stone walls and many courtyards of a great house. This was no country gentleman's manor, with a modest gabling and an upper storey half-timbered; this was a Norman keep, hallowed by centuries of upheaval endured. At the first sight of its noble outlines I stopped short, arrested and open-mouthed. I had possessed no notion that Penfolds Hall was such a grand old pile. From its appearance it might have been formed in the time of the Black Prince, and survived the years of Tudor Wars. It had gloried in Elizabeth, and sheltered Charles I; it stood silent while Cromwell's armies marched like so many ill-clad ants over the landscape, and felt its crenellated towers crumble under the reign of Hanover. Regarding the estate, with its vanished moat filled in by time, I had an idea of the first John d'Arcy, heir to the Earl of Holderness, plotting a Glorious Revolution by its hearth-stones.

It was clear, moreover, whence arose the local legends. However venerable those halls spread out below me, they wanted the appearance of happiness. What had Lydia Danforth felt, as she watched her babes die in the stony fastnesses? And felt her own spirit ebbing with last winter's snows, into the bitter ground? Had she loved Charles Danforth enough to face the rumours of ill-fate—and been defeated at the last, so that not even love could survive her children's graves? A chill hand clutched my heart, as though merely to gaze upon Penfolds Hall was to suffer a sort of petrification; I swallowed hard, and forced myself onwards in Jennet Arnold's wake.

THE HOUSE'S APPEARANCE OF COLD DESERTION WAS IMMEDIATELY BElied, however, upon achieving the kitchen gardens.

It was through these Jennet Arnold led me—down a well-trimmed grass path, between rows of trellised beans and lavender past its bloom; along solid hedges of box and rosemary, their fragrant arms entwined to keep the rabbits from the root plants—turnips and onions, carrots and potatoes. There was an admirable glass-paned conservatory, where tomatoes and melons and lemon trees basked in captured warmth; pears and quinces were trained against the main house's walls; and every kind of herb ran riot in a knot garden outside the servants' door.

Here, the sunlight fell in a golden wash, and two bright-cheeked young maids were gossipping and laughing with the mending under an apple tree. They fell silent and looked askance as we approached; the sound of singing drifted towards me through the kitchen's leaded windows. "Greensleeves."

"Come thee through to the stillroom, miss," muttered Jennet, with her basket of elder over her arm. "That's where our Tess's book'll be found." She skirted the herb garden and pushed open a small side door set into the Great House's walls, waiting for me to follow her example. I broke off a branch of lemon balm, crushed the leaves, and held it to my nose. All the joys of my girlhood at Steventon—the long morning hours rolling down the grassy slope in company with my brothers—rushed upon me. I breathed deep, and closed my eyes.

"It's jus' through here, miss," Jennet called in a low, insistent voice.

I tossed aside the lemon balm, aware of the girl's urgency. She feared discovery—from Mrs. Haskell, probably. I stepped quickly to join her, and entered the cool dimness of Penfolds Hall.

We were standing in a stone-flagged corridor, low-ceilinged and flanked with simple plaster walls; the bones of the house were evident in the branching stone architraves that supported the upper storeys. This was the ground floor of the house, reserved for every sort of function except those of elegance and refinement: here there would be the kitchens—and I doubted not there were two, one for winter and one reserved for the airiness of summer; here were the wash-rooms, with their great tubs and mangles, the heavy irons ranked upon the shelves; here the offices and sitting-rooms of the house-keeper and the steward, where accounts were settled, rents paid, and country news exchanged; here, the pantries for china; the entrance to the wine-cellars; the storerooms for every sort of goods procured from England and abroad.

And, of course, the stillroom that had been Tess Arnold's par-ticular province.

Jennet peered over my shoulder towards the far end of the corridor. The clatter of pots and the shrill voices of several women suggested that beyond lay the kitchen.

"... a quantity of ash for the soap-making, and now's all spoilt fra' the rain. If another of they teacups goes missing, Sarah, ah'll have it fra' tha wages ..."

The maid grasped my arm, and pulled me quickly through a doorway.

It was a surprisingly small space for the size of the household— a room perhaps twelve feet by ten, lined with shelves and marble counters. Jars of preserved vegetables and fruits, of jams and cordials and candied peel, winked brilliantly from those shelves with all the enticement of a jeweller's cases. A large sink stood under a window, and an iron stove beside it; a scarred oak table ran the length of the stone floor, with fragrant bunches of herbs depending from the ceil-ing overhead. One hard wooden chair was tucked into a corner, per-petually unused from its neglected air; and a remarkable cabinet—at least as tall as myself, and filled with rank upon rank of square, iron-bound drawers—dominated the wall opposite to the door. Labels, penned in neat script, had been affixed to each shelf and each drawer of the cabinet. I crossed to where it stood, and peered at several. *Betony. Myrrh. Elixir of Roses—*

"Here it be," Jennet said, and handed me Tess Arnold's still-room book.

I held in my hands a quarto-sized ledger, bound serviceably in linen; most of the pages had already been cut.[1] She had kept her records in the same neat script as her labels, rather more crabbed due to the dearness of paper and a native economy. I turned the initial pages with care, and observed that the dates commenced in 1802.

"I thought your sister entered into service at the age of twelve," I remarked to Jennet. "This ledger encompasses only the past four years. Are there earlier volumes?"

She shook her head. "Tess only learnt her letters when she were seventeen. That's when the Mistress coom to Penfolds, and set up her school."

"The late Mrs. Danforth?"

"Aye. Full o' ideas she were, 'bout us and our letters. Those as wanted to learn, might. Our Tess was up until all hours, most nights, working on her copybook. She had the sharin' of it with two others, and didn't get the time of it she should; but happen she were quicker'n most."

"I see. And so she commenced this ledger four years ago—when she would have been about twenty."

"Our Tess knew the remedies Mam taught her by heart," Jennet said frankly, "but she reckoned it'd save a good deal o' trouble if they was writ down. So she asked the Mistress for this book, next time Master went to Derby; and the Mistress were happy to give it. The Mistress set a good deal o' store by our Tess and her healing ways."

"Did she, indeed?"

"T'were Tess got her the boy," Jennet said frankly.

"The boy?" I repeated.

"Little John d'Arcy. Him what died last spring. No more'n two he

---

[1] A quarto volume was one in which a sheet of paper was folded in four leaves, or eight pages, each of which was cut with a knife when read—or in this case, inscribed. It was roughly nine by twelve inches in size. —*Editor's note.*

were, and a fine, strong lad afore the convulsives got 'im. Apple of Master's eye."

Charles Danforth must be called the Master now, though she had spoken of him so bitterly in the hills above Miller's Dale. The boundaries of Jennet Arnold's world, I thought, must be contiguous with the extent of Danforth's fields.

"Your mistress bore a son because of Tess's remedies?"

" 'Fore that, Mistress only had girls—two what miscarried, and two what lived. Fond as he was of 'em, Miss Emma and Miss Julia did the Master no good at'all."

"I see." Simples and excessive faith had produced the coveted heir; illness and misfortune had claimed him again, and his stillborn brother. Perhaps Lydia Danforth had meddled too much in the ways of Providence.

I opened the heavy volume and began to leaf through its pages. "If the boy was but two when he died, the entry you speak of should be somewhere in 1803. And so it is—'Remedy against miscarriage' and one for conceiving a boy."

"Mistress always were prone to losin' her babes afore they time."

"Indeed." I scanned Tess's narrow lines. "And when the children fell ill?"

"Tess did 'er best," Jennet retorted sullenly. "T'weren't her fault they died. T'were the fault of they London doctors, what the Master called in. Tess weren't good enough for *him,* though the Mistress set such store by 'er. And the little'uns died apace, for all they cuppings and bleedings and fancy draughts. How Tess did laugh at they great pompous oafs fra' Buxton and London!"

I stared at Jennet, a creeping horror in my throat impeding all speech. The children of her fond mistress had died in pain and suffering—and Tess Arnold had *laughed.*

A scream from the stillroom doorway brought both our heads around. Mrs. Haskell stood there, her face as white as a sheet, and her eyes fixed upon my companion's face.

"Thought I'd seen a ghost," the housekeeper said faintly, "but it's tha', Jennet Arnold, coom back like a bad penny. I thought I'd forbid tha' the house! Tha' set that Michael Tivey on us all, and lucky we were not to be murdered in our beds! Shift thysel', girl—there's visitors coom—"

"Good morning," I said, stepping into the housekeeper's line of vision. "You must be Mrs. Haskell. I am Miss Jane Austen. I believe my friend Lord Harold Trowbridge has arrived in search of me?"

"Lord Harold? In search of *tha'*?" The good woman looked bewildered, as well she might. "And 'ow did the lady come to be 'ere, wi' out my knowing of it?"

"I confess I encountered this young woman in the grounds. I had walked some distance in the heat of the day, and felt a faintness coming on. She was so kind as to offer a glass of angelica water. Most refreshing!"

"Oh, aye." The housekeeper eyed Jennet balefully. "What right the girl has to do the honours of the house, I'd like to know—"

"Lady Harriot Cavendish sends her best respects, Mrs. Haskell, and begs that you might extend to her the Penfolds receipt for quince preserve?"

"Preserve?"

"Ah've been searchin' it out fer her," Jennet said, "froom our Tess's book."

At the sound of the maid's voice, Mrs. Haskell's eyes sought her face, then shifted uneasily away. The fear and dislike that had dogged the housekeeper at the Inquest was not entirely fled. Mrs. Haskell crossed the stillroom swiftly and snatched the quarto volume from Jennet's hands.

"Take it to Lady Harriot an' welcome—and a jar o' the preserve by way of a present," she said hurriedly.

"You are too good," I returned, with an inward exulting. Now I might peruse the stillroom book at my leisure.

"Did'na tell tha' to be off?" the housekeeper snapped furiously at Jennet.

"But—"

"Mr. Wickham!" Augusta Haskell screamed at the top of her lungs. "The constables, if you please!"

Jennet looked scathingly at Mrs. Haskell, and began muttering under her breath; the housekeeper stepped backwards, and made the sign against the evil eye. With a slight smile of scorn, Jennet turned for the door; to myself, she said not another word.

"T'were a black day for Derbyshire when that family crawled out of the hills," Mrs. Haskell whispered. "I don't say no word against Old Arnold, mind—him what's done fer garden afore I were born—but I don't have to tell the miss what that Tess was. Out for all she could get, and no better than she should be."

"My dear Miss Austen," observed Lord Harold placidly from the doorway. "I thought I heard you scream."

"How very kind of you to come to my aid! I was merely remarking upon the excellence of the Penfolds cordials." I reached for a clear glass bottle filled with a liquid like clouded brandy. "Angelica water, Lord Harold—most refreshing on such a heated day. I am sure it will do you a world of good."

"JANE," LORD HAROLD MUTTERED, AS WE FOLLOWED MRS. HASKELL above, "I would do much to support your endeavours; but do not allow me ever to sample such a concoction again. I shall be suffering the flux for a fortnight, I am sure."

Against Miscarriage

*P*ound equal amounts of cinnamon, nutmeg, mace, and cloves in a mortar, and bind up the broken spices in a bit of cotton. Place the cotton in a scarlet silk bag, with the dried petals of camomile, and tie the silk round the waist, so that the bag lies pressed against the hollow of the back.

—From the Stillroom Book of Tess Arnold,
Penfolds Hall, Derbyshire, 1802–1806

Chapter 18

A Natural History of Despair

29 August 1806, cont.

~

"AND DID YOU SPEAK TO THE STEWARD—MR. WICKHAM?" I ENQUIRED of Lord Harold as our hired curricle rolled away from Penfolds Hall.

"I did—though Mrs. Haskell would have it the man was indisposed, on account of his unhappy experience with the ruffians last night. I was obliged to expend full a quarter of an hour in attending to the lady's history of that dreadful affair; I was treated to tears, convulsive fits, and a threatened swoon, at which I gallantly applied Mrs. Haskell's vinaigrette with my own hands."

I glanced at him sidelong. "And to what purpose, my lord?"

"Are you so mistrustful of gallantry, Jane? What possible cause can the male sex have given you, for so unbridled a cynicism?"

"I do not pretend to know anything of the *general* run of men."

"Ah. Very well. Your mistrust is reserved for myself alone. Or perhaps it is applied universally to second sons? In either case—I commend your ruthless opinion. I managed to convey to Mrs. Haskell my infinite concern for her late difficulties—dropped a word or two as to the wild character of so many young women—the world of trouble devolving from the management of a great household—the sadness attendant upon the Danforth family—"

"And Mrs. Haskell poured out to you her soul."

"The sum of the matter is this: She had long suspected the nature of Tess Arnold's interest in her employer's brother, and set a tenant's child to the task of following the stillroom maid whenever she should have occasion to quit the Hall. This infant—being early schooled in extortion and deceit—so informed upon Tess Arnold, that Mrs. Haskell contrived to discover the girl Monday in a state of undress in an abandoned ice-house on the western boundary of the Penfolds property—"

"Playacting," I murmured.

"—taking care, one imagines, to watch Mr. Andrew safely away before visiting her wrath. She claims that Tess denied the liaison—'bold as brass,' was Mrs. Haskell's encomium—and so she dismissed the girl from service on the spot."

"Tess Arnold was not admitted back into the house?"

"Not by Mrs. Haskell—or at least, not with her knowledge. She swears she never saw the girl again."

Lord Harold did not need to inform me of how readily a way might be found into Penfolds Hall. I had entered it myself this morning, without the housekeeper's being in the least aware. "So she could offer no notion, I collect, of how the maid came by Charles Danforth's clothes that evening?"

"None whatsoever. She has interrogated most acutely the two maids who shared Tess's garret quarters—and though either might be sworn to silence, or feel themselves allied with the dead maid against their superior, Mrs. Haskell believes they know nothing more than they have said. I gather she did not scruple to lay the rod against their backs—and what the rod does not reveal, is not worth our consideration."

I shuddered. "And all this you learned in a mere quarter-hour? I should better have left Jennet Arnold in your care! Rather than dark hints and brooding surmises, you should already have won the name of Tess's murderer! But what does Mr. Wickham say to such disorder? Did Mrs. Haskell overcome her scruples, and disturb the steward's rest?"

"Upon learning that I was come direct from Chatsworth, ostensibly with instructions from Charles Danforth intended for Wickham's ears alone, Mrs. Haskell let me to him. A most amiable fellow, and quite the gentleman. We had a good deal of conversation, while you mused on the nature of tansy and bergamot."

"—Without recourse to fits and vinaigrettes?"

"Wickham did not swoon, I gather, even in the noose's mouth. He reserves a just and noble rage for the men of Bakewell, who nearly had his neck last night; but knows nothing of stillroom maids and their schemes, profitable or amorous. He regards Charles Danforth as the most amiable of men; considers his recent history lamentable in the extreme, and deserving of pity rather than malice; and hopes that the appearance of a new mistress among the household might turn the tide of public sentiment in his master's favour."

I regarded Lord Harold steadily. "Is Mr. Wickham so close in his master's confidence, as to speak the name of Lady Harriot?"

"A man cannot always be observing his fellows on horseback, riding over the fields to Chatsworth, without drawing the proper conclusion," Lord Harold replied. His countenance preserved an admirable gravity. "I gather Wickham has been urging marriage on the mourning widower, though Lydia Danforth is but four months in the grave."

"Curious," I commented. "Did he give any reason for such haste?"

Lord Harold snapped the reins over the backs of our borrowed horses. "You never fail to amaze, my excellent Jane! A thousand women should have exclaimed at the indignity visited upon the dead lady, in thus driving her husband to the altar; a thousand more should have berated Mr. Wickham, or Mr. Danforth, as dishonourable and unfeeling brutes. You merely wish to know the reason *why*. Very well—I shall tell you. Or perhaps, I may say, I shall tell you why *not*."

"Exclusion is the better part of reason, my lord."

"I endeavoured to learn, with infinite discretion, whether Mr. Danforth is embarrassed in his circumstances, and requires a wealthy wife with a considerable fortune to save him—but Mr. Wickham assures me that, in addition to the comfortable rents of the Penfolds estate, Charles may depend upon his late wife's income. Lydia Danforth, it seems, was the only child of a prosperous textile-mill owner, such as are prevalent in these Midland parts; and though her birth was inferior to her husband's, she brought Charles Danforth no less than an hundred thousand pounds. Lydia possessed only a life-interest in the sum, however; by stipulation of her father's will, the principal was to be settled upon her children. At her death—all such children having predeceased the lady—the wealth became Charles Danforth's to command."

"Good Lord!" I cried. "If ever there were a motive for murder, *there* is one! Had the maid and her mistress exchanged places, we might look no further for the cause! But though a man might often be blamed for his wife's death in childbed, I have not heard it called *murder.*"

"Not in an English court of law, in any case," his lordship replied. "But such a vast sum of money *does* give rise to speculation. Had the children not preceded their mother to the grave—"

"Had the babe not been stillborn, and carried his mother with him—"

"Then Charles Danforth should be a much poorer man." Lord Harold tapped the squarish parcel that rested on the curricle seat between us. "What did you spirit away from Penfolds Hall, my dear Jane?"

"Tess Arnold's stillroom book," I replied. "In which she recorded the histories of each of her cases, the dates on which the poor sufferers sought her aid, and the remedies she availed them."

"Compelling reading," Lord Harold observed. "Do not neglect to study her account of the Danforth progeny. Precarious though childhood may be—and beset with every danger from contagion to accident—I cannot quite credit the parade of misfortune that has dogged Penfolds Hall. It strains the bounds of human belief, does it not?"

"But may be well within the bounds of human infamy," I replied.

I WAS SET DOWN AT THE RUTLAND ARMS AT THREE O'CLOCK. MY SISter and Mr. Cooper had walked out in the direction of All Saints Church—a difficult, though rewarding, climb up a considerable eminence in Bakewell—Mr. Cooper being most desirous of showing Cassandra the tombs in the Vernon transept, recommended to his notice by Sir James Villiers. My mother was dozing in her chair in the upstairs parlour given over to our comfort; but at my entrance, came to her senses with a start.

"And so Lord Harold has been carrying you off into the countryside, Jane," she cried by way of greeting. "We are fortunate this outing did not end in a report of your death!"

"He is a most cautious and proficient handler of horseflesh, ma'am," I replied.

"And yet murder and every sort of disgrace are forever nipping at that gentleman's heels! He cannot be in the country, without a body being found under every hedgerow! It bears a most suspicious aspect, my dear; and if your father were alive, I am sure he would agree. I am sure Mr. Austen would forbid you that gentleman's company, being most anxiously concerned for your health. He should certainly not wish you to enter a closed carriage. Any sort of mischief might ensue, in such company."

"It was a curricle, ma'am," I told her. "There can be nothing disgraceful in a summer airing, amidst the beauties of the Peaks."

My mother looked darkly and said, "I suppose Lord Harold denies all part in that unfortunate maid's end?"

"Naturally, ma'am—having learned of her existence only Tuesday, in company with ourselves."

"You are far too artless, Jane! You ought not to believe everything you are told," my mother returned. "It is necessary to give the *appearance* of belief when one is young, and in the world—anything else should be immodest in the extreme. The arch and knowing woman will drive off every eligible prospect that offers. But among your family, Jane, I hope you will always speak frankly."

"You may be assured of that, dear ma'am. I have not the slightest doubt of Lord Harold's being other than a murderer; and I cannot think that any ill should attach to my name, from being known to have driven out in his company, nor to have dined at his invitation at Chatsworth. I should rather be the object of envy from our entire acquaintance, and serve to raise our credit wherever we are known."

"I have sent the grey silk to Sally for airing"—my mother sighed—"and have told Mr. Cooper that does he wish to quit this place for Staffordshire on the morrow, he must do so alone. You are not growing any younger, Jane—and against such an extremity as spinsterhood, a trifling affair of whooping cough must be accounted as nothing."

After dinner, I settled myself beside a tallow candle with Tess Arnold's stillroom book. The cooling air crept softly through the open casement, and all the horror of yesterday evening—the drunken shouting, the gathering of men like a bated storm—might never have happened. Had the Danforth brothers returned to Penfolds? I wondered. Or did they remain at Chatsworth, in respect of tomorrow's dinner party? My heart quickened at the idea of being once more in the midst of that brilliant company. There should be much to enjoy—and much to observe. Purposefully, I opened the dead maid's book.

11 November 1803. Gave Mistress, at her wish, a draught of oil of sweet almonds just before bed; labour begun hard and fast three hours after. Gave mistress a purge at lying-in, of boiled milk and beaten eggs, with a little sugar.

12 November 1803. Mistress brought to bed, hard on one o'clock, of a fine, healthy boy. He is named John d'Arcy Danforth. Saw birth along with Dr. Bascomb of Buxton. Gave mistress a posset of pennyworth of Mummy in warmed white wine, to clear the Secundine.

13 November 1803. Haskell complains of breathing; gave a little of the armoniac and hyssop water. Miss Julia yellow about the eyes; gave celandine and madder water against the jaundice. Old Matthew feels gout coming on, and is spitting blood. Sent Comfrey water to stables and a little Duke of Portland's Remedy.

Tess Arnold had been a most active stillroom maid, between the demands of her employers, their several children, and a house full of servants. It was a wonder that she could spare any time from her duties to attend to the ills of all and sundry in the Peaks—much less go playacting with Andrew Danforth; but spare the time, she had. A brisk trade in draughts and powders, steel pills and plasters was managed from the Penfolds stillroom. Tess had turned a pretty penny.

21 May 1804. Gave wine whey and spirits of Hartshorn against the sore throat to Maggie Watchit; one shilling fivepence. For a

sour stomach, draughts of gum Arabick and chalk, to Michael Tivey, fivepence. To Daisy Marlebone of Tissington, Musk and Damask Rose Water, for they histerick fits. Sixpence.

This was the first mention I had found of Michael Tivey, though I assumed their association was an ancient one; nobody raised in so confined a society, with a mutual concern in curing the sick, could fail to learn of one another. I wondered at the surgeon seeking out a simple healer for his ills; but then recollected that he was supposed to be enamoured of the maid—and perhaps it was no uncommon thing to find a surgeon seeking the skills of another as apothecary. But surely there were apothecaries enough in Bakewell? So large a town—and so well patronised by a comfortable gentry roundabouts—must boast at least two or three.

The entries in the journal ran on through the years from 1802 until the summer of 1805, with just such a mixture of trifling incident and common ailments—here a case of the dropsy, there an attack of the rheumaticks; until August of 1805, when I noted an entry that must alert all my senses.

2 August 1805. Had of Michael Tivey tincture of opium, for the mixing with sulphate of zinc, in a wash for tired eyes; sent the same to the Duchess of Devonshire, against her dread ailment, by way of Lady Elizabeth Foster, one shilling. For Lady Elizabeth Foster, against the blockage of the menses, Mugwort pap and Rhubarb water, to be taken at bedtime, fivepence.

This was the first time I had noticed an entry regarding the intimates of Chatsworth, and I found it in every respect extraordinary. That Her Grace the Duchess—who could command the finest physicians in the land, and must employ a stillroom maid herself at Chatsworth—should attempt to find aid from the servant of a neighbour, confounded belief. Had Tess Arnold's reputation for healing merited such sponsorship? Or had Lady Elizabeth, whose hand had carried the tincture to her bosom friend, gone far afield in search of discretion?

5 September 1805. Lord Hartington, for the healing of deafness, applications of warm oyster likker to both ears. Three shillings. Miss Emma, Russia Castor and Milk in black cherry water, against they convulsive fits, three draughts the day.

Here was one mystery solved at least; Lord Hartington had met Tess Arnold first under the guise of treatment.

"Will you not retire, Jane?" my mother enquired, breaking into my thoughts. "It has grown very late, and you shall strain your eyes, in reading by such a poor candle! They were never very strong in any case; and you must look your best tomorrow."

"Coming, Mamma." I pressed my fingers against my eyelids—they were, as my mother suspected, reddened and sore with reading—and flipped rapidly through the remainder of the autumn. Lord Harting- ton had contrived to visit Penfolds at least once each week. Some- times the oyster liquor was applied; at others, warm almond oil to which spirits of juniper were added. A gap of over a month oc- curred in late November; presumably, his lordship had been absent in Town. One visit occurred in March of 1806—but by this period, more disturbing entries demanded my attention. I read through them once more.

25 September 1805. Miss Emma, for the convulsive fits, black cherry water.

26 September. Miss Emma, a clyster of washing starch, linseed oil, and laudanum, which I had of Michael Tivey, for the bloody flux. Extract of belladona in strong tea against vomiting.

27 September. Miss Emma bled today by Dr. Bascomb of Buxton.

A similar series of entries occurred in October and November. I read them with a gathering disquiet in my mind and a vice tightening around my heart.

27 November 1805. Mistress believes herself increasing again. Spearmint water and Naples biscuit against the sickness at morning.

28 November. Tincture of morphia against vomiting, in black cherry water, for Miss Emma. Dr. Bascomb cupped and bled her. At quarter past eleven in the evening, she died, aged five years, seven months, three days.

That was all Tess Arnold had thought fit to record; the words told nothing of Lydia Danforth's agony, or Charles Danforth's despair; nothing of the other children left silent and bewildered with their nurse upstairs; nothing of the dreadful building of so small a coffin, or the pain of leaving it, solitary in the autumn cold, in the Danforth tomb. Tess Arnold had said very little, I reflected, regarding the nature of the little girl's illness. Her pen was reserved for the remedies she had prescribed. But there had been others in attendance who might well know more. Dr. Bascomb of Buxton, for one.

I read on, as the hours of night fled away; I exchanged a guttering tallow candle for a fresh; I fought back weariness with the sick horror of one who cannot turn her eyes from disaster. The second eldest child—a girl of four named Julia—succumbed in February to a persistent fever and coughing; a wasting disease not unlike consumption, but far swifter in its effect. Dr. Bascomb, I observed, was not in attendance. He had been replaced by a London physician, who could do nothing to save little Julia; after three weeks of worsening ills—of morphia drops and Tess's draughts—the child gave way to a violent sickness in her bowels, much as Miss Emma had done.

I set aside the book at half-past two in the morning, unable to read any more—or to face the minutiae of small John d'Arcy's end. I understood, now, why the people of Bakewell wished Lydia Danforth at peace. Her final months on earth had proved a living hell. And how had Charles Danforth sustained his soul through such an onslaught of unspeakable misery? How could he not have thrown himself into the earth, that day in May when Lydia died, along with all his family? His survival beggared belief.

And with that final thought I stopped short on the threshold of my bedchamber, staring mutely into the darkness. How long would Charles Danforth have continued in health, had Tess Arnold remained alive?

A Wash for Tired Eyes

Take one pint rose water, add one teaspoonful of spirits of camphor and one teaspoonful of laudanum. Mix and bottle. To be shaken and applied to the eyes as often as necessary.

—From the Stillroom Book of Tess Arnold,
Penfolds Hall, Derbyshire, 1802–1806

Chapter 19

A Pleasure Party, Interrupted

Saturday
30 August 1806
~

THE SUN WAS HIGH BY THE TIME I APPEARED IN THE PARLOUR, BUT AS Mr. Davies only served breakfast at ten, I was able to scavenge some rolls and order a fresh pot of tea for my refreshment. Cassandra was seated over a book near the front window; Mr. Cooper had gone to pay a call of condolence upon George Hemming—a call that would undoubtedly involve the entire gaol in a good deal of singing—and my mother had walked out in the direction of the confectioner's, intent upon procuring some little iced cakes for her dinner. After five days, she had grown tired of Bakewell pudding.

"You look rather pale this morning, Jane. Did you sleep well?"

"Well enough, Cassandra." I raised one hand to my head and peered doubtfully at the harsh sunlight flooding the parlour. I would pay for the abuse to my eyes with a headache, and I was not careful. There could be no reading today.

"I hope you are not going to be indisposed," she observed, "on the very day of Lady Harriot's party."

"Never! I shall be carried senseless into the dining parlor, if need be. All I require is a little breakfast."

"And perhaps a change of scene," she suggested. "You have spent a good deal of this visit to Derbyshire in racing over the countryside in Lord Harold's company, and very little of it in mine! I feel myself outrageously neglected. Not to mention ill-used. The management of Mr. Cooper and my mother has been all my own, Jane, and I have not derived unalloyed pleasure from the task!"

The words were reproachful—but the tone was lighthearted; and I felt a welling of gratitude towards my sister, whose sacrifices were always borne with the best will in the world. I had hoped to spend a good part of the morning in perusing Tess Arnold's stillroom book— but all such selfish notions should be put aside. I reached instead for Cassandra's hand and squeezed it.

"I owe you a thousand apologies, my dearest. Such arrears in attention as I owe shall be totted up, with interest. Are you worn to a thread between the efforts of my mother and Mr. Cooper both?"

"Mr. Cooper—having accepted with ill grace the deferral of his departure until Monday at the earliest—has taken the notion that he must stand friend to Mr. George Hemming in his hour of need." She snapped together the covers of her book and set it upon the table. "You may thank me for having begun the idea, Jane, with many hints and careful surmises as to the nature of a soul in darkest torment, and the obligations of Christian charity, and the conduct his noble patron, Sir George Mumps, might reasonably expect. Our cousin presently regards himself in the light of a saviour. I daresay, if Mr. Hemming is reduced to a pitiable jelly by the effects of Mr. Cooper's plainsong, we may win another four-and-twenty hours."

"Delightful creature!" I cried. "What plans of pleasure have you drawn up for the day?"

"My mother begins to tire easily," Cassandra mused. "I do not think she will like to drive out, once her errand with the confectioner's is done. She will spend the period before dinner quite comfortably, in reading her correspondence and writing letters. I think we may regard the day as ours, Jane—and I am perishing for a breath of air, and a glimpse of the hills!"

"Then you shall have them. The cost of a pony trap and driver should not exceed the combined weight of our purses, and Mr. Davies is most obliging in the provision of horses." I pulled on the bell-rope to summon Sally. "I have two pounds, five shillings, and seven pence I may call my own; and I shall speak to the innkeeper directly. Where should you like to drive?"

"I have heard that there are caverns in the hills," Cassandra said wistfully, "large enough to hold a banquet in; that there are torrents above the dales, and villages famous for the plague; that one might climb, with effort, along paths that rim the abyss, and reward with endless beauty."

"Then we shall endeavour to find them all," I told her decidedly. "Sally! We require a pony trap, a driver, and a provisions hamper with the greatest despatch!"

WE DEPARTED LESS THAN AN HOUR LATER—MY MOTHER HAVING INterceded upon her return to The Rutland Arms, and requiring a full account of all our plans, and the wasting of precious moments while she hung in agonised indecision, uncertain whether to claim the peace of the empty parlour or join us in our wandering. Peace at last won out; and we were suffered to drive away with an enormous basket of victuals at our feet, a variety of lap-robes against the dust, Cassandra's sketching-pad and box of crayons, several novels, two sunshades, and an enormous blunderbuss of ancient vintage, which Mr. Davies propped on the box beside our driver—"for with these murderin', godless ruffians abaht, miss, tha'll be wantin' a sound piece."

Our driver was the selfsame Nate who had carried my urgent missive to Sir James Villiers two nights before, a strong young fellow of perhaps twenty, whose wall-eyed stare was roundly disconcerting. I wondered which eye he trained upon the road, and determined not to ask.

He pushed his cap to the crown of his head as we settled ourselves within the trap, and scratched ruminatively at his thick reddish hair.

"The Blue John Cave is what tha' ladies be wanting, ah'm thinkin'," he observed ponderously, "wit' all tha' talk o' bankets underground, but it's a good twenty mile fra' here, an ah've never been, myself. The Plague Village'll be Eyam, what lost so many a good bit ago, and that's no more nor less than five mile. As fer they abysses"—in his mouth, the word was nearer *abbesses,* as though it were a nunnery we sought—"I reckon tha'll find such along the Hucklow road, above Eyam. We might just do it, an' tha' has time."

Cassandra sighed over the lost Blue John Cave, but upon hearing that Nate could produce a Stone Circle for her delectation—a scattering of monoliths, from an ancient burial ground, not far from Eyam—she learned to be happy.

The sun was hot, and the wind stirred by the horse not worth mentioning; the pony trap wanted cushions for its hard wood seats. We swayed along the stony road at a drowsing pace, our sunshades propped against our shoulders, while the scents of drying grass and soiled sheep's wool drifted across the fields to either side. I had tucked Tess Arnold's stillroom book, wrapped in an embroidered shawl, under the mattress of my bed; and though my person was at leisure, my mind would often return to the closely-written pages. Not a glimpse of them should I have before tomorrow; but much might be elucidated at Chatsworth this evening. Various of the Devonshire family had known a good deal of the stillroom maid.

We passed through the town of Baslow and the hamlet of Stoney Middleton. Cassandra's eyes were bright and her colour fresh; I should never mistake her today for the younger image of my mother. She kept her sketchbook open upon her lap as we drove, and despite the swaying of the equipage and the necessity of keeping a firm handhold on the seat, managed a fair likeness of Nate, as viewed from the rear. In the Plague Village of Eyam, the horse was let to grass for an hour while we walked the narrow streets and exclaimed over the plaques on every side, that recounted the melancholy history of 1665, when two-thirds of the villagers succumbed to disease. A little girl with golden curls hanging down her back found us resting in the shade of an elm, and brought us spring water in a dipper made of tin.

Two hours out of Bakewell, we found ourselves ascending the Hucklow road, where we intended to rest a while among the standing-stones. The country fell sheer away on either side of our cart-track, in much the fashion of Nate's promised "abbesses." Cassandra had given over her expressions of delight at every turning, and was now gripping the sides of the swaying trap as though her very life depended upon it. She had suffered one carriage overturning two years since, and the experience did not rest lightly with her; frequent headaches from a considerable knock on the head were the fruit of disaster, and a consequent anxiety each time she trusted herself to an unknown conveyance and driver.

"You might as well get down, my dear, and walk," I suggested. "I shall do the same. We should both benefit from the exercise, and the horse from the lightened load. You there! Driver! Pull up your horse!"

Nate turned his head around and stared at me. "Tha's niver askin' to halt the beast when he's strainin' up sich a hill? Tha's a woman, for ye. Bide bit, till tha's at the top."

He had no sooner uttered the words, than the report of a gun set the horse to plunging in its harness. The frightened animal neighed wildly and attempted to bolt—Cassandra screamed, and clutched with both hands at my arm—Nate swore aloud, and dropped the reins to seize his antique blunderbuss—at which the horse, being given its head, plunged forward with a great lurch, spilling Cassandra and me backwards over the pony trap's seat, along with a quantity of sunshades, novels, sketchbooks, and lap-robes.

The hamper of food, mercifully enough, remained within the equipage.

I tumbled down upon the stony roadbed, felt my head strike an inconvenient outcropping, and struggled to my feet. I looked for Cassandra—espied her bewildered countenance, and reached out my hand—when a shouted halloo from the road ahead drew both our heads around.

A man on horseback, his face masked in a scarf of India cotton, his hat-brim pulled low, was fixed at the head of Nate's horse with a pistol raised. Nate himself was braced in the pony trap's seat, his unwieldy weapon levelled upon the highwayman; and the two appeared to have achieved an impasse. I considered whether the wisest course might not be to run—when Cassandra observed, in a voice only barely discomposed, "What sort of highwayman plies his trade in broad daylight, Jane? The fool might be discovered by anyone along the Hucklow road."

"True enough," I murmured, and took a step forward.

The highwayman's eyes shifted slightly from our driver's wall-eyed glare to my own flushed cheeks, my disarranged sunbonnet. I untied the strings of my leghorn straw and removed it. I took a moment to smooth my hair. And felt Cassandra approaching slowly behind me.

I enquired: "What do you mean, sirrah, by incommoding us in this dreadful fashion?"

"No incommoding meant, and I'm sure, only I did need so as to halt yer trap," he promptly replied. "I'm under orders to fetch that there book as you carried away from Penfolds Hall yesterday, and I'm obliged to keep you here until you do give it up."

"The stillroom book? You must be mad! Who are you?" I took a step closer, thinking swiftly of the quarto volume secreted under my mattress.

"Who I be makes no matter, miss," the highwayman replied. "I'll be taking that book now."

"I haven't got it," I retorted stoutly. "I gave it into the keeping of Sir James Villiers, the Bakewell Justice—but perhaps you are already ac-quainted with *him*."

"Not so's to speak to," the ruffian replied equably. "You wouldn't be spinning me a falsehood, miss?"

"My sister will tell you the same," I replied, with what I thought was admirable evasion.

Cassandra nodded vigorously.

The highwayman relaxed his vigilance a trifle, in consideration of our veracity; and without a second's hesitation, Nate fired his blun-derbuss full at the fellow's head.

The shot went wide—the gun's recoil knocked Nate backwards into the body of the trap—the highwayman's horse reared, and tossed him neatly to the ground; and the man went skittering down the side of the Hucklow road, bouncing and cursing and tumbling with a fearful force until he fetched up against a large boulder some thirty feet below. He lay, inert, while Cassandra assisted the faithful Nate out of the body of the trap.

"Held on't the horse's reins, any road," he muttered proudly.

"You did quite well, my dear sir. We were both quite thankful to have you at the fore," Cassandra gasped.

"I should recommend aiming for some other part of the anatomy than the head, however," I counseled. "Even in the case of defence against highwaymen, a judge may not look kindly upon outright murder."

" 'Tisn't murder, when the gun fires wild," Nate returned indignantly. "There was nivver a chance of it. But yon fellah's done for hisself, by the look o' things."

"He is certainly suffering from a nasty blow to the skull," I observed, "if not a broken neck."

"I'd best fetch a bit rope and tie 'im into the trap. Justice'll be wantin' to see him."

"I suppose there's no other course open to us"—Cassandra sighed—"but I had hoped for the standing-stones, Jane. And consider of that lovely hamper! I'm positively famished!"

Poor Man's Plaster

*T*ake one part beeswax, three parts tar, and three parts resin, and melt all together. Spread the plaster on paper or muslin, and cut into strips two inches wide. Tie the strips firmly around a bruised or aching joint.

—From the Stillroom Book of Tess Arnold
Penfolds Hall, Derbyshire, 1802–1806

Chapter 20

The Fate of Chamber Pots

~

WITH A MISCREANT INSENSIBLE AT OUR FEET AND THE PICNIC HAMPER perched upon our laps, we achieved Bakewell in less than two-thirds of the period required for quitting it. Perhaps twenty minutes into our journey, a series of groans could be heard emanating from the pony trap's floor; the highwayman was once more in the land of the living, and by the sound of his mournful tones, regretting the privilege. He was too securely bound to occasion alarm; I resisted the impulse to set my feet upon his head; but with such music in our ears, neither Cassandra nor I could summon the energy for conversation. The remainder of our pleasure drive was spent in the grimmest silence, while the beauties of Derbyshire passed away unnoticed.

Nate drove straight through the town from the Baslow road and made directly for the constables' watchhouse, where our burden was deposited amidst cries of wonder and consternation; the watchmen could no more recognise the fellow, when deprived of his India cotton scarf, than Nate had been able to do. Cassandra insisted at this juncture upon walking the last few hundred yards to the head of Matlock Street, where all the comfort and sustenance of The Rutland Arms awaited; we left the picnic hamper to Nate's attention, and thanked him profusely that we had not come to greater harm.

"And I shall send immediately for Sir James Villiers," I informed the constable, "with the instruction that he must seek you out, and question narrowly this fellow in your keeping; do be certain to keep him close, and watch him well, for he seems to me the slipperiest of brigands."

The highwayman positively swelled with pride at this encomium, and the constables looked all their confidence; I left the whole party in rousing good spirits, and determined to enjoy themselves.

"What did that ruffian mean," Cassandra enquired at last, "when he spoke of a book you had taken from Penfolds Hall, Jane? I had not known that you found occasion to visit the place."

"I presume the fellow would mean the stillroom book belonging to the murdered maid," I replied. "Her sister placed it in my keeping only yesterday." *Her sister.* If the masked highwayman had known to follow me from Bakewell, as I must presume he had done, then Jennet Arnold must have set him on me. Whether she had done so with the intent to harm remained open to question. At the very least, she had been pressed for her knowledge; but who could wish to secure the stillroom book so desperately, that he should send out a man with a pistol in broad daylight? The highwayman himself—or one who employed him?

One lesson, however, I had learned: The stillroom book must be secured against theft or injury, if I had to carry it myself to Chatsworth that evening in a reticule the size of a carter's dray.

"MY DEAR CASSANDRA!—JANE! THE OUTRAGE THAT HAS OCCURRED IN your absence!"

My mother cried these words as we appeared on the parlour threshold, and immediately sank back into her chair, a square of lawn pressed to her eyes. Sally bent most anxiously over her, waving a vinaigrette, while Lord Harold Trowbridge himself appeared to be occupied chiefly in collecting shards of pottery from the parlour floor. My cousin Mr. Cooper was singing. The volume of sound in that small place was sufficient to drive out every other thought.

Cassandra set down her sunshade—which alone she had retrieved from Nate's trap, the rest of our things being intended to arrive with the driver—and untied her bonnet strings. "My dear mother, have you suffered on our account? Has some news of our mishap travelled already to your ears? But we are perfectly well, I assure you—neither Jane nor I regard the indignity as being in the least out of the ordinary way."

"Not *out* of the ordinary way?" my mother cried, with a wild look. "Such spasms in my side—such palpitations of my heart—when a respectable woman is robbed in her own rooms, in a decent inn managed by worthy people? I should call it very much out of the way!"

"Robbed?" Cassandra pressed her fingers against her ears, as though to ward off the bellowing chorus from Mr. Cooper, and glanced anxiously at me.

"Lord Harold," I called out, "I had not looked for the honour of this visit. Would you be so good as to tell us who has been robbed?"

"Michael Tivey," he replied, "and of the better part of his reason."

"Michael Tivey! The surgeon?"

"I fancy he appeared more in the role of blacksmith this morning. But yes. The same Michael Tivey." Lord Harold stood up and carried the shards of crockery over to the parlour table. The devoted Sally—whom my mother had waved peremptorily away at the first sight of her daughters—set down the vinaigrette and commenced loading a kitchen tray with smashed earthenware.

"It is the chamber pot, Jane," Cassandra murmured with twitching lips. "We seem destined to destroy them all."

"Mrs. Austen has been troubled this morning by an unwelcome visitor," Lord Harold explained. He crossed to the corner near the parlour window, where my cousin still stood, drawing breath for a fourth verse, and seized him by the arm. "My good fellow—if you do not leave off that dreadful noise at once, I shall be forced to call you out; and though it has been my habit, in affairs of honour, never to aim for the heart—in your case, my dear sir, I should be sorely tempted."

Mr. Cooper paused, his mouth agape; allowed an expression of mortification and sheer terror to fill his countenance; and then exited the parlour without another refrain.

"I have affronted him," Lord Harold observed. "That is very well.

Nothing so becomes a man as a sensation of injured pride. He will set himself to drafting letters to my direction; he will consider the naming of seconds; and when Mr. Cooper comes to realise that the only possible second remaining to him is presently residing in Bake-well gaol, and thus beyond all power of a dawn meeting—he will drown his injury in a quantity of hock. A far preferable recourse than pistols for any self-respecting clergyman." Lord Harold dusted a few fragments of pottery from his fingers and raised an eyebrow in Cassandra's direction.

My sister choked on what might have been a laugh.

"Does no one spare a thought for me?" my mother exclaimed indignantly.

"Most certainly, ma'am," Lord Harold assured her. "My own thoughts at present are full of admiration for a lady of such advanced years, and indifferent health, who is yet capable of defending her ho-nour with a chamber pot so soundly, that she lays a man of fifteen stone insensible at her feet."

"My lord," I said, "pray enlighten us."

"Michael Tivey, being long familiar with The Rutland Arms, having assisted in its construction not two years ago through the manufac-ture of some iron implements and grillwork, engaged to enter the premises by the servants' door, just off the stableyard, when the cook and the benighted Mr. Davies were otherwise diverted by the cares attendant upon the management of a posting inn. Tivey mounted to this corridor by the servants' stair, and forced his way into the parlour—whose door, it must be admitted, was undoubtedly left on the latch. Your mother, being thoroughly wearied by the hurly-burly of trade, and the consumption of a rather heavy dinner, com-plete with iced cakes, had given way to the arms of Morpheus; when the stealthy footfall of Tivey in an adjoining room alerted all her senses. She called out, believing herself to have been joined by Mr. Cooper; and the footfall fell instantly silent. No answer did Mr. Tivey make. Alarm seizing the excellent lady—"

"—I took up the chamber pot and made immediately for your bed-room, Jane, where the scoundrel had hidden himself. He thought to push past me—he thrust himself savagely out of the door, my dear, so that I very nearly fainted—and with all my strength, I threw the pot at him!"

"You succeeded in striking him in the head?"

"Not at all," my mother cried. "But the pot, in tumbling at his feet, quite tripped up the rogue; and he dashed his head against the corner of that table. There was a quantity of blood; but as I fainted away myself at that moment, I had no cause to regard it."

"The blood fell to my lot," Lord Harold observed, "or rather, to the excellent Sally's; for the girl had just been conveying me to this room along the front passage while Tivey commanded the rear. She found the door already thrown open, and two bodies lying as if dead within; but happily, all such mortal fears were laid to rest with Mrs. Austen's regaining her senses. I restrained the blacksmith, while Sally cried out for Mr. Davies, who was instantly in attendance—Davies summoned another man—and in a matter of minutes, the offending Tivey was removed to the kitchens below. Sir James Villiers is already summoned."

"And have you enquired what the blackguard meant by invading our rooms in such a manner?" Cassandra demanded indignantly.

"I have not, because I rather fancy I know. He wanted the book your sister saw fit to carry away from Penfolds Hall; and he meant to have it."

"Tivey!" I cried. "Then it must have been *he* who placed that highwayman in our way!"

"Highwayman?" gasped my mother, turning pale. "Whatever is to become of us? Whooping cough is nothing to it!"

I dashed towards my bedchamber, but stopped short on the threshold. The mattress had been tumbled from the bedframe. The quarto volume I had wrapped in a shawl was nowhere in evidence.

"But what possible use could the Coroner make of such a thing?" I asked despairingly.

Lord Harold touched my shoulder in a gesture of comfort. "Perhaps he regarded it in the light of evidence, Jane."

"But against whom?"

"For that, we must peruse its pages."

I turned—and saw the very volume resting in his hands.

"I wonder who first discovered the efficacy of the mattress as a hiding place—Adam, or Eve? No matter. I pried the stillroom book from Tivey's clutches while he was as yet insensible. I advise you not to let it out of your sight."

I could have kissed Lord Harold's grave and inscrutable face; but instead, I clutched the volume to my breast and said only, "Thank you, my lord."

"Thank your mother, my dear," he advised. "It was she who was beforehand with the chamber pot."

It was only as I conducted his lordship towards the coaching inn's door that I thought to enquire after his purpose in paying his call.

"Merely to offer these," he said carelessly; "they should go very well, I think, with your hair."

He held out a small velvet box, such as one might obtain from the dearest of London jewellers. I looked up at him wordlessly, my arms at my sides. It was impossible that such a man should make a gift of something precious to *me;* and impossible that I might keep them, if he did.

"They are ornamental combs belonging to my niece, Desdemona," he said. Something flickered in his eyes—an understanding, harsh and painful, of my predicament. My cheeks flamed red.

"She enquired as to your dress"—he still held out the box in his gloved hand—"and I confess I could tell her nothing. Please accept them. Mona was most anxious that you should be happy on such an occasion—your first evening at Chatsworth."

"The Countess is very good," I said haltingly. I should have felt relief at the little parcel being anything but a gift; instead, a wave of shame and vexation at my mistake swept over me. I reached with trembling hand to accept the box.

"What is it, Jane?" Lord Harold enquired gently.

I shook my head, and opened the lid. The combs were ebony, and set with a pair of sapphires; they should look charmingly against Mona's hair, and would do very well, indeed, with grey silk. I managed a smile. "Pray offer my deepest thanks to Lady Swithin," I told Lord Harold. "I shall wear her combs with pleasure."

"I have ordered His Grace's carriage for your comfort," he said. "It shall be standing at the door at six o'clock."

And tipping his hat, he was gone.

A Remedy for Sun-burn

Tan may be removed from the face by mixing magnesia in soft water to the consistency of paste, which should then be spread on the face and allowed to remain a minute or two. Wash off with soap and rinse in soft water.

A preparation composed of equal parts olive oil and lime water is also an excellent remedy for sun-burn.

—From the Stillroom Book of Tess Arnold,
Penfolds Hall, Derbyshire, 1802–1806

Chapter 21

A Macabre Masquerade

30 August 1806, cont.

~

"Miss Austen! I am told that you have met with the most abominable behaviour in the world this morning! Are you entirely well?"

Sir James Villiers, his countenance animated by the liveliest anxiety for my welfare, hailed me thus from the swinging door that separated the public rooms of the inn from Mr. Davies's quarters. I assured the Justice that I was in perfect health and spirits, though justifiably apprehensive. I should prefer the experience of highwaymen and robbers to remain marked by its singularity.

"Naturally!" he cried. "And for that very reason I have instructed my men to throw Michael Tivey into the watchhouse, alongside his confederate Will Pickle. Tivey has been responsible for too many disturbances of late, and should benefit from a period of sober reflection."

"Will Pickle, I presume, acted today as highwayman?"

"He did, and confessed the whole at my interrogation. He is a cousin of Tivey's from over the Buxton way, and so was not likely to be recognised in this part of the world. I am assured he meant you no harm; but, however, he appeared on the road and brandished a firearm, and thus must be tried as a desperate and violent man. He shall be fortunate to escape hanging."

"For that, I should have to lay charges against him, I suppose."

Sir James appeared surprised. "I had not thought that was open to question. You will surely wish to do so."

"I should rather show clemency, and perhaps obtain valuable information in exchange. Michael Tivey, too, I presume, is open to the laying of a charge? For there were several witnesses as to his thieving entry into our chambers."

"Certainly." Sir James's eyes narrowed. "What is it you would propose, Miss Austen?"

"Mr. Tivey sought to obtain the stillroom book compiled by the murdered maid, Tess Arnold. There can be only one purpose in his elaborate subterfuge: he regards the book as a threat to his own security. I have already perused nearly half of the maid's entries, and may attest that there was considerable collusion between herself and the surgeon; she often obtained medicines from Mr. Tivey that should belong more properly in an apothecary's establishment. But I can find no evidence of any real wrongdoing on the surgeon's part. I must suppose, therefore, that Tivey has no idea what Tess might have written in the book—and that it is his own guilty knowledge which drives him to secure and destroy it."

"What would you have me do with the fellow?"

"Is he still detained there, in Mr. Davies's kitchen?"

"He is."

"Then I should very much like to speak to him, Sir James—if you would be so good as to bear me company."

The Justice smiled, and held wide the kitchen door. "With the very greatest pleasure, Miss Austen—provided you will undertake to leave in peace, any crockery you are tempted to fling at Mr. Tivey's head."

"If it must be so, it must." I sighed, and preceded him through the door.

The inn's kitchen and adjoining scullery were of a size commensurate with the needs of a coaching establishment. A cook and two scullery-maids, sweat glistening at their temples, were huddled between the hearth and a double stove set into the wall at its side; Sally our parlour-maid sat darning a sock by the open back door. Michael Tivey, his powerful arms bound tightly to his sides with a length of twine, was perched on a stool; Nate stared balefully at him, blunderbuss levelled, from a distance of perhaps five feet. Mr. Davies appeared too harassed by his several duties, and the signal honour of a Justice in the kitchen, to spare Michael Tivey a thought.

"Here we are," I declared, "and none the worse for a trifling fall from a pony trap, on my side, nor a blow to the head on yours, Mr. Tivey. I did not think that I should meet the respected Coroner of Bakewell again in such circumstances—but life is replete with irony, is it not?"

"Get the woman out of 'ere, Joostice," Tivey muttered at Sir James. "Ah've no time fer a deal o' palaver."

"I should lend Miss Austen your ear, Tivey," Sir James replied in a severe tone; "she has your interest—and liberty—at heart."

The surgeon's head came up, his countenance a sketch in canny hostility. "Wha' joo want wit' me, then?" He made no effort to speak, I noticed, with the deliberate care of the Inquest's proceedings. Discovery and disgrace had returned him to a baser realm.

"Mr. Davies," I suggested, "would you be so good as to afford us the liberty of the kitchen for a period? Mr. Tivey might prefer to speak for the Justice's ears alone."

Davies sought Sir James's face, then cleared his throat noisily. "Now then, girls," he ordered. "Into the yard wit' thee. You, too, Nate. Happen we might fetch that load o' flour Miller 'as waitin'."

The serving members of The Rutland Arms filed dutifully—and not at all unwillingly—through the back kitchen door, and Sir James saw it fastened securely with the bolt. The warmth of the kitchen was swiftly stifling; but my own discomfort could not be allowed to matter. I folded my hands and looked at Michael Tivey.

"You sought this morning, by various stratagems, to obtain the stillroom book compiled by the dead maid, Tess Arnold. You did so because you fear what the woman wrote concerning yourself. Your activity came too late, however, and fell far short of your objective; I had already perused the book's pages, and what Tess knew of your nefarious habits, Michael Tivey, you may be assured that I now comprehend as well."

For an instant, the most naked fear could be glimpsed in the surgeon's small, dark eyes; I felt a surge of satisfaction within. A man afraid for his life is a man who may be bent to purpose.

"Ah've told Sir James what ah know."

"Of Tess Arnold's death, perhaps—but it is her life that concerns us now. I shall not scruple to say that circumstances have informed against you. Your case looks black, indeed. The Justice has agreed to offer you a chance at winning some leniency from the Law. But you must be frank and open, Mr. Tivey—you must speak without reserve or hesitation. Nothing else is likely to save you."

"Ah'll speak," he cried out, before I had barely concluded my sentence. "Ah'll tell tha' what ah can."

I glanced at Sir James. His expression was wooden; but from a flicker of his eyelids I judged I should be allowed to proceed. I drew forth a vacant stool and settled myself upon it.

"Very well. You procured for the maid a quantity of medicines, such as should properly be in the keeping of a professional surgeon or physician. That much is clear. But you gave her other things as well, did you not? You instructed her in methods of healing that were far beyond her station."

"Tess'd learnt 'er letters," he explained.

"She borrowed books from you," I declared, with greater certainty than I possessed; I must tread carefully now, and never disclose to Tivey how little I actually knew.

"Yes!" he cried. "I lent her my books. There was noo 'arm in it. She was hungry fer learning, and books is scarce to coom by. She'd askt the Master up t'a Hall, and Mr. Andrew. They'd gone through libree for 'er. But they'm old books, in Latin; and neither Tess nor I were properly learnt in they dead tongues."

"Naturally." I kept my eyes trained upon the surgeon's head. His own gaze was steadfastly bent upon his knees; the bluster of former days was gone. I saw again in memory the strong forearms and the heat of the blacksmith's bellows, Tivey amidst a crowd in Water Street, careless about his effect. *If no one claims 'im, ah'll be wanting the body for study. . . .* A good corpse was hard to come by. The students of London physicians must pay a pretty penny for the remains of beggars; and even then the hue and cry of the pauper's family could be fearsome to behold. There had been riots in the streets of Town on the strength of a common criminal's being turned over to the College of Physicians; it was hardly unusual for God-fearing folk to regard the dismemberment of a corpse with superstitious terror.

"You lent Tess Arnold books about herbs and simples; and about the workings of various medicines," I suggested, my eyes on his face. "But I have an idea, Mr. Tivey, that you must also have spoken to her regarding the subject of . . . anatomisation?"

He drew a shuddering breath, and thrust his face in his hands. "Oh, God! And I told her to breathe not a word! The stupid bitch . . . the stupid *cow*! She went an' wrote of it in her book!"

I looked to Sir James. He raised an eyebrow in confused enquiry.

"Did you manage to study corpses together, Mr. Tivey?"

No answer but a sob from behind the splayed fingers.

Sir James's voice was like a lash. "Speak, man, lest you hang for offences that dare not be uttered! Speak honestly of what you know!"

"We only went but twice," Tivey muttered. "Twice, when Tess were able to steal out of the Hall. It had to be when a grave was freshly dug, and on a night of no moon. She wore a man's clothes—dark, so's to move quickly, and not be seen. We'd dig oop the coffin and carry the body to a field in a carter's dray. Nobody were the wiser."

He swallowed hard, and raised beseeching eyes to Sir James's face. "We always poot the corpse back in't grave. We meant no 'arm by it. How else is a man to know the way o' the body?"

"You did this twice," the Justice said between his teeth. "*Twice* you violated a hallowed grave in consecrated ground. Did you intend to effect a similar abomination on the night of the maid's death?"

The surgeon nodded once in despair. "There was a suicide," he told us, "along oot Taddington way. A young fool lost a deal o' brass at cards and blew 'is brains oot in 'is father's barn. Parson meant to bury'm at the crossroads near Taddington, just where the road meets the fork down fra' Miller's Dale. Tess could walk over right easy fra' the Hall."

"And so you required her to come."

"I sent bit o' note in some morphia she'd ordered."

And Tess had walked out through the hills from Tideswell, wearing her borrowed suit of black clothes, a spectral figure under a fitful moon. Only she had never arrived for her dreadful assignation.

"I found the grave right enough," Tivey went on. "And who's to care, what befalls the corpse of a sinner? 'E weren't in churchyard, any road. I waited more'n two hour fer Tess. She nivver coom, she nivver sent no word."

"And then?"

Tivey hesitated, and dropped his eyes from Sir James's face. "I weren't aboot to let a good corpse go to waste. I opened the grave and took'm out."

"May God have mercy on your soul, Michael Tivey," the Justice muttered; and turned away in revulsion.

We learned little more from the surgeon after that, though we pressed him closely for particulars of all he had taught Tess Arnold. A formidable character emerged from Michael Tivey's words: intent upon her skill, with the toughness of a man twice her years; ruthless in pursuit of knowledge, and possessed of a heart of stone. Tess Arnold, I judged, should use any tool that fortune placed within her power, whether the tool possessed a soul or no; but perhaps it was her unswerving passion that had proved her downfall.

"We must have, at least, the names of those they anatomised," Sir James said in a voice full low. "Did their families learn of the violation in the churchyard, any form of violence might well result. The most respectable of folk might well find it in their hearts to murder with such a cause—and to visit upon the maid's corpse, the very savagery that their own Deceased had suffered at her hands."

I nodded, and studied Michael Tivey's crestfallen countenance. Sir James should be left to secure this final intelligence; it was he who must pursue the bereaved families, and visit further anguish upon those already torn with loss. Tivey looked, to me, to have divulged the worst part of his guilty knowledge; he huddled now, drained of all emotion, on his hard wooden stool.

The great bell of All Saints tolled the hour of five o'clock. The kitchen maids were hovering beyond the door; the innkeeper's dinner should be decidedly behind-hand. I informed Sir James of my engagement for the evening, received his ardent thanks on the room's threshold, and fled without a backwards glance.

Though murder will out, and the guilty must pay, I sometimes fear the turn of my own understanding. I had possessed not an idea of Tivey's secret when first I undertook to persuade; but the apprehension of all that he had done arose in my mind as swift and sure as a passage of vows between two lovers, such as I might pen on paper with my own hand. It was extraordinary—by any construction, extraordinary; and I knew, as I sped towards my bedchamber and Cassandra's grey silk, that I should not rid myself of the horror of Tivey's confession for many nights to come.

AT SIX O'CLOCK I ONCE MORE DESCENDED THE FRONT STAIRS, A woman transformed in her outer garb, however shaken she remained within. I found myself already expected—Dawson the coachman stood correct by the door of an elegant crane-necked coach. And so, in borrowed combs and a gown rather breathless through the bodice, I set off for Chatsworth House. Being absolved of the burden of conversation on this second journey along the Baslow road, I had leisure to think; but such thoughts as must come ensured a violent headache. Better to banish reason, and peer instead through the closed carriage's octagonal side-lights—to admire the verdant folds of Manners Wood, the stone enclosures of the fields, the long rays of sun gilding the saddles of the hills. I found that I should be sad to leave Derbyshire on the Monday. It was a landscape that beguiled without intending—a harsh and lovely fall of ground that inspired passion, but cared nothing for those who would claim it. One might be suffered to pass unscathed through the Peaks, but one could never claim to own them, whatever the Devonshires might say.

The country was not unlike the character of those it bred. I considered Tess Arnold—a girl grown more inscrutable, the more I learned of her. We knew, now, *why* she had worn a man's clothes on the night of her murder, but not why she had been killed. Had some grieving person, entirely unknown to us—whose late wife, or dead child, or long-suffering parent she had torn from an open grave—taken up his gun, and despatched her as brutally as she had served his kin? Then why leave Michael Tivey at liberty, to plunder graves anew?

And what, exactly, had been the maid's relations with Andrew Danforth? Had she loved him—or merely used him to obtain her borrowed feathers? The state of undress Mrs. Haskell had observed in the privacy of the ice-house, might have been nothing more than an opportunity seized for the exchange of a maid's habit for that of a gentleman; seduction might have been the farthest thing from Tess Arnold's mind.

The carriage jolted over a dry rut in the road, and I clutched at the edge of my seat. Reveries about unknown persons, and their possible grievances, were all very well in their way; they might serve quite admirably to divert Sir James Villiers' attention from the man who now sat in the Bakewell gaol. But the story, to my way of thinking, would not do. Had Tess been despatched by an outraged mourner, in revenge for crimes of anatomisation, why then should George Hemming confess to murder? All Michael Tivey's talk of churchyards and suicide threw not the slightest light on Hemming's anguish. I shook my head. Whatever Tess Arnold had intended in her gentleman's clothes on Monday night, it had played no part in her death.

IT WAS AS WE APPROACHED PILSLEY, AND THE TURNING IN OUR ROAD for Chatsworth, that I espied the lone horseman. He had pulled up his mount on a little rise above, and was staring keenly down at my equipage as it approached the western gates of the park. Both horse and rider were utterly still, their figures suggesting the statue rather than life; and something chilling there was in so undisguised, and so acute, a scrutiny. Indiscernible myself behind the shutters of my coach, I stared implacably back. Only one person in Derbyshire was plunged in so profound a mourning; and only one bore that air of grief, even in stillness. The Marquess of Hartington, Devonshire's heir.

But why was he not already at home, and dressing for his sister's dinner?

He wheeled the horse's head—raised one arm—a whip flashed out, and as swift as a bird in flight, the boy and his mount had put Chatsworth to their backs. I watched, until a turning in the road swept them both from my sight; and knew that it was the last glimpse of the Marquess I should have, that evening.

A Draught to Bring on Labour

*M*ix together three spoonfuls of white wine and one spoonful of Oil of Sweet Almonds; take this every night before going to bed for a fortnight or three weeks before the expected Time.

Or take a little rye that has been spurred or covered with ergot, and boil in one pint sweet wine; strain the whole and let it cool. The dose is one-quarter pint, and the draught thus taken will bring on the pains in half an hour.

—From the Stillroom Book of Tess Arnold, Penfolds Hall, Derbyshire, 1802–1806

Chapter 22

Lady Harriot's Celebration

30 August 1806, cont.

~

THE PROSPECT OF A FINE MEAL AMIDST ELEGANT COMPANY MUST give rise to the most pleasurable anticipation in the dullest of times; but when set in the frame of recent events, and coupled with the knowledge that one or more of my companions might be guilty of murder—it gains considerably in piquancy.

I had occasion to reflect upon this when Mr. Charles Danforth vied with his brother for the honour of taking Lady Harriot Cavendish into dinner, only to be supplanted—as must be natural—by Lord Harold Trowbridge, his senior in both years and consequence. Lord Harold preserved his command of countenance, and Mr. Charles was too well-bred to cavil. He turned instead to the Countess of Swithin, our dear Desdemona, who accepted his arm with alacrity and the greatest good-humour in the world. Mr. Andrew Danforth was consigned to me—the eldest, least attractive, and most impoverished of the lot. But such is the fate of younger sons. He bore his duty well, and was so obliging in his manner, that I nearly forgave him the role of chief suspect in a heinous crime. Mr. Andrew's attentions drew Lord Harold's eye so often during the course of dinner, in fact, that I felt myself in the slightest measure repaid for his lordship's own excessive devotion to Lady Harriot.

We were twelve at table—I had not looked for so great a crowd with the family in mourning, but Lady Harriot's native day had drawn nearly every relation to her. Georgiana Morpeth, Lady Harriot's elder sister, sat to her father's left. Lord Morpeth had brought his wife down from their home at Castle Howard, in Yorkshire, and intended to return thence on the Monday—Lady Morpeth's three little children being constantly in want of her. The Countess of Bessborough, younger sister to the late Duchess of Devonshire, was but lately arrived from her home at Roehampton; *she* intended a stay at Chatsworth of some weeks.

Lady Bessborough is a bewitching woman, with Hary-O's rapier wit and a faded beauty that is nonetheless enchanting. Here was the mold from which Hary-O had been struck; and I should not be greatly surprised to learn that Lord Harold had once been as enslaved to the charms of *this* Harriot as he was now thoroughly devoted to her niece. Though she was a Countess (and the Earl yet lived), the burdens of public rectitude had never weighed overly-heavy on Lady Bessborough's white shoulders; she had brought an excessively handsome young man, Granville Leveson-Gower, in her train from Roehampton. All at the Chatsworth dining table acknowledged him as her lover, despite the twelve-year difference in their ages; and as Leveson-Gower might command a fortune, and the notice of any woman in the world, we may adjudge his attachment a tribute to Lady Bessborough's fascination.

The Duke sat at the head of the great dining table, but the chair to his right—the late Duchess's place—was draped with black crepe. Lady Elizabeth, I saw with some relief, had not yet attempted to seize her dear friend's empty chair. One other seat had gone unfilled, as though reluctant to disturb the symmetry of our arrangement: the Marquess of Hartington's. The boy had not appeared at dinner; and I was not alone in remarking upon the absence.

"Where has young Hart hid himself, Your Grace?" Lord Morpeth cried to his father-in-law, when the first congratulations and wishes for returns of the day had been offered to Lady Harriot. "I should not have thought he would neglect his sister on so signal an occasion."

"No doubt he'll turn up," the Duke returned vaguely. "Always out until all hours. Can't drag the fellow off his mounts. Sportsman. Think he sleeps in his riding breeches."

"Did Hart know of the excessive anxiety he causes," managed Lady Elizabeth, "I am certain he would make amends, dear Morpeth; but he is of an age where the claims of Society are as nothing. The boy is heedless, foolhardy, and given over to the very worst sorts of humours—but possessed, I am sure, of the dearest heart in the world! There is nothing to his grief for our beloved Georgiana. Indeed, as I said to Lady Bessborough only this morning, I must forgive Hart every unfeeling wound when I consider of the depth of his loss."

"You are too good to us all, I am sure, Lady E.," retorted Hary-O, with barely suppressed rage. "What my brother might be, without your influence in this household, does not bear thinking of."

Granville Leveson-Gower regarded Lady Harriot narrowly—he was seated immediately to her left—then looked all his enquiry at Lady Bessborough directly opposite. The Countess gave a barely discernible shake of the head, and reached for her wineglass. Leveson-Gower sat back, his eyes yet fixed on Hary-O. There was curiosity in his gaze, I thought—but anxiety, too, for her welfare.

"And has grief entirely blasted your twenty-first summer, Lady Harriot?" he asked her gently.

She fixed her eyes upon her lap as she replied; but a warmth suffused her countenance. "It should be very strange, sir, had it not. Though I do not make a parade of sorrow, as *some* do, I must feel my mother's loss as deeply."

"I'm sure you must," he returned. "No more excellent lady lived. And the continued torments of Chatsworth—the thousand unquiet memories of happiness, now gone forever!—must deepen your pain. Lady Bessborough, I think, intends to carry you back with us to London; and there, I am sure, the diversions of Town, and the novelties of a new Season, must invariably raise your spirits."

"Carry Hary-O into Town!" cried Lady Elizabeth, before the young lady could express her thanks. "What an excellent notion, Lady Bessborough! The very thing! We are excessively obliged to you! For Lady Harriot cannot have many eligible young men thrown in her way in Derbyshire, you know," she added, with cruel disregard for the Danforth brothers, "and she does not grow the younger, as our happy occasion must only emphasise."

"I see you regard the improvement of her circumstances in the proper light," murmured Lady Bessborough ironically.

"Canis and I shall be at Devonshire House by Christmas," Lady Elizabeth continued insensibly. "I should dearly love to chaperone our little Hary-O this winter, and I am sure that Georgiana would have wished me to stand in her place—but I fear my delicate condition of health forbids it." At this, Lady Elizabeth managed an example of her peculiar, hacking cough.

That she should put herself forward, as Hary-O's chaperone—an office belonging first to the married elder sister, and more properly to Lady Harriot's aunt—defied belief! That the Duke's *mistress* should carry his *daughter* into Society! Was Lady Elizabeth so blind to the impropriety of her own position, as to imagine it went unnoticed by all around her?

Lady Harriot rolled her eyes towards Heaven. Lord Harold's composure was excessively correct; but his eyes met mine with the most satiric look.

"We may take it as settled, then," interposed Leveson-Gower briskly. "When the Duke is once more in residence at Devonshire House, Lady Harriot shall naturally make her home there; but until that time, she shall remain with the Countess."

Lady Bessborough reached across the table and squeezed Hary-O's hand. "You must let us spoil you a little, my dear—and afford us all the pleasure of your wit and intelligence during a most dullish period. Parliament is in recess, you know, and everyone off shooting; but if you consent to remain with us until December—"

"Then you shall succeed in drawing every available *parti* to Town, and shooting be damned," Lord Harold concluded.

"What are birds, to the most fascinating young lady in London?" enquired Andrew Danforth. "I have had enough of country life! Charles may moulder in the Midlands all he cares—it suits his temperament to be melancholy and retired. But *I* am for Town!"

However teazing the gentleman's looks—however lighthearted his air—I judged him to speak in the greatest earnestness. Lady Elizabeth might consider Andrew Danforth the least eligible match in Derbyshire; but that gentleman was not about to let slip his chance at a Duke's daughter.

"And you will have your career in Parliament to prepare for," I observed. "There must be all the formality of the hustings, to be sure; but with His Grace's influence, much might be done in a very little time. Of course you must go to London, Mr. Danforth! There is not a moment to be lost, if you would take your borough at the next offering!"

"Do you mean to stand, then?" Leveson-Gower's gaze was arrested. He stared first at Andrew, and then at the silent, absorbed face of his brother, Charles, who had contributed nothing to the conversation. At the question, however, Charles Danforth stirred.

"You might better enquire, Granville, how he intends to fund his bid! My brother's taste in horseflesh and wine—not to mention the cost of his tailor and his hounds!—runs to considerable expense. A commission in the Life Guards might better suit his style; but we may regard public office as a luxury he may ill-afford."

The words were as biting as a schoolmaster's to an errant head-boy; and Andrew Danforth flushed. It was the first evidence of discomposure I had ever witnessed in that smooth and plausible gentleman—but an instant only was suffered to pass, before he summoned his answer.

"Were we all as close with the purse-strings as Charles, my dear Leveson-Gower, the kingdom would falter for lack of commerce! Besides—he must know quite well that sitting Members cannot be seized for debt! Who would account the cost of attaining office, when it affords such liberal terms?"

Everyone laughed at this sally; and Andrew Danforth was acquitted of folly. His brother, however, had emerged the worse from the exchange—for where Andrew retained his charm in the face of insult, Charles could appear only grasping and mean. I wondered how often the ill-disposed talents of both served the elder to disadvantage.

"You shall be following in your dear mother's path, Lady Harriot, do you intend to take up the cause of politics," observed Granville Leveson-Gower quietly, "for there was never a greater hostess, nor a better judge of a man's character, than the late Duchess. Pray inform me when you set up your *salon*—for I shall be constantly in attendance."

Lady Harriot smiled—she cast a wistful, searching gaze at the handsome Leveson-Gower—and so their conversation ended. I do not think they exchanged more than ten words for the remainder of that dinner; but Lady Harriot was able to lift up her eyes, and throw off her contempt for her mother's rival, and enjoy the attentions of all at the party who wished her well. For this, if nothing else, I regarded Granville Leveson-Gower with gratitude—whatever his reprehensible attentions to another man's wife. There is more disinterested good in the fellow than reputation would allow.

WE SURFEITED OURSELVES ON WHITE SOUP AND PLAICE, CHICKENS AND tongue, a fricasee of turnips and buttered prawns. There were forcemeat balls and macaroni, a ragout of celery with wine, dressed lamb and asparagus; sole with mushrooms. There was a gooseberry pie, and a quince preserve; a jaune mange and a marmalade of apricots; almonds and raisins and lemon ice. We drank negus and Madeira and smugglers' claret; we sat while the covers were twice exchanged. And at last, when nearly three hours had been suffered to pass away, the ladies retired and left the men to discuss the prospects for government and Charles James Fox.

I felt myself to have grown quite flushed with food and spirits, and suspected that not even Cassandra's grey silk might disguise the damage to my complexion. The great French windows had been thrown open to the night, affording a pleasant coolness. While Lady Swithin went cheerfully in search of her needlework, and Lady Harriot stood in closest conversation with her aunt, and Lady Elizabeth enquired fretfully of Georgiana Morpeth how her youngest child did—whether the danger of quinsy was *entirely* past—I wandered over to the open window, and saw that a broad stone terrace lay just beyond. It overlooked the parterres of the formal garden that flanked the eastern facade of the Great House. A wave of scent rose up from the boxhedge and flowers; I stepped out into the darkness, and breathed deep.

The moon was now fuller and stronger than it had been on the night of the maid's death. The stars shone out, in a bewildering pattern overhead; owls called from the Spanish oaks, from the heavy coverts of trees lapping Chatsworth for mile upon mile; a deep stillness lay over the countryside, beautiful in its peace—an ageless stillness,

such as must have obtained in this part of the world from time im-
memorial. Its illusion of measureless happiness was utterly bewitching. Great power was sunk in the stones of this house, great brilliance
and talent in those who commanded its halls. I could not deny its se-
ductive force; everything in my heart and soul longed to claim a part
of this world. *Lord Harold's world.*

Naked with ambition, grasping in its ruthless drive for self, and
glittering in its possibilities, the chances it risked. There was great
happiness—great sorrow—but always *passion* in such a world. Better
to throw oneself on the wheel, to rise and fall with its whims, than remain forever bound to the earth—

Perhaps the Madeira and the French wine had quite gone to my
head. The age of thirty was a trifle late to adopt the role of romantic
heroine—to pin all of life on an excess of sensibility, and die when
the object of love was denied. As I stood in the darkness above the
spreading parterre, awash in that tide of scent, I acknowledged that
Lord Harold alone could form my idea of happiness; and knew, with
all the finality of earth thudding down upon the grave, that such happiness must be denied.

"Your ladyship has ever been the soul of forbearance."

His voice, as though I had conjured him from the darkness, spoke
softly from the shelter of the neighbouring window.

"It is just that I feel it my *severe duty,* Lord Harold, to be the next
Duchess of Devonshire," Lady Elizabeth replied, her voice breaking
with tears. "Poor Canis is quite lost without me! But no one knows
with what *dread* I regard the prospect! No one takes my part—no one
feels the depth of my suffering, to stand in the place of *she* who was
dearest to me in all the world!"

"I am sure we can none of us be in ignorance of what you feel,
Bess," Lord Harold equably replied. "Perhaps with time—"

"Yes," she faltered. "Perhaps with time, I shall see better what path
I must follow—which duty should be regarded as the most pressing. I
do not speak of one's duty to *oneself*—that cannot be held in the balance. I learned long ago to disregard *self* entirely."

"You were always a creature of sacrifice," Lord Harold murmured.

"And it is in the nature of sacrifice to be misjudged, and ill-
regarded," she returned bitterly. "I am sure I should be quite lost

without such good friends as you and Lady Bessborough. The young people positively blame me for their mother's death!"

"Surely not."

"Lord Hartington most certainly does! As though I, who nursed Her Grace to the last—through those horrible final hours, when she neither spoke nor knew anyone, and suffered the most fearful agony—as though I could have wished Georgiana ill! I cannot tell you, Harry, how the cloud of suspicion and neglect has deepened my grief! It is a wonder I have not already found my own grave!" Lady Elizabeth blew her nose rather noisily into a handkerchief. "But for the thought of dear Canis, and his helplessness—I believe I should have been carried off!"

"Lord Hartington must be very foolish," Lord Harold observed. "There can be no possible cause for accusation. Indeed, I cannot believe it even of *him*. Though I know the young fellow to be yet in the grip of grief, surely his reason must urge restraint."

"It is all on account of that wretched maid." Lady Elizabeth sighed. "I wish that she had never been born, with her schemes and her remedies and her incantations!"

"Of whom are you speaking?"

I knew that note in Lord Harold's voice; he was instantly alive to every possibility, and determined never to betray it. Lady Elizabeth was the merest trout—a slippery fish that had taken the Rogue's lure. I waited, my breath suspended, for my lord to play the line.

"The stillroom maid, from Penfolds Hall," Lady Elizabeth retorted peevishly. "The great healer you all cannot be done talking of—the girl so viciously murdered. Young Hart made quite a pet of her, you know."

"Did he, indeed?" Lord Harold managed to suggest the faintest air of distaste, as though schoolboys who dallied with maidservants were decidedly *not* the thing.

"It is vastly shocking, I am sure—Hart is rather young, and so awkward in his ways—but I assure you, Harry, that we knew nothing of the matter until last month! Canis had occasion to run across the boy on horseback, and observed him parting from the maid. It seems that Hart had been riding over to Tideswell to see the girl ever since his dear mother died."

No word to Lord Harold, of her own use for the stillroom witch. Lady Bess, I thought, was a subtle character, and vicious in her manipulation.

"Did Hart offer an explanation for such attentions?"

"Not at all. Canis and I both demanded the entire history of the affair, in separate applications; we threatened and cajoled him by turns; and it ended in Hart's being forbidden to ride in the direction of Tideswell. I persuaded Canis to forbid the boy the use of his horses, indeed, did he contrive to disobey his father. And the sum of it is, that Hart has taken me in severe dislike!"

"I do understand. It is a most prickly age. At fifteen a boy may be wounded by every trifle, and harbour unreasonable resentments."

Lord Harold's mind was revolving the intelligence as thoroughly as my own; but he had not yet read the stillroom book. He knew nothing of Lord Hartington's attempts to cure his deafness, and must assume the visits to Tess Arnold—which I knew to have long predated his mother's death—were nothing more than infatuation.

Had there been such a calf love, indeed? Had the Marquess fallen in love with a woman ten years his senior, and followed her about with silent devotion? Until he discovered her one day, as Mrs. Haskell had done, in a state of undress or another man's arms?

I'd hoped the witch had died in agony.

What would such a boy have done, at the prickly age of fifteen? I saw again in memory the hideous gouts of blood at the rock's base. Did the delivery of *one* wound demand the blow of another?

And what kind of shot had the Duke taught his heir to be?

"Not a kind word have I heard from Hartington's lips since April," Lady Elizabeth cried fretfully, "when we buried Georgiana in the Devonshire crypt! He, who has been almost a *son*—"

Here she broke off, with the faintest suggestion of having been caught out in an indelicacy. Whatever the true nature of the Marquess's parentage, it would not be Lady Elizabeth who dispelled the mystery. It should be in her interest, I surmised, to foster doubt; and she was never the lady to disregard her own interest.

"Perhaps when all your friends have left you," Lord Harold said comfortingly, "you may be quiet for a little, Bess, and recover your spirits."

"Yes," she gasped. "Solitude is all I require. It is a great thing, Hary-O's going with her aunt."

"You will not be lonely?"

"Lonely! With Canis for company!"

I could imagine the scene: Lady Elizabeth's eyes wide with shock at her friend Harry's suggestion, one hand pressed against her palpitating heart.

"His Grace will be often in the fields, at sport, over the next few months."

"To be sure—but it is not as though we shall remain in Derbyshire indefinitely. We shall be often coming and going to London. And it is not as though Hary-O were a considerable *comfort,* you know—she may look the angel, Harry, but she is a most selfish and cold-hearted little—" Here, the last word was cut off by a bout of coughing. Lord Harold, I noticed, did not leap to his beloved's defence; but neither did he join in Lady Elizabeth's condemnation.

"Grief is a capricious mistress, Bess."

"Oh, yes—I do not deny that she is *excessively* grieved—but I should think that her heightened sense of what is due to her mother's memory, would make her ever more eager to show kindness to her mother's oldest friend! And yet she *will* not do the civil, and appear in public with Canis and me—which might quell the hideous nonsense everybody speaks behind our backs, you know; that the family is all in disorder, and entirely on my account."

"It is possible that any appearance in public is distasteful to Hary-O at present."

"Oh—as to that—I do not derive any pleasure from it myself, I assure you! But one must consider the obligations of a ducal house! It is vastly unpleasant to parade before the eyes of the *ton,* and know the vicious things that must be said of one; to feel that the purest conduct in the world—the devotion of an old family friend at such a melancholy time—must be trammelled in the mud of vulgar opinion!"

"I am sure you have suffered a good deal."

"And so *tenacious* as Hary-O must be on the subject of *place!* Canis and I have never paid much heed to those things; everything with us is easy—but Lady Harriot must have the proper deference paid to rank and authority. She, who is the merest *child*—! It should do her a world of good, I daresay, to throw herself away on a nobody like Andrew Danforth, and then see what *place* the world afforded her! She should not be so nice in her distinctions *then*, once the protection of her father's house was lost to her!"

This sudden access of spite—and Lord Harold's ominous silence—must have warned even one so insensible as Lady Elizabeth; she broke out once more in a fit of coughing.

"Bess, I fear the night air does not agree with you," Lord Harold observed, and led her gently away.

I tarried another moment or two, alone under the stars—thinking of all that had passed, and wishing foolishly that the Gentleman Rogue might return. My cheeks had lost their heat, and the tumult in my brain receded; a buzz of determined conversation told me that all the gentlemen had now joined the ladies. It would be as well, I thought, to discover what I could of Lord Hartington's movements on the night of the murder; I should never have such an opportunity again.

I smoothed my grey silk, touched a hand to the borrowed combs, and turned my face to the light—towards the tea service, the card tables, and the conversation—all the claims of Lord Harold's glittering world.

A Remedy for Persistent Coughing

*T*ake two ounces each of barley, figs, and raisins, a half ounce of liquorice, and a half ounce of Florentine iris root. Put the iris root and barley into two quarts of water, and boil them well, then put in the raisins, figs, and liquorice. Let it boil up again, and after eight or ten minutes strain it off.

A coffee cup full is the dose, and is to be taken twice each day.

—From the Stillroom Book of Tess Arnold,
Penfolds Hall, Derbyshire, 1802–1806

Chapter 23

A Bit of Ivory
Two Inches Wide

"I UNDERSTAND, MISS AUSTEN, THAT YOU ARE ACQUAINTED WITH George Hemming," said Mr. Charles Danforth as I emerged from the moonlit terrace.

"A little," I concurred with a quickening of interest, "but hardly so well as yourself. He has served your family in the capacity of solicitor, I believe?"

Danforth accepted a cup of tea from Lady Swithin, handed it in turn to myself, and steered me gently towards a settee placed comfortably in an alcove. "Such a term does not begin to describe the loyalty and devotion he has shown to Penfolds Hall," he said. "In the course of thirty years, Hemming has served my family in nearly every capacity one can name. I owe him every measure of gratitude and respect—nay, of friendship. I am greatly disturbed in my mind at his present circumstances."

I seated myself and studied Charles Danforth's countenance. It was sober and reflective; and though stamped with the lines of old pain, suggested nothing of a willful duplicity. "You were surprised, then, to learn of Mr. Hemming's confession?"

"Nothing could have a greater power to astonish! I was told of it only yesterday before dinner, the morning having been entirely consumed with anxieties of my own—but perhaps you will have heard of the despicable attack on Penfolds."

"Yes."

He looked a trifle conscious, and seemed unable to resume the thread of conversation; if I knew of the attack, presumably I knew that all of Bakewell believed Charles Danforth a murderer.

"And can you account for Mr. Hemming's extraordinary behaviour? For I must tell you, Mr. Danforth, that I regard his claims as entirely false."

He sat down beside me, and eased his lame foot straight out before him. "It does not sit well with a man of my temperament to skulk here, under the Duke's protection, as though I were afraid to enter my own house. Had I not been pressed to remain for Hary-O's native day, I should have ridden out long ago."

It was hardly a reply to my question. I let his words fall without remark, and took a sip of tea.

"Miss Austen—have you spoken with George—Mr. Hemming?"

"I have. I was present at his confession, if one may thus describe an admission so thoroughly disguised in drink. I told him then that I believed him to be shielding another—to have claimed the murder of the maid in the belief that Sir James Villiers would be satisfied. But Sir James is not. Too many aspects of Tess Arnold's death do not accord with Mr. Hemming's story."

"Aspects?" he enquired, with a penetrating look. "And may I ask—? But no. You shall not be pressed to an indiscretion."

"Sir James is of my opinion, Mr. Danforth, that Mr. Hemming would act in the guise of scapegoat. But for whom? Have you any idea?"

I observed the gentleman so coolly, and yet so narrowly, that I could not mistake the turn of his countenance. Charles Danforth was consumed with anxiety; and his fears were inspired by whatever George Hemming might know.

"I can well believe that he would place a noose around his own neck, if it might save another whom he loved," the gentleman said in a voice hollow and low. "Hemming is the best-hearted and best-intentioned fellow in the world. I can conceive of no reason on earth why he should have harmed Tess Arnold—but neither have I ever known George Hemming to *lie*."

"And so you turn on the horns of paradox," I murmured.

"*One* of his actions must be false," Danforth exclaimed. "But which? Having admitted falseness to be impossible, I cannot rightly say."

"Perhaps, if Mr. Hemming could explain his actions—either his purpose in lying, or his purpose in killing the maid—we might comprehend his behaviour."

"Naturally," Charles Danforth agreed, "but it is just that sort of explanation we cannot expect. I understand from Sir James—who rode out here yesterday to impart the news of Hemming's confession—that he will offer no reason for his violence or its result."

"I suppose," I said tentatively, "that if the person truly responsible were forced to acknowledge his guilt, Mr. Hemming would regard himself as released from silence; but any declaration *then* on his part should no longer seem useful."

Charles Danforth clasped his hands uneasily on his knee. "My father and his second wife died in a carriage accident, Miss Austen, when I was but eighteen years of age, and intending Cambridge. It was Hemming who travelled to London to inform me of the tragedy himself, Hemming who comforted me in my first paroxysm of grief. For months thereafter, when I was a lost and frightened boy, it was Hemming who served as guide through a world of care I had not hoped to assume for decades together. I should be a very different man but for his influence; I have reason to regard him with affection all my life. If I can in any measure serve as friend in his present turmoil, then I shall. I owe him that much."

"Charles!" cried the Countess of Bessborough, approaching with a glow of animation, "you must save us all from the most dreadful ennui, and partner me at the whist table! I cannot drag Granville away from the charms of Lord Harold's conversation."

Mr. Danforth rose with good grace, nodded unsmilingly to me, and went immediately to Lady Bessborough's side; and I did not speak to him for the remainder of the evening. But his words—the force of his expressions, and the manner in which he uttered them—lay powerfully in my mind. He had formed a desperate resolution, I should judge, and required only the opportunity to act.

His Grace preferred, when sitting down to cards, to play at faro—a game whose sole purpose may be described as the loss of as much of one's purse as one is willing to wager. It is a game played by two people alone, one of them serving as dealer and bank; Lady Elizabeth Foster served in this capacity for the Duke, sitting opposite him at the green baize table and turning over cards very prettily with her thin white hands. The Morpeths sat down to whist, and claimed Lady Bessborough for a third; her partner was the dutiful Charles Danforth. Lord Harold was engrossed in conversation with Granville Leveson-Gower; and that left Lady Harriot, the Countess of Swithin, Andrew Danforth, and myself at leisure.

"Well, Hary-O, and how shall we mark so signal an occasion? Should you like to play at *vingt-et-un*, macao, or loo?" Danforth enquired in a cavalier tone. "Though my brother has callously revealed that my pockets are entirely to let, I shall wager my pitiful pence in honour of your native day."

"Do not beggar yourself on my account, I beg. I am sure that I am sick of cards. Losses at the *tapis-vert* reduced my mother to a walking shadow. I should much rather amuse myself with music than anything."

"Then pray let us open the instrument!" Danforth cried. "I do not think, Miss Austen, that you have seen the music room as yet, but it may justly be described as one of Chatsworth's glories; though nothing in the room is so much an ornament as she who is accustomed to play there."

Lady Harriot looked archly, and slipped her arm through Desdemona's. "My father cannot bear the sound of the pianoforte when he is at cards, Miss Austen, so I am afraid we must hurry ourselves away. Do you play?"

"A little." I had not touched an instrument in months, however; though I had hired one for my use in Bath, it was an indifferent article. "I should dearly love to hear a true proficient."

"I cannot claim to be so much—and dear Mona is always flying about, she cannot sit still for the length of a concerto! But Mr. Danforth sings. Perhaps we may attempt a duet."

The gentleman bowed; and without further ado we followed Lady Harriot from the grand salon into the music room at Chatsworth.

It was an excessively elegant chamber—the sort of place that should be reserved for public concerts, with its draperies of gold, its little French chairs, its massive harp and violins in cases. The pianoforte to which Hary-O turned was of rosewood, beautifully inlaid—and but one of the instruments displayed in the room.

"A present from my father," she observed, "sent down from London only three days ago. Though he can be said to possess not the slightest interest in music, he is still capable of spending ridiculous sums. I have not yet grown accustomed to the keys."

She sat down at the instrument and trilled her fingers over the ivories. It was the first occasion on which I had chanced to remark her hands: long, thin, speaking fingers, expressive of all the fire and passion in her soul. *These* should never be tanned from neglect of a glove, nor coarsened by exposure to a scullery; they were hands designed for the fluttering of a fan or a pen, for the wearing of precious jewels, for the offering of a caress. Hands that might hold in a phaeton's team or curb a wild horse as well—for there was strength unsuspected in their lines.

"I await your command," she said with an eye for Andrew Danforth.

"Would that those words were true," he murmured caressingly.

"That depends upon the construction one chooses," Desdemona said briskly. "I would wish you to sing airs in the Italian; if you *must* descend into sentiment before us all, Mr. Danforth, you had much better do so unintelligibly."

It occurred to me that the Countess—though preserving her manners with the grace that was second nature—did not approve of her friend's suitor.

Mr. Danforth did not choose to remark her dislike; he obligingly turned over some sheets of music, and settled them before the fair performer; she commenced to play, with an infinitely superior taste than I should ever manage. Her voice was a little less equal to her fingering; but Mr. Danforth's being strong and rich, the effect was charming. I resolved at once to cede all display to Lady Harriot, and heard her with pleasure.

Two songs were thus suffered to fall away, in rapt attention from myself and Desdemona, when an interval occurred in which Mr. Danforth must find a particular song—one he had attempted before in Lady Harriot's hearing—one he would not be satisfied without attempting again—and the lady's fingers fell silent.

"He will be searching out a tender embarrassment," Desdemona confided in a lowered tone, "and I declare I shall be sick. A diversion, I think, is necessary." And raising her voice slightly she said, "I make it the third night this week, Hary-O, that Hart has disappeared without a word. Perhaps he is gone a-trysting, and is ashamed to acknowledge it! We may declare that the result of Mr. Danforth's example."

"I suspect that young Hart is poaching," Danforth declared from his place among the sheet-music; "it is the preferred entanglement of every country youth. He will be presently crouching in the under-brush of the Vernon grounds, in the company of a most disgraceful companion, intent upon the snaring of a brace of rabbits."

"Is it quite safe for such a young fellow to be abroad, when murder has been done?" I enquired, with an air of idle curiosity. "But perhaps he confines himself to the park, and writes poetry in the Grotto."

"Poetry! Hart?" Lady Harriot managed an expression of unaffected amusement; it softened the unyielding structure of her face, and made her appear suddenly more amiable. "It is meaning no disrespect to say that poor Hart is possessed of a tin ear. It is much to elicit two words from him, indeed; but on paper, he is an utter blank!"

"How very sad!" Desdemona cried. "It has been my experience that those young men who cannot pronounce a word, are the most eloquent hands at a love letter! Your easy and arrogant fellows, who may spout off an entire volume, have no time to waste in putting words to paper. I do not think I possess a single *billet-doux* in Swithin's fist, however ardent his vows by moonlight."

"Whoever murdered poor Tess is unlikely to concern himself with the heir to a dukedom," Danforth added, for my ears. "The Marquess must enjoy such protection, by virtue of his birth and his manhood, as a stillroom maid could never know."

"I will confess that I worry about Hart," Lady Harriot murmured. Her long fingers spasmed slightly where they sat idle in her lap; she clutched them together, ever the mistress of control. "When I learned that murder had been done so recently as Monday night, my thoughts flew immediately to my brother. He was abroad until dawn."

I stared at Lady Harriot, my breath suspended. Surely she must apprehend the cruel force of such a speech?

"He should *not* be allowed to wander alone," she went on, in a fretful tone. "It would never have been permitted in my mother's time. He should be forced to keep a groom at his heels—"

"I cannot think that Hart would thank you for your concern," Danforth told her lightly. "No lad of fifteen wishes to be followed by a nursemaid."

"If Lord Hartington *was* abroad on Monday night, how thankful you must have been to discover him safe—when first you learned of Tess Arnold's death," I added. "In so vast a house as this, I imagine it must be possible for a legion to come and go unnoticed."

"I should never know if Hart had found his bed or slept in the stables," Lady Harriot confirmed. "Fifteen is such a trying age! I will not scruple to admit that the boy has run completely wild this summer, Miss Austen."

"Perhaps when he has got over the worst of his grief," I suggested delicately, "you may observe a change. Perhaps if he were sent away to school—"

"Now *that* is a remedy I cannot hear of, without the most strenuous objection in the world," Andrew Danforth declared with heat. "Whoever first conceived of an exile among schoolboys, far from the comforts of all that is familiar, as a remedy for grief, can never have known what beasts young boys may be."

"You speak with all the force of experience, Mr. Danforth."

"I do. My brother, Charles, saw fit to send me to Winchester, when my parents died; and it was many years before I could forgive his interference."

"And yet," I persisted, "a man must receive an education."

"But why he must be educated at so great a distance from his home—alien to everything that must have a claim on his heart—is something I will never understand," he replied, with less of anger than he had previously shown. "When I reflect that a woman may be schooled in her own attics, by the comfort of a fire, at the hands of domestics she has known all her life—I might almost exchange my Hessians for stays, Miss Austen!"

We all laughed; but Mona could not allow the argument to rest in Danforth's hands. "It will not do, Mr. Danforth—you know that it will not do. The chief purpose in attending a school such as you describe, is not to be found in the Latin or Greek that is beaten into your head; but in the acquaintance one forms and the relations of friendship or reliance that may extend a lifetime. Hart must certainly benefit from *these*."

"Tell me, Mr. Danforth," I enquired, "did you regret your exile to Winchester so deeply, once you had been there the length of a term?"

"I hated it without qualification or exception for the whole three months I endured," he retorted. "Had poor old Hemming not appeared as my saviour, I should hate it still."

"Hemming?—Not Mr. George Hemming?"

"Naturally. Whom else should I mean? It was always Hemming Charles employed whenever anything distasteful had to be faced; and rather than come in search of me himself, and answer to the Headmaster, he sent his solicitor in his stead."

"I see." His solicitor, it would seem, was yet serving in that capacity; and having faced a Headmaster of Winchester, and stood his ground, perhaps George Hemming could find nothing very awful in the gallows after all.

"But I was forgetting," Danforth continued. "You are a little acquainted with Mr. Hemming, I think, Miss Austen."

"I was in his company on the day I found Tess Arnold," I told him starkly, "and still cannot credit that Mr. Hemming is languishing in Bakewell gaol, on a charge of murder."

"Not because of the maid?" Lady Harriot cried. Her isolation within the grounds of Chatsworth, it seemed, had extended so far as a complete ignorance of events that had animated all Derbyshire. "But why should he have done her any harm?"

"Even now, I cannot support the idea," Danforth said. "It is in every respect impossible."

"Because Mr. Hemming has been your saviour?" enquired Desdemona with interest, "or because you regard his character as incapable of violence? I merely ask as a student of human nature, and one who has witnessed murder done before. In this, you may observe the foundation of my friendship for Miss Austen."

"When the maid's body was first discovered, and believed to be that of a young gentleman," I said, "George Hemming was astonished to find a corpse above Miller's Dale. On this basis alone I do not believe him when he claims to have shot Tess Arnold; and I shall never be convinced of his having mutilated her body."

"My father has invited Mr. Hemming to dine in our company some once or twice," Lady Harriot said. "He seemed an amiable and decent fellow. But I cannot profess to know him well; and how may any of us claim to know of what another is capable? I should not admit such knowledge of my dearest relations. Indeed, if my family is to serve as example—then we may safely state that each of us is capable of the greatest good, and the deepest harm, in the world."

"Hemming sustained me through a most difficult period," Danforth said with diffidence. "He has been a steady friend to all my family. But I cannot profess to know his conscience. I cannot profess to know my own, if it comes to that."

"This is serious speaking, indeed!" Lady Swithin cried, with a satiric look for Lady Harriot; "if you may command half so much eloquence on behalf of slavery or taxation, Mr. Danforth, your success in Parliament is assured! But perhaps we cannot hope for so much. It is rare for our English gentleman to summon much love for matters of finance."

"What reason do you find for Mr. Hemming to have murdered the maid?" I asked.

He shook his head with a fine expression of distaste. "I wonder that they were even acquainted! I am as amazed as all of Bakewell, Miss Austen."

"And this is how steadiness is repaid!" observed Lady Swithin tartly. "If ever I stand in need of stout defence, Mr. Danforth, pray remind me not to look for it from your quarter."

"I shall be only too happy to speak to Hemming's excellent character at the Derby Assizes," Danforth returned. "Unless it be that he enters a plea of guilt. That is certainly the course that Sir James believes he will adopt, for I have spoken with the Justice regarding the case. He has never seen a man so determined, he says, to assume responsibility for his crime. Hemming appears to having nothing further in view, than a swift judgement."

Lady Harriot heaved a troubled sigh. "How dreadful, to have your good opinion of the man entirely overthrown! It is wretched, indeed, to feel that all one's ideas of childhood—the happy innocence of one's earliest associations—must be destroyed with age! The more I know of the world, the less I am pleased with it. There are few people I really love; and even fewer of whom I think well."

"That is because you are formed for discernment," Andrew Danforth told her gently. "You are made of such unblemished gold yourself, that all the rest of the world must appear as base, and tarnished."

Lady Harriot closed her instrument with a gesture of impatience. "Pray do not toad-eat me this evening, Andrew! I have not the temper for it."

"He is merely practising, Hary-O, for his career in politics." Lady Swithin made this observation with amusement. "You must know, Mr. Danforth, that the road to greatness is paved with seduction. You must endeavour to be the toast of all the great ladies in the Whig establishment, for it is they who wield the true power! Their husbands merely effect it."

The Countess's tone was lighthearted; but I detected something of her uncle's irony in its depths. The easy expression on Desdemona's face must belie the cutting edge to her words. She was a subtle creature—a playful and charming girl, whose manners had always been captivating. But she was nonetheless a Trowbridge. And I saw, with an inner exulting, that she did not intend her friend Lady Harriot to throw herself away. However desperate the case of the Duke's daughter—however miserable she might find herself in the prison of her home—Lady Swithin should ensure that she made a brilliant match. And Andrew Danforth was too ambitious—too insinuating in his ways—and too duplicitous for Mona's taste.

He flushed under the silken lash of her words. "A head that is turned by mere flattery cannot be made for Influence. Allow me to believe, Countess, that your long familiarity with the Great has misled you—it has jaded you to bitterness. I may hope that when Lady Harriot comes into her reign—when she is the queen of the *ton,* as her mother was before her—that she will not be swayed by hypocrites. We who wish for nothing but her happiness, cannot consign her to so miserable a fate."

"Hary-O may spot a hypocrite at thirty paces," agreed Mona with relish, "having learned to despise them from her birth. I daresay you have been fortunate, Mr. Danforth, in the ease of your Derbyshire conquests; but London-bred ladies may prove a difficult case."

"My Derbyshire conquests," he repeated, with an air of puzzlement. "I cannot think what you would mean."

Lady Harriot gathered her music with a petulant little slap, her countenance averted. "Let us have no more of this sparring, Mona. You both make my head ache."

"I believe you dropped this, Mr. Danforth, in your haste to lead Lady Harriot from the dining parlour." The Countess held out a small gold jeweller's case with an air of offering a beggar tuppence. "The lady who presented it should never wish you to leave it on the carpet, disregarded."

Mr. Danforth took the token from her and caressed it with his fingertips. "No," he said slowly, "I am sure she would not."

He snapped open the case and showed us what it held—a bit of ivory, two inches wide. The miniature of a lady, painted in watercolours.

"My late mother," he said simply, and snapped the case closed. He left the music room without another word.

Desdemona stared after him, for once bereft of speech. There was an expression of calculation on her countenance, however, very like to what I had observed in Lord Harold. It was probable that the Countess of Swithin suspected her uncle's attachment to her friend; and with the best heart in the world, would further his suit. Whatever knowledge he possessed of Andrew Danforth, Mona probably comprehended as well.

Except, it would seem, the most intriguing fact of all. That intelligence belonged to me alone. For I knew, now, why George Hemming languished in the Bakewell gaol. The lady in Danforth's portrait—with her golden hair, her high cheekbones, and her slanting eyes of green—was the selfsame one he kept close to his heart, the miniature let slip on the night of his confession. I had thought then that the portrait was his wife's. I was wrong.

A Remedy for Inward Bruises

*B*oil half an ounce of ivy leaves and half an ounce of plantain in three pints of spring water, until it has boiled away to four cups. Then add an ounce of white sugar. The patient is to take a cup three times each day, warmed. It is very restringent, and will stop inward bleedings.

—From the Stillroom Book of Tess Arnold
Penfolds Hall, Derbyshire, 1802–1806

Chapter 24

Motives for Murder

I DID NOT FIND MY OWN BED UNTIL NEARLY THREE O'CLOCK IN THE morning. Lady Harriot would have had me stay the night at Chatsworth, but I declined the honour most vociferously—being little disposed to tarry too long in Paradise, lest it make me ill-suited to my usual realm. Besides, I had brought no change of clothing, and could not appear at the breakfast table in evening dress.

His Grace the Duke was so kind as to send me back into Bakewell behind his own horses, the moonlight being strong enough to permit of driving, even at so advanced an hour. Dawson the coachman having been summoned from his bed, he vented his grievance in pounding soundly at the broad front door of The Rutland Arms. Stumbling and weary, I mounted the stairs behind the candle of the unprotesting Mr. Davies—who must be said to possess experience of Dukes and their shocking hours. I do not think I was suffered even to dream.

But I awoke with a start at seven o'clock, as though the presence of a stranger in the room had unnerved me. All was still; only birdsong and sunlight crept through the window-curtains. Without hesitation I reached under my pillow for the stillroom book of Tess Arnold, and began to read where I had left off Friday evening.

23 January 1806. Met LH above Miller's Dale.

LH: Lord Hartington? Lady Harriot? Or—Lord Harold Trowbridge? The appearance of no one among Tess Arnold's patients should surprise me now. I suspected, however, that LH signified one person only; and though Tess offered no hint of what she had supplied or charged for her services, there was reason for secrecy in their meetings.

1 February 1806. LH with tutor. Saw one hour above Miller's Dale.

Of course the boy possessed a tutor, one who might go with him from London to Derbyshire and back again; one more suited to the instruction of a pupil with impaired hearing, than a host of Eton masters should be. I did not need Andrew Danforth's indignation to fear Lord Hartington's fate among schoolboys; they should despise him for his awkwardness, and taunt him cruelly for infirmity. But what a lonely life the Marquess seemed to have led! No small matter, then, the attentions of a worldly young woman; and well worth a winter ride to the heights of Miller's Dale.

14 February 1806. Ten draughts against the Gravel to Lady Elizabeth, of burdock root, vitriolated Tartar, and syrup of Marshmallows, five shillings. Also one for liverish complaints, of celandine, turmeric, madder, and bruised woodlice, to which added, twenty-five drops morphia from Michael Tivey, one guinea.

Bruised woodlice? I shuddered. Lady Elizabeth appeared to have suffered from a variety of ailments, and to have dosed herself most liberally; there were further entries for the liverish concoction, each with increasing amounts of morphia. I had not thought she should have found occasion to visit Chatsworth during the London Season; but in fact I knew very little of her movements.

27 February 1806. Master John seized with vomiting and a bloody flux. Mistress hysterick. Administered salt of wormwood in lemon juice to the child, with hartshorn and diascordium against

the stools; to the Mistress, asafetida in rue-water. Urged Dr. Bascomb be called.

3 March 1806. Master John wasting in fever. Dr. Bascomb bled
him to reduce the heat of the blood. I applied the leeches.

5 March 1806. John d'Arcy Danforth, aged two years, five months,
and nineteen days, died this morning of a malignant fever.

14 March 1806. To Lady Elizabeth, by post, Tincture of Bitter Almonds in Juniper Water, one shilling.

By post. The malingering Bess had not, then, been in residence at
Chatsworth. No mention of what use might be found for Tincture of
Bitter Almonds.

28 March 1806. Mistress thrown this morning into early labour,
several weeks before she expected. Placed Tansy steeped in Sack in
cloth bag against the navel, and gave posset of milk and Oil of
Sweet Almonds. As Master was absent on business in London, askt
Mrs. Haskell to send to Buxton for Dr. Bascomb. Doctor came, and
at eight o'clock in the evening, Mistress brought to bed of a dead
child. Gave Mistress bruised millipede in white wine against sore
breasts, and Hartshorn water against histericks.

How sick Lydia Danforth must have been, of these useless
draughts for ills no human hand could cure! How desolate that last,
and most dreadful, lying-in, with her faint hopes of happiness staring
sightless from the eyes of a stillborn babe!
There was a further episode in the Danforth tragedy; and I found
it not long thereafter.

8 April 1806. Mistress taken today with malignant fever. Gave
powder of Bark and Virginian Snakeroot in strong cinnamon
water. Dr. Bascomb called, and bled her.

10 April 1806. At a quarter past one o'clock this morning, Mistress taken to God. Mr. Charles has shut himself up in his room and sees no one.

There were entries enough after this—Tess Arnold's careful hand ran all the way up to the twenty-second of August, when she had applied a poultice of elder-berries against a scullery-maid's burn; but none of them afforded me so much interest. It was singular, I reflected, that Andrew Danforth had suffered not the slightest indisposition in nearly four years of record-keeping; and Charles Danforth had been ill only once. The entry that referred to him was the very last one contained in the stillroom book.

23 August 1806. Master seized with vomiting after dinner. Offered red surfeit water but he would have none of it.

Charles Danforth had refused the maid's physick; and Charles Danforth was still alive.

I sat upright in bed for close to an hour, while the light and bird-song of morning strengthened beyond my window, and considered of the nature of the Danforth ailments. Of Lady Elizabeth's peculiar combination of liverish complaints and blocked menses. Of Lord Hartington's loves and Lord Hartington's silent rages.

I thought of Michael Tivey, and how useful a friend he had proved; I thought of the lies Tess Arnold had told her sister, of Freemasons and sacrifice in the hills above Miller's Dale.

Lastly I considered of George Hemming. There was but one reason I could think of for his perilous course towards judgement and execution—for if Tess Arnold had blackmailed the solicitor, she had taken his secret to the grave. The stillroom book betrayed not the slightest hint of the reasons for his shame and misery. But I thought I could conceive of explanation enough.

I closed the quarto volume at last and set it carefully to one side. Then I got up and went in search of paper and a pen. Before I might dress for Sunday service—before I might do up my hair, or petition Mr. Davies for hot tea—there was a letter to be drafted to Dr. Bascomb of Buxton. The innkeeper must certainly know the physician's direction; and Sunday or no, I would have the answers I required.

"YOU WILL BE SURE TO OBSERVE THE TOMBS IN THE VERNON CHAPEL, Jane," observed my cousin Mr. Cooper as we toiled up the hill to All Saints Church.

The day was cloudy and promised rain; the first cool breeze of autumn fingered the leaves overhead. Services were at ten o'clock, and all of Bakewell seemed bent upon the old Norman edifice—all except those who inhabited the great estates. Chatsworth House boasted its own chapel, where the family attended each Sunday; services were held as well in the little village of Edensor, that the fourth Duke had seen fit to demolish and reassemble at a convenient remove. I understood from Lord Harold that it had been Georgiana Duchess's practise to visit both chapels each Sunday, as an example to the estate's dependants—a fact that had recommended that lady to my good opinion more than anything I had yet heard of her. It was a custom I could imagine Lady Harriot continuing; she was the sort to understand the power of example, as Lady Elizabeth never should.

"Did you enjoy your evening at Chatsworth, Jane?" Cassandra enquired.

"Very much," I replied, feeling again the rush of guilt at my own selfish joys. "Your grey silk was much admired."

"I cannot suppose it was anything out of the ordinary way, in such a company—but for the fact that *you* were wearing it," she said simply. "I am glad to know it did not disgrace you."

"Not at all!"

"And . . . did Lord *Harold* admire it, Jane?"

I shrugged a little, as though it could not matter to me if he did. "You have been indulging our mother's fond hopes, Cassandra. Or should I say, *fears?* Lord Harold is not in the way of admiring me— unless it be for the keenness of my understanding."

"You have been acquainted now a number of years," my sister observed in a lowered tone, "and neither of you has married. He disappears for months at a time—and then, when chance throws you in his way, renews his attentions. I cannot think that such behaviour is suggestive of true ardour—"

"No, indeed!"

"—but any woman should consider it most marked."

Any woman, but one who had observed how he looked at Lady Harriot Cavendish. Could I have seen even half so much passion in Lord Harold for myself, I should have ordered my wedding-clothes long ago.

There was a moment, last evening—when the whist tables had just broken up, and the ladies were strolling idly about the room, and the gentlemen were lost in conversation with their boots propped up on the hearth-fender—a moment just before the cold supper was laid out at midnight—when Andrew Danforth bent his golden head over Lady Harriot's fiery one, and drew her with him out onto the darkened terrace. No one should dare to follow them there; but I observed the eyes of more than one person in the room stray most speculatively towards the French windows.

Charles Danforth stood correctly with Lord and Lady Morpeth by the drawing-room's far wall—a strained smile upon his face while they talked insensibly of their *children*. Granville Leveson-Gower maintained the liveliest conversation with His Grace the Duke, regarding the foibles of a common acquaintance—but so arranged himself that his gaze was fixed upon that open French door. The Countess of Bessborough, his avowed love, watched Leveson-Gower most narrowly over the head of a talkative Lady Elizabeth, whom I am sure she had not the slightest trouble disregarding. They were all alive to the possibilities inherent in moonlight and passion. But Lord Harold—

Lord Harold approached no one, Lord Harold said not a word. He resolutely ignored the balcony scene played out for the party's amusement, and poured himself a glass of Port. As he stood sipping at it speculatively, his eyes rose to meet mine. I do not think there was another person in the room—besides myself—so much in the grip of agony at that moment; no other person who failed to seek relief in converse with another. His grey eyes were blank; even to myself they disclosed nothing; but one muscle of his jaw commenced to twitch.

And then Hary-O walked swiftly back through the doorway, her face flushed and her eyes alight.

"I have had a little too much of happiness tonight, and must own that I am dreadfully tired," she told the room in general. "I would beg you all to forgive and excuse me, when I would retire. No one ever had such a family, or such friends; and I thank God that I have lived so many years among you, and pray that I may witness as many more. God bless you all—and good night!"

Then she swept away, not as a little girl over-excited by a party; but as a young and powerful woman will cede the stage, secure in the knowledge that it is hers for the asking whenever she should wish to tread its boards again. I could read nothing in her face of Andrew Danforth's fate—nothing of whether she had accepted what must surely have been an offer for her hand, or slapped him for presumption. The gentleman in question merely took up a position by his elder brother without a word. And in Andrew Danforth's countenance? Only the unvaried charm, the perpetual softness that must weary with time.

Lord Harold's looks were as fixed as stone. He set down his empty glass, and devoted himself to my amusement for the half-hour remaining before my carriage was called; but in all his remarks I detected an absence of mind, as though he played a role long familiar from habit, a role that demanded nothing. His thoughts and his heart were moving through the upper halls, clutched in Hary-O's elegant hands; they drew off her silk dress in the company of her maid, they brushed her red-gold hair in the candlelight. They stood with her in the darkened chamber, when her maid had long since gone away, and stared out once more at the moonlight that silvered the lawns of Chatsworth; and when she cried for the mother who had not lived to see her twenty-first birthday—they kissed her tears away.

"—nine children," my mother was saying, "including an infant in swaddling clothes, who is possessed of the most malicious countenance in the world. I must suppose him to have died of colic."

"Of what are you speaking, madam?" I enquired with effort.

"Of the tombs your cousin refers to, Jane, along the south wall of the church. They memorialise Sir George Manners and his wife, along with their nine children. But as they died in Elizabeth's time, or thereabouts, I cannot find it very tragic. *Everyone* died in that period, you know."

"And sooner rather than later," I murmured. "Mr. Cooper—"

My cousin mopped his reddened brow with a square of lawn. "Yes, Jane?"

"Did your excellent wife disclose in her letter the reason for her apothecary's abhorrence of black cherry water?"

"She did not. But I suspect Mr. Greene to possess a very natural distaste for the interference of females—and the strength of mind to declare it. Were the general run of gentlemen so forthright, the general run of ladies might appear to greater advantage: their conduct seemly, their ambitions modest." Mr. Cooper eyed me with disfavour. I was not to be forgiven my insertion in the affairs of his friend, Mr. Hemming, it seemed, nor absolved of culpability for the disaster that had followed.

We had achieved the threshold of All Saints. I sent a prayer Heavenwards for all the babes who are fated to die too soon, and stepped into the dimness peculiar to God.

Red Surfeit Water

*C*lean half a bushel of fresh-cut red poppies, and put them into three gallons of fine French brandy. Cover the pan and let them stand two days and two nights steeping, then strain off the liquor.

Put into this liquor two pounds of thinly-sliced figs, two pounds of prunes, four ounces of fresh licorice root pared and pounded flat, three ounces of aniseed beaten small, and half a pound of brown sugar candy. Stir well together and set in the sun for six days, then strain off the liquor, and bottle it up for use.

This is a very rich tincture of Poppies. A glass of it drunk at any time is conducive to health, particularly when a person fears a cold, or suffers an oppression of the stomach. It will also throw out the Measles, or Small Pox, or any other scrofulous marks, with small doses oft repeated.

—From the Stillroom Book of Tess Arnold,
Penfolds Hall, Derbyshire, 1802–1806

Chapter 25

Playing Truant with Purpose

WE DINED EARLY AND HEAVILY AFTER THE SERVICE, THOUGH I POS-
sessed little appetite. Mr. Davies, the landlord, sent a message by Sally,
among the covered dishes and the rolls, to inform me that my urgent
letter to Dr. Bascomb had been carried into Buxton. I could expect
an answer during the course of the day, did the messenger discover
the physician to be at home; or at the very latest, that evening. I
hoped that Bascomb was the sort of gentleman to take an unknown
lady's anxiety to heart, rather than to disregard it as the product of
an over-active mind; I should know, I reasoned, from the form of
his reply.

The dishes had not been very long cleared away, and the Bakewell
clocks were tolling the hour of one, when the noise of a carriage
in the street below drew me to the window. I peered out—saw the
Devonshire livery—exclaimed aloud at the thought of its being possible that Lady Harriot should drive into Bakewell—and was in time
to observe a black silk hat emerge from the crane-necked coach.
Lord Harold Trowbridge. This should be fuel for my sister's speculation, did she require anything further.

"Visiting on *Sunday?*" enquired my cousin Mr. Cooper, in a voice of signal disdain. He had not yet learned to forgive Lord Harold's biting remarks as to hymns, though he should never be so absurd as to demand satisfaction.

"It must be something particular that brings him here," Cassandra said. "It cannot be a social call. Should you like us to walk out into the town, Jane, while he speaks to you?"

"I do not expect a declaration, Cassandra—I think I may meet him with equanimity, and in the company of my whole family."

She took up her needlework and said nothing more; but my mother was not so easily satisfied.

"Lord, Jane—and you would put off your new gown after church," she exclaimed in dismay. "How you expect to see that man in a turned muslin, three years behind the fashion and faded with washing, I cannot think. You should not have purchased those ten yards of pink stuff so cheaply; pink never became you as it does your sister, and if I had been consulted, I should have advised most strenuously against it. A lady with a reddened complexion cannot support the colour."

"But being at present so grossly tanned," I returned with some complaisance, "I cannot be anxious on that account. Provided I am decently clothed and tidy, it cannot matter to Lord Harold what I wear."

A knock upon the parlour door forestalled her reply; the door swung open, and revealed the Gentleman Rogue himself, with an expression of haste and concern upon his countenance.

"How very kind of you to pay a call, Lord Harold!" my mother cried. "I am afraid, however, that we were all of us just walking out. Were we not, Mr. Cooper? To visit your friend, Mr. Hemming, at the gaol? I cannot consider it a pleasant duty, but one very well suited to a Sunday morning, provided one has first partaken of a hearty meal. Come along, Cassandra! Fetch your bonnet!"

"My bonnet?" Cassandra repeated, as one dazed by events.

"Naturally! Would you grow as tanned as your sister? I have no hope for Jane—her skin is become so coarse and brown—but I will not have your complexion ruined. Make haste, my love!"

Cassandra stared at me beseechingly; I raised an impervious brow; and so the offending headgear was retrieved from her chamber.

"Do not hurry yourself away, my lord, on our account. I am sure that Jane will be vastly happy to oblige you with a little conversation— or perhaps some of Mr. Davies' beer." And with the most deferential air, my mother nodded and smiled her way out of the room, one hand gripped fiercely on Mr. Cooper, and the other on my sister.

"A formidable will animates that woman," his lordship observed, "however much she would affect a decline. Having learned to know her a little better, I perceive the wellspring of your own resolve, Jane."

"How may I account for the honour of seeing you here, my lord?"

"I bear tidings, Jane, that I would not have you know of any other."

My heart sank at his sombre aspect. "Lady Harriot is to marry Andrew Danforth, then?"

Lord Harold stared. "Good God, no! It has always been Charles she admired. Although I suspect there is more of pity, and less of love, in her affections than she understands. But to marry Andrew— how could you conceive of such an idea?"

"Last evening, it appeared that he petitioned for her hand—when he led Lady Harriot out onto the balcony, just before she retired."

"I am sure that he did," Lord Harold replied with thinly veiled contempt. "He is always dogging the girl's footsteps—enquiring whether he may have cause to hope, whenever she affords him a spare moment! He has requested the honour of her hand in the Orangery, and in the stableyard, after a morning's ride; he has popped the question around the potted plants, and while taking her into dinner. To my certain knowledge, Jane, this is the second application the gentleman has made this week—for on Monday evening, he tarried barely five minutes in the dining parlour after the ladies had retired, before excusing himself."

"Did he, indeed?" I cried, much struck.

"No doubt Hary-O refused the scrub on that occasion, too, as she has certainly refused him now. His Grace was quite put out at Danforth's desertion of the gentlemen; but his absence did not prevent the Duke from embarking upon a discussion of Fox's program, and the Whig strategy once Parliament sits, that any young fool with a heart for politics should never have missed. But I did not come to speak of that young cub's pretensions. I came to allay what fears I could."

"Fears?"

"From your expression, I perceive that you are as yet in ignorance of events that have animated all Chatsworth for the past several hours."

He spoke too gently, as though he would protect me from hurt. I thought of Lady Swithin and her unborn child—and in the fear of sudden death, sat down hard upon a vacant chair. "What has happened?"

"Lord Hartington has not yet returned home, and being absent now nearly a day, must be regarded with considerable suspense. His Grace's servants have stood watch for the better part of the night, in both the stables and the main house; but Hart has not appeared, and nothing is known of his intended direction."

"But I espied his lordship myself last evening," I cried, "above the Baslow road, not much past Manners Wood."

"So near the house as that." Lord Harold declined the offer of a chair; he had no intention of stopping very long. "I must inform the Duke. Such a direction had not entered into His Grace's calculations, it being expressly forbidden."

"Because the Duke did not wish Lord Hartington to ride towards Tideswell?"

"Exactly." He smiled at me faintly. "You overlistened my conversation with Lady Elizabeth last evening; I suspected as much."

"While his lordship was yet under my gaze, he spurred his mount to the west, and vanished into a fold of the landscape," I said quickly. "Moreover, I have learned from Tess Arnold's stillroom book that he was much in the habit of meeting her—in the rocks above Miller's Dale, where she was later murdered."

"That is unfortunate," Lord Harold muttered, "for Tideswell is some distance from the village of Hartington itself, whence His Grace directed the search party."

"Search party! The Marquess will not thank you for it. I understand he is much given to playing the truant. And knowing the country so well as he does—surely he can have come to no harm!"

"I should have said the same—until this morning, just after eight o'clock, when the boy's black horse limped into the yard. The beast bore bruised knees, and had obviously been down. Of Hart's fate, we remain in doubt."

"Dear God! I had no notion it was so bad as this! But what has been done—what is being attempted, to recover him?"

"A stable lad detected limestone in the horse's hooves, such as is prevalent upon the White Moor, not far from the village of Hartington. The Duke has organised a body of men to work over the ground."

I studied his lordship's countenance; he had held somewhat in reserve. "What is it that troubles you? What do you fail to say?"

He hesitated; then bowed his head in submission. "The limestone of the White Moor has long been quarried, Jane, for a legion of purposes. There are, as a result, any number of pits and eroded cliffs that might do mischief to a wandering lad—particularly if he were not entirely himself, and darkness were coming on. Melancholy—rage—even a guilty conscience, Jane—might drive Hart to recklessness."

"Are you suggesting, Lord Harold," I slowly replied, "that the Marquess of Hartington has done away with himself?"

Lord Harold's eyelids flickered, but he did not directly reply. "I know I may depend upon your discretion. Not a word of this has been uttered by the Duke or myself; but the thought hangs heavy in the air of the Great House. The Danforths have exchanged idleness for action at last, and are gone out on horseback; the Morpeths are disposed to be anxious, and talk overmuch; Lady Elizabeth is insensible to everything that does not directly affect her; but Hary-O is afraid, Jane. She knows Hart better than anyone in his family—and *Hary-O is afraid.*"

Lord Harold looked at me, all his feeling speaking in his face. "It is this that causes me to wonder *what* Lady Harriot fears—and just how much in Lord Hartington's confidence she has been."

"But surely, my lord, if she knew something that might assist in her brother's recovery—surely she would speak it without reserve!"

He turned away. "Such a thought is obvious to someone like yourself, Jane, who has never been schooled in any but the severest honesty. Deception—particularly the deceit of divided loyalty—is as foreign to you as French bread. But that is not Hary-O's case. She was raised in a house where the most simple exchange of daily pleasantries is fraught with several meanings, and where those she should naturally trust—her closest relations—have always formed a shifting alliance. Hary-O learned from birth to guard her soul, and display nothing like its true self to the world, lest it be trampled."

"You believe she is protecting the Marquess? —Against whom?"

"—the influence of Lady Elizabeth, perhaps—the violence of the Law—possibly she even protects him from *me*." Lord Harold paced towards the parlour window in an agony of frustration. "I am the truest friend that Hary-O possesses, Jane, but she will not trust me with her brother's life, if she fears him guilty of some horror. She learned the lesson of reserve from her mother—an open-hearted, laughing beauty of a woman who paid too deeply the price of innocence."

"Her Grace had better have taught her daughter to hold the world in contempt, than to purchase it at such a cost."

Lord Harold's head lashed swiftly around, and for the first time in my life, I glimpsed the full force of his power for love and hate. "Before you would judge Georgiana too harshly, Jane, know this: at seventeen she was a Duchess, a toast, and a beauty—and *wholly neglected* by her husband. Whatever occurred in her life from that point, must be laid entirely at Devonshire's account."

I was silenced.

Lord Harold drew breath; he reached for his gloves and hat; he drew on the former and settled the latter over his eye. Only then did he look at me.

"I shall end by driving my last friend away with my bitter tongue. Forgive me, Jane."

"That is something I should never presume to do, my lord. It might justly make you hate me."

He touched my chin with his gloved hand, and would have stepped out into the passage—but that I clutched at his wrist.

"Take me with you."

"You cannot expect to do anything in Hart's case."

I reached for the stillroom book and held it before his eyes. "But I know why his lordship exulted in the maid's death. If you would prove he did not kill her, we must ensnare her true murderer. Nothing else will end this folly of guilt and mutual suspicion."

For an instant he said nothing; then he took the book from my hands.

"Leave word for your mother where you are gone, Jane. And do not neglect of your sunbonnet. Having disappointed Mrs. Austen in so much else, I owe her this small gesture of attention."

A Wash for the Complexion

Grate a quantity of horseradish into sweet milk, and allow to stand for six or eight hours. Then apply to the skin with a clean linen rag, and rinse with clear spring water.

—From the Stillroom Book of Tess Arnold,
Penfolds Hall, Derbyshire, 1802–1806

Chapter 26

Death Among the Rocks

31 August 1806, cont.

~

BEING A GENTLEMAN OF SOME DESPATCH, LORD HAROLD UNDERTOOK to pen a note to His Grace at Chatsworth, informing the Duke of his intelligence regarding the Marquess, and instructing a party of men to turn their efforts towards Miller's Dale. He suffered the Duke to know that we should proceed thence ourselves, in an effort to locate Lord Hartington without delay; and that if the search were unavailing, we should await assistance in the miller's cottage.

"Now tell me all you know, Jane—or all you suspect," he commanded, when we were settled in the Devonshire equipage.

For this once, despite the heat of August, I must own I valued the discretion of a closed carriage; no one should overlisten my conversation with Lord Harold.

"Lord Hartington was acquainted with the stillroom maid," I said, "for nearly a twelvemonth. He first undertook to ride over to Penfolds Hall, in secret; and as Tess Arnold's notations are entirely concerned with remedies for deafness, I must imagine him to have been preoccupied with these."

"Deafness? But surely he is not so very troubled by the impairment to his hearing?" Lord Harold remarked.

"I suspect that few are privileged to know just how far the difficulty extends. A person such as Lord Hartington—the sole heir to a princely realm, with all the burdens of wealth and birth, all the expectations of Society placed upon him—cannot admit to infirmity. He must struggle against it from a boy; and disguise what he cannot help. From the little I observed him, I should say that he is an adept at the reading of speech. Though he cannot hear, he may often comprehend, provided the speaker's face is turned towards him."

"I see. And yet he was troubled enough by infirmity that he sought help from the stillroom maid."

"She makes no reference to the success or failure of her remedies; but certainly his lordship continued to seek them. Whether he eventually met with Tess Arnold from *other motives*, I cannot say; but I presume as much, from the place of the meeting having changed."

"He no longer rode to Penfolds?"

"Last winter, he began to meet his witch in the rocks above Miller's Dale. The meetings, from this date, grow less frequent—you will recollect that he was often from Derbyshire during that period, Her Grace the Duchess having been in Town for most of the winter."

"Georgiana fell ill there in March," Lord Harold said soberly. "Lord Hartington, I believe, was much by her side. He did not return to Derbyshire until she was interred at Chatsworth, in early April."

"He met with Tess infrequently during the course of the summer, and always in secret; though once, at least, he appears to have been accompanied by a tutor. Perhaps he could not throw that gentleman off."

"No tutor worth his pay would neglect the charge of his employer, nor the confidence of his pupil," Lord Harold observed. "We may consider the gentleman present, but sworn to silence. He is no longer in the Duke's employ, in any case, and may not speak against the Marquess. But I interrupt: you have obviously formed an idea of young Hartington's purpose. Was he dallying with the maid?"

"I do not believe so. It should be a chilly place for such a purpose, in the depths of January; and by the summer he had clearly learned to hate her. No, Lord Harold—I believe the Marquess required information. You will recollect that he must have observed his mother's decline."

"Georgiana? What can she have had to do with Tess Arnold?"

"Her Grace was being steadily dosed by the stillroom maid, for a variety of liverish complaints, from the late summer of last year up to her death."

Lord Harold's expression hardened. "That book tells you so much?"

"It records the frequent remedies sought by Lady Elizabeth, for a variety of ills she does not appear to have suffered. Lady Elizabeth would carry off the gravel, and her stomach was much indisposed; she required eyewash, and remedies for the liver—and once, it must be said, for a persistent cough. This, at least, we may impute to have been Lady Elizabeth's own. The rest I believe were purchased on behalf of Georgiana Duchess. The remedies contained an increasing quantity of morphia, such as must relieve the most acute suffering; and the oil of bitter almonds, which I believe is poisonous over time. It is possible her London physicians were unwilling to prescribe what must certainly kill her."

Lord Harold reflected upon this in silence. "Bess told me that Hart certainly blamed her for Georgiana's death."

"Whatever charge his mother laid upon her bosom friend— whatever Lady Elizabeth chose to take upon herself—should never have been meant for the boy's ears. But Lord Hartington's ears are not his only means of acquiring intelligence. I assume he observed an exchange between the two ladies that was not intended for him."

Lord Harold sighed heavily and passed a thin hand over his brow. "*I'd hoped the witch had died in agony.* Hart hated the girl, Tess Arnold, because he thought her remedies killed his mother. Is that what you would say, Jane?"

"I would go further, my lord. I believe that the Marquess suspects the maid and Lady Elizabeth between them of having colluded to *murder* his mother—so that Lady Elizabeth might be Duchess in Georgiana's stead."

"Impossible!" Lord Harold's eyes blazed darkly in his pallid face. "You may suspect poor Bess of every indelicacy—of a want of tact, and a self-absorption that may border on the criminal—but she was honestly devoted to Georgiana. Whatever remedies she purchased on Her Grace's behalf, were purchased at Georgiana's insistence. You may be assured of that."

"But I am not fifteen. I am not destroyed by the severest grief. I have not the spectre of illegitimacy to haunt me—I need never regard my father's despised mistress as being quite possibly my parent. I need never know the agony of being twice dispossessed: once, of the mother I adore; and yet again, of the certainty that I may rightly call her mother. When I consider the burdens under which Lord Hartington has laboured, I must find it surpassing odd that he has not done violence before—to himself, or another. Indeed, he has been an example of restraint."

Lord Harold stared. "You mean to say, Jane, that it was *not* Hart who savaged the girl's body among the rocks?"

"Not at all. That horror belongs entirely to another; for it was not the Marquess who summoned Tess from Penfolds Hall; he can have had no reason to look for her that night above Miller's Dale. You have not heard, my lord, of the robbing of graves, or the uses the maid found for a gentleman's clothing—but as we have time and road enough for a story, I will consent to tell you all."

IT WAS WELL AFTER THREE O'CLOCK WHEN WE REACHED THE VALLEY of the River Wye, and the splashing white of the miller's weir; all was peacefulness, as it had been nearly a week before, and I might almost have looked to find George Hemming's upright figure etched against the trees. But no one stood with rod and tackle—only the miller's wife, her hands perpetually twisting in her threadbare apron.

"He's not 'ere," she called from the doorway before we had even thought to step out of the carriage, "he've gone out Buxton way."

"Thank you, my good woman," Lord Harold replied. "We require only your consent to leave our coach under your eye. We intend to walk up into the hills. A party of men under the Duke of Devonshire's direction may presently appear; pray afford them every refreshment in your power, and conduct them towards that path above the weir."

He pointed in the direction I had taken now twice before, and the miller's wife closed her palm over Lord Harold's coin. As we turned away, however, I observed her to cross herself with averted eyes; here was one who would believe the stories of Satanic sacrifice.

We hurried along the path that rose towards the crags above the river, neither of us speaking for some time. Lord Harold cupped his hands to his lips, and called out the Marquess's name; at the sound of his harsh voice, birds rose out of the surrounding brush with a clatter of wings. The sound had the power to raise gooseflesh along my arm, and curl the hairs at the back of my neck; the urgency of disaster sped our footsteps. Though Lord Hartington might not be guilty of murder, he might yet have done himself violence from despair: I dreaded to think what we might find among the rocks above.

"Hart!"

Lord Harold paused at the brow of the last hill. The grey tor where I had found the maid's body rose jaggedly in the distance. He peered at it, eyes narrowed, and discerned the figure sprawled at its foot; and then, without a word, he began to run.

THE SCENE WAS THE SAME, AND YET NOT THE SAME, AS IT HAD BEEN five days before. I stood gasping at the foot of the tor, my gloved hand to my mouth, and stared at the figure dressed all in black, the welter of blood about the rocks. There was the mark of a lead ball in the forehead, and the staring eyes; but the birds had not yet descended. He clutched a fowling piece in one hand, and a scrap of paper in the other. But this time Charles Danforth's clothes were properly his own.

His brother knelt in the dust, hands covering his face, and wept with the horrible, tearing sound of a man unaccustomed to tears. A horse whinnied; I turned, and saw the two gentlemen's mounts tethered side by side under a tree some thirty yards distant. The same tree, I noted with half my mind, beneath which Lord Harold had found the marks of hoofprints on Friday.

"Good God," Lord Harold murmured. He bent to Andrew Danforth and gripped his shoulder firmly. "What has happened here?"

Danforth raised a streaming countenance and failed to utter a word. If he saw us clearly, I should be greatly surprised.

"Speak to me, man!"

He shook his head brokenly. "I was . . . over there. Towards Penfolds. In the copse." He drew a shuddering breath and mopped at his eyes with a glove. "Charles was before me. We had come out with the intention of looking for Hart. He suggested we traverse the ground separately, in order to cover the better part of the terrain—"

"Why here?" Lord Harold enquired sharply. "The Duke had no notion of sending you, surely."

"Charles said that he believed the Marquess was much in the habit of coming here. It was his idea to search the place. I heard the shot—I feared for Hart's life—I spurred my horse down the path and emerged to see—*this*."

We stared down at Charles Danforth. His dark eyes gazed sightlessly at the blue August sky; his mouth was slack. All the power for good or ill that had been etched in that countenance, was fled; only the pitiful shell of the man remained. Slowly, Lord Harold reached out and took the scrap of paper from the corpse's hand.

He read it aloud.

31 August 1806
Chatsworth

I, Charles Edgar Danforth of Penfolds Hall, do hereby testify that I am guilty of having killed the stillroom maid Tess Arnold on Monday night, the 25th of August 1806. I followed her into the hills above Tideswell with the intention of shooting her, because I was convinced that she had murdered my children and my wife. Her reasons for so doing I will not name, lest they embroil the innocent; but having lost all that held meaning for me in the whole world, I have no longing for anything but the grave. I am sorry for having caused unpleasantness for anyone; and hope, most sincerely, that Mr. George Hemming will find it in his heart to forgive me. A truer gentleman never lived.

Charles Edgar Danforth

A General Caution

In the use of these family cordials, we thought it proper to begin with a general account of their use, and the needful caution. Without such care, a book of Medicines may become a book of Poison. . . .

—Martha Bradley, The British Housewife, or Cook, Housekeeper's and Gardiner's Companion, 1756

Chapter 27

Dr. Bascomb of Buxton

31 August 1806, cont.

~

THE MARQUESS OF HARTINGTON, WHETHER HE WERE ABOVE MILLER'S
Dale or no, was no longer our object. Lord Harold sent Andrew Danforth at a run to the miller's cottage, where he found a party of men
despatched by the Duke of Devonshire. Danforth tarried only long
enough to send a message to His Grace, before urging the better part
of the search party back up into the hills. It was a sober company that
soon appeared, with a makeshift litter among them, to bear Charles
Danforth home.

He was placed on the litter, and his eyes closed; and then, with a
heave, six men lifted the body high upon their shoulders. Andrew
Danforth loosed his brother's horse, and led it in tandem with his own
behind the grim procession. They would walk thus, down the path
Tess Arnold had so often trod, towards Tideswell and Penfolds Hall.

I had remained in Lord Harold's company while the men were
summoned; but I did not wish to make another of the melancholy
group struggling through the fields. My heart was at present too full.
I turned to his lordship, who lingered only long enough to watch the
men out of sight, before hastening to the tree where the Danforth
mounts had been tethered. He studied the ground, nodded once,
and then made his way back to me.

"Do you wish to return to Bakewell this evening, Jane?"

"Not at all. Where do you intend to proceed, my lord?"

"To Penfolds! However indolent His Grace may appear in the general way—however consumed with worry for his son and heir—he remains Lord Lieutenant of the County. He will know exactly how to act. If I am not greatly mistaken, Sir James Villiers will presently make his way to the Hall; and I should wish to be on hand when he appears."

"Then I shall accompany you."

His lordship nodded distractedly. In his hand he still held the last words of Charles Danforth; he folded the piece of paper and tucked it inside his coat. "At the very least, I must be sure to give Sir James *this*. For it is certainly in Danforth's handwriting."

"Of course. He was a man to do a thing properly, if he would undertake it at all," I observed.

Lord Harold's gaze raked over me keenly; but he said nothing—and so we descended the hills above Miller's Dale for the last time in silence.

HALFWAY TO PENFOLDS, THE RAIN THAT HAD THREATENED ALL DAY burst in a great roar over our heads, so that the patient Devonshire horses, so long pressed into Lord Harold's service, were steaming with wet at our arrival. We found the great door thrown open, and a miscellany of carriages standing before it; more than one bore the crest of serpent and stag. Naturally, Lady Harriot would come at the first word of tragedy. Before the wheels of our own conveyance had ceased to turn, Lord Harold had thrust back the carriage door and alighted.

Mrs. Haskell stood grim-faced and silent in the front entry. Under the livid glare of the summer storm, the old stone of Penfolds closed in like a tomb. I shuddered, my eyes on the housekeeper's rigid form. She took his lordship's hat and stick without a word, and waited for me to untie my bonnet strings. "His Grace the Duke is in the parlour, my lord."

We followed a footman through one of the doors leading from the hall. A fire had just been lit in a massive hearth, against the chill of the sudden rain; the Duke stood with bent head, staring into the flames. In a chair drawn close to the fire sat Lady Harriot; the Countess of Swithin clasped her hand. I could detect no tears on Hary-O's face; her countenance was terrible in its self-possession. Andrew Danforth stood by the window, framed in the red folds of a velvet drapery; Sir James Villiers resplendent in a lavender waistcoat and buff pantaloons, had adopted a place on the sofa. The Justice appeared the most easy of the party. All five looked around as the footman threw open the door, and revealed us to their sight; and I discerned immediately that we were not the persons expected.

"Uncle! And Miss Austen!" Lady Swithin cried; she squeezed Hary-O's hand and came swiftly across to us. "Is everything not dreadful! I still cannot believe it possible of Charles!"

Lord Harold touched his niece's cheek; she gazed at him imploringly, as though even now he might be capable of restoring Charles Danforth to life. "Stay with Hary-O, Mona—there's a good girl."

The Countess nodded once and returned to her position by Lady Harriot's chair.

"Your Grace," Lord Harold said formally. "Any word of Lord Hartington?"

"Young fool stumbled home an hour since," the Duke of Devonshire muttered, "with some tale of poachers in the woods near Haddon Hall. Gun was fired—mount threw him—dashed his head against a rock. Slept off the worst and walked twelve miles back. Lucky he wasn't left for dead. Teach him to go hunting on another man's turf."

"That is excellent news," his lordship replied.

The Duke peered around at the assembled company. "Bess's with him now. Do the boy a world of good."

No one vouchsafed a reply.

The drawing-room doors were thrust wide again, and a stranger was admitted to our midst.

"Well, Bascomb?" Andrew Danforth enquired. "What is your opinion?"

"Life was extinct from the instant the ball was fired," the gentleman replied with a bow. "I cannot think that he suffered. The shot was certainly fired from the fowling piece."

"Are you Dr. Bascomb?" I cried. "Of Buxton?"

"The same. But I confess that you have the advantage of me, madam, for I do not recall our meeting."

"My name is Jane Austen. You are come into the neighbourhood at my summons, I think."

"Ah!" the doctor returned, with a look of quickened interest. "The very lady. I looked for you first at The Rutland Arms, and was told that you were thought to have gone to Chatsworth. No sooner did I arrive there, than the Duke informed me of the sad events above Miller's Dale. I have often served as physician to the Danforth family—as well you know; and so I availed myself of His Grace's kind invitation, and made another of the party. Did you chance, Miss Austen, to carry with you the interesting stillroom book?"

"I did. It is even now in the carriage. But you will wish, I think, to peruse the letter Charles Danforth left at his death."

Lord Harold reached for the paper he had thrust into his coat and handed it to Dr. Bascomb. The rest of the party were staring at us in obvious perplexity; Andrew Danforth abandoned his position by the window and came to stand near Hary-O's chair.

"Forgive me," I said hastily. "Your Grace, Mr. Danforth—I beg your pardon. I requested Dr. Bascomb's opinion regarding the Danforth children, and he has been so kind as to sacrifice his Sunday to my benefit. You will not protest, I hope, if he satisfies our curiosity?"

"Eh?" the Duke replied. "Oh—of course. Very well. Proceed, man—proceed."

Dr. Bascomb gazed keenly around the room. He nodded once, then adopted a position by the fire.

"I see from this letter," he began, holding it aloft, "that Charles Danforth suspected the nature of his children's deaths. Miss Austen has already discerned that I was in attendance upon little Emma, the eldest of the three; so much is noted in the stillroom maid's book. I was called, as well, when Lydia Danforth was thrown into labour two months before her time; but in that case, I could do nothing. At the Duke's insistence, a London doctor was called when Miss Julia fell ill in February; and though I looked in upon John d'Arcy in March, he was already too far gone for my physick to save him."

Lady Harriot's countenance twisted; she threw her face in her hands.

"I was troubled by what I observed in Emma's case. The child suffered a series of feverish attacks, each worsening in nature, over the course of a month; a slight indisposition became a gradual wasting; vomiting and violent purges ensued; and at the end, dehydration and death. In the intervals between these attacks, however, she appeared in complete health.

"Our Hary-O had a similar passage," the Duke observed, "and three nursemaids were dismissed on the strength of it, until Georgiana discovered the child surfeiting on sweetmeats in the pantry corner. Greedy little minx."

"It was possible that the girl suffered from the sort of wasting complaints that every childhood is prey to," Dr. Bascomb continued with a deferential bow. "I cannot number the young lives taken suddenly off, by a host of ills that plague every town in England. It is not even unusual for entire families to be lost. But in Emma's case I suspected poison—arsenical poisoning, to be exact. I confided my fears to Charles Danforth. He was greatly disturbed in his mind, as should only be natural; but to his wife, who suffered greatly from her daughter's death, he imparted nothing of my fears."

"Were you well acquainted with the late and lamented Lydia," said Andrew Danforth, "you would not question my brother's decision. His wife was excessively fearful for the health of her children."

"With cause," murmured Lady Harriot.

"Danforth undertook to search out any supplies of arsenic that might be lying about the Hall, and ordered them destroyed," Dr. Bascomb said. "The gardener's shed was the most obvious culprit, as arsenic is often employed in the control of rats and other vermin; but the gardener himself could not be suspected of malice towards any of the children. He had been first employed in old Mr. Danforth's time, and was a great favourite; his grandchildren, the Arnold girls, had grown up on the estate. I believe that Danforth was inclined to regard my words as fanciful—or worse, as the result of my unwillingness to accept responsibility for having lost the child. Mr. Danforth destroyed the poison he found, and ceased to consult or confide in me.

I heard nothing further of the Penfolds household, until word was received of the second daughter's death.

"It is significant, I think, that Charles Danforth was absent in London when Julia became ill. He was absent when John d'Arcy died suddenly, as well. The person responsible for their deaths made certain that she was unobserved by the one most likely to suspect her."

"Are you saying," Andrew Danforth broke in, "that you believe my brother's claim that poor Tess intended to murder his family? I must regard that accusation as nothing more than the delusion of a broken mind—a mind destroyed by the effects of grief and unaccountable misfortune. Surely the maid can have had no reason to wish my nieces and nephew dead?"

Dr. Bascomb made no reply. His gaze, however, drifted over the room and came to rest upon me.

"Tess Arnold did not kill the children with arsenic," I told Danforth, "but with a common solution that has been used for time out of mind in the administration of medicinal draughts to children. Black cherry water, Mr. Danforth—the distilled essence of cherry bark boiled in spring water. It has a palatable taste, and may disguise whatever is given to the patient; but I believe I am correct in thinking, Dr. Bascomb, that it has only lately been judged a poison in its own right?"

"Highly poisonous, Miss Austen. A single draught should be unremarkable, though vomiting might result; but when the application is repeated, and the doses increased, it is probable that the effect over time should be death."

"But Tess could have possessed no notion of the pernicious effect!" Danforth objected. "She learned her stillcraft at her mother's feet. Her remedies were the stuff of incantation, passed down through generations of healing women; she merely did as she had observed others to have done. If she killed Emma and Julia with the intention of healing them, surely we may absolve her of guilt!"

Dr. Bascomb merely lifted his shoulders. "I cannot profess to know the girl's mind," he said. "I only know that I had instructed her myself, most strenuously, never to give a draught in the common bitter waters to children. And yet, Miss Austen has found repeated references in the stillroom book to the employment of these very waters."

A silence settled over the room, broken only by the crackling of a log upon the fire.

"But why?"

Lady Harriot's deep and penetrating voice carried across the room. "Why kill those children Charles loved so well?"

I looked at Lord Harold and raised an enquiring brow.

"It is possible," he answered slowly, "that she did so at Charles's bidding."

"Ridiculous!" Andrew Danforth cried.

"Is it? He stood to inherit a fortune if his heirs predeceased his wife; and you will observe that they did. He was warned by Bascomb that the illnesses looked like poison; and so he contrived never to have Bascomb in attendance again. Two of his children died, moreover, when Charles was himself away—so that he might never be suspected of guilt, should questions arise. And finally, he silenced Tess Arnold—the only party to his crimes."

"He had no need of such a fortune," Lady Harriot protested. "Charles was a wealthy man!"

"But he may, my dear Hary-O, have felt desperately in need of *you*," Lord Harold said harshly, "and his wife and children stood in the way."

She drew a sharp breath; her beautiful eyes blazed. "That is an unpardonable thing to say."

Lord Harold inclined his head, but failed to apologise.

"I will never believe it!" Danforth exclaimed.

"Naturally you will not." I summoned courage for what must come. "For it was to *your* benefit that the children died, and not your brother's. Emma and Julia and little John d'Arcy—they stood between you and your inheritance, Mr. Danforth. And Tess Arnold had great ambition for you. Or should I say—for you *both*?"

Andrew Danforth went white. "Think well before you utter another word, Miss Austen, lest your speech disgrace you! A familiarity with Lord Harold may have taught you to forget what is due to civility; but a moment will suffice to recall it."

"The spectre of disgrace has no power over me, Mr. Danforth," I replied calmly. "Your brother's sacrifice has absolved us all. You will recall what he said in his final letter? *Her reasons for so doing I will not name, lest they embroil the innocent.* Charles Danforth suspected that Tess would murder his heirs and place *you* in his stead. In the interval provided after his wife's death, he had time enough for reflection; it was not the maid's habit to act precipitately. Tess had allowed months between the children's passing away. And so your brother was suffered to remain in health throughout the first part of the summer. And then, two days before the maid was killed, he endured a bout of vomiting himself."

"That was the day he despatched a letter to me," Dr. Bascomb explained, "and informed me that he had looked into the stillroom book. He described the remedies the maid had administered; he described the solution she gave at his wife's labour, well before I arrived. His wife, I did not scruple to advise him by return of post, should never have gone into labour, but for the draught against histericks that Tess administered when young John d'Arcy died. It contained a quantity of rye, in addition to its healing effects; rye that had spoiled from the action of ergot. It is the most powerful spur to labour that is known."

"Your brother knew, then, how his children had died," I told Andrew Danforth. "He knew that Tess Arnold was your friend of old; you had played together as children, when Charles was banished to the south. She should naturally have your interests at heart. He may even have observed the two of you meeting in an abandoned ice-house at the estate's extent, and wondered at the nature of your connexion."

"This is abominable," Danforth muttered between his teeth. "I would that Charles could hear you! What indignation you should arouse!"

"He never suspected, however, that Tess acted at your behest," I concluded softly. "Charles believed you innocent of the worst. And in that, Mr. Danforth, I fear your brother was a nobler soul than you yourself have proved."

"Are you suggesting—" Lady Harriot cried, in an accent of shock.

"—that Andrew Danforth encouraged the maid to murder his nieces and nephew? Naturally. He taught Tess Arnold to hope for everything. And when she had played her part, he killed her."

"*I* killed her?" Danforth stared about the room as one amazed.

"In the interval between the ladies withdrawing from the Chatsworth dining parlour Monday evening, and the gentlemen rejoining them over an hour later."

Lord Harold tore his eyes from Andrew Danforth's face and stared at me. "Good God," he said. "So that was how it was done."

"Sir James chanced to mention to me the entire program of that evening," I said. "It was only later, in conversation with Lord Harold, that I detected the discrepancy. You left Penfolds, Mr. Danforth, for Chatsworth at about five o'clock, on a swift horse that might gallop the distance in half an hour. You dined at seven, and the ladies withdrew at half-past ten, much as we did the night of Lady Harriot's birthday. Sir James was told that the gentlemen quitted the dining parlour at a quarter to twelve, having been much engrossed in a discussion of politics, and the prospects of Charles James Fox—a discussion that you, as a man ambitious in politics, might have been expected to join. But you did not."

"Andrew?" Lady Harriot gasped.

"I thought you had gone after her," Lord Harold muttered, his eyes on Andrew Danforth, "to dance attendance. You excused yourself not five minutes after the ladies retired. It never occurred to me that you quitted the house entirely—"

"This story is absurd!" Danforth burst out. "If you will credit the notion that a man might race across open country, under a fitful moon, in order to shoot a girl he had no notion should be walking the hills at such an hour—"

"But you did know, Mr. Danforth," I persisted. "Because you supplied Tess Arnold with your brother's clothes in the ice-house that very morning. She told you where she would be, and all that she intended, as a very good joke. You had often engaged in playacting together, as children. You are playacting now, I think."

Andrew Danforth emitted a choking sound.

"You quitted the dining parlour perhaps five minutes after the ladies. You went swiftly out the West Entrance to the stableyard, and saddled your horse. The stable lads should never have been disturbed; Lord Hartington was much given to coming and going about the loose boxes at all hours of the night. You galloped hard across the country to the hills above Miller's Dale, and tethered your horse beneath the same tree you chose for your brother's mount today. We found your hoofprints there on Friday. You waited in a pile of rock for the maid to appear; and when you had shot her, you rode at great speed back to Chatsworth, and joined the ladies a few minutes in advance of the other gentlemen."

"Deuced cheek!" ejaculated His Grace the Duke.

"You took a considerable risk, to be sure; but one that very nearly succeeded," I went on. "An enquiry among the stable lads, however, will suffice. One at least must have remarked the curious fact that your horse was already damp with sweat, when you called for it at one o'clock, and quitted Chatsworth for your road home."

Danforth turned his head wildly, as though in search of a friend. The Duke stared with bulging eyes; Lady Harriot had buried her face in Lady Swithin's gown; and a cruel smile played about Lord Harold's lips.

Danforth's eyes came to rest on the amiable countenance of Sir James Villiers.

"But Charles—You read the letter yourself—"

"Charles confessed to a crime he did not commit," I said implacably. "He did so from the same motives that have placed your solicitor, Mr. George Hemming, in the Bakewell gaol. Your brother took *your* guilt upon himself, Andrew Danforth, because he believed too much in your goodness."

His lips began to work, but no sound came.

"Charles believed that you discovered the maid's hideous work, and cut off her life like a poisonous snake's. Why else should she have been killed so soon after her attempt on his life? He regarded you with gratitude; he thought you a man of honour. To kill from such a motive is no different in a gentleman's mind, I suspect, than death should be in a duel. And having exposed your neck to the noose on behalf of his children, Charles determined that you should receive a similar testament of loyalty. He suspected the reasons for George Hemming's sacrifice—the solicitor was devoted to you. He saw that Lady Harriot looked upon you with favour. His own prospects of happiness had gone forward into the grave. Why not end such misery with a snatch at honour, and take upon himself your guilt? And so he wrote his letter.

"Did he show it to you, in the hills above Miller's Dale?"

Danforth sank into a vacant chair, as though his legs would no longer support him.

"I wonder if he understood what you really were, in that last moment before you killed him?"

To Prevent Nightmare

*E*at nothing after three o'clock, and no night-mare will ever assert its suffocating presence.

—*From the Stillroom Book of Tess Arnold,*
Penfolds Hall, Derbyshire, 1802–1806

Chapter 28

Cages We Cannot Help

Monday
1 September 1806
~

"MICHAEL TIVEY HAS CONFESSED," SIR JAMES VILLIERS INFORMED ME, "to having anatomised the body of the stillroom maid. It is as you suspected—having gone in search of Tess Arnold when she failed to appear for their midnight appointment, Tivey discovered her dead body, and made use of it for his own despicable purposes. He thought to throw suspicion for the girl's death upon the Freemasons, whom he cordially disliked for having rejected him; and thus endeavoured, as soon as her body was found, to put about the story of ritual murder. Being denied the full knowledge of Masonic rites himself, however, he could effect the wounds of a traitor's execution only imperfectly. And so we suspected the tale's veracity from the first."

Sir James sat in one of the hard-backed chairs of our parlour at The Rutland Arms this morning as the trunks were brought out. My cousin Mr. Cooper had carried his point; and but for this brief visit from the Law, I should have quitted Bakewell without learning how matters were disposed.

"Mr. Hemming is at liberty?"

"He is—and will soon leave the district with the intention of seeking a holiday. I am sure he will have returned for the Derby Assizes, however."

Where Andrew Danforth should be tried for the murders of Tess Arnold and Charles Danforth. I could no longer consider the latter his brother; for indeed, they had not the slightest particle of blood in common.

Sir James peered at me narrowly. "I cannot entirely reconcile George Hemming's willingness to shoulder Andrew Danforth's guilt. Such dedication in a solicitor for one of his clients is beyond the bounds of my experience."

"But you may have known a similar loyalty in a father for his son," I observed gently. "Mr. Hemming's feeling for Andrew Danforth, I should judge, was just that strong in degree and kind."

"I see," Sir James returned thoughtfully. From the rapid change in his countenance, I discerned that he would consider new sources of information, that must invert the nature of the problem. But no word of that lovely old miniature, borne by both father and son, did I offer. Andrew Danforth might have sacrificed every consideration of civility, by his vicious conduct; but George Hemming yet deserved my protection and silence. I suspected that he had paid already for his indiscretions, in years of blackmail to Betty Arnold, who had known the truth of Andrew's origins. Her daughter Tess had undoubtedly shared them with Andrew himself—and in fear that his illegitimacy should be proclaimed, and his eventual right to inherit Penfolds disputed, he had been moved to murder.

George Hemming would continue to pay for that single great love, that rash act of youth, until he found his own grave; I had no wish to add to his burdens by publishing his past before all of Bakewell. I had already won Hemming's enmity, by stilling the hand of the executioner and placing the noose around his son's neck. Far from expressing gratitude at his deliverance, and a proper sense of respect for the working of justice, he had taken no leave of the Austen family.

My cousin Mr. Cooper was greatly surprised by this rude parting; but reflected with satisfaction that he had behaved blamelessly himself throughout the entire affair, and might expect a glowing commendation from so great a personage as Sir George Mumps, when that gentleman knew the whole. He would continue, he informed me, to pray for his sad friend.

Sir James stood up and held out his hand. "I hope, Miss Austen, that if you ever find it possible to take Bakewell in your way, that you will not hesitate to call at Villiers Hall. I should have engaged you for dinner at Monyash, had your visit been prolonged; but the duties of justice—"

"—and the claims of a friend with a Scottish manor," I added, "should never go neglected. I am honoured by your invitation, Sir James, and shall avail myself of the opportunity of accepting it, whenever the occasion may offer."

He bowed—begged to be remembered to my mother and sister, already established in the carriage below—and took himself off.

I tarried for a last look from the parlour window, as if in expectation of observing a glossy equipage, in the First Stare of Fashion, emblazoned with the serpent and the stag—but Matlock Street was empty of life, but for our own post chaise bulging with baggage and a quantity of dried trout.

I turned away from the window, and found him standing in the door. "Lord Harold!"

"My dearest Jane."

He crossed swiftly and seized my hand; held it to his lips, and closed his eyes. The ravaged looks of the previous few days were gone; he might rest now in the certainty that his duty to Georgiana's children had been discharged. But I detected no joy in his countenance—only resignation and the hollowness of loss.

"You have asked for her hand," I said, "and she has refused you."

His grey eyes flew open and gazed into my own. I was pleased to observe no tragedy in their depths; the hint of self-mockery prevailed. "It is ridiculous for a man of eight-and-forty to expect such a creature to return his affection. She must regard me as almost a father."

"Do not sell yourself so cheap, my lord. Fathers, in Lady Harriot's estimation, cannot be accounted highly."

He released my hand. "No matter. I should not have taught myself to hope. It is the effect of old love, you know—unrequited love for her mother; and the sensation of seeing the woman reborn once more in Hary-O. Such a union must have ended in folly."

"You may find that with time, the lady's sentiments may undergo a revolution. She is very young, and has suffered much in recent months; perhaps when another twelvemonth has passed away—"

"—I shall be merely another year older. No, Jane—however much I may esteem her—however much I regard her as exactly the sort of woman to suit me—we should not have gone on well together. She is at the very beginning of her powers, while I approach their end."

"Fiddlesticks!" I cried. "You are worth ten young men put together—in understanding, knowledge of the world, *brilliance*. There is charm and flattery enough, my lord—but *nobody* is brilliant any more."

"Thank you, my dear," he replied with a trace of amusement. "I know you well enough to value your frankness. But truth to tell, I should have been tempted to put Hary-O in a gilded cage; and she has spent most of her life in one already. What she desires now is flight—and a man who might give her wings."

His expression, as he uttered the words, became fixed and closed to me; and in this I sensed the depth of his regret. There was nothing more to be said. He had resigned all pretension to the woman he loved.

The Gentleman Rogue, however, was not yet done. In a tone of some briskness he declared, "I must congratulate myself, Jane, in having discharged this last service to Georgiana—in having saved her beloved Harriot from a *most* unsuitable marriage. Who knows where Andrew Danforth's rapacity might have led?"

"To the murder of his wife, perhaps, against the vastness of her fortune?"

"I have *you* to thank for Hary-O's present safety. I shall always think of you with gratitude and fondness, Jane—for this, as for so many past examples of your goodness."

"As I shall think of you," I managed. And stifled all other words that might have come. I reached for a small packet that yet stood upon the parlour table, and presented it to him. "Pray extend my thanks to the Countess for the use of her combs."

"I believe she intended to make a present of them to you."

"Lady Swithin is very good—but I could never accept anything so fine."

He gave me a long look, then slipped the jeweller's box into his coat. "Shall I escort you below? The dissipation of a giddy watering-place, and a thousand gallant sailors, await you in Southampton."

He offered his arm; I tucked my hand between the folds of sleeve and coat; and so was carried off quite handsomely to the waiting chaise. He handed me in, and lifted his hat; and as the carriage creaked to life, I summoned resources enough to wave.

But it was a considerable period before I could utter a word, or appear sensible to my mother's cries of delight as the carriage slipped south with the autumn leaves; and of Mr. Cooper's voice lifted fulsomely in hymns of praise, I heard not a syllable. The image of a silver head and a whipcord form—of one last, serious parting look—were all that filled my sight. I suppose more than one young woman has been sustained a twelvemonth on so little.

Editor's Afterword

REMEDIES SIMILAR TO THOSE FOUND IN TESS ARNOLD'S STILLROOM book appear in a variety of facsimile publications of old cooking guides. Those chiefly useful for this editor's purposes were: *The British House-wife, or, the Cook, Housekeeper's and Gardiner's Companion, by Mrs. Martha Bradley, late of Bath (1756);* Volumes I, II, and III (Prospect Books, 1997). Also consulted was *Healthy Living, 1850–1870,* compiled by Katie F. Hamilton from A. E. Youman's *Dictionary of Every-Day Wants,* first published in New York in 1878, and now available from Metheglin Press, Phoenix, AZ. Although the remedies offered in Thomas Dawson's *The Good Huswifes Jewell* of 1596 (Maggie Black, editor, Southover Press, 1997) might be thought dated by Austen's period, the stillroom tradition evident in the volume finds it heirs in women like Tess Arnold.

DURING HER JOURNEY DOWN FROM THE MIDLANDS IN SEPTEMBER 1806, Jane Austen succumbed to whooping cough. The illness lingered through the fall as she attempted to set up house in Southampton, in company with her brother Captain Francis Austen and his new bride. Though relations between the Austens and the Coopers remained cordial, there is no record of Jane ever visiting Hamstall Ridware or Derbyshire again.

The Whig party luminary Charles James Fox died suddenly at his home outside London on September 13, 1806. It was a signal blow to his lifelong friends and political colleagues, who had looked to Fox to lead the Whigs into power. Lady Elizabeth Foster was present at Fox's death; the fifth Duke of Devonshire walked behind his coffin through Pall Mall to Westminster Abbey. The Whig strategy plotted that summer at the Chatsworth dinner table, during which Andrew Danforth was suspiciously absent, was thus never put into effect.

Readers new to the history of the Devonshire ménage during the late-eighteenth and early-nineteenth centuries may be interested to learn that Lady Elizabeth Foster became the fifth duke's second duchess in the fall of 1809.

William, Lord Hartington, was eventually reconciled to his father's choice of wife; but despite the family's firm insistence that Hart was Georgiana's son, he is rumored to have harbored doubts regarding his inheritance of the dukedom. When Canis died in 1811, Hart duly became the sixth Duke of Devonshire; but he never married, and never produced an heir, so that at Hart's death the dukedom passed to a cousin. In this small way, legend has it, William Cavendish rectified any errors of legitimacy compounded by his extraordinary parents.

Lady Harriot Cavendish married Granville Leveson-Gower on Christmas Eve, 1809. It is possible that her father's marriage two months previous made Hary-O's position within the family intolerable, and that the prospect of union with a man twelve years her senior was no longer a source of alarm. The fact that her aunt, the Countess of Bessborough, had by this time borne Leveson-Gower two illegitimate children, is something she may not even have known; but certainly she learned of it later.

Leveson-Gower was created Earl Granville in 1833, so that Hary-O, like her dear friend Desdemona Trowbridge, left off being a duke's daughter in order to become a countess. Earl Granville served as British ambassador to Paris, where we may assume Lady Granville presided over a most diplomatic household. She had been trained for such an occupation from birth.

The opinion of Lord Harold Trowbridge regarding Hary-O's marriage is nowhere recorded. He is thought to have spent Christmas Eve, 1809, somewhere along the Iberian Peninsula on behalf of the Crown. At the time, news of his lordship had not reached the *ton* for nearly a year—although certainly his secret dispatches found their way into competent hands. It is best, perhaps, that Lord Harold was saved the unfortunate duty of toasting the bride and groom; but a very fine portable writing desk, of Spanish origin and craftsmanship, eventually appeared among the wedding gifts displayed at Devonshire House.

Lady Harriot was, after all, one of the greatest letter writers of her period—in print, she rivals even Jane Austen for sharpness and sagacity.